A Wedding
in December

ALSO BY ANITA SHREVE

Eden Close
Strange Fits of Passion
Where or When
Resistance
The Weight of Water
The Pilot's Wife
Fortune's Rocks
The Last Time They Met
Sea Glass
All He Ever Wanted
Light on Snow

A Wedding in December

A NOVEL

Anita Shreve

LITTLE, BROWN

LITTLE, BROWN

First published in the United States of America in October 2005
by Little, Brown and Company
First published in Great Britain in September 2005 by Little, Brown
Reprinted 2005 (five times), 2006

A CIP catalogue record for this book
is available from the British Library.

HB ISBN 0 316 72777 6
C FORMAT ISBN 0 316 72778 4

Printed and bound in Great Britain by
Clays Ltd, St Ives plc

Little, Brown
An imprint of
Time Warner Book Group UK
Brettenham House
Lancaster Place
London WC2E 7EN

www.twbg.co.uk

for my father

Friday

⸙

The glaciers are receding," she said. Nora peered through the window as if she could see the progress of said glaciers some ten thousand miles north. "I read it in the paper. This morning."

The view, Harrison had noted before he'd sat down, was of still-green lawns and dormant rosebushes, of a wrought iron fence and a garden bench, of ornamental grasses and white pines. Beyond the considerable acreage was a steel ribbon of river and beyond that a range of mountains, blue-gray in the morning light.

"The birds must be confused," he said.

"They are. I . . . I see them flying north all the time."

"Is it bad for business?"

"No. Not really. No one's canceled. Though the ski areas are suffering."

Nora left the window and moved to the chair opposite. He watched her cross her legs, a cuff riding just above the edge of a black leather boot and making a slim bracelet of smooth white skin. Harrison superimposed the woman he saw now over the memory of the seventeen-year-old girl he'd once known, a girl with a soft face and large almond-shaped eyes, a girl who had been graceful in her movements. The woman before him was forty-four, and some of the softness had left her face. Her hair was different, too. She wore it short, swept behind her ears, a cut that looked more European than American.

When they'd met just moments earlier at the foot of the stairs in the front hallway, Nora had been standing at a small reception desk. She'd glanced up and seen Harrison, and for a moment she'd examined him as an innkeeper might a guest one had not yet attended to. *Harrison,* she'd said then, advancing, and his own smile had begun. As Nora had embraced him, Harrison had felt both unnerved and buoyant — a cork floating in uncharted waters.

"Your . . . your room is comfortable?" she asked.

He remembered this about her. The slight stutter, as if hesitant to speak. No, not a stutter; more a stutter step.

"Very," he said. "Great views."

"Can I get you something? Tea? Coffee?"

"Coffee would be fine. That's quite a machine there."

"It makes espresso with a lot of crema," she said, standing. "It's a draw, actually. Some of the guests have said they've come back for the coffee in the library. Well, for that and for the dumbwaiter. I put the dining room upstairs. To take advantage of the views."

On either side of the bookshelves were half columns, and below those shelves were cabinets. On one wall, there was a built-in bench upholstered in lichen stripes. The windows — a set of three facing west — had panes in the tops only, so that from the leather couch on which Harrison was seated he had an unobstructed view of the mountains.

"How long has this been an inn?" he asked.

"Two years."

"I was sorry to hear about your husband."

"You sent a card."

He nodded, surprised that Nora remembered. There must have been hundreds, perhaps thousands, of cards for such a distinguished man.

"Renovations," she said, making a gesture so as to take in the entire building. "Renovations had to be made."

"You've done a terrific job," he replied, slightly jarred by the non sequitur.

Harrison had followed signs from the center of town to the inn and then had taken the long drive up the hill to the top. When he'd reached the parking lot, the view of the Berkshire Mountains had opened up and stopped his heart in the same way that, as a boy at Cinerama, his heart had always paused as the camera had soared up and over a cliff edge to reveal the Grand Canyon or the Rift Valley or the ice fields of Antarctica.

He'd walked with his suitcase to the front steps, noting along the way the pruned bushes, the raked lawns, and, in a maze that had perhaps lost its challenge, the expertly trimmed hedges. The inn was sheathed in white clapboards and shingles and sported a chimney that tilted slightly forward. The windows, unadorned, shone in the morning light. Like many houses built at the turn of the century, it had gables of differing widths and porches sprouting unconventionally at odd angles. The outline of the roof, Harrison thought, would be almost impossible to draw from memory.

Inside, the inn had a crisp edge that had been accomplished in part, Harrison thought, with a great deal of white paint and chrome. Much as he admired the inn, however, he wondered if visitors ever lamented the lost house, the one Carl Laski had inhabited.

"This used to be an inn. Years ago," Nora said. "After World War II, it became a private home. There's an early photograph. Behind you on the wall."

Harrison stood and leaned in toward the wall, balancing himself with his hand on the back of the couch. The photograph, framed in dark walnut, was remarkably detailed and clear, every blade of grass and twig made distinct with a kind of vision denied the naked eye. The picture was of a white shingled building with a cupola on its roof. It looked to be November or early March, to judge from the light dusting of snow that outlined the furrows of a garden. At the river's edge, there was a trail of mist, but he saw, on closer inspection, that it was really smoke from a moving train, the train itself a blur, merely a shadow.

"The photograph dates from 1912," Nora said. "It was made from a glass negative. There's a rose garden there. And a racetrack."

Harrison sat again on the couch and wondered if anyone else had arrived yet. He had wanted to be the first, to see Nora without the noise of the others. "It was an inn, then a house, and then an inn again?" he asked.

She smiled at his confusion. "When Carl and I moved here, it was a private house. We lived here for fifteen years. After he died . . . after he died, I had the idea of reconverting it to an inn. It had always wanted to be an inn. Even when it was a house."

"How many rooms are there?"

"There used to be twenty-two."

"How did you manage?"

"We closed most of the rooms off. Would you like more coffee?"

"No thanks. I'm fine. Any of the others here yet?"

"Agnes said she'd be here by lunch. Bill and Bridget, too. Rob . . . Rob won't be here until later."

"Rob's coming?" Harrison asked with pleasure. He hadn't seen Rob Zoar in . . . well, in twenty-seven years. Harrison was startled by the number and recalculated. Yes, twenty-seven. "He's in Boston now, isn't he? I think I read that."

"He performs all over the world. He gets wonderful reviews."

"I was surprised to hear he was a pianist. He kept it quiet at Kidd, didn't he?"

"I think he tried to resist it."

"It seems like this wedding came together very fast," he said.

"It did."

Too fast for Harrison's wife, Evelyn, to rearrange her schedule. Bill had sent Harrison an e-mail saying that he and Bridget were getting married — at the inn — and he wanted Harrison and Evelyn to come. Harrison and Bill had for a time kept in touch (their families had gone skiing together twice), but Harrison had had no idea at all about Bill and Bridget.

"Bridget's sick," Nora added. "It's why Bill wants to do it now."

"How sick?" Harrison asked.

"Very," Nora said, her face tight. "Do you remember them together?"

"At school? Of course." Bill had been a muscular catcher, a consistent hitter with power who had routinely sent the baseball over the fence. Bridget, a serious girl, was pretty in a slightly plump way. In another era, she'd have been a beauty. The couple used to cross the campus so entwined it was as if they were one creature. Harrison recalled how disillusioned he had been when he'd heard that each had married someone else.

"How did they reconnect?" he asked now.

"Our twenty-fifth. Did you ever go to any of the reunions?"

He shook his head. He'd told himself that he hadn't gone for Evelyn's sake. She was Canadian, she wouldn't have known anyone, the journey would have consumed too many of her precious days off. But Harrison couldn't satisfactorily explain why he hadn't gone by himself. The simple answer, he supposed, was that he hadn't wanted to. The sight of the invitations had produced in him an anxiety he had no intention of exploring. Even this small reunion — this hasty wedding — had made him hesitate.

"You?" he asked.

Nora shook her head, and Harrison was not surprised. He could not imagine Carl Laski at a Kidd reunion.

"Have you seen any of the others?" Nora asked. "Since school, I mean?"

"Well, Bill," he said. "And I met Jerry in New York about five years ago. We had drinks."

"He's coming with his wife, Julie," Nora said. "What was it like, meeting Jerry?"

"He mostly wanted me to know how successful he'd become," Harrison said and then shrugged to take the edge off the unkind comment.

"You're staying until Sunday?" Nora asked.

"I think that's the plan."

Harrison had flown from Toronto to Hartford, rented a car, and driven to the Massachusetts Turnpike, which he had followed west. He'd realized, as he'd driven, that he'd never been to western Massachusetts. When he had visited New England before, it had always been to Boston and then straight on to Kidd in Maine. Never inland. He'd known of the Berkshires, of course. Tanglewood, the summer home of the Boston Symphony Orchestra, was world famous. Edith Wharton had summered in Lenox. Melville had written *Moby Dick* in Pittsfield.

"There are some good walks," Nora said, gesturing toward the windows. "The weather . . . the weather is amazing."

"It's been unseasonable in Toronto as well. Very mild."

"Each day has been more beautiful than the last," she said. "I think Nature means to mock us."

"How so?"

"9/11."

Harrison nodded slowly.

"All that horror. All that grief." She paused. "People . . . people are stopping one another on the streets and saying, *Can you imagine?* and *Isn't this extraordinary?* and *Enjoy it while you can.*"

"They say the temperature is breaking all records."

"I think it will reach seventy-two today," she said.

"Surely a record for the first week in December."

"I wonder . . . I wonder if the idea is that the sins of man, more terrible than anyone's ability to imagine them, are nothing in the face of Nature's bounty and serenity," Nora said.

"Nature a supreme being?" Harrison asked, puzzled.

"Entity?"

"A terrible one at times."

"Not today."

"No, not today," Harrison said.

"Or . . . or are we meant to be reminded of a reason to stay alive? To savor each day as if it might be the last?"

"Nature capable of grace?" Harrison asked. "I like that."

Nora laughed, reached forward, and touched him lightly at the tip of his knee. "Listen to us," she said. "We're so pretentious. We used to do this all the time in Mr. Mitchell's class, didn't we?"

"We did," he said, glad that she remembered, more gladdened by her sudden touch.

"It's great to see you," she said with seemingly genuine pleasure.

"Where were you when it happened?" he asked.

"Here. In the kitchen. I turned on the TV just before the second plane hit. Judy, my assistant — you're bound to meet her — came in and told me. What about you?"

"I was in Toronto," he said. "I was eating breakfast. I had a cup of coffee and the newspaper. On the television, the announcer's voice changed in pitch, and I looked up in time to see a plane hit the second tower."

The images of that day had played and replayed for hours, Canadian television more willing to air the most horrific images — those falling bodies — than American stations had been.

"Were you frightened?" he asked.

"Here? No. Not really. Upset. Very upset. But not frightened. I thought of Carl. I was glad he wasn't alive. To see it."

Nora began to nibble at the skin at the top of her index finger.

Abruptly she stopped, putting her hands in her lap with a decisive gesture. From behind the shut door of the library, Harrison could hear a vacuum cleaner.

"They say it's the death of literature," she added.

"I think that's a little extreme," he said, shifting his position on the couch. In the days following the tragedy, he'd been greatly annoyed by such dramatic remarks. "I admired your husband's work very much," he added, feeling remiss that he hadn't mentioned this earlier.

"He . . . he was a wonderful man," Nora said. "A wonderful poet and a wonderful man."

"Yes."

"I was the helpmeet," Nora said, surprising Harrison with the archaic word. "I've . . . I've never understood what that means exactly. Helpmeet. *Help. Meet.*"

"I'll look it up for you," he offered.

"I could do it myself. I must have a dictionary. Somewhere . . ." She gazed at the spines of the books that lined the shelves.

For Harrison, the brilliance of Carl Laski's work lay in its oblique nature, the way the point of a poem was often a glancing blow: a glimpsed headline across the breakfast table while a woman tells her husband she has a lover, or a man berating his wife on a cell phone in an airport lounge as he passes a small child sitting alone with a bright red suitcase. Later it will be the memory of the child with the suitcase that will bring the man to his knees in his hotel room.

Harrison, of course, knew of Laski's reputation. The poet had won numerous international prizes, had been the recipient of honorary degrees, had been — when he'd died — professor emeritus at St. Martin's College, at which he had founded the celebrated St. Martin's Writers School and from which he had sent out into the world a disproportionate share of poets. Laski, Harrison had read, regarded the writing of poetry as man's highest calling and therefore worth the inevitable squandering of happy marriages and good health, to say nothing of sound finances. Largely due to his efforts, poetry had been enjoying something of a renaissance when he'd died, though one so mild as to barely register on the North American consciousness. Not one man in forty could today name a living poet, Harrison thought. Not one in a hundred could say who Carl Laski had been.

Harrison had also read the Roscoff biography, a book that purported to be literary but showed almost no interest in the work itself. Rather, Roscoff had focused on the more lurid aspects of Laski's life: his abusive father, his early drinking problem, his nearly obsessive womanizing while a professor at New York University, his disastrous first marriage, the loss of his sons in a bitter custody battle, and his subsequent self-imposed (and somewhat misanthropic) exile to the backwater college of St. Martin's in western Massachusetts. "Your husband should have won the Nobel Prize," Harrison said.

Nora laughed. "If he were here, he'd agree with you."

"Was it difficult for him, being passed up year after year?"

"It . . . it was an *event* each time it was awarded. I mean that it would register. Like a small seismic shudder. He'd hear the news or read it in the newspaper, or someone would call and tell him, and his face, for just a moment, would cave in. Even as he was ranting about the winner or reading another part of the paper. The only time . . . the only time he didn't mind personally was when Seamus Heaney won. He loved Seamus."

Harrison set down his cup. Laski had been thirty years older than Nora. The two had met when Nora was nineteen; Laski, forty-nine. "Was it ever an issue between you — the age difference?" he asked.

"Only that he had to die before me."

Harrison listened for a note of bitterness or grief.

"We always knew it would happen," she added.

Harrison nodded.

"We just didn't know it would be so awful. One night . . . one night when it was really bad, Carl said, 'It's so easy.' I thought he meant the pain. That somehow the pain had eased up. But he meant dying. That he'd found an easy way to die."

Laski had filled his bathtub, plugged in the hair dryer, and let it drop. Harrison remembered precisely where he'd been when he learned the startling news. An editor Harrison had once worked with in Toronto had walked by his table in a New York City restaurant, bent down, and murmured, *Have you heard about Carl Laski?*

"A terrible end to a magnificent life," Harrison said now.

Nora was silent.

"The courage to do that," he added.

"Carl . . . Carl would have said 'cowardice.'"

"He had throat cancer?"

"He kept saying that he could never have described the pain. Not even at the height of his powers. That it defied words."

"It's hard for the healthy to imagine pain like that."

"But what was truly horrible, Carl always said, was the knowing. Knowing he was going to die."

Harrison agreed. He could think of few things in life worse than knowing when one was going to die, for it seemed to him that all the days in between — between the *now* and the *then* — would be tainted, poisoned by that bitter knowledge. "In the end, he picked his own time," he said.

Nora stood, smoothing the hem of her blouse across the flat of her stomach. She had the body of a woman who had not had children, and Harrison thought briefly of his wife's body: muscular and elongated from swimming, yet still there was the small curve of her belly, a swelling he loved to touch. "Want to sit outside?" Nora asked, opening the double doors.

Harrison expected a sudden chill, but the air that came in from the small veranda outside the library was warm. "You and Agnes have stayed friends, I take it," he said as he stood.

"Yes. We . . . we don't see each other much, but we write. She's kind of old-fashioned. Our Agnes. She stayed on at Kidd. She teaches there."

Harrison remembered Agnes's sturdy body, her dreamy nature, her fascination with history.

"She finally bought a computer when the school put a gun to her head," Nora said. "She hides it under the bed and takes it out only to post her grades."

Harrison laughed.

"Bridget's mother and sister will come for the wedding. Bill's family won't come. They're angry with him for . . . well, for leaving his wife and daughter for Bridget. Bridget's son is bringing a friend to keep him company. They're fifteen. It'll be a small wedding. More a wedding supper than a wedding. Though Bill is intent upon the details. I've helped him plan the flowers and the menu. He wants it to be . . . perfect. For Bridget."

"What's wrong with her?" Harrison asked.

"Breast cancer."

Harrison sucked in his breath. The mother of a fifteen-year-old boy. He didn't want to think about it.

He shaded his eyes with his hand. "What's that over there?" he asked.

"It's the top of a roller coaster," Nora said cheerfully. "In the summer, with binoculars, you can see the people in the cars. You can watch them make the long, slow climb to the top and then hurtle out of sight below the trees. Then, as if by magic, you can see them emerge again. They seem to spin off into the air."

"I've never been on a roller coaster," Harrison confessed. "The closest I've ever come is when my mother used to take me to Cinerama when I was a kid."

"I don't think I ever went to Cinerama."

"It was the first of the wide-screen movies. It made you feel as though you were right there — sitting in the car of a roller coaster, or climbing a mountain. It was meant to give you the thrill and sensation of movement."

"I can't do it anymore," she said. "The roller coaster. Carl did though. He'd snatch at any excuse to go. He'd borrow children if necessary." She looked at her watch, and Harrison thought about the notion of borrowing children. "Tell me about yourself," she said.

"Not much to tell."

"You're married."

"Yes. My wife and I live in Toronto with our two boys, Charlie and Tom. Evelyn, my wife, is an estate lawyer."

"How did you end up there? In Toronto?"

"Evelyn is from Toronto."

"You're . . . in publishing?"

"Yes."

Nora rocked herself in a chair. "Tell me more about your wife."

"Evelyn? Well, let's see. She's French Canadian. She's tall and has short blond hair. I think her hair might actually be gray now, but she never lets anyone see it. She's a very good mother."

Harrison had then a quick image of Evelyn and the boys at home. He could see the interior of their town house, particularly the small, cluttered kitchen. A jumble of laundry, including his boys' slippery red hockey shirts, would have spilled out onto the floor from the alcove where the washer and dryer were stowed. He could see the breakfast table with its boxes of American cereal that the boys favored, a tea bag rolled and hardened on a saucer. Evelyn would be in a pink cashmere robe Harrison had given her for her birthday, and her hair would be askew from sleep. In the background would be the steady patter of an early morning news show. And Harrison realized, as he saw and heard this scene, that he did not wish himself there. With that realization came an emptiness he was all too familiar with, an emptiness that opened up whenever he found himself alone in a foreign place — a sense of floating, of not being anchored in the way that chores and hockey games and engagements will do. "My older son, Charlie, who's eleven, has Evelyn's looks but my disposition," Harrison said, "while Tom, who's nine, is the spitting image of me, but has Evelyn's disposition." He paused. "It's occasionally deeply unsettling," he added, smiling.

"And what disposition would that be?" Nora asked.

"Evelyn's?"

"Yes."

"Oh, I think most people would say she tends to be somewhat more dramatic than I am," Harrison answered, feeling mildly disloyal.

"And so you would be . . ."

"More even tempered," he said.

"Yes. I can see that," Nora said.

Sometimes Evelyn seemed closer to Harrison the farther away he was from her in a strict physical sense. When they were separated, he tended to think of her with more fondness than when he was with her, and he wondered if she felt the same. He sometimes thought that he had disappointed her in marriage — or, rather, that marriage, with its promise of constant love and physical intimacy, had disappointed them both. In her most dramatic and, paradoxically, romantic moments, Evelyn reproached herself for not having loved Harrison enough; but he couldn't ease her mind on this point without admitting to the death of hope. Together, they cared for the boys, attended to their jobs, and had made, he thought, a good family. And occasionally there were moments of true joy, as when one or the other of the boys would say something winsome at the dinner table, and Harrison would catch Evelyn's eye, or as when, lying together in the bed, having made love in the forgiving half-light of an early Sunday morning, a kind of weekly hurdle crossed, Evelyn would put her head on his chest and he would stroke her shoulder, and a brief contentment would envelop them before they drifted off to sleep.

"Tell me a story," Nora said.

Harrison laughed. "You used to do this all the time."

"So I did."

He let his mind go blank. He sat in a rocker opposite and let some seconds pass.

"Once I was staying at Le Concorde in Quebec City," he said. "I had a view toward the Frontenac, down the Grande-Allée. Between my hotel and the Frontenac, there were a dozen rooftops. All shapes and sizes. And on one of these rooftops, there were four teenage boys. They had brooms, and I thought at first they'd been sent to the roof by maintenance to sweep off the snow. But it soon became apparent to me that they were making a hockey rink. The prospect of that was horrible, you see, because there was no guardrail, no barrier, and if one of the boys bodychecked the other, say, or if one simply lost his footing, he'd have slipped right off the roof. And died, presumably. The building was at least seven stories up."

Nora tilted her head, waiting for more.

"I couldn't take my eyes off them," Harrison said. "And yet, strangely, I didn't *do* anything. I didn't know what the name of the building was, and I thought that if I went out onto the street, I wouldn't be able to see which rooftop it was. So I did nothing."

"What happened?"

"Nothing."

Nora rested her chin on the back of her hand. "What else?"

Harrison thought a minute. "Before I left to come here," he said, "I watched my wife get dressed for work. She had on two different socks. One long and one short. She hadn't shaved her legs."

"How did you feel about that?"

"I was faintly repulsed," he admitted. "I love my wife, by the way."

"But you see," Nora said, "you didn't include these facts. You edited. You would have omitted those details. If you'd been asked to give an account of yourself. And then I would have . . . I would have a very different picture of you."

"How so?"

"I now know that you're willing to share small secrets. You might be a closet coward. You probably don't like to get too involved. You're capable of being faintly repulsed by someone you love."

"Didn't you know these things already?"

"We were children then," Nora said. "We're . . . we're entirely different now."

Are we? Harrison wondered.

"What's that over there?" he asked, pointing. "That plume of smoke? It looks lethal."

"A paper bag factory. They say it's perfectly safe. But I don't believe it."

"Quite a forest," he said.

"It's deceptive. You can see only the tops of the trees from here. Below them, there are houses and roads and power lines. Even a McDonald's."

"Say it isn't so," Harrison said with mock horror.

"Afraid it is. There's a real forest behind the inn, though."

He craned his neck, but the roof blocked any view of the woods behind the inn. "The inn does well?" he asked.

"Surprisingly. It works the way I hoped it would work. There are . . . there are always problems — the too-low toilet seats being the most frequent complaint."

"I hadn't noticed."

"But many of our guests have returned. And they've told their friends about it. This year we're booked through to the end of February."

"Well done."

"I hadn't meant to compete. It hadn't ever really crossed my mind. I just wanted something of my own. But I am. Competing. With a whole string of B and Bs throughout the Berkshires."

"Who makes up your clientele?" he asked.

"Mostly people from Boston and New York. Looking to escape the cities. They profess to come for the charm — a sort of New England charm I find hokey. So I don't offer it. Apart from these L.L.Bean rockers we're sitting on. Or they come with an ideal of family togetherness that invariably unravels as the weekend progresses."

"You sound a bit cynical."

"What people really come for is the promise of sex and food and material goods. Not necessarily in that order. The outlets are just ten minutes away."

"Under all those trees."

Nora nodded.

"I'm actually hot sitting here," Harrison said with some surprise.

"Take off your sweater."

"I think I will. If we were primitive people, we'd be frightened by this, wouldn't we? This freakish weather."

"The inn was reviewed last year in *New York Magazine*," Nora said. "The reviewer wrote that one could sit on the porch in December. He meant sit on the porch *in a parka,* but this year you can do it in shirtsleeves. The sun bakes the clapboards."

"The lawn is still green," he said.

"By this time of year, there's usually snow on the ground. Men who haven't been on sleds in years like to show off to their wives and children before their knees give out." She glanced at her watch. "I really have to go," she said, standing. "I have a rehearsal lunch. There's another wedding tomorrow. Agnes and Rob should be here by one. We'll have a private room for the dinner tonight. And of course one for tomorrow evening."

"Is that usual?" Harrison asked. "To have more than one wedding a weekend?"

"Oh, yes," Nora said. "I've sometimes had four in a weekend, all with rehearsal dinners. The trick . . . the trick is to keep the brides from running into one another. Each wants to think herself unique."

"Don't we all?" he said.

Nora smiled.

"I thought I might go for a walk," he said, standing as well. "I had breakfast on the way here."

"Good. So you're all set."

"I am."

Nora took a step away from him but then glanced back. "I suppose someone will mention Stephen?" she asked.

The name produced in Harrison, as it always did, a clench in his gut along with a slight oil slick of shame. He stood still and waited.

"I've been thinking about him a lot," Nora added.

Harrison was silent.

"Do you remember the funeral?"

"Of course," he said quietly.

"Grief, seen up close like that, is unbearable. It was so much worse than ours. So much more intense. It made me realize how shallowly we'd loved him."

"Perhaps," Harrison said, though at the time his love for his friend had felt intense enough.

"You and I haven't spoken to each other since the night of the party," Nora said.

"No, we haven't."

Nora looked at him for a moment, and he felt her scrutiny. "I wonder if this wasn't a mistake, agreeing to have the wedding here," she said. "Having you come is a little bit like taking a stick and poking it into a clear pond and watching the mud eddy up into the water."

"Was the pond so clear before I came?" he asked.

"It was," Nora said. "Yes, I think it was."

She turned, and Harrison watched her walk away along a narrow gravel path that circled around to the front of the inn. She moved briskly, head down, though she must have known he was looking at her. And doing so, he had a sudden and sharp memory of Nora as she had been when he'd seen her walking along a side street in Maine. He'd always remembered where and when he'd met Nora, but it had been years since he'd actually been able to *see* it as he could now. The clarity of the image took his breath away, and he thought, as he picked up his sweater from the rocker, that other such sharp pictures might reveal themselves during the weekend to come. For a moment, he stood with his hands on his hips and braced himself, even as he admired the spectacular view.

Agnes was writing about the Halifax explosion. She'd first learned about the blast early last summer while on a short vacation to Nova Scotia, a trip arranged by her local public radio station in conjunction with the history department at Kidd Academy. Halifax in early June had seemed like a good idea at the time, but as excursions go, it had been something of a strain — an unexpected tedium made worse by dismal weather, an unending rain that had so chilled her hands and feet, she'd had to warm them up each night using the hair dryer in her hotel room. Activities had been scheduled — tours into the countryside and to museums and so on — but Agnes had been happiest when on her own. In the mornings, she would do her five-mile run, shower, and breakfast, and if there were no appealing outings that day, she would walk the streets, enjoying her temporary freedom from the routine of academic life at Kidd.

On one of those walks, she stopped at a bookstore that had in its window a copy of a book entitled *A Flash Brighter than the Sun: The Halifax Explosion.* Intrigued, Agnes went inside, located the book, and riffled through its pages, paying close attention to the photographs of the city in the days immediately following the blast. She remembered in particular a picture of a child sitting on a white iron hospital bed, her eyes bandaged, her hair cut short in a manner similar to the way in which Agnes's own mother used to cut and comb her hair when Agnes was a girl: in a sort of bowl with the top of the hair drawn back into an elastic band that sat to one side of the crown of her head. There were other photographs in the book as well, of wooden buildings that had gracefully imploded and of acres of devastation, as if the city were Dresden or London in a future war.

Agnes purchased the book, tucked it into her backpack, and then walked on to a coffee shop where she ordered a cappuccino. She sat at her table, oblivious to the other patrons, and read that on the morning of December 6, 1917, a munitions ship, the *Imo* out of Belgium, collided in Halifax Harbor with a French freighter, the *Mont Blanc,* a ship carrying picric acid, benzole, and TNT to the conflict in Europe. The collision, which occurred shortly before 8:30 in the morning, caused a considerable stir in the Canadian city, the resulting fire bringing the citizens of Halifax to their windows to view the spectacle. Curiosity and a kind of compelling beauty caused them to linger, ignoring their breakfasts and the ironing and the need to go to school. Though Canada was involved in the war, Halifax had seen no action. It was instead a feeder city, supplying both men and matériel to Europe. A fire in the harbor, then, was a bit of excitement in what promised to be an otherwise uneventful day.

When the *Mont Blanc* exploded at 9:05, the windows of the houses near the harbor shattered, sending slivers of glass into the faces and eyes of many of those who were watching. Before day's end, 2,000 people died, 9,000 were wounded, and nearly 200 were completely or partially blinded, many of them children.

One of the reasons Agnes had begun writing about the Halifax explosion was that she'd had some visual disturbances of her own — odd liquid blips at the periphery of her eyesight that rose like oily bubbles in a cylinder. For a few weeks now, she'd been considering going to an ophthalmologist. Of course her eyesight was precious to her. She could hardly do her job without it. For seventeen years, she had been a history teacher as well as the coach of the girls' varsity field hockey team at Kidd Academy, a coed preparatory school located in northeastern Maine, a school to which she herself had gone.

Agnes particularly liked the history of Kidd Academy, founded in 1921 by textile manufacturer James Kidd, who had bought several of the larger summerhouses on the bluff just outside the village of Fenton, Maine, thinking to make of them a small boarding school for exceptional students — his son, of course, being one of them. Acquiring in a quiet manner most of the twenty-room "cottages" from the summer folk who'd been coming to the seacoast village for generations (but who were finding it harder and harder to keep up the behemoths without the legions of servants their own parents had employed), Kidd had the empty buildings winterized and set up as classrooms or dormitories. The old houses lent themselves to dorms, with their long corridors and many small bedrooms, and Agnes was sometimes amazed at how the school continued to have about it the air of a summer community. There were no Gothic spires at Kidd, no vast lawns. The weathered, shingled buildings were rarely taller than two or three stories. Cars were not permitted on campus, though the students managed them anyway, striking bargains with the natives for their garages in advance of the school year.

Agnes first joined the faculty of Kidd, where she had been a student, in the early 1980s, having spent five years teaching in the public schools, to which she was ill suited and vice versa. She was what she supposed people in Halifax in 1917 would have called a spinster. It was a hateful word that Agnes hesitated to say even in her thoughts, not only because of its antiquated and insulting nature but also because it suggested a bloodless woman of indeterminate age, whereas Agnes, apart from the new thing with the eyes, was in good health, excellent physical condition, and of a very precise age, which was forty-four.

When Agnes thought about the Halifax explosion, she imagined a man named Innes Finch, a young surgeon trained at the Medical School of Maine at Bowdoin, arriving in Halifax on the afternoon of December 5. So far, Agnes had written:

Innes stood on a street in the Richmond section of the city and watched the sun fall below a layer of olive cloud. The light moved along the road toward the surgeon, illuminating first a wooden house at the far corner, then a buggy with a pair of Clydesdales, and finally a woman struggling with a baby carriage on the cindered pavement. The luster of the wet street made Innes squint. He set down his cardboard suitcase — dented from its journey in the hold of the ferry and streaked with something that resembled axle grease — and covered the sun with his palm. He was preternaturally aware of clarity and color. The woman with the baby carriage gazed upward. A man in a naval uniform — a man who might have seen any number of visual phenomena on the high seas — turned to look behind him. Through a window next to Innes, a wooden mantle was set aflame, the grill of the panes making rectangular patterns on a pink-tinged wall.

The pellucid light was not an omen, Innes decided, picking up the streaked suitcase. Such displays were merely facts of physics — of luminosity and angles, of wavelengths and emissions.

Agnes didn't actually know if there was an Innes Finch in Halifax at that time. The odds would be much against it, wouldn't they, though she supposed that it was possible. More astonishing things had happened. Maybe there was only an Ian Finch or an Innes Findlay. But Agnes's Innes was now so real to her that when she thought about the incident, it was his narrative that intruded. This was a pattern, if not actually a habit, that Agnes was familiar with. Over the years, she had had to learn how to translate the global to the personal for her students, and she found she often did this in her own life as well. Whenever she witnessed or learned of an event too horrific to be absorbed, she began — not entirely subconsciously and not without some will — to imagine a specific person affected by that tragedy so that she could better understand it. She'd done it the previous spring when she'd seen, in her rearview mirror, a woman in a Volvo lose control of her vehicle, swerve erratically, and then begin to tumble end over end away from Agnes as she watched. She still thought from time to time about the woman's bewildered face, and then about her life as it might have been, even though she'd had only a second's glimpse of her. She could still see the woman's kitchen with its granite counter, and her son, perhaps fifteen, who sat at that counter eating cheddar cheese on Wheat Thins, his backpack slung against a chair, an algebra book spread out and touching an empty milk glass. Agnes imagined the boy waiting, at first oblivious and then mildly concerned, past 6:00, and then 7:00, until his father walked in the door — he, too, puzzled and then alarmed. What had happened to his wife, the boy's mother, who was just then lying in a hospital in Maine and who would, Agnes had decided, survive her horrific accident?

Agnes had done this as well after the catastrophe at the World Trade Center earlier in the fall. For days, Agnes had walked around in a kind of disbelieving daze until she'd happened to read a paragraph in the *New York Times* describing a young Hispanic woman who had died on the 102nd floor of the North Tower. As soon as Agnes had set down the paper, a life had begun to spool backward from the moment the woman had reached out toward the coffee machine and Flight 11 had struck the building. That woman was real to Agnes now, her life elaborate and complicated, and whenever someone mentioned the tragedy, Agnes had what amounted to fond memories of the woman and her daughter.

Innes Finch knocked on a door opened by a woman holding a skein of red yarn. Mrs. Fraser owned the house to which he had traveled and in which he had arranged to stay for several months. She seemed surprised to see Innes, though he had written that he would arrive before 4:00. Perhaps it was his appearance — tired, windblown, and on no account prepossessing — that made her hesitate.

"Come in," she demanded, perhaps wishing to make up for the tepid greeting. Innes stepped over the threshold and dripped onto a tiled floor. He held the suitcase, self-conscious now about the axle grease. He could have wiped it off in the harbor. He could have demanded that a steward do it for him, though Innes had never been good at giving orders. "I'm Mrs. Fraser," she added unnecessarily, her hands imprisoned in the wool.

Behind the skein of yarn was a structured bosom that Innes guessed would be hard to the touch. Mrs. Fraser was fifty-five possibly, fifty if she was unlucky in her looks. Her hair was as tightly corseted as her body, though her face creased unexpectedly into a nervous smile. Innes wondered why she might be nervous. Her posture was impressive.

"Dr. Fraser won't be home until six o'clock," she said. "He's at hospital. A complication with a surgery. Are you hungry? Do you need a bath? You could set that by the door, and I'll have it taken up to your room."

Innes had yet to say a word.

A man appeared, slow and slightly sullen. He was dressed in tie and jacket, though there was no mistaking him for anything but a servant. He took the suitcase and began to climb the stairs, treading heavily, a hand on the banister, each footfall a small and unwarranted reproach.

Innes took off his gloves and set them on the table.

"The coatrack is in the corner," Mrs. Fraser said.

"Could I give you a hand with that?" Innes asked, meaning the red yarn. He extended his arms to the twisted skein.

Mrs. Fraser hooked the coiled wool over the back of a mahogany chair. "You'd better come with me," she said. "I'll show you to your room. You must be wanting cocoa and a hot bath."

It was Agnes's opinion that at that moment in time Innes Finch wanted cocoa and a hot bath and a great deal more: challenging work and easy love; exciting risk; exceptional beauty.

Agnes didn't think that she had been particularly lucky in her own looks. Her face was prematurely weathered, a result of having stood on the sidelines of several hundred field hockey games and practices, as well as having spent nearly thirty years on the coast of Maine. She had a strong body, but not an elegant one. She was only five feet, four inches tall, which, these days, was considered short (her varsity girls towered over her). Her hair was light brown, cropped close to the head, and lately it had begun to frizz in the humidity, which she found annoying. She did have, however, beautiful eyes — deep set and dark brown in color, the only feature about which she routinely received compliments. When she first started teaching, she used to wear wool skirts with oxford cloth shirts each day to her classes. Now, with the looser dress code, she usually put on a pair of chinos and a polo shirt. She prided herself on the fact that she still had a waist.

For twelve of the seventeen years Agnes had taught at Kidd, she had resided in school housing. Some of the faculty lived on the beach in small cottages referred to as shacks, but most lived on campus in dorm apartments. After more than a decade of duty as a dorm parent, Agnes now had a condo, leased to her until she stopped teaching, at which time it would revert to the school.

It was an unusual condo, carved from one of the larger houses, and Agnes thought she could be quite happy there until she retired. She lived in a corner of the house that included a two-story turret. On the first floor, she had a kitchen and a living room, and in the turret itself a large round table surrounded by a leather banquette and windows. She lived at that table, eating, correcting papers, and composing lineups and drills for her teams. On the second floor was a large bath and, in the turret, her bed, not round, the head-board situated so that she could look out to sea, an activity that consumed an inordinate amount of her time. She also had a small balcony off the bedroom on which she could sit and do the same with a cappuccino in hand, the expensive machine a gift from her sister, who worked for Citibank in New York.

Nearly every residence on the campus had a view — of surf, of pebbled beach, of rocky coastline. The campus land had been left untended so that it was all beach scrub and footpaths between buildings. Though there was a certain drama in being perched on a bluff overlooking the ocean, the feel of the school was more homely than grand. In winter, the wind was terrific. Whole months went by when Agnes did not open her windows for fear that the wind would blow over her plants. An old golf course had been turned into playing fields, with the gymnasium situated directly in its center. From the team's practice field, Agnes could see not only the ocean but also the wild hydrangeas that surrounded the head-master's house. Most of the students quickly grew oblivious to their exhilarating surroundings, though occasionally Agnes would see one of them sitting on the rocks, looking out to sea. Despite any number of signs prohibiting it, the students sometimes rowed out to Pepperell Island to drink and party, and inevitably one would attempt to mount the narrow spiral stairway in the abandoned lighthouse. The student would make it to the top and then would blanch on the way down when it became obvious there was nothing to hold on to: one slip might send him or her plummeting into the dark well of the tower. Miraculously, no one had died doing it.

Agnes loved the campus and its cinnamon beach plums intermingled with fuchsia roses, a hardy species that managed to survive the northern New England coastal winters, the roses always in bloom in June and again during the first weeks of September. She wished she knew birds, because Fenton was a birder's paradise. They were in the marshes with the goldenrod and the stiff, clean air. It was well-known that many of the residents of Fenton — the true natives, all 148 of them — lived well into their nineties, a fact Agnes didn't think could be attributed entirely to genetics. Flowers set in Fenton water lasted for weeks. (Agnes drank a great deal of the local water, imagining it as a preservative.) She was charmed by the jumbled roofline of the village and the stretch of expensive honky-tonk beach houses. She was endlessly captivated by the squat curves of the lobster boats just offshore, with their engines thrumming and the lone silhouettes on the sterns. She even liked the 1940s look of the naked telephone wires stretching along the beach road to the village, suggesting a thread-thin link with the outside world. There was at Kidd a vast sense of natural privilege, of entitlement, of having something others spent millions to get — houses with views of the Atlantic — and which was, incidentally, no small attraction for the parents who sent their children there.

Agnes realized suddenly that she might have missed the exit. She did this all the time, daydreamed when she should be paying attention to her driving. She glanced at the handwritten directions on the seat beside her. She could get off at the next exit, at which time she could orient herself. It had been a long drive, and there was a cramp running all along her right thigh from her knee to her buttocks. She tried to maneuver the leg into a different position but couldn't. She had to apply a steady pressure to the gas pedal.

The clock on the dashboard read 12:00 noon. Agnes was hungry despite the stop in southern Maine. She couldn't imagine Nora's house as an inn. Agnes had visited the place before, but only when Carl Laski had lived there, and once again for his funeral. She remembered it as primitive and dark, with a dismal kitchen and a warren of tiny rooms upstairs. Her own bedroom had lacked sufficient heat and had had on the bed a crazy quilt of velvet and silk that Nora had found at a flea market. It was frayed at some of the seams, but it was a wonderful object to behold, the labor astonishing. Agnes hoped Nora had kept the quilt. Agnes had heard, in lengthy letters written in Nora's precise and upright hand, of all the renovations and of their exorbitant cost, and of Nora's belief that the inn would soon begin to pay off some of the monstrous debt. The money that Carl Laski had left Nora was gone now, but Nora's last letter had sounded optimistic. The inn was booked through to the end of February. Nora complained about having to write letters and not being able to reach Agnes via e-mail, but Agnes believed Nora enjoyed the letters, the writing of them as much as the receiving of them.

Agnes drove for what seemed like a long stretch and then pulled into a rest area. She parked her car, grabbed her backpack, and went inside the building. After visiting the bathroom, she stood in line for a coffee and a doughnut and then found a table at which to sit. When she'd finished the doughnut, she wiped her hands on a paper napkin and rummaged through her backpack. She took out her notebook and a pen.

Agnes had never written a short story before, despite having taught both English and history. The writing was a secret. She hadn't even told Jim. Perhaps one day, if she finished the story, she would send it to him.

Mrs. Fraser lingered for a moment in the doorway of the room she had assigned to Innes, as if impressing his face and form to her memory, as if the man might vanish as quickly as he had come. Mrs. Fraser had two daughters, and young men of good appearance produced in her a double-pronged anxiety: her daughters currently had no husbands, and the Frasers had no sons. Mrs. Fraser announced that dinner would be at 8:00. At Innes's school, the students had dressed for dinner, trailing whiffs of formaldehyde to the dining room. At home, his family had dressed only on Sundays. The place where dinner was called "supper" seemed very far away now, farther even than the distance that five years of medical school and a war had put between them.

His brother, Martin, was in France; Innes was in Halifax. Innes had imperfect feet and a childhood asthma that inexplicably had disappeared in the months after he had failed his military physical. He thought often of trying again. It was said they didn't care about the feet now. But his professors had insisted that he could better serve his country by honing his surgical skills. Soldiers were taking shrapnel to the eyes. A man's sight might be saved. If the war was still on when he finished his training *(though dear God let's hope not),* Innes could go abroad and do some good.

Innes was twenty-seven, late to his vocation.

He touched a small stain on the marble top of a dresser and wondered whose room he had usurped. The mirror above the bureau tilted in its frame, and Innes adjusted it so that he could see himself. Years of studying and northern light had left his skin pale, his hair dark. His eyes were a Prussian blue that seemed genetically wrong in such an unremarkable face. Looking at him, one was reminded of coming upon the ocean in the middle of the winter. Though the color had leached itself from the landscape, the blue of the water was just as vivid as in July.

He set his books upon the marble dresser top. Inside were all the words he had had to study. He brushed his palm against the pebbled leather. The books were well-made. A thousand times they'd been opened, and yet the spines still held.

The texts had taught him some of what he had to know. The rest he had learned during his clinical studies. He now understood, for example, how a man was likely to react to the news that he would be blind for the rest of his life. First there would be the facial paralysis, descending to the body, an eerie immobility that could last for minutes. Then there would be the shock that blotted out physical and emotional pain, a kind of merciful interlude. Innes had hardly ever heard a patient cry out immediately. Instead the mind created images and scenes of how it would be to live without one's sight, to be forever blind, trying it on like a suit of clothes. And then, finally, the weakened limbs, the need to put a hand to a chair for support. Even the youngest and strongest of them walked away as if bludgeoned.

Innes had gravitated to surgery and to ophthalmology in particular because his mother had begun to go blind when Innes was thirteen. This caused him to think about eyes all the time and, as he grew older, to try to invent ingenious methods to help his mother to see. Once he fashioned a kind of metal corona that she was to wear around her face so as to trap more light. Another time, he went to a druggist to learn how to grind a pair of lenses. The lenses were so heavy, however, that his mother couldn't keep the spectacles on the bridge of her nose. She finally told him to stop: it was enough, she said, that Innes himself had perfect vision.

Innes went south to Maine to medical school, but now he had come home. Not to the fishing village in Cape Breton where his mother and sister made nets and sweaters, but to the city he had always longed for. He would complete his training at Dalhousie with Dr. Fraser. And then he would go out into the world.

History, Agnes always told her students on the first day of school, was not a matter of dates and battles, but rather one of stories. She would tell them stories, she announced, and they would listen. But as Agnes put her pen and notebook away, she wondered this: Is imagination dependent upon experience, or is experience influenced by the imagination?

Agnes left the rest area and drove in the direction of the inn. After a short time, she spotted the sign she was looking for. She realized, as she slowed for the exit, that she was excited. Who would be there? Harrison, for one. And Bill and Bridget. Rob. Jerry and his wife, whom Agnes had never met — had any of them met the wife? Agnes hadn't seen Harrison or Rob or Jerry in more than twenty years. She would hug them, of course, but they would be strangers to her. She thought about all the days that had intervened since they'd last spoken to one another. And it was then that she recognized the source of her excitement. They would know Jim. She would actually be able to say Jim's name aloud to them. Of course, they would know him only as Mr. Mitchell, the young English teacher who had introduced them first to Whitman and O'Neill and then to Kerouac and to Sylvia Plath. He had made them laugh even as they had imagined themselves budding intellectuals. Agnes would be able to say — oh so casually — *Remember Mr. Mitchell?*

(A muscular chest, a gap between a belt buckle and his pelvic bones. A pang — a longing as familiar to Agnes as breathing — moved through her body, and she waited for it to pass.)

Would she tell them? Did it matter now? Yes, of course it mattered. Jim was still married. But if she'd been able to tell them, what would they say? They would be shocked. Their Agnes — sturdy, studious, and sometimes stubborn (though surely they had never thought her sexy) — involved in an affair with a man who had once been their teacher.

Jim. In her bones and in her blood. She would tell them of how it had all begun, of the challenge of keeping the affair a secret, of the places she and Jim had gone to be together. And later, when she was teaching in the public schools, of how they would meet in motels and hotels in anonymous towns and cities. She remembered — indeed, fed off of — the thrill of driving to a place she had never been before, checking into a hotel, and then finding Jim, as they had agreed, in the bar at a prearranged time. And later still, of how she had interviewed at Kidd and surprised Jim with the news, and how she saw him then every day for three years until finally he'd left to go to Wisconsin, after which they'd had to resume their intermittent rendezvous. Nora and Harrison and Bridget and the others would remember that Jim had been married. And when they learned that he still was, would they then want to know how Agnes had lived with this fact all these years? Twenty-six years, to be precise?

She would answer their questions with a question: Why was a marriage the only possible happy ending?

(No, she wouldn't discuss this, she realized suddenly. This was Bridget's wedding, after all.)

But still. Agnes would like to ask what they thought was more real, the living of a love affair or the imagining of it? Wasn't it more delicious to engage in a transcendental passion than to endure the messy and boring mechanics of actual marriage? In Agnes's ideal scenario, she and Jim would continue to meet in anonymous rooms in anonymous hotels. Agnes had little desire to be a wife. Rather, she wanted to be the steady mistress. If only she could be certain that the affair would last, that Jim would be there on a consistent basis.

Agnes desired certitude.

Maybe it was not entirely true that Agnes would not have chosen marriage had she been given the opportunity. The difficulty was that Jim sometimes had doubts. He was occasionally overcome by guilt. He wrestled with moral quandaries. That struggle kept him apart from Agnes, usually for months, occasionally for years.

Agnes would ask another question then. If a man didn't have the courage of his convictions, was he still a good man?

But how did one define "good"? Agnes wondered. She thought of Bill and Bridget, grasping at a bit of happiness before what might become a dreadful time for both of them. Could a woman truly love a man who had left his wife and child to be with her? Was Bill a *good* man? Was the romance real, even though the man had shown himself to be capable of betrayal? What price was Bill's wife paying for his happiness? And conversely, what price was Jim's wife — *Carol,* such a cold name — paying as she unwittingly lived with a man who didn't love her?

Of course, Agnes would say none of this.

Jim's last letter to Agnes had been in June. Agnes had written to Jim twice since 9/11, but she had had no reply.

Agnes cherished Jim's letters. They were full of declarations of love and passion. They were full of remembering. He was the only person on the other side of their shared history. Agnes believed in Jim's letters wholeheartedly.

Agnes had waited for so long. She could wait some more.

Stories, Agnes thought, were usually about things that had occurred. Her particular story was about things that had not occurred.

What had not occurred was the sum of all the days and years she and Jim had not had together, the days and years that could never be returned. But, she thought, her story wasn't over yet. Possibilities remained. Sometimes Agnes felt frozen in the expectation of a remarkable destiny that might still materialize.

Agnes followed well-posted signs for the inn (tasteful gold lettering on a dark green background) through small villages and then along a narrow road and finally up a long drive. She pulled into the parking area, relieved to have found the place with no wrong turns. She got out of her Honda Civic, her knee stiff from having remained so long in one position, and limped a bit as she retrieved her luggage from the backseat. Briefly she admired the view, which had not changed, before turning her attention to the house that now gleamed in the sunlight.

My God, she thought, what a transformation!

The house she remembered, Carl Laski's house, had been in near derelict condition, the paint peeling, the sills rotting, the porch floor tentative in places. Now the facade of the inn, with its new cottage windows, fresh paint, and remade porch, resembled a spread one might see in a magazine. Tubs of thriving yellow mums flanked the entrance. The front door, on which there was a Christmas wreath, had been propped open. What day was this anyway? December 7? December 8?

Agnes hoisted her orange nylon duffel bag and her backpack over her shoulder and made her way up the steps and into the lobby. Before her was a long hallway with a highly polished dark wood floor, a stairway with intricately curved posts, and to her right, a reception desk, uninhabited. Agnes set down her luggage. She could hear voices from behind the reception desk. She wandered, arms crossed against her chest, to the sitting room at the right. Two sofas and several armchairs had been arranged in three groupings. Instantly Agnes wanted to lie down. There was a fire-place, not lit, at one end of the room, and at the other, an octago-nal game table of black wood. Agnes recalled for a moment the old sitting room, dark with walnut furniture, an upright piano against one wall, the tables and floor covered with books and magazines, wineglasses and ashtrays.

Agnes crossed the hallway and entered another room, one wall of which was a bank of windows that looked out to the shallow mountains in the distance, the sky above them blue dust. She tried to remember what the room had been before the renovation: Carl's office maybe? She heard footsteps on the wooden floor and re-turned to the hallway. A young woman with thin blond hair was standing behind the desk running her finger down a page of a large guest book. She looked up and noticed Agnes.

"Oh, hi," the woman said. "You just got here?" Her glance slid to the orange duffel bag, which looked garishly out of place in the muted lobby.

Agnes nodded.

"And you are?"

Agnes gave her name.

The woman bent toward the guest book and flipped a page. "There's a note here that says I should go get Nora when you arrive. You're a friend?"

"I am," Agnes said.

"Do you want to be shown to your room? Or would you rather wait while I find Nora?"

Agnes was torn. Nora might be busy now, and Agnes's arrival would be an inconvenience. Though wouldn't it be rude not to see her?

"I'll wait for her," Agnes said.

"I think Nora's in the kitchen."

While she waited, Agnes examined the hallway again. She noted the chair-rail molding and above it a series of black-and-white photos tastefully matted and framed in thin black wood. They were of village scenes from the 1920s and 1930s, to judge from the automobiles in the pictures. One was of a drugstore, with a woman in a suit and hat emerging. Another was of a house perched on a hill. Edith Wharton's house, if memory served.

"Agnes."

She turned, and Nora embraced her.

"Look at you!" Nora said, stepping back.

"Look at me? Look at the house!" Agnes said. "Nora, what have you done? It's amazing. I hardly recognize it."

"Do you like it?"

Agnes saw at once that Nora might be slightly vulnerable here, having anticipated and perhaps feared reviews. "What I've seen so far is beautiful," Agnes said at once to ease her mind. "You've done so much work."

"I have," Nora said, not dissembling. "Yes. I have. Well, not always me. Mostly it was the contractor and the architect and the craftsmen. But it *feels* as though I hammered in every nail, scraped every wall. Come. Let me show you the rest."

Nora turned to the woman behind the desk. "Judy, have Dennis take Agnes's suitcase — is this everything?" she asked Agnes, and Agnes nodded — "up to room twenty-two.

"I think you'll like your room," Nora added to Agnes.

"Not my old room then."

"It doesn't exist. I . . . I had several of the smaller rooms combined into suites. You'll have one of those."

"Will it still have the quilt?" Agnes asked, allowing herself to be shown into the sitting room she'd visited just minutes before.

"What quilt?"

"The crazy quilt with the velvet and silk?"

"I think I packed that away. Maybe I'll get it out again. It was frayed, wasn't it?"

"It was lovely," Agnes said. "I loved it anyway," she added.

"We broke through a wall here and opened up this room," Nora said, pointing. "We . . . they . . . finally got the fireplace to work, after all these years."

Agnes remembered that the old house had been impossible to heat and that she, Carl, and Nora had often sat around with thick sweaters and blankets. Mostly, though, it had been just Agnes and Nora, Carl usually elsewhere, across the hallway writing or at school.

"Come see the kitchen," Nora said.

Agnes followed Nora through swinging doors. Though Nora was dressed simply in a white shirt and black pants, Agnes couldn't help but notice the chic cut of the shirt, the way it slipped just so over Nora's slim hips, the way the pants were tailored so as to fall perfectly straight and narrow to the expensive black leather boots. "Your hair," Agnes said.

Nora put a hand to the back of her head. "I got rid of it," she said. "Too much work."

Agnes could not imagine what work Nora was referring to. She remembered Nora's hair as thick and chestnut colored, with red threads catching the light. She absentmindedly fingered her own hair, short because it had to be. With any length it would look lank and stringy. Why, if you had such riches, Agnes wondered, would you divest yourself of them? "How have you been?" Agnes asked, meaning Carl.

"Fine," Nora said with a firmness that was new to Agnes. "Fine," she repeated, and Agnes could hear a distracted note. As owner of the inn, Nora could be expected to be preoccupied. "Harrison is here," Nora added.

"Is he?" Agnes asked, surveying a room in which the old dismal kitchen was only a faded memory. Two men were working at a pair of stoves set into an island topped with black granite. There were as well two large stainless steel refrigerators, a massive porcelain sink, two stainless steel dishwashers, and a set of white shelves on which dozens of ivory dishes had been stacked.

"I've had fun collecting these," Nora said, making a sweeping gesture to include the dishes. "I go to flea markets and junk shops to find them. Some are very old. They're all mismatched. Which is to me their charm. Any one table setting in the dining room might contain several different patterns."

A long bank of cottage windows let in natural light, though overhead, glass globes hung over the stoves and countertop. For a moment, Agnes flashed on the old kitchen, a narrow room with a table under a small window at one end and a fridge at the other. The cabinets had been painted a 1950s aqua; the floor had been a dark linoleum that Nora could never get entirely clean, no matter how hard she scrubbed. Empty wine bottles with candles in them were perched on ledges, and there had been no view from that kitchen window, just the one glimpse of the front porch. Agnes, as was her habit everywhere, had always been first down to make the coffee. She much enjoyed those solitary moments, watching the light come up, the night turning into day. Nora would join her around 8:30, Carl not at all. He worked until noon, after which he would drive his green VW to St. Martin's for his classes. She remembered dinners that began at nine and lasted until midnight, Agnes begging off in search of her bed with the crazy quilt, leaving the couple downstairs still drinking and smoking and sometimes arguing, a single word occasionally climbing the narrow staircase and making its way down the hall to her ears.

Though it hadn't registered at the time and was now apparent only by contrast, Nora hadn't been entirely well then. Agnes remembered a pale face, translucent bluish shadows under the eyes, the body thin but not strong. Nora had worn long skirts and boots and sweaters and large silver hoop earrings. Carl had always treated Agnes decently (she'd had the feeling he'd been asked to do so), though it was his nature to pry and to scrutinize even the most seemingly innocuous reply. One learned to speak carefully around Carl Laski, unless one was very drunk, which sometimes happened, in which case recklessness might lead to heedlessness and then almost certainly to an argument disguised, as they could all do so well, as intellectual debate. Despite being decidedly looped upon occasion, however, Agnes had never been tempted to tell either of them about Jim, not even Nora, whom she genuinely loved.

Agnes briefly closed her eyes. Where would Jim be now? She glanced at the oversize wooden clock set amid the shelves. He would be at an early lunch, in the dining hall, she guessed, or perhaps taking a walk around the vast grounds of the private school at which he now taught. Would he have a thought of her today?

"You kept that," Agnes said, pointing to the clock.

"Yes, I did. Harrison's here. Did I say that already? He got here about an hour ago. Let me show you to your room."

"Oh, Nora," Agnes said, clearly pleased for her friend, her old roommate from Kidd. "I'm happy to see you looking so well."

"I am well," Nora said with a quick smile. "I'm very well."

Agnes followed Nora up the back stairs — not as grand as the staircase in the front hallway — and along a corridor of polished hardwood floors with small tables set at intervals on which sat bouquets of fresh flowers. Nora stopped at one door and opened it with a key — a real gold-colored key — and held the door so that Agnes could enter first.

It was not the standard-issue country inn room, Agnes thought. No chintz, no patterned curtains, no ruffled bedspreads. Instead, a feeling of simplicity and calm overtook her, and once again she had a strong desire to lie down. The bed and side tables were of a black wood. The bedding was a simple white duvet with a black border, the motif repeated on the pillowcases and shams. Chrome reading lights protruded from the wall, which had been painted a pale taupe. Under the bank of three windows was a white chaise with a chenille throw and on the other side of the room, a black desk with a chair. On a valise stand rested Agnes's orange duffel bag, the only wrong note in this pleasing sonata.

"This could be in *House & Garden,*" Agnes said. "Have you had photographs taken?"

"Oh," Nora said. "A few."

In the bathroom was a tumbled marble counter with polished chrome fixtures that looked as though they'd come from England. Tucked into an alcove and under another bank of windows was an oval bathtub, a Jacuzzi. The linens as well as the bath mats underfoot were plush and white.

"I'm simply amazed," Agnes said, unable any longer to keep from walking to the bed and sitting down.

"You must be tired," Nora said. "I'll let you rest." Nora checked her watch, a gesture Agnes couldn't ever remember Nora making before. Had she even owned a watch?

"To think of you with all of this," Agnes said. She thought about how it might take years to find the thing you really wanted, at which you were really good.

Nora moved toward the door, setting the gold key on the desk. "I'll see you at drinks tonight. If not before. Six-thirty in the library?"

Agnes laughed. "How nice for us that Bill and Bridget decided to get married." She paused. "How *is* Bridget?" she asked.

"I think it will be a strain for her," Nora said. "But Bill . . . Bill insists he has enough energy and desire for the two of them. We're trying to keep this simple. Bridget may have to leave from time to time to rest. But that's fine. We'll all manage."

"I'm sure it will be lovely," Agnes said.

"If you just go to the dining room, whatever the time, someone will find you and feed you."

Nora shut the door behind her. Alone, Agnes lay down on the bed and then scuttled along the duvet so that her head rested upon the silky-crisp pillowcase. She thought immediately of Jim, of how she wished he were with her. Agnes imagined surprising Nora and the others with her lover, the instant celebrity that would attend her for having brought a former teacher to their gathering — and carrying with her the whiff of scandal, too. But again, *no*, Agnes would not do that. It would be wrong to upstage Bridget at her own wedding. So there would be no Jim at the inn, though she longed for him. She fanned her arm along the duvet, touching the space where Jim might have lain. Sometimes, the longing was keen and rough-edged, and in an instant could turn to rage or self-pity. *Why me?* Agnes would sometimes cry out. Why could she not have the one thing she really wanted? She would give up everything else. Really she would. Even if she only had a year. Would she take that? A year of frequent and regular meetings and then never again? Yes, she thought she would. For no matter how hard it would be to part after that year, at least she would have had *something*.

But then again, she thought, she did have *something*. It was a something large and indefinable, but it was her life.

Agnes sighed and rolled over onto her stomach. She wished she could forget.

Agnes did not have the luxury of forgetting.

She got up off the bed and walked to the window. She leaned her forehead against the glass. At least, she thought, she would be able to write to Jim again without seeming too pushy, without first having had a reply from him. For how could she not write to him of this reunion of his former students? He would want to hear of them, wouldn't he? She would write him a long letter, describing the inn and Nora and all of the others as best she could. She would write a chatty letter — no, a witty letter, one that would make him laugh. There would be no words of love in the letter. It would simply be a missive from one friend to another, multilayered, rich, and detailed.

Agnes saw a man emerging from the entrance. He walked with his hands in the pockets of his trousers. He had on a navy sweater over a white dress shirt. His hair was dark and thinning just at the crown. The man made a turn where a path curved around to the back of the inn, and Agnes saw then that it was Harrison Branch. Agnes pushed at the window to open it and realized it was locked. By the time she unlocked the window, Harrison had turned the corner. Agnes would have liked to call to Harrison, would have liked to surprise him with her voice and face. They might have had lunch together. She remembered the boy, diffident and talented, an athlete who didn't make her nervous in the way the other boys sometimes could and did. A boy who was not exceptionally good-looking — not in the way Stephen was, for example — but whose face was immediately appealing. Harrison had been a friend of the popular boys and yet somehow had not been one of them. Agnes imagined that had it not been for his athleticism, particularly on the baseball diamond, he might have been something of a loner. Often she had seen him walking the streets of Fenton by himself.

But Stephen. One could not have a thought of Harrison and not immediately afterward think about Stephen. Stephen, whose deep fear of boredom had sometimes pushed him blindly forward. Stephen, who had managed to remain lovable despite his popularity, whose desire for risk, which they all had found so appealing, had often got the better of him. Stephen, who remained fixed in place, while all the others had gone on — grown older, married, had children, had affairs, failed in both love and work — whereas Stephen had simply stopped. Like all those people at the World Trade Center had simply stopped. Like all those people in Halifax had simply stopped.

Agnes sat at the desk, and Innes checked his tie in the mirror over the bureau. She picked up her pen.

He wondered if he would be the only man at dinner not in uniform, and he hoped that Dr. Fraser hadn't signed on in some reserve capacity. The lack of a uniform begged explanation, which Innes didn't like to give, since the asthma was plainly absent and the rest sounded either feeble or self-serving. He hadn't had to explain himself often because he had lived in a universe of American students and physicians (their numbers dwindling after April, when America had entered the war), but he could see that he might have to invent, for the casual acquaintance, an ironclad reason why he was not in service dress. It occurred to him that apart from Dr. Fraser, there might be no men at dinner at all, since so many had been sent abroad.

He opened the door of his room and glanced to either side of the hallway. He saw no other activity, no one to guide him to the sitting room. It was a modest house, though he had a sense of many rooms. He saw himself already slightly lost, opening doors and closing them in search of another human being. He hoped not a servant. Decidedly not the sullen man who had carried his suitcase.

Innes descended the stairway to the front hall. From another room, he could hear voices. He heard someone say "chutney jar" at the end of a question, and from elsewhere, with some emphasis, the word "socks." The doors off the hallway were shut, reminding Innes of Mrs. Fraser's unwelcoming bosom.

Innes guessed that the large oak door to his right might lead to a sitting room. He gave it a try, and it opened to a chamber lit with a globular lamp that did little to illuminate an otherwise shadowy expanse. He noted that the heavy blackout curtains were drawn. He heard the crackle of the fire and, like a primitive, headed in its direction. As he did, he saw a woman sitting with her back to him. Innes hesitated. The woman seemed not to know he was there (was her indifference deliberate or had he really been so stealthy?) and he did not want to intrude upon her perfect immobility. On the other hand, he was a guest, expected to know little of the household, expected to be welcomed. Besides, if he left now, he would almost certainly make a sound, and then the question of why he was retreating would have to be raised.

"Good evening," he said, his throat needing a clearing.

Innes advanced, and the woman turned her head, not to Innes directly, but in profile to acknowledge him. The lamp on the console behind her lit up as much of her face as she had allowed. He was struck first by the hair, a dark mass that had been done up in an intricate knot and then let loose in a broad sweep that came low over her forehead and covered her ears. Her cheek was smooth — she was young: nineteen, twenty? — her mouth in repose. Her eyebrow sloped downward in nearly a straight line, and her eyelashes formed an exquisite curve. Eager to see the whole face, Innes walked toward her, saying, *Hello* and *I'm glad to have found someone.*

She held out her hand, and he took it.

Innes could make out all of her face now, the brief smile erasing the odd chill of the profile only. She had lustrous dark eyes. Over a dress of thin black polka-dot material, she had on an almost iridescent feathery blue wrap. Innes could see the outlines of a black corset or a slip. The collar of the dress was wide and low, suggesting a sailor's. The skirt of her dress lay in folds just below her knee.

"You must be Mr. Finch," she said. "I'm Hazel Fraser. I'm first down. I'm having a sherry. Will you join me? I'm sorry to say my father is not back yet. I know you must be eager to meet him."

"I am," Innes said. He stood with his hands at his sides. He had not been invited to sit. Should he pour his own sherry? Yes, of course he should. He bent toward the bottle on the table in front of Hazel, aware that his hand was trembling, regretting that he had not waited a decent interval or declined altogether, for she would certainly see the trembling, which was even more pronounced as he picked up the small gold-and-blue goblet from the tray. He counted six goblets and wondered who the others would be.

"Please sit," Hazel said when Innes had finally managed the business of the bottle and the glass, trembling fingers a death knell for an eye surgeon, though Innes's hands were always rock steady in the operating theater. There, a cold certainty stole over him. As a physician, he was supremely focused and, he some-times thought, gifted.

"How was your journey?" she asked.

"Uneventful," Innes said, adjusting his suit as he sat. He had only the one suit and two shirts, which would be inadequate for the city. He hoped there would be time to visit a tailor, though he would have to be frugal with his purchases. Until a salary was negotiated — Innes assumed a salary, though there had been no discussion of that eventuality — he had only the money that his sister and mother had sent, a fortune to them but barely enough to cover the expense of a new suit.

"The very best sort," Hazel said, "though one always secretly longs for adventure."

"Do you think so?" Innes asked. "I should think an absence of adventure a good thing during wartime."

"Here one longs for excitement," Hazel said. "We are a backwater city."

Innes searched for a diplomatic response.

"I've lived here all my life," she added. "But you," she said with superb manners, shifting the emphasis away from herself, "you have had an intriguing time of it — school in America, I'm told. A degree in medicine."

So Hazel knew that Innes was from Cape Breton. Doubtless she knew his circumstances as well. "If cadavers and libraries and books be thrilling," he said, meaning it to sound kindly and not arch, "then perhaps I have." He could see now that the woman he had just met (he adjusted her age to twenty-three or -four: a certain gravity about the mouth) desired risk, that it was on her mind and on her tongue, though possibly she struggled not to allow others to see it. Hence, the perfect immobility.

(Innes thought that, yes, he had had a certain kind of adventure, though not one of traveling abroad and studying for his degree. Rather, his had been one he would just as soon forget — the necessary struggle of the poor, the daily quest for food, an endeavor that held risk and sometimes resulted in death, as when his father, a fisherman, had been washed overboard from his vessel. Innes now belonged to the category of people who longed not for bodily adventure, for he had had that, but rather for some quite tangible adventure of the mind. That he awaited eagerly, impatiently.)

"There you are," Innes heard behind him. He pictured the rapidly advancing figure of Mrs. Fraser even before he saw her. He was surprised by how much he minded the abrupt interruption. He had not even begun to have a proper conversation with Hazel, a conversation that could not be continued now in Mrs. Fraser's presence, a fact that admitted of a certain kind of intimacy between himself and the woman sitting across from him, however slight, a conversation that suddenly seemed urgent to Innes, not because of its content, which might, after all, turn out to be banal, but because he had not heard enough of Hazel's voice.

"You've found the sherry, I see," Mrs. Fraser added, implying an act of poaching. Innes stood, as good manners demanded. He couldn't sit unless Mrs. Fraser sat, and she showed no inclination to do so. Indeed, she seemed agitated, even slightly affronted, which couldn't be, Innes reasoned, simply the sherry.

"May I pour you a glass?" Innes asked, bending slightly toward the bottle, catching Hazel's bemused eye as he did so. Innes also saw, in the firelight, a circle of tiny diamonds on a finger of the hand holding the blue-and-gold goblet.

"Not just now," Mrs. Fraser said, suggesting that possibly the hour for drinks had not yet arrived (another small affront?). "Hazel," she added, looking pointedly from the young woman to the still-standing Innes, "wherever is *Louise?*"

And it was then, as Innes straightened to his full height (he was not exceptionally tall, though he towered over the diminutive Mrs. Fraser), that he began to understand that in Mrs. Fraser's eyes, and perhaps implying some fault of his own, he had introduced himself to the wrong sister.

As it should be, Agnes thought, setting down her pen and standing up from the desk. With some satisfaction, she moved to the bed and began to unpack her duffel bag.

Bridget studied the two fifteen-year-old boys in the backseat: both asleep, bodies sprawled, mouths open, the tinny sound of music audible through the headphones that covered their ears. Matt, her son, had smooth skin despite the expected legacy of his father's acne. His friend's face was nearly ravaged, a cruel announcement of the arrival of adolescence. Bridget wanted to tell Brian about BenzaClin and tetracycline, but could one do that without insulting him? Probably not. Perhaps Bridget could mention the antibiotics to Brian's mother? No, that might be just as bad. Bridget would stay out of it, then. And didn't she have enough to worry about without taking on the burden of Brian's complexion?

Still though. The miracles of modern medicine.

Bridget lingered on Matt's sleeping face, something she was seldom able to do now. More often than not, her son was still awake when she went to bed, his circadian rhythms wildly out of sync with her own. Though Bridget saw him sleeping in the mornings when she went upstairs to fetch him for school, it was a chore she dreaded. Matt woke sullen and uncooperative, a deep resistance to being snatched from his dreams evident in his heavy footsteps to the bathroom, his overlong showers, and his maddening inability to pick out a shirt and a pair of pants in a timely fashion. Rarely would he eat breakfast, and trying to engage Matt in conversation in the early morning brought little joy. Instead, mother and son communicated in short interrogatives that Bridget suspected were being repeated throughout North America. *You have your back-*

*pack? Your cleats? Did you finish your homework? What time is prac-
tice over?* Answers might come in the form of grunts that could es-
calate to snappish replies if Bridget asked one question too many.
She had learned over the last year and a half to be present if
needed, invisible if not, a skill she had nearly mastered.

Afternoons were better. Matt, more sociable when he got home
from school, charged through the door, smelling of the gym or the
playing fields, ravenous and willing to consume almost any food
put in front of him. It was the only time Bridget could get him to
eat vegetables — raw with a dip. Matt would talk to her, her questions accepted as valid, though she rationed them and never asked
the same thing two days in a row. Since she had become ill, Matt
was, upon occasion, solicitous. He might ask her (suddenly looking
up at her from his guitar) how she was, or Bridget might catch him
studying her face when he thought she wasn't looking. Bridget had
attempted to hide as much of the illness as she could from her son,
Bill getting the brunt of it and accepting it without complaint.

It was Bill who stayed home from work on the days Bridget received the chemotherapy, who sat with her while the medicine was
fed through the IV. Bridget could not think of it as poison, which
many patients did and which she supposed it was. Rather, she pre-
ferred to think of the three chemicals that dripped into her body as
beneficent potions. And it was Bill who was in the house during
the afternoons and evenings when Bridget could not raise her head
from the pillow. On treatment days, Bill brought her ricotta cheese
and fruit, oddly the only food that appealed to her. He left her
alone when she wanted, or stood in the bedroom, hands on his
hips, while she threw up in the bathroom. She did not like him to
see, though she knew he could hear. Occasionally, when she was
nauseated, a terrible sensation of panic would overtake her, and she
would call out to him, and he would come. His presence, just outside the bathroom door, would be enough to calm her. He would

remind her that the ordeal would be over soon and that the medicine was doing its job, platitudes she just as easily could have told herself.

She glanced at Bill behind the wheel — at his steely hair, at his round face, sculpting itself with age; at the other sculpture of his torso, coming undone with the years, like ice slowly melting. Bridget loved Bill. Not fiercely, as she loved her son. Not all-consumingly, as she had once loved Bill as a teenager. But, rather, solidly and knowingly, a deep undercurrent of passion and memory running below a grateful surface.

Aware of her attention, he turned his head and reached out with his hand, giving her something between a pat and a poke, the touch both automatic and reassuring. "How are you doing?" he asked.

"Fine," she said, knowing Bill would accept her answer, even as she knew *he* knew she might be lying.

Bridget wasn't fine. Since the chemo, long drives made her carsick. She ached to get out and to stretch her legs, to breathe fresh air. She was hungry, too, another consequence of the chemo, the constant need to put food in her stomach as well as a perfectly justifiable desire to indulge herself from time to time causing a weight gain of twelve pounds in six weeks. The weight gain struck Bridget as egregiously insulting. She particularly minded now on her way to her own wedding. Bridget thought of the pink bouclé wool suit she would wear to the ceremony, of the way the waistband of the skirt pinched and caused the skirt to rise up higher than it should. And that thought led to a dispirited one of the ironlike underwear she would need to put on under the suit to smooth out the new swells and rolls: the one-piece, the panty hose, the skirt girdle. Too much architecture, and yet Bridget was unwilling to let herself go entirely.

She didn't want to reveal, for example, her nearly bald head.

She'd told herself that the wig was for her son's sake, that if she didn't look sick he wouldn't worry about her as much. And it was better, too, for the sake of her colleagues at the school department. But of course the wig was for herself. In the middle week of the three-week treatments, when she had recovered some of her energy, she could almost believe that she was well. Her skin tone had changed (she was paler, and she'd been told that might be permanent), but with the wig and a sweep of blush, she thought she could pass for normal. Fear was counterproductive, Bridget had learned. One couldn't spend every minute thinking about death.

She fingered the wig now, the stiff netting that lifted slightly off the back of her neck. It was made of real European hair, colored light brown, thicker than hers had ever been. But Bridget could not get used to the strange otherness of this head of hair that was not her own, that was really more of a hat.

The wig had been terrifically expensive, and Bridget had gone to great lengths to find it. During her first three-week treatment, she had traveled from the Boston suburb in which she lived to New York City on the advice of a friend who'd known of a wig shop in Brooklyn that was supposed to be the Rolls-Royce of wig makers (*sheitel machers,* Bridget had learned). Bridget had spent the night at a hotel in Manhattan and then had taken a long taxi ride to the Flatbush section of Brooklyn, noting the sharp demarcation of the neighborhood with its Hebrew signs and kosher shops. She'd entered the unprepossessing wig shop full of doubts, aware of herself as an outsider and yet welcomed in a kind of chaotic way to the back room. There, as she had waited for the owner, who would tend to her and who would become something of a confidante in the weeks following the initial fitting, Bridget had stared into the mirror, unable to keep from watching a drama that was unfolding in the chair next to her. A woman who could not have been older than eighteen was trying on a newly made wig for the first time.

The girl seemed young for her age, about to spiral out of control in the way that adolescent girls sometimes could — alternately delighted with her wig, and then snapping at her mother, snatching the wig off her head as if it were diseased, and then sobbing. The girl would be married in two days, Bridget learned (calculating that the wedding date would be a Wednesday; odd to get married on a Wednesday), and would have her head shaved just before the ceremony. The Orthodox tradition to which the girl belonged forbade a married woman from showing her hair to anyone but her husband. The young woman would wear her wig for the rest of her life. The girl had an astonishingly beautiful head of hair, thick and long and shiny, and Bridget could not believe that she would in two days' time allow someone to cut it off, the image harsh and reminiscent of Jewish concentration camps or of French female collaborators during World War II. The minutes that Bridget had spent in that back room had seemed among the most foreign of her life (the most difficult to translate), and it was only when the owner came in and gently put her fingers through Bridget's short (and surely foreign in this setting) hair that Bridget had rattled back to the reality of her cancer and to the reason why she was visiting the shop.

It had taken three trips to Brooklyn to complete the process, each journey more arduous than the last as Bridget had progressed through the treatments — the last trip nearly desperate since she was by then losing her hair at a rapid clip. Bill had arranged for a car to pick Bridget up at home and deliver her to the now-familiar, even comfortable, *sheitel macher,* where the staff had greeted her like an old friend. The car had waited for Bridget and then had taken her home, a round-trip of thirteen hours and costing Bill nearly a thousand dollars, every penny of which, Bridget later decided, was worth it.

Bridget was used to the wig now and even liked its convenience (she could wake up, put it on, and have instantly perfect hair), though it became an unwelcome inanimate object in the bed on the nights when Bill slept over. The most difficult part of the cancer was not the fear of death or the treatments themselves but rather, Bridget had decided, the loss of dignity, particularly excruciating in the run-up to a wedding.

The cancer had taken Bridget by surprise, and she'd been slow to accept its reality. She remembered the routine appointment for a mammogram in late August, her third since she'd turned forty, and the way she'd casually whined to Bill beforehand about how tedious and uncomfortable the process was. After the mammogram, Bridget had waited in a claustrophobic cubicle at the radiologist's, feeling naked in her hospital gown. She'd half read an article in *Family Circle* about how to stretch three meals into nine, all the while expecting to be dismissed as had happened on her two previous visits. This time, however, Bridget was summoned back for another set of pictures with the reassurance that it was the technique itself that had failed. She waited once again in the cubicle, unable to read, the magazine tightly clasped and leaving a smear of red and black on her fingers. A technician announced that a sonogram would be necessary, the diagnostic test presented without fanfare, suggesting no reason for alarm: it was more a matter of Bridget's having cystic breasts. Bridget lay in a darkened room, gel spread upon her right breast, while the technician ran a paddle around and over her nipple. Again and again, the technician made the circuitous journey, finally putting down the paddle and fetching the radiologist. Bridget's questions — *Is everything all right? Do you see anything?* — went unanswered as the physician and the technician spoke in hushed tones about a "shadow."

Lights snapped back on, and Bridget was asked to get dressed and to meet with the radiologist in his office. Even though her hands trembled as she buttoned her blouse, Bridget still thought she would be told essentially good news. Removal of a cyst or even a biopsy might be necessary, though one expected a routine result.

In the darkened and cramped office of the radiologist, Bridget was asked to look at her X-ray. She was shown a spot that looked, in the doctor's words, "suspicious." A code word, Bridget would later learn, for "bad."

"You see the star?" he asked, pointing to a shape but looking straight at Bridget. And it was only that afternoon, as she was telling Bill, that she realized that "star" was a euphemism for "crab," for she *had* seen the crab, the oval with the tentacles reaching into her flesh. Still, even as she said the dreaded word to Bill, she did not believe in it. The tumor would turn out to be benign.

In the weeks that followed, Bridget absorbed the increasingly dismal bulletins as a series of shocks: first the biopsy (malignant); the findings after the lumpectomy (the tumor slightly larger than anticipated); the decidedly bad news about the lymph nodes (five of them implicated); followed by the realization that radiation and rigorous chemotherapy would be necessary. And even the messy reality of those treatments had not fully registered until Bridget had attended a grisly orientation session with a nurse who spoke of anal hygiene and sexual atrophy until Bridget had put up her hand and said, quietly, *Stop.* She did not want to hear another word, fearful of the power of suggestion. Denial, she was learning, was not only effective but sometimes essential.

Bridget returned home to face a difficult task: Matt needed to be told. Though he'd been vaguely aware that his mother had had some kind of procedure done earlier, he did not know yet about the cancer. She asked Matt to come with her to the living room, the request itself disturbing since Bridget seldom asked for a formal sit-down.

"What?" he asked. And again as he sat down, "What?"

"I have breast cancer," she told her son, knowing that the word "breast" and the word "cancer" might, initially, carry an equal charge, his mother's breasts and cancer being entities Matt would not, at fifteen, want to think about.

Matt, who'd had a unit on cancer the year before in science and who knew all about the disease, cried out, "I don't want to be there when they tell you it's come back!" He then went rigid with shock and fear, and Bridget had had a time of it reassuring her son that, against the odds, all would be well, a physically arduous task that had ended with the two of them eating tacos and watching *Sports-Center* at 10:00 that night.

Bridget put a foot up on the dashboard and rested her right arm on the windowsill. The few weeks following that night with Matt had been difficult, her son growing increasingly withdrawn, refusing to discuss what was bothering him, as if he, too, knew that to talk about a thing was to make it real. Though Bridget and Bill had decided that for Matt's sake Bill would not move out of his Boston apartment and into Bridget's house (a nostalgic and illogical decision given any teenager's understanding of broken and blended families), Bill took to spending more evenings and nights at the house in order to get Bridget through the treatments and to cook and help Matt with his homework. Bridget was sleeping odd hours and sometimes had to go to bed before 8:00. It comforted her to know that Bill was in the house, even if Matt did not actually need him.

Bill had *not* been there, however, when the incident with the alcohol had occurred. That was how Bridget thought of it now: The Incident with the Alcohol.

Bridget had woken on a Monday morning with the intention of making French toast for Matt and Lucas Frye, a friend of her son's who had slept over the night before. Lucas's parents — and Bill as well — were traveling. Feeling peppier than usual, Bridget had gone into the kitchen in her bathrobe, set out the ingredients, and then climbed the stairs to rouse the two boys. She called from the open door into Matt's bedroom, Lucas answering groggily. Bridget thought, with some relief, that Lucas would get Matt up and into the shower without her having to do anything, an unexpected boon on a Monday morning. But it was Lucas alone, sheepish and bleary-eyed, who appeared twenty minutes later at the breakfast table. Bridget chastised herself for not having stayed up to make sure the boys got to bed on time.

"Where's Matt?"

"He won't get up."

"Seriously?"

"I can't get him up" was all Lucas would say, trying not to look at the frying bacon.

"You feel okay?" she asked, and Lucas shrugged. Bridget assumed that Lucas was simply as intractable on school mornings as her son.

Once again, Bridget mounted the stairs and walked into Matt's room. He was not in the bed. She called his name, left the bedroom, checked the bathroom, and then returned to his room. It was then that Bridget noticed, in the center of a tangle of jeans and T-shirts and video games, an oval of vomit, orange colored and dried, on the carpet. Bridget called her son's name again and walked further into the room so that she could see between the twin beds. Matt was lying on his side, wearing a pair of mesh basketball shorts and a T-shirt, his feet ensnared in his jeans as if he had made an effort to get dressed. Frightened, Bridget shouted his name. She knelt beside her son and tried unsuccessfully to rouse him. She sat back with a jolt that ran from her throat to her stomach. Had Matt had a seizure?

She ran to the top of the stairs and called Lucas's name, in hopes of discovering what the boys had been doing, but, as she later discovered, Lucas had already let himself out of the house and was walking to school. Bridget dialed 911, returned to Matt's room, and felt for his pulse, which, alarmingly, was racing. Oddly, her son did not smell of alcohol, which both the EMTs and the police commented upon, asking her repeatedly if her son was prone to seizures. Bridget thought of all the reasons a fifteen-year-old boy might have had a seizure, none of them good. The EMTs put Matt on a stretcher and carried him down the stairs and out the door to the waiting ambulance. Bridget thought, as she pulled on jeans and a sweater, *This can't be happening.*

Two police cars and an ambulance were in her driveway, the lights of all three vehicles flashing, a small circus certain to bring every neighbor to the window. A mild drizzle fell, and Bridget, though shaking now, worried about Lucas. She told one of the policemen that he should try to find the boy.

Bridget took a seat in the front of the ambulance. No sirens wailed as they drove to the hospital, a silence that alternately alarmed and soothed her. She peered through the narrow opening to the back of the vehicle and saw an EMT rub hard on Matt's sternum, rousing her son long enough for him to utter a word Bridget had never heard her son say and which nearly caused her to demand that he watch his language, despite the ludicrousness of the reprimand. Before they got to the hospital, news reached the driver via the radio that Lucas had been found on his way to school and had confessed: the boys had together drunk a fifth of vodka that Bridget had had in the freezer for months, the bottle left over from a small summer dinner party she and Bill had given. She hadn't even remembered the vodka was there. It had become, like the boxes of frozen peas and the Ziploc bags of unidentifiable meat, simply part of the refrigerator's furniture. Lucas, strenuously questioned, insisted that both boys had drunk the same amount, and

Bridget wondered how it was that Lucas had been able to walk to school. She thought the vodka had to have been Matt's idea, because his friend wouldn't have known it was in the freezer. Well, he might have seen it on a hunt for an ice-cream bar, but what boy would presume to ask for it? On the other hand, anything was possible. Who'd have thought two fifteen-year-olds would have wanted to become blind drunk on a Sunday night?

Matt was taken from her at the hospital. Bridget sat in a waiting room with televisions in the corners, each showing perky early morning talk shows. When Bridget was finally allowed into the ER to see her son, she found Matt unconscious in the bed, dressed in a hospital gown, and hooked up to several monitors. An IV had been inserted into the back of his hand, an image that chilled her. This was, of course, the same hospital at which Bridget received her chemotherapy treatments. She asked a nurse if Matt's stomach had been pumped and was told that it was too late for that. Her son had already absorbed all the alcohol.

For seven hours, Bridget sat at the end of Matt's bed while nurses and doctors jostled against her in the cramped emergency room, its various smells identifiable and often unpleasant. In the next cubicle, not three feet from where Bridget sat, an elderly man complained of agonizing pain in his abdomen. A doctor came to tell Bridget that Matt's alcohol level was still remarkably high. The physician calculated that at 1:00 in the morning, it would have been nearly lethal. Her son, Bridget was told, had come very close to shutting down his kidneys.

Reeking of alcohol now, Matt occasionally regained consciousness, though he spoke incoherently. Bridget alternated between anger and heartache. *What were you thinking?* she would cry, and then immediately afterward would whisper, *I love you so much.* As long as her son was on the IV, Bridget was told, he would not have the terrible hangover she found herself wishing upon him, if only to allow him to feel the punishing effects of what he'd done.

Phone calls were made. To Bill (stunned). To Lucas's parents (stunned and baffled). And to Matt's school (they'd already been informed by the police). Gradually, what had earlier been terrifying — another two swigs of Absolut and might Matt have died? blown out his kidneys? inhaled his vomit? — became tedious as Bridget watched Matt's urine drip into a plastic bag by her knee. By 3:00 that afternoon, Bridget had to remind herself of the gravity of the incident, repeating the words "he almost died" to shock herself into a more alert state.

In silence, mother and son had driven home, Matt at first refusing to enter the house. For most of an hour, he'd sat cross-legged in the driveway, sobbing, and Bridget could not get him to say why. Away from the IV, Matt began to experience the nausea and headache of a hangover, and she could hear him vomiting from time to time in the upstairs bathroom. (*Good,* she thought.) Bridget, hypervigilant, could not go to bed until after 3:00 in the morning, needing to check on her son's sleeping form, waking him briefly each time. Her final task, before she crawled into her own bed, was to pour out all the alcohol in the house: two bottles of red wine, one bottle of white, a small bottle of Chivas she hadn't even known was in the cupboard, and, finally, a six-pack of Sam Adams in the fridge, a silly and empty gesture since Bill would almost certainly replace it after his trip. Sam Adams wasn't the problem.

The next morning, Matt dressed willingly and, subdued, ate a full breakfast. When he returned home that afternoon, he devoured guacamole dip with celery sticks while he sheepishly told her what had happened. A dare had turned into a lark, neither boy having any idea how much alcohol was too much, until each had become thrillingly drunk. They'd passed the bottle back and forth, more of a good thing being a good thing. After the Incident with the Alcohol, Matt had gradually regained his more-or-less agreeable disposition, and Bridget sometimes wondered if the experience hadn't been cathartic for her son, if his nearly fatal binge and subsequent survival hadn't purged him of his fear of death (hers).

"Should we stop for coffee?" Bridget asked, lowering her foot from the dashboard.

"These guys must be starving."

"They're always starving," Bridget said, staring at Bill. She hadn't had a husband for almost a decade. Bill, she had discovered, was that rare man who had an extraordinary gift for bringing out the best in people. In herself. In Matt. And doubtless in the two hundred or so employees he had under him in his software business.

"What?" Bill asked, a smile beginning.

"Nothing," she said.

"What?" he repeated.

"I can't believe we're doing this," she said.

With his free arm, he pulled her toward him. She leaned briefly into Bill despite the awkward maneuver over the console. He kissed her quickly, taking his eyes off the road.

"You'll kill us," she said.

Bill pulled into the parking lot of a rest area, and the boys roused themselves. Dressed nearly identically in North Face fleeces and Abercrombie & Fitch jeans, they stepped out of the van and stretched. Each had grown half an inch while sleeping.

"Where are we?" Matt asked.

"I thought we'd get some lunch," Bill said.

Waking from hibernation, the boys walked across the parking lot and into the fast-food complex. Bill put his arm around Bridget. "You're sure you're okay?" he asked.

"Coffee," she said, trying to keep pace with his stride.

"Matt wanted to rent a tux."

"He did?" Bridget asked, surprised that her son thought the occasion merited the formal wear.

"So we did," Bill said.

"You and Matt are wearing tuxes?"

"And Brian, too."

"To a wedding with twelve guests?"

Bill grinned.

"You guys," Bridget said. "How did you pull this off? When did you get them?"

"That night Matt asked me to take him to get basketball sneakers? The tuxes were his idea, and he wants it to be a surprise. But I'm telling you now. Just in case you hate the idea, you'll have time to get used to it. Because, baby, we are wearing those tuxes."

"But I love the idea," Bridget said.

They found the boys in line for Burger King, and Bill joined them. Bridget, who had never been able to stomach fast food, even before she'd gotten sick, gravitated to the frozen yogurt stand. She asked for a medium-size cup of vanilla with nuts on it (no wonder the twelve pounds, she thought). She turned with her cup and saw Bill waving her over to a table where the boys were already deeply into their Double Whoppers with extra cheese. The fat! Not to worry, she thought. The combustion engines inside Matt and Brian would burn off all the calories before they'd even reached the Berkshires. As Bridget walked to their table, she pictured Nora's place, remembering the trip she and Bill had made two months ago both to visit their old friend and to see her new creation. In late October, when Bill and Bridget had decided to get married, Bill had thought of the inn and had written to Nora. There was romance in the idea of inviting old friends only, those who had known Bill and Bridget years ago when they'd been high school sweethearts. Bridget had told her friends from home that the wedding would be just family, a small white lie that bothered her only a little.

"Coffee," Bill announced as Bridget sat down, the boys reining in the clutter of waxed papers and plastic cups, packets of ketchup and straw wrappers. Bill slid the overlarge cup toward her, and, instinctively, she drew her head away. The smell of the coffee was offensive. Slowly, so that Bill wouldn't notice, she pushed the coffee to one side and dug into the yogurt with her plastic spoon. The frozen pudding felt like silk on her tongue, the icy cold welcome, for she had suddenly grown overly warm in the rest area. She slipped her fleece from her shoulders, securing it with her back to the chair. She wiped her forehead and her upper lip.

"You okay?" Bill asked.

"A little hot is all," she said.

"Thanks for lunch," Brian said, a boy who remembered his manners at odd moments, sometimes an hour after the meal, running downstairs from Matt's room to thank Bridget in the kitchen after she had washed all the dishes.

"You're welcome," Bridget said, hoping that Brian would have a reasonably good time this weekend, that he and Matt would find activities to keep themselves busy until the wedding itself.

"What's wrong?" Bill asked quietly.

"I think I just have to go to the ladies' room," she said. "I'll be right back."

Bridget hated public bathrooms with their germs, the toilet paper on the floor, the blocked toilets. She loathed the automatic faucets that refused to produce water, the hot-air dryers that made her desperate for hand lotion. As she reached the door that said WOMEN, sweat beaded on her forehead, and she felt a familiar panic and dizziness. She searched for the last cubicle in the second row, a need to be as far away from others as possible.

She shut the door and bent over. She raised the toilet seat with her boot. She closed her eyes and braced herself, two fists up against the opposing metal walls, and waited. A wave of nausea overtook her. She coughed experimentally. Nothing. The sweat had soaked her hair under the wig and trickled down her spine.

Oh God, she thought. She would have to do this alone. Bill could not come in here. How soon would he begin to worry? Would he send someone after her? Another wave rose, and she bent further over. She should try to vomit, get rid of it, but she didn't dare put a finger in her mouth. She might have touched something dirty. She had to be particularly careful about germs now and had learned to wash her hands a dozen times a day. A third wave passed through her, and she tried once more to vomit.

After a time, Bridget straightened up. A momentary lull? She waited a minute and then dared to open her eyes. She took a fistful of toilet paper and wiped her forehead and face. She lifted the back of the wig and mopped up the sweat that had accumulated there. She felt distinctly better. Had she won a reprieve? On her wedding weekend? She tossed the tissue into the bowl.

She emerged from the stall and stood before a mirror to wash her hands. Her face was pale and undefined, the extra pounds (ounces on her face) blurring her jawline. The wig had been washed this month and blown into a flip. Bridget never knew when she opened the small square cardboard box from Brooklyn exactly who she'd be that month. A matron with a turned-under pageboy? An aging in-genue with curls? Or someone more hip, the hair falling straight to her shoulders? Bridget had written "no flip" on her notes when she returned the wig for cleaning each month (FedEx: if Bridget sent it out at 6:00 p.m. on Monday night, she got it back before 10:00 on Wednesday morning — forty hours without her wig, during which she sometimes wore a synthetic backup), but the word "flip" must not translate well into Yiddish, she had decided. Bridget had been mildly distraught, a week ago, to see that she would have to be married in a flip, but she knew enough not to try to wash it herself, which she had once done, the outcome disastrous and resulting in a shoulder-length Afro.

When she left the ladies' room, she found the boys sitting at the table with their chairs tipped back. They were satiated and would sleep again. Bill had been watching for her, but it was possible she hadn't been gone long enough to worry him. She put a smile on her face, one that grew more genuine with gratitude for the reprieve. (Grateful to whom? God? Could he possibly care about Bridget and her nausea with 9/11 and terrorists to think about? She could hear her father say, he used to say it all the time — *we don't amount to a hill of beans* — a phrase that could disturb or soothe, depending upon one's point of view.)

"Guys," she said, stopping short the question she knew was on Bill's tongue. "Ready?"

The boys shrugged their chairs away and stood with their trays. Bill wiped up a spill and took his trash to the container. They would all travel on to the Berkshires and find their rooms at the inn. The boys would wear tuxedos, and Bridget would squeeze herself into her pink bouclé suit. Agnes and Harrison and Rob would raise a toast, and tomorrow Bill and Bridget would be married.

The two adults and two boys stepped out into the sunshine. Bridget felt soft air on her throat and at the back of her neck. She was relieved — so relieved! — not to feel sick at this moment. She took Bill's arm, which he freely gave. Was there anything better, she wanted to know, than feeling well? Simply feeling well?

Harrison set out on foot up the slope behind the inn. The bare trees suggested winter, the warm air felt like spring, and it was pleasantly disorienting to have to remind himself that Christmas was less than three weeks away. He followed a well-worn path that meandered through birch groves and around rocky outcroppings and occasionally was steep enough to warrant a handhold. The sun bathed the woods, and, for a time, Harrison was entranced by the mild midwinter light.

The hill grew gentler as he climbed. He came to a stone wall that reached to his knees and was remarkably intact despite the appearance of age. He followed the wall for a time and was surprised to discover that it simply ended, giving no indication of what it had once enclosed. He turned and sat on its rough edge and saw that he had an exceptional view not only of the inn but also of the Berkshires in the distance. Perhaps the wall had been designed for this purpose.

He wondered where Nora was, what she was doing at that very moment. He remembered the image he had had earlier, of the first time he'd ever seen her up close. The way the picture had come to him with vivid clarity.

It was a Sunday, he recalled, and he'd been walking in the village as he sometimes did when he'd been studying for several hours and needed a break. Late October of his junior year, he thought, because there was the smell of burning leaves in the air. Unlike his roommate, Stephen, Harrison woke early on Sunday mornings and tried to get as much of the week's homework out of the way as he could. Harrison was not a skilled sleeper, whereas Stephen had a knack for it, as, indeed, he had for nearly everything else. Harrison remembered Stephen hanging upside down from his bunk explicating Randall Jarrell's "The Death of the Ball Turret Gunner" even though he'd only glanced at the poem. He recalled Stephen making the entire senior class laugh at his brilliantly timed jokes during his pitch to become class president — and this to a student body who valued cool and irony above all other qualities. He could still picture Stephen nodding respectfully, even eagerly, at a few words his father had to say about finding the talent one was truly good at and making something of it — pitcher of old-fashioneds at Dad's side, glass in hand — Harrison having the sense that direct attention from father to son had been in short supply and was therefore all the more coveted.

So it had to have been before the Sunday meal, Harrison decided, that he took that walk. Yes, absolutely, because there was a short but steady stream of cars starting their engines and leaving the Congregational church. 11:15? Was Nora coming from church? Odd that he'd never thought of that before.

Harrison walked often then — on Sundays, occasionally at dusk after practice, sometimes in the early morning before his first class — not for exercise, because he had plenty of that with the mandatory sports at Kidd. No, it was more to clear his head and to be in nature. He had always, even at a young age, understood himself to be a lover of the natural world, and he had often wondered if he hadn't gravitated to it to assuage some great loss — a longing for his father perhaps? — though he had not followed the hypothesis much further than that.

The girl, Harrison remembered now, was walking across the street, slightly ahead of him. Harrison could see the pale blue of her cloth coat, the way her woolen scarf was wound around her neck several times, pushing her hair into a chestnut bubble that rocked gently from side to side as she strode. Unlike Harrison, she didn't seem to notice the cottages and the piles of leaves around her. She didn't look into windows or into backyards. Rather, she seemed instead to be staring at a spot perpetually five feet ahead of her on the road.

Harrison increased his pace, ratcheting it up from stroll to walk. He wanted to overtake the girl, if only to see her face. He thought he knew who she was. She was new to his class that year. She had come from somewhere in the Midwest. He'd seen her crossing the campus and in the dining hall. Her name was . . . Sarah? No, something else. *Nora.*

She walked with her hands in the pockets of her coat, and she never broke her stride. Harrison easily drew even with her but was reluctant to close the gap. If he glanced over at her, and she at him, he would then have to speak to her and possibly even walk with her. And though he found the prospect of that conversation and walk exciting, he sensed that the girl might not welcome the intrusion.

Harrison was near enough now to see her chin and a fan of dark eyelashes. The carbon-laden smoke was thick and delicious in the cold air. She was the girl he had imagined. Nora. Nora what? He wondered what so preoccupied her thoughts that she did not even glance up.

As he drew closer to her, it occurred to Harrison that the girl could not possibly be unaware of his presence. At the very least, she had to have heard his footsteps. He could not remain slightly behind her and *not* speak to her, because to do so might seem as though he were following her. The girl would be bound to increase her own pace, or, worse, whip around and confront him. Harrison had a dilemma.

In the end, he had little choice. Reluctantly, he drew even and glanced across the street. He said *hello,* hesitated a second, and then kept walking.

Aware of her gaze on his back — a gaze that burned and seemed to cause a concavity there — Harrison moved with a false sense of purpose, as if he had a destination. He had had just a glimpse of her face (the dark eyes not startled but slightly wary; she had not returned his greeting), and too soon he reached the gate at Kidd. He did not want to enter the school grounds, and only a tremendous physical effort kept him, as he paused at the gate that was not really a gate but more of a wrought iron arch, from turning around to look in her direction. He ought to have done so, he thought now. What would have been the harm? He might have pretended to have to tie a shoelace. However lame and transparent the excuse, the delay might have given him a chance to speak to her. He would have asked her what dorm she lived in. If she ever walked the beach instead of the road. And (screw Stephen) they'd have gone together to the dining hall and had their lunch, sitting across from each other and, he imagined, finding connections — teachers they might have shared, classes they liked or did not.

Of such momentary decisions, Harrison thought now, were entire universes constructed. Had he spoken to Nora that day, she might have become his girlfriend instead of Stephen's. There would not have been the scene at the cottage.

He got up from the stone wall and searched for the place where the path headed back to the inn. Chance constructions could not be undone, Harrison knew. Momentary decisions could not be disowned.

Though the trip up the hill had taken nearly forty minutes, it was only fifteen down, and Harrison returned to the inn with sore knees and a good appetite. He wondered if he'd missed lunch. He noted a sign in the lobby for another wedding (had it been there earlier?): KAROLA-JUNGBACKER REHEARSAL DINNER, PIERCE ROOM, 7:00. When he entered the dining room and sat down, a waitress appeared with a menu. The lunch entrées were few but varied: Raclette with Cornichons and Roasted Potatoes; Baked Eggplant Crepes; Misty Knoll Free-Range Chicken Livers. He ordered a spinach-and-fig salad to start, followed by the raclette. He sipped a glass of cabernet sauvignon. Through the windows, he had a pleasant view of the mountains to the west. Three other tables were occupied, one by a couple who seemed inured to the boundless enthusiasms of a boy who looked to be about Tom's age, who was coloring with Magic Markers and pressing his parents repeatedly for assurances that they would go up a certain gondola and visit the North Face Outlet Store and make it back to the inn in time for a predinner swim. Harrison tried to catch the father's eye, hoping to convey a kind of parental empathy.

Harrison's good mood was marred only slightly with the arrival of the salad and the presence of a dead fly lurking at the perimeter under a spinach leaf. The waitress had missed this at first, and since Harrison did not want to embarrass her (or Nora, for that matter), he decided not to point it out. It wasn't until the girl came to clear the mostly uneaten salad away that she noticed the fly.

"Oh God," she said at once, "you should have said something."

"No trouble," he said.

"Can I bring you another salad?"

The waitress had blond hair pulled tight to her head and fastened at the back. A prominent eyetooth was smudged with lipstick. She seemed so flustered that Harrison wished he had hidden the fly simply to save her the confusion.

"Really," he said, "it's no trouble at all. You could bring me another glass of the cabernet, though, if you really want to."

The girl seemed relieved and whisked away the offending plate, which had given little offense, Harrison thought, the presence of the fly in mid-December but one more indication of the freakishness of the season. Almost immediately, she brought another glass of wine, which he took his time enjoying as he ate his raclette. He thought again about the day he'd met Nora.

Without a backward glance, Harrison had entered the gate, returned to his room, and waited until 1:00 so that he could wake Stephen. Harrison was beset with a nagging sense of irresolution. He longed to crawl back into the moment he'd passed Nora and do it over, to choose not to walk straight past the girl in the blue cloth coat but to begin a conversation, or, even less subtly, to wait for her at the gate. But having missed his chance, he did not, as another boy might have, seek immediate redress. Harrison saw Nora in the dining hall that afternoon but did not speak to her, the sheer dazzle and demands of Stephen's presence gradually obliterating Harrison's view of her in the corner (when Harrison looked up, she was gone). And later, as the day progressed, there was the weekly poker game at 3:00, then a quick supper followed by study hall at 8:00, during which time Harrison read *The Old Man and the Sea,* having finished all of his homework that morning.

Harrison could remember that day well, but he could not see the next or the next, and whole months were lost to him now. He could recall certain key moments at Kidd, most having to do with sports and later with Nora, and if pressed and given a few hints, he could recall a given incident — but huge segments of his last two years at school remained a blur. He remembered another girl, Maria, with whom he'd gone skiing during Christmas break of his junior year, staying at Maria's parents' condo at Sunday River. Much to Harrison's surprise, he'd been awakened shortly after 1:00 in the morning by an athletic Maria slipping into his bed. He'd at first been hyperalert to the sounds of parents waking and walking along the corridor, an alertness that had competed with and lost out to the excitement of the girl in his bed and to the thrill of her remarkable expertise, not, as it happened, much needed, since Harrison was a willing if bumbling partner, eager to relieve himself of his virginity. And having done that together, Harrison and Maria were for a time something of a couple, though Harrison sensed that Maria, with her long blond hair and overdeveloped breasts, might at any moment slip into someone else's bed. The girl in the blue cloth coat — which had given way to a denim jacket as winter moved toward spring — receded even further into the past, that past now growing fat with missed opportunities, lost chances, and mild regret.

In early April, at the beginning of the baseball season, Harrison remembered a game against North Fenton High School, a tough team, though a game Kidd was supposed to win. Harrison's memory intercepted the game in the fourth inning, the play before that a blur, though he recalled that Kidd was down by five. Jerry Leyden, on the mound, was an exercise in pure frustration. Earlier, in the dugout, the pitcher had snapped, "Guys, let's get it together," the rest of the team having given him no run support. For once, Harrison hadn't blamed the defense that day. In his opinion, it was all down to lousy pitching, Jerry leaving the ball up, unable to make his sinker sink. North Fenton knew it, too, and had gotten their five runs with patience: two walks, a triple that brought in two runs, a hit batter, and a homer. When Harrison's fickle memory interrupted the game, he was playing second and there was a man on first, the guy driving Harrison nuts, he was so far off the bag. If Jerry would just whip around with the ball, the first baseman could make the pickoff easy.

Harrison wondered why Coach D. hadn't made his way out to the mound yet, why he hadn't put another pitcher in. Stephen, in the hole between second and third, was thwacking his fist into his mitt. The only one who would hate this loss more than Jerry would be Stephen. The shortstop bent, put his hands on his knees, and swayed from side to side, keeping loose. Harrison was hovering behind the base path, wanting some action. Baseball in Maine was a winter sport, with its muddy fields, freezing temperatures, and fierce winds straight off the Atlantic sending any decent hit over the fence in right field, though Rob Zoar was as good an outfielder as Harrison had ever seen.

A gust rattled over the mound. Jerry stalled, waiting for a lull. The ump told him to play ball. Jerry went into his windup, his leg kick theatrically high, and, Harrison thought, uneconomical. Any decent runner on first could steal second before the ball hit the catcher's mitt. The ball stayed up, and the batter hit a line drive through the gap between second and third. Harrison watched Stephen arch over at a seemingly impossible angle, glove the ball as it bounced in the dust, and whip it across his body even as he was rising in the air, a play that no high school kid should have been able to make. Harrison, waiting for it, got it out of his glove as he leaped over the runner and snapped it to first, getting the batter there. Two out. Their patented double play, the one Harrison and Stephen had fine-tuned the year before, had talked about all winter, and had practiced incessantly, Stephen being the key, the pivot, his spin making it work. It was the first time they'd had a shot at it all day.

Stephen, lighter on his feet now and pumped, his blond hair blowing straight back from under his cap, his uniform flattened against his chest, gave Harrison the thumbs-up, a gesture undetectable to anyone else. If Jerry could keep the ball down this last at bat, they could retire the side and start again at the top of the order: Harrison, leadoff batter; Rob Zoar batting second for his uncanny ability to make contact; Billy Ricci, catcher, phenomenal hitter with power, batting third; and then Stephen, batting cleanup. There was still a chance to get into the game.

Harrison could see the fat pitch as it left Jerry's fingers. The batter knew a good thing when he saw it. The ball went high and long and so far over the fence into the dense scrub brush that there was no point even trying to retrieve it.

0–6.

Jerry was yanked, and a new pitcher came to the mound to warm up. Harrison glanced over to the small hillock on which the fans sat — fewer in April than in May, many more at home games than away — and saw a smattering of parents, some of whom he knew had driven more than a hundred miles to see their sons play baseball. And set apart, resting on the steepest part of the slope, her elbows dug into the new grass as she half reclined, was Nora in her denim jacket, a pink scarf loose at her neck. Harrison made note of the khaki skirt, the long black boots, the heels of which she was ruining. She had a hand to her forehead to shade her eyes, but Harrison could see clearly her line of sight. She had come for Stephen.

Even now, in the dining room of the inn, Harrison experienced a slight aftershock of the quake he had felt that afternoon. First the bewilderment. Then the stunning surprise. Finally, his outrage at Stephen, even though Harrison knew Stephen's betrayal to have been unwitting: Harrison had never spoken to Stephen of his missed opportunity — a missed opportunity being, by definition, a nonstory.

Harrison, stunningly preoccupied, could not get into the crouch, could not get loose, as the new pitcher threw his first pitch. Strike one. Harrison glanced from Stephen to Nora and back again, a comic-book swivel, Harrison's intuition confirmed when he saw Stephen glance over at the hillock and smile. How had Harrison not seen that smile before? Surely, it was not the first of the game?

The batter swung at a bad pitch — strike two — which should have lifted Harrison up onto his toes, ready for a grounder and a third out. The batter swung at the third pitch, high and outside, improbably making contact and sending it on a hop to Harrison, who booted it behind the first baseman, a senior, who in turn had to run for it, trying to field it as it ricocheted against a wooden fence.

Man on second.

Harrison, glancing at Stephen, saw a puzzled look on his friend's face. Harrison turned away, furious. North Fenton's pitcher was at the plate, an easy out by all accounts, though now it was a ground ball right through the legs of Kidd's pitcher. Harrison fielded it but was slow to get it out of his glove, and the runner beat the throw. When Harrison glanced up, he saw that the runner from second had scored.

0–7.

Harrison's memory could not retrieve the rest of the game, though he recalled that afterward, as they picked up their bats and helmets and ate the brownies and drank the lemonade a team parent had brought, he saw Stephen walk to where Nora reclined. She stood up and brushed the back of her skirt. Stephen hovered over her and spoke. Of the pitiful game? Of his own beautiful but wasted play? Nora looked up once and smiled. And though the pair did not touch, Harrison knew, by the way Nora let Stephen stand so close to her, that they *had* touched, had perhaps even kissed. Was it possible they were already lovers?

Harrison felt a brief touch on his left shoulder and looked up. Nora moved into view. "The fly appears not merely to have alighted on the fruit," she said. "Nor . . . nor even to have inadvertently drowned. But . . . it would seem from the insect's supine and slightly sensual posture . . . to have wallowed in the viscous syrup of the dressing." She had on a slim black skirt and a white blouse through which Harrison could see her camisole. He stood, but she waved him down and sat across from him. "This . . . this is not, strictly speaking, a crime," she added. "Nor can this event entirely obliterate the sense of well-being I had earlier on the porch. Not in the way blocked plumbing can, for example. But I wonder if it isn't, if it isn't a harbinger of the weekend to come. 'Well-being' a fruit one can peel away, layer by layer."

Harrison smiled at the baroque apology.

"I'm joking," Nora said, "but I just wanted to say I'm sorry about the fly."

"Don't be," Harrison said, "if the result is that charmingly obscene image."

"Judy brought the plate to me for my inspection." Nora had on pearl earrings and, unlike earlier this morning, a suggestion of makeup. Her lips looked glossy. Her eyes were darker, more defined.

"Judy is very honest, then, and you should employ her forever. She was apologetic enough for both of you."

"Judy is a pretty girl with no charm whatsoever," Nora said. "She's so quick and bright, though, I dare not offend her."

"I imagine the fly, dazzled by the unseasonable weather, flew into the kitchen and was seduced by the luscious-looking fig," Harrison said.

"Will you tell the others?"

"Very funny. You seem in good spirits."

"Despite the fly, I am."

"Why?"

She sat back in her chair. "I'm . . . I'm amazed by this day. And being amazed, I'm filled with an incredible sense of happiness."

"I'm glad. The raclette is very good, by the way. My compliments to the chef."

"Eddie. I'll tell him. May I?" she asked, indicating Harrison's untouched water glass.

Harrison pushed the glass toward her. "I was just wondering. Why take on an inn? Surely your husband's royalties . . ."

"Carl's royalties were pitiful," Nora said, crossing her legs. "You . . . *you* . . . of all people should know that." Harrison was struck by her poise. "But that's not the real reason. The real reason is that I wanted to."

Nora took a long sip.

"How did you and your husband meet?" Harrison asked, aware of a slight problem of nomenclature. To call the man "Carl" assumed a familiarity Harrison did not have. Yet to refer to him in Nora's presence as "Mr. Laski" felt bizarre. And Harrison couldn't keep referring to Laski as "your husband" either.

"I wish you wouldn't keep asking me questions you already know the answers to," Nora said.

Rebuffed, Harrison took a sip of wine.

Nora set down the water glass. "I thought *Poetic License* a work of spite. I refused to cooperate with Alan Roscoff. Did you read it?"

"Yes."

"It . . . it wasn't so much that it wasn't as respectful as a widow would have wanted. It was that it was *insipid*. And uninformed. I don't believe he had the faintest idea of what Carl's work was all about."

"I thought the book thin and rushed," Harrison said loyally. "Deliberately sensational."

"I've been wondering if I should have a serious portrait of Carl done," Nora mused. She nibbled on her finger, and Harrison found this break in her poise endearing. "Perhaps you could help me suggest a writer? Someone you respect?"

Harrison was flattered by the invitation, but wondered if it wasn't slightly disingenuous. Surely Nora Laski was flooded with requests for interviews, for access to the poet's files. Harrison guessed that there might be two or three literary biographies of Laski in the works already. "I'd be happy to," he said.

"I . . . I was sitting on a park bench," Nora said, "in Washington Square Park. I was eating a sandwich when Carl sat down. He asked me if he could have half. I knew him then as Professor Laski.

For a few minutes, I couldn't speak. I was a sophomore at NYU. Professor Laski was . . . well, he was a presence. I'd taken a lecture course with him the year before. Though he claimed that day to remember me, he later confessed that he had not."

Harrison could not imagine any man failing to remember a young Nora.

"Carl would come by every day to the park at the same time. And it was understood that I would give him lunch. I started making more and more elaborate lunches until they began to be full-blown picnics. I was aware that he was married. I was also aware of his reputation. I thought . . . I thought that as long as nothing progressed beyond the park bench, we were fine. And, for a long time, it didn't."

Nora paused. "I didn't think much about his age," she continued. "It didn't seem as fraught then as it does now. If anything, there was a kind of conferred status upon girls who slept with their professors."

"For how long did this go on?" Harrison asked.

"Weeks," she said. "I met him in the spring. It went on until I left for the summer."

"Where did you go?"

"I worked as a waitress in Provincetown. I shared a room with another girl. It was the thing to do then. We'd spend our tips in the bars after work. In July, I saw a poster announcing a reading by Carl Laski at the Unitarian church. I think I may have bragged to my friends that I knew him. And once I'd done that, I had to go. To prove it. I thought I'd make a picnic and bring it. It would be a sort of joke."

Nora smiled.

"Carl read from the pulpit. There was no other place for him to stand. And, well, you can imagine. That man, that head of hair, that booming voice. Did you ever hear Carl read?"

"Yes. Once, I think. In New York."

"He . . . he was magnificent," Nora said. "It was a performance. And the words . . . *the words* . . ." She put a hand to her chest, as if even now, after all these years, she was still slightly stunned by those long-ago words. "He read from *Bones of Sand*. He saw me from the pulpit. I don't think he took his eyes off me during the entire reading. He never actually read, you know. He would memorize everything in advance. So that the performance, if you want to call it that, was riveting."

"I'm imagining a charismatic Calvinist in a New England pulpit," Harrison said.

Nora glanced at her watch, and Harrison found he was beginning to mind this constant gesture. "He had a hotel," she said. "You don't want to hear all this."

Harrison did, and he did not. "As an editor, I find this fascinating," he said. "Sometimes there's a fact that sheds light on the work."

"A poem," Nora said, "is an act of the imagination. It's rarely, if ever, an act of straight reportage."

Harrison wasn't sure he agreed. "You don't think your husband once saw the girl with the red suitcase waiting at the airport?"

"No," Nora said with an air of fatigue that surprised Harrison. "I gave up trying to make straight connections years ago. I don't think . . . I don't think readers give writers enough credit for the imagination. They always want to know, Did this happen to the writer? When, of course, it probably didn't. Not literally. Not exactly as described. It's the imagination. That makes a work come alive."

"But the chestnut hair," Harrison said gently. "I assume you're the model for 'Monday Morning' and 'Talk After Supper'?"

"Actually not," Nora said, looking away. "The ideal preceded me."

The sentence was full of implication, and Harrison let it go. "By the way," he said, "I looked up 'helpmeet.' *I will make an help meet for him.* Genesis. Adam and Eve. I will make a partner suitable for him. I gather it's appropriate to you and Carl?"

"Some men need women to feel as though they exist."

Harrison set his napkin at the side of his plate.

"Would you like some coffee?" Nora asked.

"Yes, thank you, I would."

Harrison watched as Nora made a gesture to someone standing behind him.

"You don't seem like an innkeeper," he said.

"How so?"

"I think of an innkeeper as a red-faced publican or a starchy spinster, not . . ." But here he faltered, for to tell her how he saw her was to assume too great an intimacy. "In another age, you'd have been the mother of war heroes," he said instead, "or the wife of a distinguished physician or perhaps even a poet yourself."

"They'd have said 'poetess' then."

"So they would."

"One could argue that being an innkeeper . . . with its financial independence and only the self to answer to . . . is a better job than being merely a wife and mother. Better than being a poet."

"True," Harrison said. His plate was whisked away, and a cup of coffee was set before him. "You won't have any?" he asked.

"I . . . I drink too much caffeine already."

"I went for a walk earlier," Harrison said, stirring in some milk. "I got as far as a stone wall. It seemed to end in the middle of nowhere."

"It used to be part of an estate."

"Odd place to have an estate."

"There are lots of access roads in these woods. That seem to lead to nowhere."

"I assume this is your wedding-rehearsal uniform?" he asked, pointing with his teaspoon.

"It is."

"Very pretty," he added, keeping it light. "What happened to you when you returned to NYU after Provincetown?"

"Carl was married, and he had sons. His wife had more or less tolerated his previous affairs. But now Carl wanted to move out. She wouldn't stand for that. She wouldn't forgive him for leaving her alone with the two children and humiliating her. Though one could argue she'd been thoroughly humiliated long ago."

"You seem sympathetic to her."

"I am," she said. "Now, I am. But I wasn't then. Nothing makes a person more selfish than being in love. Carl's wife retaliated by suing for sole custody of the boys. He hired a good lawyer, and he was sure he would win, but that's not how it worked out."

"That must have been hard on both of you."

"When . . . when a man leaves his wife and children for another woman, there's a burden on that woman. She has to be worth the sacrifice."

Harrison blew over the top of his coffee cup. "I'm sure you were."

"No one is worth that kind of sacrifice. In Carl's case, it was even worse. To be worth the sacrifice, every word had to be incandescent."

In the corner, Harrison could see Judy clearing away dishes.

"If the work was extraordinary, one might be able to say later that artistic greatness had come from the sacrifice," Nora added.

"I would think to be worth the sacrifice, as you put it, there has to be only one truly great poem."

"You think there is?" Nora asked.

"Of course I do," he said. "There are many truly great poems. I know 'The Red Suitcase' is widely regarded to be his best work, but personally I think 'The Fourth Canto' is."

Nora said nothing, a silence Harrison took to be dissent.

"I imagine you know the work intimately," he said.

"I *should*. I had to type them all a hundred times."

"Literally type?"

"In the early days, yes."

"Carbon papers and all that?"

"Carl was slow to take up the computer. I think it was the promise of pornography that intrigued him finally."

Harrison was taken aback by this intimate revelation, an entire universe contained within. Unhappy marital sex? Bitterness? Betrayal? Or was it simply a joke, and only Harrison had missed the punch line?

"Carl wrote in his study in the mornings," Nora said. "He would go there immediately after waking up, and I wouldn't see him until around noon or so."

"He always wrote in the mornings?"

"He used to say that anything written after twelve noon wasn't worth keeping. He could be very bristly when he came out of his study, and it was usually impossible to talk to him. I think he hated pulling out of the dream state in which he wrote. I used to tell him to take a shower. Mostly, though, he just wanted to sit and stare out the window. I really didn't like being around him during that time. If I started to talk to him, or he to me, we would invariably end up arguing. So I avoided him." Nora glanced at her watch again. "Agnes is here," she said.

"Is she?"

"I'm surprised you didn't see her at lunch."

"How is she?"

"Does our Agnes ever change?"

"I don't know," Harrison said. "I'd like to think she's had some great adventure."

Nora smiled. "She looked very well. Healthy and fit."

"You've stayed friends with her?"

"Yes," Nora said. "She used to come here often. When Carl was alive. They had fabulous arguments."

"They fought, you mean."

"Not quite. I think of their debates like verbal spirals, circling inward but moving forward in another dimension. Carl could out-argue anyone."

"Even you?"

"Oh. Especially me," Nora said lightly. "I have to get some papers in my office. Want to come?"

Harrison followed Nora along a corridor, up a short set of steps, along another corridor, and down an equivalent number of steps. Her suite began with a vestibule that opened onto a sitting room / bedroom with French doors to a private veranda. Off the room, Harrison had a glimpse of a large white bathroom. Cut glass cruets of exotic colored oils lined the marble surround of the tub.

"This is your apartment?" Harrison asked.

"Just a bedroom and a bathroom. I eat all my meals in the kitchen. I never cook."

"Not such a bad life."

"Not if you're fond of fifteen-hour days."

"Seriously?"

"Weekends, yes," she said, walking to her desk and opening a drawer. "The parties often go on until midnight. You can try to end them at eleven, but it hardly ever works. They'd go on longer if we let them. Whatever happened to the notion of the bride and groom leaving before the end of the reception and going off on their honeymoon? Today . . . today it's prewedding lunches, rehearsal dinners, golf, tennis, shopping, after-parties in the bar, bride's breakfasts in the morning. I should think it would sour any marriage right from the get-go. If *I'm* exhausted by Sunday afternoon, the brides must be comatose."

"But isn't this good for your business?"

"Well. Yes." She laughed. "I encourage it, actually."

The crisp, clean look of the inn had been continued in Nora's quarters. Harrison glanced at the chairs and the cocktail table with its objets — a vase, a stack of books, a small photograph that might have been of Nora's mother — and at a chaise near a window. One wall was covered in paintings and prints and photographs, arranged not so much artlessly as haphazardly, as if Nora had simply hung them as she'd found them, utilizing whatever space was available. He was drawn immediately to the photographs.

"Is this you?" he asked, pointing to a picture of a man he recognized as Carl Laski and a woman who was clearly a very young Nora.

"Yes," she said, looking up. "That was our wedding day."

Harrison studied the photo. Nora, who looked barely twenty, had on a blue-and-orange flower-print dress, her long chestnut hair done up in a bun. Laski's hair was also long — wild and unkempt. He had on a white shirt and a sport coat and a pair of jeans. His eyes seemed unfocused, as if he might already have been drinking. Looking at the picture, Harrison was aware of a vulnerability in Nora he had missed, that of a young child wanting to be reassured, or of a bereaved wife needing comfort. And he suddenly understood how it was that she might be taken advantage of. Harrison had an urge to enter the photograph and put an arm between Nora and Carl Laski.

"There," Nora said, finding a sheet of paper in a folder. She turned to face Harrison, a question on her lips. She hesitated a moment and then spoke. "Do you . . . do you ever think about what would have become of Stephen?"

Harrison forced himself not to look away. "Had he lived, you mean?"

"Yes."

"I imagine he'd have gone to Stanford on a baseball scholarship, as he was supposed to have done, then been drafted by the Blue Jays. He'd have been traded to the Twins and later would have ended up playing shortstop for the Red Sox — pre-Nomar, that is. Stephen would be a four-time Gold Glove winner and have an all-time batting average of .301, and any minute now he'd be on the ballot for the Hall of Fame."

"Was he that good?" she asked.

"Oh yes," Harrison said, running his fingers along the edge of a mahogany console table.

"Were you that good?"

"No. I only looked good because of Stephen. The two of us could turn a double play better than anyone in the league. But it was all Stephen — the way he'd snag the ball and whip around midair and rocket it to me. The only other player I've ever seen do it as well as Stephen *was* Nomar, actually."

Nora sat in the desk chair. "It's all so . . ."

"Sad?" Harrison asked.

"That, yes, but more than that. *Pointless.*"

Yes, Harrison thought. Absolutely pointless. "When I think about Stephen," he said, "I worry about my own two boys."

"They say it's worse now even than back then," Nora said.

"The drinking, you mean."

"We . . . we had a group of boys here in town last year who went joyriding, skidded on the ice, and hit a telephone pole. One of them was decapitated. All six died."

The image squeezed at Harrison. "It's a wonder any of us make it," he said quietly.

"Enough," Nora said, standing. "It's almost three. I have to go." She moved toward the doorway and stood at its entrance. "Will you be all right until six-thirty?"

"Of course," Harrison said, getting up from the chair and moving to the door as well. "I brought some work with me. I might look for Agnes."

He stood so close to Nora that he could smell her shampoo.

"That night," she said.

Harrison shook his head.

"No. You're right." Nora touched Harrison with the flat of her palm in the slight hollow between his shoulder and his collar bone, a touch that Harrison experienced as if on naked skin. As soon as he registered the touch, however, it was gone, and Nora was again leading the way along the corridor. "I can't wait to see Rob," she was saying from somewhere miles ahead of him.

Agnes unpacked the orange duffel bag, laying out her clothes on the bed. Jeans and a hand-knit sweater. A rose-colored suit for the cocktail party that evening. A blue wool dress she would wear to the wedding tomorrow. She sat at the edge of the bed and ate a PowerBar. She knew the inn served lunch — hadn't Nora said so? — but Agnes, on a tight budget, the budget made necessary by a modest salary from Kidd, had brought her own lunch, not knowing if meals were included in Nora's generous offer to put up everyone in the wedding party. Agnes had not liked to ask.

As she ate, she thought about the tour she had had earlier of the inn, of the sitting room, austere and yet inviting, of the splendid kitchen with its new appliances, of the corridors with their fresh white paint. Had Nora had a designer, or did the decor represent her own aesthetic? It was a kind of cleansing, Agnes thought, as if the inn had been put through a washer and the wringer had spit out something new. Yes, it was the *newness* — an entity with weight and texture — that so unnerved.

But something else nagged at Agnes, a half thought she had had in the kitchen before she'd been interrupted. What was it? Though the kitchen was magnificent, something struck her as *wrong*. Agnes closed her eyes. Yes, that was it: the smell of meat. Delicious in itself, but foreign to the kitchen of old. Carl had been a vegetarian, a purist. Agnes recalled with a shudder the bars of homemade soap, slimy and sandy at once, in the tiny bathroom at the end of the hall.

The smell of meat in the kitchen. Carl Laski would turn over in his grave. Where was his grave, come to think of it?

Agnes, who had arrived in her best school clothes, not knowing if she'd immediately run into Jerry or Bill or Bridget, changed into the sweater and jeans and a pair of L.L.Bean boots, finished off the PowerBar, took a swig of water from a bottle provided by the inn, and slipped the gold key into her pocket. She hooked her backpack over her shoulder.

At the desk in the lobby, she found a trail map for hikers. She paused for a moment on the front steps, studying the map and trying to orient herself. She was hot in her sweater but reluctant to return to her room to change. Surely it would grow cooler as the afternoon progressed, and she might find herself in the shade of the hill. It was an extraordinary day, and she wanted to make the most of it. It was a novelty to be able to walk without the wind biting at her face, as it nearly always did at Kidd in December.

Agnes took off impatiently, anxious to exercise muscles that had tightened and complained during the long ride from Maine. She had an image of herself running up the side of the hill but found, as she went, that the path was steeper than it had first appeared. A gentle light sifted through the trees, the limbs creating a gauzy view of the inn and of the mountains in the distance. If Jim had come with her this weekend, he would not be with her on this hike. A contemplative man, he did not like to exercise. He could be cajoled into a walk, but he seldom seemed to enjoy it. Never, in Agnes's memory, had Jim initiated a walk or a hike — something a wife, but not a lover, might begin to nag about, might learn to despise.

Agnes skirted a stone wall and followed the path, which grew steeper still. She was panting now, sweating inside her sweater (her own handiwork), and was cross with herself for not having worn layers, which she might have been able to peel off. Her unsuitable wardrobe was hardly her fault, though, was it? Who'd have predicted seventy-degree temperatures in December in New England? She leaned against a tree trunk, needing to catch her breath. Sweat trickled down her neck and under her arms, and it occurred to her that she might have forgotten to put on deodorant this morning. If so, she'd ruin the sweater. One could never get the smell out, not entirely. She glanced about her for signs of other human beings, but knew from the utter stillness of the woods that she was alone. She lifted the sweater over her head.

Immediately the sweat began to dry on her skin. She sat in her jeans and her bra on a rock, mildly tickled by the thought of herself half naked in the woods, slightly disconcerted by a narrow roll of fat hovering above the waistband of her jeans. She would have to increase her sit-ups from fifty to a hundred a day. She had a horror of Jim calling to arrange a rendezvous and Agnes finding herself overweight. If a woman had a man every day in her bed, Agnes wondered, was she then able to stop worrying about an extra pound or two?

Tonight, someone would ask Agnes why she had never married, why she hadn't wanted children. Someone would assume, but not say, that she was a lesbian. It was bound to cross the mind. Never married. No observable boyfriend. Field hockey coach. Agnes had been asked these questions before, had even been the recipient of passes from other women (one on the Nova Scotia trip). The questions, which Agnes used to try to dodge or dismiss, had lately begun to annoy her for their repeated assumptions. Agnes did not hunger for a child. Sometimes she wondered if this wasn't a failure of her imagination. She could no more picture herself with a child than she could with a horse.

A slight breeze rose and passed across her skin and cotton bra. She put a hand to her chest and was reminded of how smooth and taut her skin was there, of how long it had been since it had been touched. More than a year. How many years, Agnes wondered, before her skin was no longer smooth but crepey in the cleavage, as she had noted on underdressed older women? It would be all lost then, this skin, this loveliness, a dismal thought that gave rise to another one. Did a woman who had been fully loved mind the loss of her youth less than a woman who had not?

They'd all been together in Jim's class their senior year. Harrison and Nora and Rob and Jerry and Bill and Stephen. Not Bridget, who was a year behind them, the only junior in their circle of friends. Contemporary American literature was a class with a waiting list, and those who got in considered themselves privileged. They sat on sofas in Bloomfield Lounge, discussing Bellow and Kerouac and Ginsberg. Stephen, who seldom did the reading, had a gift for arguing a point. Nora, a true scholar, wrote papers she was sometimes asked to read aloud to the group. Agnes remembered Harrison as the thoughtful one; ideas and deft debate were Stephen's forte. Rob kept up a barely audible running commentary on the commentary, amusing anyone lucky enough to sit next to him, sometimes even Mr. Mitchell. Jerry, Agnes remembered, was always well prepared and brusque, occasionally resorting to ad hominem attacks when all else failed; yet just when you thought he'd gone too far, he would graciously concede the point and ask the one brilliant question that none of them had quite been able to formulate. And Mr. Mitchell (not yet Jim) would attempt to answer it, gently moving the conversation toward a kind of conclusion, allowing them their intellectual theatrics. Beneath the posturing, real learning was going on. It was only later, when Agnes herself became a teacher, that she understood the quiet skill of his methods.

It was November of their senior year, November 13 to be precise, a date Agnes had observed every year since as a kind of private anniversary. She'd walked into Mr. Mitchell's office after school to argue a grade on a paper. She had not, during her years at Kidd, made a habit of harassing teachers (as some of the students had), and so she had thought herself perfectly justified in her assault. She went in ready for a battle and did not allow Mr. Mitchell a word until she was done. By the end, she was sputtering, red and blotchy in the face. Jim, sitting across an oak desk while she stood and delivered, pushed his chair back and crossed his arms over his chest.

"Miss O'Connor," he said, everyone "Miss" or "Mr." then, "that was the most cogent argument I've ever heard in favor of changing a grade. More cogent, I might add, than anything you have so far written for this class. I am impressed. So impressed that I will change the grade. On one condition."

"Really?" Agnes asked, exhausted and slightly bewildered by her easy success.

"I want you to promise me that you'll work yourself into a similar state when marshaling your thoughts in writing."

Agnes wondered if this was a trick. "Okay," she said.

"Good," Mr. Mitchell said. "You'll write the paper over, and you'll get an A." He stood and gave his belt a little hitch. He put his hands on his hips. Agnes looked at his hips, saw the way his shirt billowed a bit over the belt, noticed as well the four or five inches of bare skin on his wrists where the man had rolled his sleeves, and she experienced desire. Pure. Unfamiliar. Uncorrupted. Her eyes rose to his face, to the blue irises she had not noted before. Agnes had been in this man's class twenty or thirty times, and she had never really looked at his face. Impossible.

Mr. Mitchell, clearly puzzled by Agnes's demeanor, tilted his head. "Well," he said.

Agnes could not move.

"So then," he said, made uncomfortable now by Agnes's odd behavior, "if I give you until next Wednesday, will that be enough time?"

Agnes nodded but made no move to pick up the paper she had set upon the desk with a snap in the middle of her argument.

"Anything else?" he asked.

Agnes tried to calculate his age. He was not old. Possibly thirty. She would find out. She could one day ask him where he'd gone to college — so much to learn about the man! — and what year he'd graduated.

"No," she said. "I'm just . . ."

Mr. Mitchell waited for his student to finish her sentence.

"Just what?" he asked in a gentle voice, dipping his head.

(Later, Jim would tell Agnes that he thought the generosity of his gesture had unleashed in her a desire to unburden herself of teenage angst — that she might reveal a tortured home life, an altercation with a roommate, a love affair gone bad, none of which he felt equipped to deal with, none of which he wanted to hear.)

"I've got to run," he said when Agnes didn't answer him.

Agnes collected her paper from the desk. "Thank you," she said. "Wednesday is fine."

"Good," he said, as though already congratulating himself for having successfully negotiated a tricky moment with a student.

But Agnes knew differently.

Leaning against a tree in the woods, remembering that day, Agnes realized she had to short-circuit the longing. If she didn't, she would cry, and she was not a lovely crier. Her eyes would vein up, and her lids would turn the color of uncooked bacon. No amount of makeup would disguise the mess. She put her sweater back on and took several deep breaths. She thought about the papers she had not yet graded, about her bank balance, about the roll of fat over her jeans. She thought about the Halifax disaster, that comfortable place to which her mind lately traveled. She reached into her backpack for her notebook and pen.

At dinner, Innes was seated across from Louise, a smaller woman than her sister. Louise had remarkable hazel eyes (yes, there was no other word for their color; Innes was a connoisseur of eye color), a fact that caused a slight dissonance, the actual Hazel having brown eyes. Did the Frasers regret their firstborn's name when Louise had come along? Or had they appreciated the little genetic joke?

"We are so happy to have you," Louise said in a rush, her nervousness betrayed in a tightness about her mouth. "Though heaven knows there's no shortage of men about with the war on. Droves of them, in fact. Coming and going. Simply droves."

An odd remark, Innes thought, begging the question of why Louise had remained unattached. Or perhaps Innes had got it wrong and Louise, too, had a ring. He could not just now see her hands.

"Few with Mr. Finch's qualifications to be sure." This from Dr. Fraser, who was missing at drinks but prompt for dinner. He was a man with military bearing of his own, the high collar, dotted tie, and neatly brushed mustache a sort of uniform. Innes wished that he and Dr. Fraser had had a moment to speak before the meal, not only so that the apprentice could properly introduce himself but also because Innes had large gaps in his understanding of his precise duties.

"How was your journey?" Louise asked.

"Cold, but remarkably easy," Innes replied, thinking that Louise would be prettier if her face relaxed, the nervousness inherited from the mother, certainly not the father, who had shown himself throughout the meal to be taciturn, immune to the chattering of his younger daughter and his wife, a private moving picture show of wounds perhaps or of surgical instruments or of soldiers' faces preoccupying him instead. For the wounded and dead soldiers were coming in "in boatloads,"

Innes was informed in one of Dr. Fraser's few pronouncements, a grim counterpart to Louise's "droves."

As the liver and bacon were served, Mrs. Fraser spoke of a new house, away from Richmond, in a better neighborhood, Young Street, did Innes know it? No, he did not. Mrs. Fraser registered her disappointment and added, in case Innes had missed the point, "where the better people are." Innes, of course, was not one of the better people, though he had prospects to recommend him, which Mrs. Fraser, the wife of a physician, knew only too well. Did Hazel, hearing this exchange, smile? Innes thought she did. He wondered if the circlet of diamonds was a gift from a grandmother. But almost immediately, the name Edward was mentioned in close proximity to Hazel's, the coupling causing a frown on Louise's brow. So it was true, Innes thought. Hazel gone before a dozen sentences exchanged. Gone even before his arrival. He was aware of the absurdity of his claim, entirely out of proportion to the length of time he had spent in her presence. She had given him nothing except, perhaps, for that half smile. She was a stranger.

Innes's attraction, however, was visceral.

"I inherited this house from my uncle," Mrs. Fraser said in another attempt to remove herself from Richmond. "He owned a sugar refinery."

"Will you be here long, Mr. Finch?" Louise asked, passing him the bowl of root vegetables.

"I'm to stay six months," he said with a question lobbed in Dr. Fraser's direction. Dr. Fraser did not respond.

"Through Christmas then," Louise said. "Will you be here over Christmas, or will you have to return to your family? They are where?"

"Cape Breton."

"Too long a journey," Louise said.

95

"My work might prevent a journey home at that time," Innes said carefully, embarrassed by Louise's question. Very likely, the Frasers, wishing to be alone over the holiday, would want him away for a few days. In truth, Innes could not afford the journey to Cape Breton.

The elder Frasers ate with relish. Louise, eager to please, filled in all the gaps, her rapid speech more than just nervousness. Innes diagnosed mild hysteria. Louise's hair, light brown, had been cut short and waved at either side of her face.

"We would welcome Mr. Finch at Christmastime," Mrs. Fraser said politely, albeit a bit late.

Innes imagined Hazel's fiancé. A man in uniform. A surgeon? An officer in France? Louise was speaking of a dance aboard a ship in the harbor and wondered aloud if Innes would like to go. Innes was reminded of his civilian suit, his one civilian suit that would not take itself aboard a ship full of naval officers in uniform.

"Mr. Finch," Dr. Fraser said, rousing himself in the moments after the liver and bacon and before the pudding, "I have some papers I should like you to look over this evening. Meet me in the front hallway at nine-thirty in the morning. We will have a rigorous day. New wounds from France."

The phrase, a low gas floating across the table, smothered conversation. The silence drew itself out, approaching unendurable. Even the voluble Louise was quiet, though she glanced sideways at Hazel. A guess was confirmed. Hazel was engaged to an officer in France.

"Fifteen ships lost last week," Dr. Fraser added, seemingly oblivious to the effects of his remarks. Perhaps the women of the table were used to them. "They say a man at the front has a three-month life expectancy. A horse, one month."

Oddly, it was Hazel who broke the ghastly silence. "Do you play cards, Mr. Finch?"

Innes Finch, as it happened, was rather good at cards. "Yes, I do," he said.

"We'll play gin rummy," Louise said as they all stood. She moved to take Innes's arm. "We'll be a team, you and I, because Hazel is simply too good. Aren't you, Hazel? We'll have some cocoa and make an evening of it."

The three returned to the sitting room where earlier drinks had been served. An electric lamp had been lit near a hexagonal table. The low light and the blackout curtains gave the impression of a fortune-teller's parlor, and Innes had the bizarre sense that a séance was about to take place. He was reassured by the sight of a ball of yarn perched on the wide arm of a chair. Louise would be knitting socks for the war effort. Hazel, he was certain, would not.

The two women seated themselves at either side of Innes. Mrs. Fraser would not be joining them. Mention was made of a mild stomach upset. Louise kept up a running commentary on the war. A thousand British ships lost. John Ferguson killed. Mary's father had made a bundle in munitions. Hazel seemed unmoved by her sister's insensitive pronouncements.

Innes noted, even in the low light, a shabbiness to the room he hadn't before, not in its furnishings, which seemed too grand for the homely simplicity of the room, but rather in the absence of moldings, the narrow floorboards, a place just above a door where a chunk of plaster had been dislodged. Through the window at his back, there was a draft. Innes felt the house shudder as a motorcar rumbled by.

Innes won for Louise, the card game a stream running below conscious thought, his play automatic and deft, even when he intentionally lost the next game to Hazel. In medical school, they had played for pennies, earning or forfeiting beer money. Innes had been trained to think methodically and precisely on one level, intuitively on another, a trick his mentor had made him practice evenings in his office. A skill available to anyone, but consciously retrieved and employed when interviewing patients for surgery.

The sullen manservant who had hoisted Innes's luggage up the stairs as if it had contained dead cod appeared at a distant door asking for Louise. Louise left the table to speak to the man, and immediately Innes and Hazel exchanged glances — she raised her eyes just as he looked away. A thrumming began in his chest as Hazel stood to see to Louise at the door. Innes heard the sisters murmuring, then Louise's mild distress. She disappeared with the sullen servant.

Hazel, stopping by the fire, said, "My mother is not well and needs Louise. My sister has a tonic she makes that alleviates my mother's discomfort."

Innes diagnosed constipation. "I'm sorry she's feeling poorly," he said, standing up from the hexagonal table.

"You don't love cards, do you?" Hazel asked, putting her back to the fire.

"Under some circumstances, but not tonight."

"I work with my father in the clinic."

"Do you?" Innes asked with genuine surprise.

"Would you like another drink?"

"Not if I'm to be alert in the morning," Innes said as he moved toward the fire.

Hazel sat at one end of the leather sofa. Innes, not sure where to put himself, chose a chair near the sofa's opposite end. He had a view of Hazel's face in the firelight. "What do you do at the clinic?" he asked.

"I roll bandages. I soothe frightened patients."

"I would find your presence soothing," Innes dared to say.

"Why did you not stay on in America?" Hazel asked, ignoring the compliment.

"I felt my place to be here," Innes said. "There's a keen sense of nationalism everywhere now, isn't there? Also, it is a great honor to train with your father."

"The war is taxing his reserves," Hazel said, frowning. "And his spirits. He has seen many die of their wounds. I should warn you that he will be a hard taskmaster."

"I look forward to the challenge," Innes said.

"I'm sure you do, Mr. Finch."

"Would you consider," Innes asked, "since I am to live here for the duration, calling me by my given name?" Not waiting for the answer, he added, "Shall I stoke the fire?"

"I'm off to bed soon, but do if you plan to remain here."

Innes, too, would be off to bed soon. He hoped a fire had been made up in his room. If not, the sheets would be frigid. At school, ice had sometimes formed in the pitchers beside the beds.

"Louise has a slight nervous condition," Hazel said.

Harrison nodded, wondering if this was treachery on Hazel's part, quashing Louise's chances, or was it merely a warning? Innes did not say what he thought, that Louise was desperate to love whomever might love her in return. Attention, Innes could see, had all been given to the older sister. "I gather you're engaged," Innes said.

There was a kind of dull anxiety about Halifax evenings. The knitting of socks. The rubbers of bridge. The shipboard dances. An officer in France, if he made it back, would offer an escape.

"You wouldn't be a suitable candidate for medicine had you not deduced that," Hazel said.

"Tell me about him."

"In a sentence? He is a lieutenant commander with the British Royal Navy."

Innes, thinking that if he loved someone, a sentence would never do, asked, "He's not a surgeon then?"

"No," Hazel answered, glancing away from Innes and toward the fire. "He's in manufacturing."

Money or good looks must have attracted, Innes thought, knowing even as he had this thought that attraction defied logic, just as it was doing now in the Fraser sitting room.

"Will you settle here?" Innes asked.

"That is a decision for Edward to make," Hazel answered, raising her chin.

Hazel would move away then. Even Young Street, with its better sort of person, would not suit. Already, Innes found he minded Hazel's future absence. Halifax, full of possibility just hours ago, would seem empty without her.

"Mr. Finch — Innes — I think you will do well in your profession."

"I hope you are right."

"You have intuition and empathy. I saw it at dinner and again at cards."

"Thank you."

Hazel gestured toward the windows. "I hate the curtains," she said with feeling. "There's a lovely view out there of the harbor and the ships in the moonlight. When the war ends, and I have my own house, there will be no curtains on the windows. I'll want to see the lights, the stars." She stood. "I'm off to bed now."

Innes, jealous of that future house with its naked windows, rose with her.

"I'll see you at breakfast," she said. "Ellen, our cook, will do a Scottish breakfast in your honor."

"I will be honored then."

"Do you miss your family?"

"More so as the years pass," he confessed. "In the beginning, I was impatient to be away. I was cruel in that, I think. I have a brother in France."

There was a pause while each imagined the brother in France, a country neither of them had ever seen.

"Did you ever think of medical training yourself?" he asked.

"It was not encouraged," she said, moving toward the door. "Louise will be sorry not to have said good night to you. My mother must be worse than I thought."

"I hope to see them both at breakfast."

"I hate this war," Hazel said, turning. "Hate it."

Innes was surprised by the ferocity of the statement. "We all do," he said.

"No. Not all. Some prosper."

Innes wondered if she was thinking of Edward, who was in manufacturing. "One could say that physicians prosper," Innes offered. "Careers can be made."

"For physicians, I believe it exhausts more than it enhances," she said.

"Is your father exhausted?"

"Yes, and I worry about him. But he is a man of discipline."

"And are you?" Innes asked, opening the door for Hazel. She crossed the threshold, moving close to him.

"Not at all," Hazel replied. "No, not in the slightest."

Soon Innes would go to bed, Agnes thought. He would sleep between frigid — no, warm — sheets. In the morning he would have his Scottish breakfast, and then the unthinkable would happen. Some of the Fraser family would die. One would be blinded. The power that Agnes had over Innes and Hazel and Louise — Agnes, who was powerless to affect her own life — was both frightening and quietly thrilling.

Agnes returned to the inn with little memory of the trip down the hill. It was nearly dark when she crossed the threshold, shutting the door behind her. She took the stairs two at a time, not wanting anyone to see her in her sweater, her stringy hair. She shut the door behind her like a fugitive and caught her breath. She peeled off her clothes as she made her way to the shower. She looked at the Jacuzzi. Did all the rooms come with a Jacuzzi? Her first thought was one of pleasure. Her second one of pain. Must everything in life be referential? Was there nothing that would not remind her of Jim?

Agnes stepped out of her underwear and studied her face in the mirror over the sink. Her eyes were clear. Her skin was slightly flushed. She would not, under any circumstances, cry. She would, in fact, disregard the tub entirely. She saw, on a silver tray on the shelf under the mirror, containers of shampoo and shower gel. She twisted off the cap of the shampoo and inhaled. She smelled rosemary, grapefruit.

Harrison returned to his room, the treble note of Nora's palm on his shoulder drowning out thought, intention, rest. Unwilling yet to go in search of Agnes, though that would have been the plan, he stood at the window and saw intermittently, as it appeared and disappeared from view around curves and below hillocks, a stretch limo making its way up the drive. The limo snagged his attention, for he thought it had to be Bill and Bridget, that they had arrived in grand style (good for Bill, Harrison thought). Harrison crossed his room so that he could have a view of the front of the inn. A woman, not Bridget, emerged from the right rear door of the limo. She was smartly dressed in a black sweater and black pants, the solid line accentuating her height, which must have been near six feet. The woman had sleek blond hair, though Harrison could see, when she turned around, that she was nearing forty if not there already. From within the dark expanse of the car, the woman was handed a fur, which she draped over one arm. Harrison watched as she walked directly into the inn without a backward glance.

From the other side of the limo, a man Harrison recognized — for his height, for his trim build, for the head of tamed reddish curls — stepped out onto the gravel and surveyed the property as if he might buy it. It was not entirely illogical that Jerry should have come by limo — he lived in Manhattan and clearly didn't want the fuss of a car — but had the stretch really been necessary?

There would be no grand entrance for Jerry, however, no doorman, no porter for that matter. The limo driver took out the luggage — camel leather, supple, and impressive — and set it neatly on the first step of the inn, his task completed. The chauffeur had the air of a man whose strict business code barely masked his impatience to be away. (Was he hungry? Did he need a bathroom? Had Jerry been obnoxious in the car?) Jerry would be annoyed at having to manage his own luggage (or would Judy have to fetch the bags and haul them up the stairs?), and Nora, in Jerry's book, would be down a point or two before she'd even begun. Harrison was tempted to open his door and walk to the top of the stairs simply to overhear what Jerry had to say when he stepped into the lobby and there was no one there to greet him. Or would the sight of the limo have roused the troops?

Harrison supposed he ought to go for another walk. He needed to order his thoughts. The prospect of seeing faces one had known intimately in another universe — the unsettling illusion that these people were truly his closest friends, though he had not seen some of them in twenty-seven years — as well as the notion of presenting oneself to one's peers for judgment (was Harrison doing well? was he happy in marriage? did he look forty-four?) disturbed him. Though not as much as Nora's quick touches, on the knee and on his shoulder, surely meaningless at their age, merely a way of making a point, and yet sounding that note that was still quivering in the air. And then there was the twice-mentioned Stephen, whose ghostly form was filling in like a special effect in a B movie. There would be talk of Stephen, and Harrison would have to prepare himself for it. Men and women Harrison hadn't seen in more than two decades would look at him and think, *Stephen*. It was natural. It was to be expected. Harrison had been, after all, Stephen's best friend and roommate.

Harrison sat at the desk with its lamp and blotter and telephone.

He removed the inn cards (the promotions, the list of local attractions) so that the desk was as uncluttered as he could make it. He'd have liked a second cup of coffee and thought about the espresso machine in the library, but he might meet Bridget or Agnes or even Jerry there, which he was not yet ready to do. No, now he needed to make a connection to his family — to Evelyn — however tenuous, however quixotic (Harrison would arrive home before the letter did). He could call, but he didn't want to hear his wife's rushed voice, her perfunctory questions: *How are you? How was the flight? What's the inn like?* Rather he would like to see Evelyn in repose, curled up on the leather couch in what passed in his house for a library, a third of the shelves filled with children's books, sitting with a cup of coffee (lucky girl) while she read Harrison's words. The effort of a letter seemed atavistic in an age of e-mail — deliberately Luddite and time-consuming — and yet it was this image of Evelyn, one he hardly ever saw in real life, that inspired him to rummage through the desk drawer to find the inn's stationery: large sheets of heavy white paper with the name of the inn embossed white on white on the back flap of the envelope so as not to intrude commercially upon the letter writer's thoughts.

Pure Nora, Harrison thought.

Dear Evelyn,

How long has it been since I sat down to write to you? A year? That trip to London? I'm inspired to do so again and hope you don't mind this rambling letter, nor the fact that I'll be within Toronto's city limits when you receive it. As always, I think back to the days when you were living in Toronto and I was in Montreal, and we wrote incessantly. I remember listening for the postman's steps along the sidewalk (I was like a dog in that; I could tell his gait three houses away) and bounding down the stairs to snatch the envelope — always gray —

from him, and carrying it with care, as if it might crumble, to my squalid room. I'd fall into a swoon of pure emotion as I read. Possibly it's that feeling I'm trying to recapture now: rare as I grow older. More likely to happen when watching the boys, I think. By the way, how are they? (Absurd to be asking a question I'll already know the answer to when you read this.) Not too annoying while I'm gone, I hope. Though secretly I think both they and we like the holiday of an absent parent, any novelty being preferable during the school year to the same old.

I arrived at the inn this morning. It's quite unique — all gables and porches and improbable rooflines, which might sound Gothic but isn't really. Maybe it was in the days when Carl Laski lived here, but Nora, his widow, the woman who owns the inn and has arranged for Bill and Bridget's wedding (you remember I mentioned Nora) has made the place terrifically inviting — very up-to-the-minute with espresso machines and Jacuzzis in the bathrooms. The rooms feel calm, and one has a sense of "having arrived." I think Nora's a genius at this. Perhaps she's found her true calling. Certainly she seems happy, if distracted, and we are all amazed by this incredible weather — sunny and seventy degrees. Is it glorious there as well? I see this as a good omen for Bill and Bridget, for whom I wish only the best. Bridget has a fifteen-year-old boy I'm looking forward to meeting. Wonder if Bill's put a glove in his hand yet.

I've never talked much about my days at Kidd. You once asked me why. I think — no, I know — it's because my time there ended so badly. I told you that my roommate died a month before graduation, but I'm not sure I ever told you how.

All of us were friends. Stephen (who was my roommate),

A Wedding in December

Bill, Jerry, Rob, and I had been on the varsity baseball team since our sophomore year. Stephen, among us, was truly gifted, the one who would have gone to college on a baseball scholarship — a better college than he deserved, I might add, since he was only an average student, sliding through mostly on his dazzle and debating skills. As you can imagine, this was a constant source of tension between us, I being the plodder, the one who did all the reading, probably three or four days before it was due. But we were tight despite our academic differences. Stephen was unique, a guy who could see the bigger picture, who made us think. And, of course, we all wanted to be him. Handsome doesn't really do him justice. The word is too static, I think. His face could come alive in an instant, and his smile was truly encompassing. You wanted to be standing somewhere within its perimeter. He had money, which not all of us did (Kidd wasn't that kind of school). His father had made a fortune in the early years of telecommunications and had an enormous house in Wellesley. I believe it had seven bathrooms. His father had divorced and remarried a younger woman — Angelica, I think her name was. She was only ten years older than we were, which was always slightly disconcerting (I may have had a crush on her my freshman year). It was in Stephen's father's house that I had my first drink (decidedly not Stephen's first), sneaking down one night during our junior year and unlocking his father's liquor cabinet and together putting away nearly a fifth of Jack Daniel's. Not sure I've ever been that sick since.

Bill and Jerry were roommates. You remember Bill from the two skiing trips with the kids. At school, Bill was quiet and unassuming, while Jerry was "in-your-face" long before we even knew what the term meant. He was a terrific sinker-ball pitcher, though, and if he could keep the ball down, the other team couldn't get a hit out of the infield. When Jerry was at school, he was half a blowhard, half a genuinely inquisitive kid. I always hoped the genuinely inquisitive kid would win out, but I met him about five years ago in New York for lunch and was disappointed to see that not only had the blowhard won out but it had taken over like a virus. I'm not sure much has changed, since I just saw him pull up to the inn a few minutes ago in a stretch limo. I thought it was the bride- and groom-to-be until Jerry, with his long neck and gangly limbs (now cosseted in expensive tailoring), stepped out of the car. For all his braggadocio, though, he's the smartest among us, and I look forward to seeing what he does to the mix tonight.

Rob, a tall, skinny kid, played right field, but probably shouldn't have. We didn't know it then, but he was headed for Juilliard on the strength of his virtuosity at the piano. I'm sure once he got in (it took him two or three tries after we graduated from Kidd), they told him he could never catch a ball again. I wonder now if he even follows the games. He was an insane Red Sox fan. It's a miracle, really, that he didn't jam a finger during his time at Kidd. It happens all the time.

The other three from our group at Kidd were girls (women now, obviously): Agnes, Bridget, and Nora. Of the three, I know Bridget the least. She was a year behind us — around because Bill was there. If Bill was quiet and unassuming, Bridget was mute, deaf to anything but Bill's voice. They were the ur-couple, the pair you knew would stay faithful all through college and marry the day after graduation. I'm not sure what happened — well, I guess Jill happened, didn't she? — but I remember being shocked when I heard Bill had married someone else.

Nora, I know fairly well. She was Stephen's girlfriend and

always in and out of the dorm when visits were permitted, or on the sidelines at the games. If Kidd had been the kind of school where one elected a prom king and queen (Kidd was so low-key, we didn't even have a prom), they'd have been the pick. I think Nora must somewhere have a penchant for difficult, dysfunctional men, however. By the spring of our senior year, Stephen was becoming a serious drunk. From all accounts, Carl Laski was a drunk and a bastard. I don't know that he specifically treated Nora poorly, but he was, at the very least, a troubled man.

Toward the end of that year, Stephen began finding reasons to drink two or three times a week. "Let's have a party," he would say, or "Let's get wasted." Drinking was de rigueur on Friday and Saturday nights. He got caught once and was suspended for four days. He went home willingly to dry out. I'm not sure why Nora put up with it, except that Stephen was dangerous and exciting and ridiculously good-looking. And I don't think she got the brunt of it, as I did. The vomiting, the hangovers, the self-loathing. And, to be honest, by spring semester of our senior year, a lot of us were drinking and partying, secure, we thought, with our college acceptances. Mostly we drank in the empty beach houses, the majority so flimsy we could easily break in. We'd wait until after dark and have a party inside if it was raining, outside on the seawall or the beach if the weather was halfway decent. Those were good times, and I wish I could remember them with fondness, but I can't. It was during one of those parties that Stephen got drunk, walked into the ocean, and drowned.

No one realized he was missing until it was too late. We all assumed he'd walked back to campus along the beach, singing off-key as he had a habit of doing when he was plowed. When he didn't show up in our room that night, I alerted a proctor. I've never forgiven myself for not going out earlier to find him on the beach.

His body washed up on Pepperell Island a week later. I've spent whole weeks, months, years even trying to forget that night. There was a funeral and a listless graduation, after which we all scattered, too ashamed and heartbroken, I think, to stay in touch. It was a tragedy for Stephen and his family. A filthy, shameful sort of tragedy for the rest of us.

Harrison put down his pen and wiped his brow. These were half-truths, a gloss.

I haven't mentioned Agnes, the most grounded of us all. Nora's roommate, Agnes was always old-fashioned and frumpy, but everyone's good buddy. I'm not sure she ever had a date at Kidd. She teaches there now, the only one of us who stayed in Maine. She's never married. I don't know why. I'd like to think it's because she knows us all — we men, that is — to be assholes. She's here at the inn, but I haven't run into her yet.

So there you have it, the cast of characters. Alive to me in some deep geographical stratum of my being. I sometimes think I know them better than I know my current friends — George, for example, with whom I've worked for twenty years. You must tell me one day if you feel the same about the friends you had when you were a teenager. I remember you talking about Rowena, but I'm not sure you've ever said much about anyone else.

I miss you, Evelyn. I wish I could watch you dress for the cocktail party tonight and then walk in with you on my arm. Every man there would envy me. And then you and I could come back to this spiffy room and fall into what looks to be

*an obscenely comfortable bed and parse the evening, and
then make love. We don't make love enough, but you know
that. Every time we do, I ask myself why we don't do it more.
Our lives get in the way, don't they? And the boys, whom we
willingly wish in the way. They are treasures, and so are you.*

   Your grateful husband,

   Harrison

Harrison put the letter in an envelope and wrote his own address
on the front. He propped the letter against a lamp.

He rummaged through his luggage on the bed for his toilet kit
and headed for the bathroom, stripping as he went. Once inside
the shower, he let the hot water hit the back of his neck. With head
bent and arms hanging loose, he refused thought, humming instead a few bars from "Lady Marmalade." *Voulez-vous coucher avec
moi, ce soir?* He stood in that position for long minutes until he
began to worry about Nora's water heater, about all the other guests
trying to have simultaneous showers for their evenings out. He
soaped himself, washed his hair, and rinsed quickly. He toweled
himself dry and wiped a spot of condensation from the fogged
mirror so that he could shave. Niggling thoughts returned. Would
there be a dinner after the drinks, or would they all be on their
own? And, if so, how would they group up? Harrison hoped Nora
had taken care of that in advance. He wondered then about the
wedding. No mention had been made of a minister or a justice of
the peace. Wasn't Bridget Catholic? He wondered idly what the
ceremony would be like, if Bridget would wear white. Was getting
married in the face of cancer an act of desperation?

Shaved and clean, Harrison chose between two shirts. He'd wear
a sport coat tonight, his suit tomorrow. The mirror was clear when
he went into the bathroom to knot his tie. Did he look forty-four?
What did forty-four look like? Whatever it was, he thought, Nora

didn't look it. There was still a gamine quality about her that age hadn't buried.

Harrison checked to see that he had his key, and then he left his room. Immediately he could hear a kind of hubbub in the lobby. Of course the inn would have other guests — hadn't he seen the sign for the Karola-Jungbacker wedding? — but it was strange nevertheless to hear voices when it had seemed so quiet before. He took the stairs instead of the elevator, stepping smartly, aware now that he might be seen by someone he knew. Aware, too, of the ridiculousness of caring. In the lobby, he noticed an elderly couple heading for the elevator to the dining room — the early shift for dinner, he guessed. A younger couple seemed unanchored, having left their room too early for dinner, not sure yet where to berth themselves.

Harrison walked toward the library. He noted, as he neared it, that the double doors were open. He paused for a moment and could hear voices. He recognized only Bill's. As he turned the corner and entered the room, faces swiveled in his direction. He spotted Rob Zoar and a man he didn't know in conversation. Rob put his hand on the back of the man's neck and leaned in close to convey a private word. Harrison was slightly stunned. He hadn't realized that Rob was gay. Had he been at Kidd? Had the others known? In the corner, Jerry Leyden waved. Agnes O'Connor was approaching, her arms spread wide. Harrison heard his name repeated and was suffused with a sense of *lights up, curtains rising,* as if for some great assembly.

Harrison."

"Agnes."

"My God."

"You look great."

"And you."

Harrison bent to embrace her. In his arms, Agnes felt even more solid than he had remembered (but so was he, he thought; so was he). He held her at arm's length and studied her face. She seemed genuinely happy to see him, slightly abashed at being examined. He let her go. Her face had weathered more than one would have imagined. She had on clothing that Harrison recognized as being out-of-date. A secular nun in a rose-colored suit. He could see, simply from the athletic way she held herself, that she wasn't used to dressing up.

"How are you?" she asked.

"Well. And you?"

She laughed and took a sip of wine. "Will it be like this all night?" she asked. "All these ohmygods and youlookgreats?"

"For a while. It would be worse at a reunion."

"This is a reunion."

"Sort of."

"Amazing about Bill and Bridget," she said.

"I was surprised."

"And you know Bill. I mean, you're in touch, right?"

"We used to be. I knew his wife. Ex-wife."

"I'm happy for them. Very brave of Bridget. Of Bill, too."

Harrison sensed Nora by the door. In the corner, a bartender was standing behind a draped table. Harrison had a sudden urge for a drink. "This inn is beautiful," he said.

"Wonderful views." Together, they turned to look through the tall cottage windows at the views, which, of course, could not be seen at night. "I can't get over the transformation. Were you ever here before?"

"Except for Bill and Jerry, I haven't seen anyone in this room in twenty-seven years," Harrison said.

"You wouldn't guess it was the same place."

"I didn't know this was an interest that Nora had."

"Who could tell what Nora's interests were?"

"I thought you kept in touch."

"I did. I only mean that she was so overshadowed by Carl."

"Surely, she held her own."

"Not really."

Harrison sensed distaste. "You don't sound as though you liked him much."

"Oh, do I give that impression?" Agnes asked.

Harrison laughed. As if the bartender had read his mind — which, Harrison supposed, was what bartenders were supposed to do — he appeared at Harrison's elbow asking him what he'd like to drink. Harrison looked at Agnes's glass. "What are you drinking?" he asked.

"White wine. Considerably better than my usual."

"I'll have that then," he told the waiter.

"You're an editor," Agnes said when the bartender had gone.

"I am. I work for a small publishing firm in Toronto. We publish mostly Canadian and British authors. Audr Heinrich? Vashti Baker?"

Agnes nodded vaguely. "And you have kids," she said.

"Two boys. Charlie, eleven, and Tom, nine." Harrison was handed a delicately etched glass of cold white wine. "Nora said you're teaching at Kidd."

"I'm the one who never left. You know, there's always one in every class who never leaves? Who wants to be a perpetual student?"

"How is the old place, anyway?"

"You wouldn't recognize it, Harrison. Very multicultural now. Terrific emphasis on science. The buildings all have new additions. I have a condo in Rowan House."

"Really?" he asked. "In the turret?" Harrison took a quick glance at Rob and at the man he didn't recognize. He felt overdressed in a tie.

"Yes, as a matter of fact," Agnes said.

"I'm envious. I always wanted to see what it looked like inside the turret."

"Well, anytime you find yourself downeast . . ."

Harrison smiled.

"You've never been to a reunion," she said, and from her matter-of-fact and slightly scolding tone, Harrison deduced that Agnes had been to all of them.

"No."

"All the really interesting people never go."

Harrison took a sip of wine. Rob and his guest were talking with Jerry and Julie. Rob looked elegant in a dark gray suit with an open collar. "Who's the guy with Rob?"

"His name is Josh. He's a cellist."

"I didn't realize about Rob . . ."

"No, I didn't either," Agnes said.

"Would he have known at Kidd?" Harrison asked, knowing even as he posed the question that it was none of his business. He tried to remember whom Rob had dated.

"I suppose," Agnes said. "Biologically speaking, from what I've read, he would have to have known. In those days, though, he couldn't have acted on it, could he? Well, not so that anyone noticed. Now, of course, we have a Gay and Lesbian Coalition. It's good, and I'm glad we have it, but I worry that the really young students who are just discovering their sexuality will gravitate to the group before they know what they're about." Agnes fixed something inside her blouse, a bra strap gone awry. "Rob and Josh want to go to the outlets tomorrow. There's an Armani for them, a J.Crew for me. I might do some Christmas shopping. Want to come with us?"

"Thanks. I might."

Agnes leaned back, making a show of surveying him from head to toe. "Let's see, button-down shirt, blue blazer — Brooks Brothers, right?"

Harrison smiled. "Is it that bad?"

Through a wall or from down a corridor, Harrison could hear the lively sounds of another party, a bigger gathering, one with music. Jerry, standing by the drinks table, said to his wife, *Do what you want. I don't care.*

"How's your mother?" Agnes asked.

The question surprised Harrison. No one from Toronto ever asked about his family. They simply didn't know him as having a family. "She's still living in the old house in Tinley Park, just outside Chicago. My sister, Alison, is in LA. She's a scriptwriter."

"Really," Agnes said, her eyebrows raised at this unexpected bit of glamour. "Anything I'd have seen?"

"When we were in LA just recently, Alison was working on a movie with Ben Affleck and Morgan Freeman. The boys got to watch the stunt doubles in harnesses film the special effects. My wife, Evelyn, got to chat with Ben Affleck, which of course made her day."

Nora, her hair tucked behind one ear, was speaking to the bartender at the drinks table. Harrison had expected her in her uniform — the sheer blouse and skirt — but she had on a dress, black with a shallow V-neck collar. Again, Harrison thought of European women.

"Did you fly?" Agnes was asking.

"There's a direct flight from Toronto to Hartford."

"Was it awful? They say it is. I haven't flown since 9/11."

"The lines were bad. Other than that . . ."

"Of course, it would have to be Portland, wouldn't it, where the trouble started," Agnes said. "I think everyone in Maine felt responsible."

"I imagine heads have rolled."

"Well, you certainly don't want to fly out of Portland right now," she warned. "The longest lines in America. Do you feel safer in Canada?"

Harrison noticed that Agnes had on incongruously sexy high-heeled shoes. He wondered if she had bought them for this occasion. "In Toronto? No, not at all."

Agnes glanced around the room. "Where are Bridget and Bill, I wonder?"

"I'm sure I saw Bill earlier," Harrison said.

"Who are the two kids in suits?"

At the table where hors d'oeuvres had been set out, two teenage boys were on a reconnaissance mission. If they were anything like his sons, they wouldn't leave the table until they'd had the equivalent of a meal. "I think one of them is Bridget's son, the other his friend. I'm not sure which is which."

"Poor Bill," Agnes said, and Harrison didn't know whether she was referring to the fact that Bill's family would not come for the wedding or the worse fact of Bridget's diagnosis. "I hope she's all right," she added, immediately answering Harrison's question. "I'm getting another drink. You want one?"

"Not just yet. But thanks."

Nora was still by the door. Harrison headed in her direction. "Delicious wine," he said when he had reached her side. "I like the glass, too."

"I find them in flea markets. I had lessons. For the wine."

"Really?"

"At a vineyard not far from here."

"I didn't know they produced wine in New England."

"There . . . there are lots of small vineyards sprinkled all through Vermont and Massachusetts and Connecticut. Some of it is very good."

"Are you still happy?" he asked.

She thought a minute. "Not ecstatic. As I was earlier. The day is gone, isn't it? But I'm excited to have everyone together. After so long."

"Is this your drinks-in-the-library uniform?" he asked, gesturing to her dress.

Nora shrugged.

Harrison was aware of a sharp and inappropriate desire to touch the bare skin of her arm. "Agnes and I were wondering where Bridget is. She got here okay?"

"She did. She's still in her room changing. She's shy. Do you remember her as shy?"

"I remember her as attached to Bill at the hip."

"Everyone thinks Bill wanted to do this for Bridget because she might die," Nora said. "But the real reason is that he's never gotten over hurting her the way he did. When he broke up with her in college and started dating Jill. I've never met her. Jill, that is."

"As I recall, Jill is an incredibly attractive woman with a healthy manipulative streak. Bill might not have had a chance."

"He thinks he and Bridget have a chance now."

"I hope that's true." Harrison paused. "Hope that's true for all of us, actually."

Nora smiled.

"How was the rehearsal?" Harrison asked.

"The bride started crying for reasons that escaped all of us."

"You don't drink?" Harrison asked, pointing to Nora's glass of sparkling water.

"I'm working."

"Doesn't seem fair."

"Well, I'm both. I'll have a glass of wine at dinner." She tucked her hair behind her ear. "Tell me a story," she said.

"What?"

"A little story. I don't have much time."

"Here?" Harrison asked.

Nora nodded.

"Okay. Well. Let's see . . ." Harrison said and paused. "Okay, here's a story," he began, thinking to best her at her own game. "One day I was taking a walk on a Sunday morning at Kidd, and I noticed across the road one of the most beautiful girls I'd ever seen. I caught up to her — I was still on my side of the road — and thought I would call over to her and talk to her and ask her her name, but I choked at the last minute. I think I said hello but then just kept walking. And you want to know something? I've regretted all my life that I didn't cross that road and start a conversation."

There was a long silence between them. Nora crossed her arms, the empty water glass dangling between her fingers by the stem. "I was disappointed when you weren't at the gate," she said finally.

Harrison could feel the heat begin in his neck and crawl up behind his ears.

"Telling the truth is erotic," Nora said. "Like opening the mouth wide for a kiss."

The thrumming sensation Harrison had had earlier in the day began again inside his chest. "It's what lovers do when they meet," he said.

"I don't ever want a lover," Nora said.

"A man can't say that," Harrison said. "Well, he can say it, but it's pretty meaningless."

"Presumably you don't want a lover because you're married."

Harrison didn't hesitate. "That would be correct," he said.

He felt a light punch to his biceps.

"Branch," Jerry said.

"Jerry," Harrison said, shaking his hand, aware as he was doing so that Nora was drifting away from him.

"You still in Toronto?" Jerry asked.

"I am," Harrison said, slightly rattled by Nora's disappearance.

"You ever think about New York? I mean, isn't that the hot center of your business? Publishing?"

"My wife is from Toronto," Harrison said, absolutely certain that he and Jerry had had this exact sequence of questions and answers in New York City five years ago.

"I know a guy at Random House you ever want an introduction."

"Let me guess. He owes you big-time."

"I made him a bundle in the early nineties," Jerry said, taking a sip of what looked to be scotch. He was expensively done up in camel cashmere, the only one of them not in a jacket.

"Didn't I see your wife just a minute ago?" Harrison asked.

"She went upstairs to powder. She'll be back. Who'd have thought Nora could pull this off? You know who's backing her?"

"I don't," Harrison said. "I more or less had the impression she's on her own."

"The toilets are for shit, and, Christ, you'd think they could scrounge up a porter. But the rooms are good. No complaint there. She kept her looks, didn't she?"

Harrison found he minded, on Nora's behalf, this mildly sexist remark. "She's lovely," Harrison said.

"Get off. You always had a thing for her," Jerry said, draining his glass. He held the glass high over his head to signal to the bartender that he needed another.

"She was Stephen's girl," Harrison said, hating that he even had to say Stephen's name aloud.

"You and Steve were best friends," Jerry said.

Harrison was pretty sure that no one had ever called Stephen *Steve*.

"And you were there, right?" Jerry asked. "That night he walked into the water? Really, is that what he did, just walked into the water? I mean, who would do that? The water couldn't have been over forty degrees. They say that lobster fishermen don't even bother to learn how to swim because if you fall overboard that time of year, you've got like a minute or two to get out before your heart stops. Swimming does no good whatsoever."

"I didn't actually see it," Harrison said.

"Really."

Harrison was silent.

"I mean," Jerry said, "if you'd seen it . . ."

"If I had seen Stephen walking toward the water," Harrison said as evenly as he could manage, "I certainly would have stopped him."

"Of course you would," Jerry said, eyeing him over the scotch. "You going to the outlets tomorrow?" he asked.

"Maybe," Harrison said.

Jerry cast an impatient glance in the waiter's direction. "Who knew Bill and Bridget had got back together? Wild, huh?"

"Wild."

"They say it's in the lymph nodes."

Harrison nodded slowly.

"If the chemo doesn't take, two years tops, according to this guy from Lenox Hill I play squash with," Jerry said.

"Then we'll just have to believe that the chemotherapy is working, won't we?" Harrison said.

"Yeah. Well," Jerry said, cocking his head to suggest that he wouldn't bet with his own money.

Harrison tried to remember an article he'd read a few months earlier in the *Wall Street Journal*. "Didn't I read," he asked Jerry, playing his one and only card, "that Bird lost big in the merger with Sanducci?"

"The press blew it all out of proportion," Jerry said quickly.

"A lot of layoffs, though," Harrison said.

"Some."

"Lucky thing you kept your job," Harrison said.

"Hey, I got eighty guys under me."

"Really," Harrison said, mildly satisfied with the exchange.

"Can you believe Rob?" Jerry asked after a time.

"What about him?"

"The guy he brought?"

"I haven't had a chance to talk to Rob yet," Harrison said.

Jerry signaled over Harrison's shoulder. "Rob," he called. "Hey."

Harrison turned as Rob walked toward them. "Harrison," Rob said, "this is Josh. Josh, this is Harrison Branch. And did I mention that Jerry Leyden here was once the best sinker-ball pitcher in Maine?"

"All New England," Jerry said.

Harrison remembered Rob as a gawky, good-natured teenager with bad skin, but he could see few signs of the boy in the man standing before him. The cut and fabric of Rob's coat were exceptionally fine, and there was no trace of that long-ago acne.

"Christ, can't anyone get a drink here?" Jerry asked, pointing with his empty glass toward the drinks table. "Talk to you later."

"Congratulations on your success," Harrison said to Rob when Jerry had left them. "I've heard you play to huge crowds."

Rob shrugged, a star in his own universe, a man used to praise. "Josh and I come out here in the summer with the BSO to Tanglewood," he said. "Now that we know Nora has this inn, we'll eat here from now on." He looked at Josh and put a hand on his shoulder. "Josh is playing with the London Symphony next week."

"Well done," Harrison said to Josh.

"I didn't know what to say to Bill," Rob confided to Harrison. "I didn't know whether to start with congratulations on the wedding or with an expression of sympathy for Bridget and what she's going through."

"I think one begins and ends with congratulations," Harrison said.

"Do you know how they met up again?"

"Someone said it was at our twenty-fifth reunion. Did you go?" Harrison asked.

"No. I forget why now. Probably I was touring. I think I would have gone. Yes, I'm sure I would have gone," he said, and Harrison wondered if it would have been to make a political statement: *Yes, there has always been gay life at Kidd.*

"I was just thinking this afternoon that the last thing you should have been doing at Kidd was playing baseball," Harrison said. "You could have jammed a finger, ruined your career."

"I think I was trying to assert my masculinity," Rob said, and Josh smiled. Harrison guessed a private joke.

"Well, you did that well enough," Harrison said, remembering Rob's spectacular dives in right field.

"Did you bring your wife?" Rob asked.

"This was such short notice, she couldn't get away. She has a case."

"She's a lawyer?"

"Yes."

"Did you bring pictures?"

Harrison shook his head. It had never crossed his mind to bring photographs of his family.

Josh whipped out an envelope. "These are the pictures of our trip to Greece," he said.

Harrison studied each snap in the packet. Rob and Josh on a white beach. Rob and Josh on a yacht too big to fit in the photo. Rob and Josh in black tie standing on a white marble balcony overlooking a lime-green sea.

"Rob gets invited all over the world," Josh explained, "by people who love the piano."

"Did you ever give a concert at Kidd?" Harrison asked.

"I used to give concerts at the Congregational church in town. I didn't tell anyone at Kidd. I was very ambivalent about the piano then. But there was a music teacher at school, Mrs. Lamb?"

"I remember her vaguely."

"Big hair? Pink glasses? She took me under her wing and coached me all during my senior year and for two years after that. I worked the register at the supermarket in town to pay for the lessons. She got me into Juilliard."

"I used to work at that supermarket," Harrison said, returning the packet of photographs to Josh.

"Nora looks great, don't you think?" Rob asked.

"Yes, I do."

"She's really got an eye."

"She certainly seems to have come into her own," Harrison offered. He wished he had another drink. He thought about the way Jerry had simply put his arm up into the air. Lot of good it had done him. "You like living in Boston?" he asked.

"Love it," Rob said. "We're in the South End. Great restaurants. Of course, I'm never there. Or it seems like I'm never there."

"Do you mind the touring?" Harrison asked, thinking of his own authors, the ones who whined about the touring and demanded the best hotels.

"Goes with the territory, doesn't it," Rob said amiably.

Harrison saw that Jerry's wife, in white wool, had been marooned near the drinks table. "You guys need a refill?" he asked. "I'm getting another drink."

Rob and Josh exchanged glances. "No, we're good," Josh said.

"Catch you later," Rob said. "You'll be there at dinner, right?"

"Yes, definitely."

Harrison moved to the drinks table. He held his glass out to the bartender, who could tell from the dregs what Harrison had been drinking. "The same?" the bartender asked, and Harrison nodded.

"Hello," Harrison said to Julie, holding out his hand. "I'm Harrison Branch. A classmate of Jerry's."

"I'm Julie," she said, taking Harrison's hand with the tips of her fingers. Julie, Harrison noted, was drinking water, too.

"You must be feeling lost," he said.

"A little." Julie's long sleek hair suited her high cheekbones and wide eyes.

"It's hard to be someplace at which you're the one outsider," Harrison said, taking the wineglass the bartender offered.

"A bit," she said, still holding back.

"Let me see if I can make this simple," Harrison said, turning to face the room. "All of the men here," Harrison said, "except for Rob's friend there in the black jacket, were on the baseball team together at Kidd. Bill and Jerry were roommates, but you probably already know that. Agnes and Nora, who owns the inn, were roommates. And Bridget and Bill were sweethearts. I think that's everybody. Those two kids over there come with Bridget and Bill. One of the boys is Bridget's son."

"Thank you," Julie said. "Where are you from?"

"Toronto. I work in publishing. And this one here," Harrison added, snagging Agnes by the sleeve of her pink jacket, "is Agnes O'Connor. Have you two met?"

"Briefly," Julie said.

Harrison watched as Agnes and Julie sized each other up. White cashmere. Off-the-rack wool blend.

"Where do you live in New York?" Agnes asked.

"We have an apartment in Tribeca," Julie said coolly, and Harrison was fairly certain that Agnes did not know Tribeca.

Harrison wanted to ask Julie what she did, but the question, put to a woman, was always a loaded one. There was simply no good way to ask it. "Wonderful weather," he said instead.

Agnes engaged Julie in a conversation about field hockey, an interest Harrison wouldn't have guessed for Julie. Perhaps she had a daughter who played. He watched as the eleven in the room met and parted and circled back, the exclamations of surprise largely diminished now. Wishing himself away, he thought of returning to his room, coming down just in time for dinner. He felt the way he did at sales conferences when he longed for fresh air. He sensed a slight dullness in the room, as if everyone in it had had enough of Part One and wanted to get on with Part Two. But Part Two couldn't begin, Harrison realized, without Bridget. He'd been aware of Bill's absences, off and on, sometimes for long periods. Harrison glanced around the room, searching for Nora. He spotted her through a set of double doors that led to a private dining room. He could see a table set with white dishes. Lit candles. White flowers.

"Is Bridget all right?" he asked when he entered the room. Nora was inspecting the silverware.

"She'll be here in a minute," Nora said. "Do you want another drink?" she asked, looking at his empty glass.

"No. Thank you. I've had quite enough for now."

"The wines at dinner will be very good."

"You're a sort of choreographer."

"I . . . I suppose."

Harrison studied Nora's face. "Tell me a story," he said suddenly, surprising both of them.

"Which one?"

"The one about being married to Carl Laski."

"That would be a very long story."

"A good one?" Harrison asked.

"Good as in entertaining?"

"No. Good as in, you loved him, and he loved you back, and you both lived happily ever after."

"I'm not sure I know that one," Nora said lightly.

Nora peered over Harrison's shoulder, and he turned. In the doorway, in a gray suit, her hair exceptionally thick and light brown, stood Bridget Kennedy — shy, pained, and now, at the sight of Nora, smiling in Harrison's direction.

Bridget, standing in the doorway to the library, saw it in their eyes. Alarm. Dismay. Pity. Curiosity. A man (Jerry Leyden?) began to sing "Here Comes the Bride." In an instant, Bill was at her side, taking her arm. The wedding, this reunion, was a terrible idea, a fiasco. These people were all strangers. *Strangers.* What on earth had she been thinking?

Nora embraced her, and Bridget was sure that her old schoolmate could feel the suit of armor beneath the gray wool. The chemo gave Bridget no-warning hot flashes that advertised themselves in a sweaty brow and flushed red cheeks, one of which she was having now.

"You look beautiful," Nora said, not for the group but just for Bridget. She pried Bridget from Bill's arm and walked with her to the drinks table. "We'll be eating soon," Nora said, "but there's time for a drink. We have sparkling water, too."

"I'll have the water," Bridget said, suddenly thirsty and not at all certain what a glass of wine might do to her.

"I was a little worried about you," Nora said.

"I got dressed, then didn't like what I was wearing, got dressed again . . ."

"Doesn't everyone? Your room is okay?"

"It's wonderful. Thank you so much."

Nora waved the thanks away. "Matt and Brian have healthy appetites," she said.

"They haven't eaten all the hors d'oeuvres, have they? I meant to tell them not to."

Nora smiled. "We have plenty."

Matt, who had moved away from the table, patted his mother awkwardly on the shoulder. "Hi, Mom," he said.

Matt's hair was combed, his face freshly scrubbed, and the sight of him in his suit sent unwanted and instant tears to her eyes. She gave her son a quick hug to disguise the moment. "You didn't eat everything," Bridget said in what she hoped was a slightly scolding voice.

Matt shrugged.

Bridget looked over at Brian and smiled. "I hope this won't be boring for you," she said to the boy.

"No, I'm good," he said.

At the drinks table, Nora ordered a sparkling water for Bridget. "I'm keeping the dinner short," Nora said. "We'll have a first course, then the entrée, and then I'm going to make everybody get up and move back into the library for coffee and dessert. At that point, it'll be easy for you to disappear to your room if you feel you've had enough."

"Thank you," Bridget said. "You've —"

"I've put you between Bill and Matt," Nora said quickly. "But I can change that if you want to sit next to someone else."

"No," Bridget said, slightly bewildered by all the decisions that had happily been made for her. "No, that sounds fine."

"And now I think I'm going to have to share you with the others. The florist called by the way and said no problem with the anemones."

When Bill and Bridget had arrived at the inn, Nora had met Bridget in the lobby, and the two of them had sat over a cup of tea in the library talking about the wedding, each determined to keep it simple. Nora, Bridget had discovered, had with Bill's help seen to all the details — the music, the flowers, the photographer, the meal — and gradually Bridget had felt a weight lift from her shoulders. (A wedding, Bridget had thought more than once over the past several weeks, was a small playlet, one with scenery, an audience, and actors playing their parts.) Nora, who seemed to have developed extrasensory empathy, had noted the exact moment Bridget had felt the need to lie down. "You take a rest," Nora had said. "Do you mind room service?"

Bridget, who had seldom had an opportunity to sample room service, simply smiled.

"I'll send up a selection of sandwiches for all of you," Nora said, rising.

Bridget had been delighted with her room. It was clearly the bridal suite, with a sitting room and a bathroom bigger than her own living room at home. In its center, on a kind of raised platform, was an enormous tub with polished chrome faucets. Matt and Brian were wide-eyed and then slightly embarrassed by the amenities offered. The lavish tub. The candles by the bed. The silver champagne bucket in a stand in the sitting room.

Bridget had a quick nap under the duvet in the bed, then roused herself when the food arrived. Nora, who did not have children of her own, seemed to understand that teenage boys came with large appetites. There was a mound of sandwiches: beef and chicken for the boys and Bill, crustless cucumber for herself. The cukes were crisp and cold, and Bridget made a mental note to buy a half dozen when she got home. They were one of the few foods that had tasted good to her in weeks. After the lunch, the boys spoke of wanting to go off for a hike, and Bridget urged Bill to join them. She wanted to be alone, she argued, to rest, to think, to let her thoughts drift.

Bridget had had a bath, letting the jets cause a froth that rose to her chin. She was wrinkled pink when she emerged, and she found herself relaxed, a state that lasted only as long as it took to start ap-plying her makeup and pulling on the severe underwear. She had two possibilities for the cocktail party. The first, a dress she had thought would fit nicely because of its loose waistline, made her think of Madeleine Albright when she put it on. Bridget tried it with the wig, thinking hair would help, but the wig, with its perfect set, made her think of Margaret Thatcher. Bridget had no choice then but to wear her gray suit, which she knew would be too tight but would have to be endured. First the one-piece, then the panty hose, then the skirt girdle. Bridget was sweating before she even drew on the skirt. From time to time, Bill knocked on the door, giving her bulletins from below. Matt and Brian had cleaned up very nicely. Jerry was having a fight with his wife. Rob had brought a date — a guy. For that, Bridget had opened the door a crack, letting the steam out. She'd insisted on all the details. After a time, Bill's knocks had become more frequent. "We're all waiting," he'd said in a slight singsong, barely controlling his concern.

In the steam, Bridget's wig frizzed. She thought that if she didn't breathe too deeply the buttonholes of her suit jacket wouldn't gape. She stepped out of the bathroom, Bill waiting by the door. "You look beautiful," he said, which was, of course, the right thing to say, but which she didn't believe for a minute. At some point, one simply had to stop caring about how one looked, she decided as she picked up her purse and stepped into her pumps. Age and ill-ness had to be accepted. This was her wedding weekend, after all. Wasn't it the event itself that mattered?

Bridget descended the stairway, teetering as she went. In a mir-ror on the landing, she saw that she had put on too much makeup, that her skirt already had stretch marks across her lap. She had a memory of herself in her childhood bedroom at eight or nine years old, following the telecast of the Miss America pageant, singing, "Here she comes . . ." to herself in the mirror, absolutely certain that one day she would be in the pageant. She had been able to imagine the moment of winning so intensely, it was as if she were actually there.

Miss America, indeed.

Bridget heard her name and turned.

Harrison held her gently by the shoulders and kissed her cheek. "Congratulations," he said.

"Harrison," she said, hardly believing it was really he standing before her. He had not grayed up as much as Bill, but his hair was thinning at the crown. She remembered the soft brown eyes, the V-like dent over one eyebrow (the legacy of having fallen out of a tree house when he was a boy, she seemed to recall), the wiry body slightly less wiry now. He was the man she'd have imagined he would become, and yet his face was not precisely the same. The difference had to be age, but Bridget thought there was something else. Regret possibly. Conceivably wisdom, though Bridget wasn't sure what wisdom looked like. Harrison was smiling and telling her that she looked wonderful. Bridget hoped not everyone would feel the need to reassure her that she was still attractive. Bridget had a clear idea of what she was and was not. What she was was sick. What she was not was healthy.

Looking at Harrison, Bridget was reminded of moments with him at school. Once he had caught up to her as she was foolishly walking from Ford Hall to dinner in a blizzard without her jacket. He'd made a tent of his own jacket for both of them (she remembered, too, that the windows facing the ocean had been an opaque white from the frozen sea spray). She recalled Harrison giving a speech in his bid to become class treasurer. Pink Floyd had played "Money" in the background. She remembered as well the day Harrison had been beaned at home plate. He'd gone down like a shot despite the helmet. And of course she could not forget Harrison Branch at that last party at the beach, the tension between him and

Stephen and Nora. She remembered, too, the awful final weeks when Harrison had retreated into himself and would not talk to anyone.

"I was stunned to get Bill's e-mail," Harrison said now, Harrison the only one of them who'd known Bill's first wife, who had spent time with Jill. Bridget wanted to ask Harrison if Bill had seemed happy in his first marriage, what he'd been like with young children, facts Bridget had no way of knowing. But Agnes was at Harrison's side now, and she was saying Bridget's name. Agnes embraced Bridget fiercely, and Bridget was glad Agnes didn't think her fragile. Agnes had aged more than Harrison. But mightn't a weathered face indicate a richer life?

"My God, I can't believe it's you," Agnes said.

(Is it me? Bridget wondered. Some of me? More of me?)

"It's such a *romantic* story," Agnes said. "Meeting up with Bill again after how many years?"

"Almost twenty-two."

"It must have been . . . was it just, like, love at second sight? I went to that reunion, but I didn't get there until Saturday."

"It was a bit more complicated than that," Bridget said, "but I think we both knew right away."

"It's such a *wonderful, wonderful* story," Agnes repeated. "Life never works out that way, does it?"

It was an unanswerable question, because, of course, life had worked out that way. But here was Rob, kissing her on each cheek and introducing her to Josh. Then Jerry enveloped her in a bear hug and introduced Bridget to his wife, Julie. Bridget, at the center of a cluster of people — more popular than she'd ever been at Kidd — felt as though she'd just won an enormous prize.

And she thought then that perhaps she had. The prize the product of possibilities and near misses. Bill's wife, Jill, coming down with the flu on the Thursday before the weekend-long reunion. Bill making the decision not to go himself. Jill talking him into it, saying that she'd be fine. Bill compromising by deciding to attend the Friday night cocktail party only. Bill wanting to have a drink with Jerry and Harrison and Rob and even their old English teacher, Jim Mitchell, who was putting in a surprise appearance. Bill's software company had finally kicked into high gear, and he'd had a selfish, nearly childish, desire to tell his old friends about this thing he had made. Bill had driven to the Back Bay town house where the event was being held. Melissa, Bill's daughter, who was seventeen at the time, was spending the night at a friend's house. Jill had said she'd be fine with a cup of tea and a rare opportunity to have the remote to herself.

Bridget had gone to the cocktail party with her friend Anne, who was a legitimate member of the class of 1974 but who hadn't the courage to walk in alone. Because many of Bridget's friends — not to mention her old boyfriend — were from that class, Bridget had allowed herself to be talked into accompanying Anne. Bridget had thought she might see Nora or Agnes or Harrison, none of whom had attended the party. And, of course, Bridget had guessed she might see Bill. She was at least as curious about Jill, however, the woman who had won him over, as she was about seeing her old love after an absence of twenty-two years.

Bridget remembered the cocktail party as a series of small shocks. Over and over again, a face would emerge from the countenance of a stranger like a photograph coming up in a bath of a chemical solution. Years would melt away, and then, in an instant, return, each encounter requiring a number of mental and emotional adjustments. It had been both a rewarding and a distressing experience, knowing that everyone who greeted her had to be making the same adjustments. (Though, of course, there were the half-dozen ageless who basked in compliments, her friend Anne being one of them — which doubtless accounted for Anne's eagerness to attend the party.)

Half an hour into the event, Bridget had felt a tap on her shoulder. When she'd turned, she'd known him at once — something magnetic in the eyes that felt nearly as intense as it had more than two decades earlier.

Bill, she had said.

He'd kissed her on the cheek.

And for a minute, possibly two, neither of them had spoken, Bridget aware of a trembling in her fingers that grew so disturbing she had had to hold the stem of her wineglass with both hands. She'd looked up and she'd looked down. She had not known where to put her eyes. Whereas Bill had simply stared.

While the experience had been literally breathtaking for Bridget, Bill had later said it was among the saddest moments of his life. For he had seen instantly what Bridget had been too bewildered to comprehend: the staggering sum of all the days and years they had missed together.

Though Bridget often thought about coincidence and fate, she and Bill discussed the reunion seldom, and then only in hushed voices, neither willing to catch the attention of the gods who had allowed them to find each other, both aware of the implied treachery of their good fortune. Matt did not yet know that Bill had left his wife to be with Bridget, and Bridget knew that she would soon have to tell her son. He was bound to learn of it, from a gleeful Melissa one day if from no one else. With a sudden chill, Bridget realized that there was every possibility Matt would learn of it this weekend. She didn't like keeping secrets from her son, believed it counterproductive to an honest relationship. But then again she wasn't sure an entirely honest relationship between a mother and a fifteen-year-old boy was possible. What secrets, for example, did Matt hold dear?

For months after the reunion, Bill and Bridget had e-mailed each other, Bridget unwilling to meet Bill for lunch because he was married, the proposed meal clearly not simply a meal, but rather signaling a willingness to proceed further. Bridget didn't doubt Bill's sincerity when he'd spoken of the years he'd spent thinking about her, about how he was certain they should be together. Her memories of Bill's honesty as a teenager were still keen. Still, she told herself, she would not enter into a relationship that required lies or sneaking around, even though she knew the waiting to be a kind of smoke screen to mask her ever-increasing feelings for Bill — feelings that emanated from a rich store of memory, triggered by that electric meeting at the reunion. And she supposed she'd known all along that eventually she would capitulate, that the self-imposed restraint was a feeble attempt to assuage her guilt, to stave off the inevitable chaos that coming together would set in motion. Eight months after the reunion, Bridget finally agreed to the lunch, *biryani* and chicken tikka at an Indian restaurant in Cambridge, the spices from the tikka somehow squirting under her contact lens and causing a brief though acutely painful episode until she washed it out in the ladies' room, ruining her eye makeup in the process.

And after that lunch, Bridget had surprised herself by discovering just how willing she was to compromise her previous ethics for love. Prior to meeting Bill, she would have said, categorically, that she would never have considered a relationship with a married man. Not only was such a relationship complicated and risky but it was simply *wrong*. A woman she did not know would be terribly hurt. Bridget knew firsthand how this worked. Had she not been terribly hurt herself six years earlier, when Arthur had walked out on her? Arthur had simply announced, an hour before Matt was to return home from school, his palms open as if he were merely reporting scientific fact, that he was leaving her. The news had been so shocking that Bridget had not been able to comprehend his words, in the same way she had not been able to understand calculus her first year in college. She could see herself as she'd been that afternoon — head shaking back and forth, mouth open, asking soap-operatic questions she would not have believed possible: *Who is she? When did you meet her? How long? Where? What about Matt?* The answer to this last question so enraging Bridget that she threw the nearest thing to hand, her pocketbook, the lipstick and hand cream and coins and supermarket receipts spilling out on its journey from her arm to Arthur's chest and then dropping to the floor as he made no effort to catch it. He no longer had any interest in her handbag or its contents or in her. He would sue for custody of Matt.

"On what grounds?" Bridget had asked.

"I can support him," Arthur had said simply, "and you can't."

Knowing it was a cliché even as she said it, Bridget had uttered the truest thing she knew: *Over my dead body.*

And it had been an ugly war, love turning to hatred overnight; in a month to disgust; in a year to pity; and finally to indifference. Bridget, her resources stretched and pummeled, had won the first two battles. Miraculously, a third had not been necessary. An arrangement had been agreed to: Matt would see Arthur on alternate weekends and for a month in the summer.

(Bridget waited, like a scientist studying lab rats, for Matt finally to act out the playlet written for him that afternoon. Where, for example, was his rage? Apart from the Incident with the Alcohol, Bridget so far had detected nothing. Matt left for his month with his father with a quick fraught hug — and until this year, tears in his eyes — and returned happy, seemingly undamaged and ready to resume his normal life. Of course, Bridget thought, visiting his father *was* his normal life, just as Bill's presence now was, children being remarkably flexible about their givens.)

Perhaps not all children, though. Bill's daughter, Melissa, had decidedly *not* been flexible. Nineteen and intractable, she had taken her mother's side, which Bridget thought perfectly understandable. Bill saw his daughter, a sophomore at Boston University, for dinner as often as he could. Bridget had met Melissa only twice, once before the diagnosis, once after, and each occasion had been disastrous. The revelation that Bridget had cancer had not produced, as Bill had hoped, a chink in the ice but rather had made Bridget somehow repellent to Melissa, a diseased thing that should not be further exposed to her father.

Bridget cringed when she recalled their second dinner together in Boston. Bridget still didn't know why Melissa had agreed to the meal. Perhaps Bill had coerced her in some way that Bridget was not allowed to know. During dinner, Melissa made a point of talking, when she spoke at all, only to Bill, and of inserting her mother into the discussion whenever possible. It was as though Bridget was not present, though her presence was implied in every reminiscence, in every bulletin from home. Melissa looked directly at her father, locking eyes when she spoke to him, as if trying to communicate an urgent message. *Come back.*

Bridget asked questions and received one-word answers. It was maddening, she thought, because she could see that in another universe she and Bill's daughter might have had true affection for each other. Melissa would be easy to like. Battle-ready armor protected an essential sweetness. Melissa had shiny dark hair that fell in a sheet down her back and would, from time to time, fan across her shoulders. She had as well a fetching way of tossing it slowly back. Bridget admired Melissa's narrow waist and the mouth that rose in a perfect curve to a point just below her nostrils. Bridget thought the look Parisian, the narrow waist and lovely mouth a legacy from her mother. Bridget supposed that she could, if she allowed it, work herself into a state of mild jealousy over Bill's first wife, whom she had seen in photographs but never in the flesh.

Over coffee, Bill broke the news of the wedding to his daughter, and Melissa responded as Bridget might have guessed. The young woman set down her water glass, wiped her mouth, stood up from the chair, and, without so much as a glance at either Bill or Bridget, left the restaurant. Since that night, she had not returned Bill's phone calls.

"She'll come around," Bill had said, though Bridget could see that Melissa might not, that it might take years for a reconciliation.

Matt had responded differently to news of the wedding. Bridget had told Bill that it was too early to talk to Matt about a marriage, but Bill had argued the opposite, reading Matt as needing *more* of a family, not less. And Bill had been right, Matt breaking into a grin with the news. Bill asked him to be best man (though a best man was hardly needed), and they'd all immediately fallen into a discussion of venues and caterers, as if it were perfectly normal to be discussing the marriage of a man to a woman whose chance of being alive in two years was only 50 percent.

Bridget looked around at the gathering in the library. Was it obscene to marry in her state? Bill and Bridget had been together only fifteen months when Bridget had received her initial diagnosis, causing her to wonder if the cancer wasn't some kind of cosmic punishment. She remembered, early in her treatments, a conversation between two women in the hematology-oncology waiting room, the first telling the second in a breathless voice that she was getting married in two weeks. Bridget attributed the breathlessness to excitement until she heard the woman tell the other that the cancer had started in her lungs and had spread to her brain. Brain cancer and a wedding. Bridget had been stunned. But wasn't her own impending marriage just as bizarre?

*　　*　　*

Nora announced that it was time to move into the private dining room. Place cards were consulted. Bridget would sit between her son and her husband-to-be, as Nora had earlier promised. Brian would be to the other side of her son. The table was a wedding in itself, with its white damask, antique ivory plates, crystal glasses, and heavy silver. Bridget was seated so that she could see the windows at the other side of the room. A twinkling light in the distance was the only visible element. Mostly what she saw was the reflection of faces. Harrison, with his chin on the back of his hand, listening to Bill. Agnes leaning in toward Julie at a sharp angle. Nora in consultation with a waiter. The evening's menu was engraved on stiff white cards set upon the plates. Bridget would have trouble with the salmon, but the beet and goat cheese salad sounded appetizing.

A waiter filled one of a small forest of glasses in front of Bridget with champagne.

"A toast," Jerry said, standing. He looked fit as he unfolded himself to his full height. His camel V-neck sweater draped appealingly from broad shoulders. Clearly, Jerry visited a gym on a regular basis.

A ripple of tension made its way along the table. Jerry, always unpredictable, might come out with anything. Bridget noticed that Matt's and Brian's glasses had been partially filled with champagne. Julie's face remained an impenetrable mask as her husband raised his glass.

"*Bill and Bridget's Wedding,*" Jerry said. "A comedy coming to a theater near you. Starring Tom Hanks and Andie MacDowell." (A smattering of laughter here.) "A feel-good movie from Universal with a surprise happy ending." (Nervous laughter, as the possibility of a not-happy ending inevitably entered each mind.) "I believe I speak for everyone," Jerry continued, "when I say that I never knew a couple so destined to be together." (An awkward pause as everyone at the table looked at Julie, clearly left out of the running for that particular award.) "When we knew you both at Kidd, you were inseparable," Jerry continued. "And, truthfully, we all envied your happiness." (*Hear, hear,* Rob said.) "Then there was a little hiccup somewhere . . . hmmm, a twenty-two-year hiccup . . . and now you're together again and about to make it legal." (Bridget glanced at Matt, wondering if he minded his birth and childhood being contained within the *hiccup*.) Jerry raised his glass a bit higher, and everyone at the table stood. Bill and Bridget remained seated. "To unions and reunions," Jerry said. "We wish you ten thousand days of happiness."

Jerry, to everyone's surprise and Julie's evident relief, had acquitted himself with grace and humor. Bill reciprocated by standing and thanking Jerry warmly and then thanking Nora for her generosity. Jerry gave a quick salute. Nora smiled. A waiter hovered next to Agnes, ready to begin taking orders. Matt and Brian drained their glasses. Bridget reminded herself to tell the waiter not to give the boys any wine. She didn't want her son getting drunk the night before the wedding, or ever again, for that matter.

Ten thousand days, Bridget calculated, was roughly thirty years. She'd be in her early seventies when the happiness ran out.

If only.

Her skirt girdle cut into her abdomen. She ordered the goat cheese salad and the salmon, wondering if she'd be able to eat any of it. She mouthed *Thank you* to Jerry across the table, and he cocked a finger gun at her. Almost immediately, the decibel level in the room was such that Bridget had to raise her voice even to speak to Bill, the noise increasing exponentially as each person discovered he or she had to shout. It sounded like a party, for which Bridget was grateful. She had feared the gathering might be stiff and dull. She would have minded for Nora's sake.

Bill had his hand on her thigh. If he could have conveyed good health through that hand, Bridget reflected, he would have, even at the cost of his own health — a kind of health transfusion he would willingly have undergone. There was a sudden lull in the conversation, during which Julie (*Julie,* of all people) asked Bridget to tell the story of how she and Bill remet. Bridget looked to Bill for help, both of them aware that the heart of the story — the secret assignations in hotels, the betrayal of Bill's wife, the passionate phone calls when Bridget's son was in bed — couldn't be told in Matt and Brian's presence. Bill gave a meaningful look in the boys' direction to convey to the group that the R-rated movie would not be shown tonight. Instead he would tell the brief and sanitized version. *I went to my twenty-fifth reunion, looked across the room, saw Bridget, and twenty-two years just melted away. It was as though we'd never been apart.*

What was not discussed was Jill's anger, Melissa's grief, and the cost to Bill, which had been considerable. If Bridget died soon — as was entirely possible, even likely according to the statistics — Bill would have risked everything for so little: three, maybe four years together at best. Would he still think it worth the cost twenty years from now?

Bridget put a hand briefly over Bill's hand on her thigh. Nora was in a huddle with Brian and Matt. Something she said made them both perk up considerably. Jerry, who might be just a little bit drunk already, was telling the group about how he'd often bragged about being practically best friends with Carl Laski's wife. Nora blinked. Bridget imagined Nora might have seen the friendship a little differently.

"Of course, I never read poetry," Jerry said, canceling out the goodwill of the flattery. "Does anyone?"

"Don't be ridiculous, Jerry," Harrison said.

"Okay, so name the last book of poetry you read."

"I publish Audr Heinrich," Harrison said.

"You don't count," Jerry said, pointing with his glass, a bit of wine sloshing out onto the tablecloth. "How about you?" he asked Rob, ignoring Julie's restraining hand on his arm.

"Oh, I don't know," Rob said, "I used to like Yeats."

"I read Billy Collins," Agnes said. "I love him, actually."

"Who's Billy Collins?" Jerry asked.

"Your poet laureate," Harrison said quietly.

"Now Robert Frost," Jerry announced. "There was a poet who deserved the laureate."

"I think your husband's work was magnificent," Rob said in Nora's direction, bringing the conversation back to where it belonged.

"Thank you," Nora said as two waiters began to serve the salads. She examined each plate as it was set down.

"I didn't even know who he was until I met Rob," Josh said, "but now I think I've read everything Carl Laski ever wrote." He smiled broadly, seemingly unaware of the backhanded compliment.

"If I could have had anyone on my list," Harrison said, "it would have been Carl Laski."

Bridget caught a look that passed between Nora and Harrison. Was this a private joke as well?

"You were always half a poet yourself," Jerry said, taking a vicious bite out of a piece of crusty French bread.

"How so?" Harrison asked.

"Oh, I don't know. Kind of dreamy. Always going off on walks of your own. Into nature and all that."

"I suppose I was," Harrison said, and even Bridget could hear the *what of it?* that was not spoken. Harrison, too, was drinking rather a lot. He hadn't yet touched his salad. A sudden feeling of — Bridget couldn't quite describe it — danger? potential danger? was in the air. She strained to think of something to say to deflect the tension.

"Not Stephen, though," Jerry said. "You wouldn't find Stephen reading a poem."

"No," Agnes said, "he'd just talk about it."

Rob gave a kind of snort, and Bill chuckled.

"You wouldn't find him reading anything," Harrison said, meaning to keep it light. Bridget noted that Harrison had glasses of both red and white in his forest. A waiter was refilling the white. Bridget wanted to reach across Bill and put a similar restraining hand on Harrison's arm. Goading Jerry would end in disaster. "He was the only person I ever knew who could intelligently discuss a piece of writing — a story, a poem — without having read it."

"How did he do that?" Julie asked.

"He'd listen for a minute and pick up on cues, and he had an uncanny knack for capturing the essence or a central theme and discussing *that,* and somehow it all worked for him. Before you knew it, Stephen was at the center of the debate."

"But it was false," Julie said.

"Well, it was and it wasn't," Harrison said.

"So tomorrow," Bill said, "we'll have a game?"

"A game of what?" Rob asked.

"You can ump," Bill said, pointing to Rob's million-dollar fingers. Bridget wondered if he had had them insured. "I brought some balls and gloves and bats," Bill explained.

"Cool," Matt said.

"We'll divide up into two teams. Agnes and Nora" — and here Bill turned to Bridget to include her as well (though he knew as well as anyone that Bridget wouldn't be able to play; she might lose the wig for one thing) — "you'll have to play, too. With Matt and Brian here, we ought to be able to get something going."

"I'm in," Jerry said. "Branch, you'll have to play shortstop. You think you can handle it?"

Harrison set down his glass with care. Jerry, chin jutting, glared at Harrison. Agnes studied her plate. Julie gazed off in the distance, doubtless wishing herself back in New York. Only Bill glanced between Jerry and Harrison as if he might, at any minute, have to leap onto the table to referee.

"Leave it," Rob said under his breath.

"Leave what?" Jerry asked, feigning ignorance.

Nora raised a hand and snapped her fingers, a sharp, skilled summons that cleared the air at once. Two waiters appeared and began to take away the salads and to set down the entrées. Bridget's salmon was translucent. Bill's was well-done. Bridget exchanged plates. Jerry had to dismantle his aggressive posture to allow his beef to be set in front of him.

"Times have changed," Nora said with a brilliant non sequitur.

"They certainly have," Rob said, arbitrarily ascribing meaning to Nora's statement. "Unfortunately, Bush is going to use it to every political advantage."

"Were you there?" Jerry asked.

"I was in Boston," Rob said.

"Well, if you weren't there, you can't judge. Julie and I were there. We saw the bodies. Giuliani was magnificent. The police, the firemen, they loved Bush when he showed up."

One might have guessed Rob a Democrat, but Jerry a Republican?

"You literally saw the bodies?" Agnes asked from her end of the table.

"Jumping," Jerry said. "Falling. You could hear the thuds. My office was right across the street."

There was a silence as each of them imagined the horror of having to jump, the moment of letting go. One hundred and two stories down. Bridget closed her eyes.

When she opened them, she glanced at Matt, who had gone pale. Matt had seen the television images, but would his imagination have encompassed thudding bodies? She looked across Matt's plate to Brian, who was poking at a carrot. This would not do.

"Jerry," Bridget said in a tone that caused everyone to look in her direction, "I'm sorry that you had to witness what you did firsthand. And I think everyone here would agree that those who lived in New York on September eleventh bore the brunt of the horror. But no one at this table was untouched or unmoved. The catastrophe hurt all of us."

"That's the thing about catastrophe," Rob said, wiping his lips with the heavy damask napkin. "It's so often the most democratic of events."

"You say you were moved by it," Jerry insisted, though Bridget could see that the steam was leaving him, "but you can't really know about it if you weren't there."

"Jerry," Julie said, "I don't think anyone here wants to *own* it."

Jerry scowled at his wife.

"Jim Mitchell once said that," Agnes added from her end of the table. "*The democracy of catastrophe.* Don't you remember? When we were reading *All Quiet on the Western Front?*"

"Your memory is better than mine," Harrison said.

"Of all the teachers I ever had," Agnes said, "he was the best."

"Yeah. Mitchell," Jerry said. "He was the man. He still teaching at Kidd?"

"No," Agnes said. "He moved to Wisconsin. He's teaching at a private school there."

"Wisconsin," Jerry said. "Was Mitchell from there?"

"No," Agnes said. "He was from Massachusetts. We overlapped for three years when I first went back to Kidd."

"Was it weird being a colleague of a teacher you'd had yourself?" Josh asked.

"A little. At first. But you quickly get used to it."

Agnes's face flushed pink. She must get hot flashes, too, Bridget thought, though it might be a little soon for menopause for Agnes.

Other teachers were remembered. The spray painting of the front of Ford Hall was recalled. Bill mentioned the night Rob "borrowed" a truck from the work shed and drove all the way to Portland and back. Four years at Kidd were retrieved in bits and pieces, making a kind of memory mosaic: not the whole picture, just the highlights. The night Jerry rented a motel room and gave a party and the cops came. The time Harrison got up on the stage and did a Mick Jagger impression ("I never did that," Harrison said). Julie seemed as lost in this litany of anecdotes as Matt and Brian were. Nora, with impeccable timing, told the assembled that they would now move back into the library for coffee and dessert. There would be after-dinner drinks for those who wanted them. Predictably, Bridget guessed, it would be those who had had the most to drink already who would ask for the cognac or the Drambuie. Harrison stood with care. Jerry blew his nose into what looked like his dinner napkin.

How did Julie stand it?

Bridget thought she would make her exit. She would not say good night because that would simply call attention to the fact that she was abandoning them. So far, no one had said the word "cancer," for which Bridget was grateful. It was a miracle, considering Jerry and his penchant for the jugular.

Bill held back. Nora disappeared into the kitchen. Bridget wanted to thank Nora again for the meal, but it would have to wait until the morning.

"Where are Matt and Brian?" Bridget asked.

"Apparently there's a pool table in the basement," Bill said.

"That's what made them perk up so. Make sure they hang up their jackets." If the boys started off playing pool in their suits, she knew, a jacket would end up on a chair, then slip to the floor, and a boy, cue in hand, would back up and step on it. The scenario demanded it.

"What about you?" Bill asked.

"I think I'll go lie down," she said.

"I'll go with you."

"No," Bridget said. "You stay with the others. Keep Jerry and Harrison in line."

Bill laughed. Bridget saw, in the doorway, Josh running his fingers down the back of Rob's impeccable jacket. The hand stopped just below the waistline. Julie bent to retrieve an earring that had fallen to the floor. Jerry announced that he had to take a piss. Agnes was asking Harrison if he had ever heard of the Halifax disaster.

Bridget turned toward Bill so that her right knee was touching his left. He put his hand again on her thigh. He had his chin propped in his other hand, his elbow resting on the table. "You *do* look beautiful tonight," he said.

Bridget sighed and then smiled. There was simply no adequate response. "Jerry's really something," she said.

"Some people never change. Maybe none of us ever do. That was a nice toast, though."

"What's with his wife?"

"Ice queen?"

"Maybe it's just around him," Bridget said. "Is she his first wife?"

"I think so."

"I like Josh. He's cute," Bridget said. "I always think gay men — the couples — seem to care about each other in a way you don't always see with straight couples. It's as though they treasure the small moments, assign meaning to them, whereas they so often pass us by."

"The unexamined life," Bill said.

"It might be because they don't have children," Bridget said.

"Children take up all the oxygen, don't they? Create chaos. I didn't know Jerry and Harrison had a thing."

"I'm not sure they ever did," Bill said. "This feels new to me. Sometimes Jerry sees a weakness, and he pounces."

"He was always a little like that."

"More so now, I think," Bill said.

Bridget thought about the way age could chisel away at a person so that only the most prominent characteristics remained.

She wanted to get out of her clothes. "Nora has been amazing," she said. "I know it's partly her wanting to show what she's done with the place, what she's made, but it's so much more than that. She's been extraordinarily generous."

"We'll have to do something for her," Bill said. "Have her out to our house some night."

"Oh, sure," Bridget said. "And second prize is two nights at our house."

Bill bent toward Bridget and kissed her. It was an unexpectedly hard kiss, and Bridget put a palm on his chest.

"Kiss, kiss," Jerry said, passing behind them.

So you don't know that story," Harrison was saying.

They were sitting on stools in the center of the kitchen. Only one light was burning, a globe over the island. Harrison had an impression of cream paint, tongue-and-groove boards, shelves of antique white dishes, a wash of stainless steel. Under a bank of windows was a built-in bench with an upholstered cushion. Off the kitchen, Harrison could see the dark interior of a pantry, closed up for the night.

He took a sip of coffee made from a machine similar to the one in the library. Coffee. He'd be lucky if he fell asleep before morning. He'd had more coffee today than he'd had in years. On the other hand, he'd had more to drink than he'd had in years. He thought the combination would make for a spectacular hangover, the beginnings of which he could already feel at the edges of his vision.

The inn was quiet. The big wooden clock set among the shelves of dishes read 1:25. Harrison briefly imagined the guests in their rooms. Jerry and Julie, their backs to each other, hugging their separate edges of the bed. Bill curled around Bridget, snoring lightly into her neck (was that a wig Bridget had on? did she sleep in it?). Agnes lying on her back, hands folded across her chest, a woman with a clear conscience who didn't move in her sleep. Rob and Josh: one was curled up within the other; Harrison couldn't take the thought further than that. Or perhaps he was wrong. Perhaps Jerry and Julie, antagonistic in public, were passionate in bed. Maybe

Bridget and Bill slept separately while she was on chemo. Possibly Agnes's duvet was twisted in a knot, her dreams troubled and nightmarish. If Harrison had learned anything about private lives, it was that anyone looking in from the outside could never know the reality.

Nora seemed exhausted, and Harrison knew he should let her go to bed. She would have to be up early, to see to the Saturday breakfast.

"The one about Carl and me?" she asked. "No." She looked past him through the windows. "It's snowing," she said.

Harrison turned. Fat flakes were drifting in the light of a lantern. "Wow," Harrison said, standing. He walked to the door and opened it and could feel the sharp, wet cold. While they had been dining and having after-dinner drinks, the temperature had plummeted. Harrison looked at a thermometer just outside the door. "It's only thirty-one," he said. "That's what . . . ? A drop of forty degrees?"

He shut the door and moved back to the island. He perched an unsteady hip on the stool and took a sip of coffee. Nora's lipstick had worn off, and there was a smudge of something dark just below her eye.

"A twenty-two-year marriage is a long story," Nora said. "It's . . . it's a continuum with moments of drama, periods of stupefying boredom. Passages of tremendous hope. Passages of resignation. One can never tell the story of a marriage. There's no narrative that encompasses it. Even a daily diary wouldn't tell you what you wanted to know. Who thought what when. Who had what dreams. At the very least, a marriage is two intersecting stories, one of which we will never know."

All of Harrison's questions died on his tongue. What would the narrative of his own marriage be? Would it encompass the weekend he and Evelyn spent at the Château Frontenac exhausting their budget on room service because they never left the bed? Or would it include the fight they'd had over snow tires in the parking lot of Harrison's apartment building at the end of that weekend? Would it be incomplete without the ennui Harrison felt and dreaded on Sunday evenings when the boys were busy and Evelyn and he no longer had anything to say to each other? Or would that narrative be defined by the one moment of perfect joy he experienced when he and Evelyn and the boys had boarded the Canadian excursion train at the beginning of their trip from Calgary to Vancouver last spring?

"I just wanted to know if you were happy," he said.

"I was happy. Sometimes," Nora answered.

"Fair enough."

"Jerry was on a tear, wasn't he?" Nora asked. "Would you like some water?"

"I'd love some," Harrison said. "I'm starting a killer hangover."

Nora fetched two glasses from the shelves, turned the faucet on, and let it run. She fingered the water to test its temperature and filled the glasses.

"If Jerry had said one more word about Stephen, I swear I'd have decked him," Harrison said.

Nora laughed as she set the glasses on the counter.

"Don't laugh. I would have."

"I'd faint if I ever saw you hit someone. I don't doubt you have other ways of eviscerating opponents. But decking isn't one of them."

"How does Julie stand him?"

"She was a good sport to stay as long as she did. To put up with all our stories. It must have been mind-numbing for her."

"How old do you think she is?"

"Thirty-six? Forty? I enjoyed Josh. I'm . . . I'm happy for Rob."

"I don't think any of us knew. At school."

"He may not really have known himself," Nora said, taking a sip of coffee. "He's very elegant, very polished, isn't he?"

"It must be the European influence," Harrison said. "What happened exactly? He just discovered this talent out of the blue?"

"No. No," Nora said. "He'd taken lessons since he was a boy. They discovered his talent early. He just decided he wanted no part of it — through high school. The first time he tried out for Juilliard, he got turned down. That's when he started to take it seriously."

"I always loved Rob," Harrison said.

"Oh, I think we all did."

"What I don't get is how Bill and Jerry have stayed friends."

"There's more to Jerry than all that posturing," Nora said. "He gives away millions — and I do mean millions — to charity."

"He does?"

"Doctors Without Borders is his particular interest. Julie was telling me."

"I didn't know that."

"You and he are going to have to come to some kind of truce before the wedding," Nora said. "Jerry might be willing to upstage Bridget, but I don't think you are."

"No, of course not," Harrison said, chastened.

"Would you like some cake? We have a lot of it left over from the Jungbacker lunch. It's delicious. You don't mind coconut, do you?"

"I love coconut."

Nora walked into the murk of the pantry and emerged with a partly cut cake on a glass pedestal.

"That was interesting," Harrison said, "what Agnes was saying about having to switch from teaching English to teaching history when she got the job at Kidd. That it was all stories anyway, so it didn't matter much. I imagine she's a great teacher."

"Her field hockey team won a big conference," Nora said, lifting two cake plates from a shelf. "You should ask her about it sometime."

"She was telling me about the Halifax disaster. Do you know about it?"

"No."

"Apparently, during World War I, there was a fire on a ship in Halifax Harbor. The sight drew everyone in the city to his or her window to look at it. Seconds later, the ship exploded — the biggest man-made explosion in history until the atomic bomb — and everyone standing at the windows was blinded by flying glass. Well, not everyone, but many."

Nora cut two generous slices and handed one to Harrison.

"Is *she* gay?" Harrison asked.

"Agnes?" Nora asked, opening the silverware drawer. "No."

"How do you know?"

"The way she talks about men," Nora said, handing Harrison a fork.

"Has she ever had a relationship?"

"I think she has," Nora said. "I think it might have been with a married man. She sometimes refers to it obliquely."

Harrison bit into the rich cake. The frosting was a kind of whipped cream with flakes of coconut contained within. "This is delicious," he said.

"I've found a wonderful baker in town. She's seventy-three. She's been making cakes for her family for years. I heard about her from her daughter-in-law. So I asked her if she'd like to make them for us. She's been terrific to work with. Each cake has been better than the last."

"Nice arrangement for both of you," Harrison said.

"The boys are certainly good eaters."

"I like Bridget's son. His friend, too. The boy's a hustler, though. Beat me at pool after suckering me into a game. Lost ten bucks."

Nora smiled.

"Are you capable of remembering," Harrison asked, "who you thought you'd be when you were seventeen? Who you imagined you'd be in twenty-seven years' time?"

Nora turned her head to the windows. There was a smudge of something white on the sleeve of her black dress, flour maybe. Once inside the kitchen, she had raked her hair, as if letting go for the night, and as a consequence, it looked mussed, as if she'd just woken up. "I suppose . . . I suppose I thought I'd be a teacher," she said. "I think that was the plan. What about you?"

"I thought I'd be a chemical engineer," Harrison said. "I went to Northeastern for their work-study program."

"You were on scholarship at Kidd."

"Yes," he said, watching Nora lick her fork clean.

"What happened at Northeastern?"

"The old story. I had a wonderful teacher for freshman English, realized I hated math, and that was that. I went to graduate school at McGill."

"Why Canada?"

"Cheaper."

"And that's how you met your wife?" Nora asked, scraping the last of the frosting from the plate with her fork.

"You really like that cake," Harrison said.

Nora looked up and smiled. "I do, as a matter of fact."

"Yes, it's where I met Evelyn."

There was a silence in the kitchen. Harrison could hear the big wooden clock ticking the seconds. He wanted to tell Nora that when he was seventeen, he'd thought he and she would end up together. More drunk than he should be, he said it aloud. "Actually, I thought you and I would end up together."

Nora said nothing.

"You remember that night in the kitchen of the beach house?"

"Of course I remember," she said.

"It was just a matter of time," Harrison said.

Nora walked her plate to the sink. "I never saw Stephen after that," she said.

"No."

"This . . . this does us no good," Nora said.

"I wonder if that's the purpose of these reunions," Harrison said. "To unburden ourselves of secrets. To say what couldn't be said then."

"If it keeps snowing at this rate," Nora said, "we'll have at least three or four inches by morning. They say four."

"You knew about the snow?"

Nora nodded.

"Even this morning, when we were talking about how beautiful the day was, you knew the forecast?"

"Front coming down from Canada."

"Oh, go ahead," Harrison said, "blame Canada."

Nora laughed. Harrison walked to the sink and stood behind her. He wanted to kiss the back of her neck. It seemed to Harrison that every moment of the day had been leading to this one. That it would be the end of one particular narrative. Possibly the beginning of another one.

"This is none of my business, but was Carl faithful to you?" Harrison asked.

"In reality, yes," she said quickly. "In his imagination, no."

Harrison was silenced by her answer.

"It's quarter to two," Nora said. Noticing the smudge of flour on her sleeve, she tried to brush it off.

Harrison sensed that Nora might be free now to let him touch her. That power, and his understanding of the consequences — for him, for her, for Evelyn — made him slightly lightheaded. His desire, apparent from the moment he'd first seen her in the lobby, had been, throughout the day, both sharpened by proximity and memory and dulled by alcohol and experience. If he let her go, he knew that he would regret it. For months. Possibly for years. If he kissed her, he would also regret it. Perhaps for years.

She squirted dishwashing liquid onto a plate and took up a sponge. He put a hand on her shoulder. "You go to bed," he said. "I'll take care of these."

They might have been married for years. A recompense of sorts.

Nora slid away from him. She tore off a sheet of paper towel from a roll and dried her hands. "You should sleep, too," she said.

In his jacket and dress shoes, Harrison walked out into the snow. Should anyone be looking from an upstairs window, he was a man who'd left his briefcase in his car. It couldn't wait until morning. What Harrison couldn't wait for was the medicinal air, the pinging frost on his face. He felt his vision clearing. The cold air punished his lungs. Nora had been right when she'd spoken of the stick and the pond, the muck disturbed and eddying up into the water. It had been dangerous to come here, he who had avoided danger for years. He slipped a little on the accumulating snow. An inch, two inches already. He opened the back door of the rented Taurus and took out his briefcase. In it, there was a manuscript by an English novelist that was absorbing and superbly written. Harrison already knew the work was good. He'd read the British reviews. He could have published it without giving it a glance, but tonight, with any luck, the book would be his ticket to a world away from the Berkshires. With any luck, it would be his ticket to sleep.

Harrison stepped away from the car. In his shoes with their leather soles, the walking was treacherous. He made his way past the front steps of the inn and across a lawn that had only this afternoon been green. Should his fellow insomniac be watching from the window, Harrison's footprints in the snow would give away his trajectory. Harrison moved until he could see around the corner of the inn itself to the little annex in which Nora had her apartment. The lights were still on. He thought of the veranda door to her room, of a possibly theatrical entrance, the odds that she might allow him in. He believed that they were high.

He had no gloves on. His jacket was made for fall. His head was bare, wet now with melted snow. Harrison didn't want a life filled with regret. He believed himself too old for romance. What he wanted was a second chance, an opportunity to turn back the clock. But almost instantly, he took that wish back, for to have it would be to erase the lives of his sons, Charlie and Tom. One could never regret anything that had led to the births of one's children: it was as axiomatic as any mathematical formula. But that truth, as pure and as stark as it was, didn't muffle desire. What Harrison wanted tonight was to live in two parallel universes: one in Toronto with his boys, one with Nora inside her room.

But only one life could be experienced. The other had to be imagined. Harrison brushed the snow off his head and retraced his footsteps in the snow. He glanced up at the rooms of the inn. On the second floor, there was a light but no one standing at the window.

Saturday

❧❧

Innes woke cold and hungry. For an instant, before he had his bearings, he thought himself back at medical school. He raised his head and remembered that he was in his room at the top of the Fraser house in the Richmond neighborhood of Halifax. When he looked at his watch, he discovered that he had overslept. He had meant to be up by seven at the latest to read over the papers that Dr. Fraser had given him. At best, Innes would be able only to glance at them.

Shivering, Innes washed himself and dressed in his sole suit, the shirt clean, not the one he'd worn yesterday. He must ask about the laundry arrangements. He must also find a decent tailor. Mrs. Fraser would know of both. Unable to locate his socks on the carpet, Innes walked to the window and drew back the heavy blackout drapes. The view, coruscating and harsh, was of the harbor. The water scintillated between freighters, transport ships, and fishing boats. Despite the steam and smoke from dozens of boilers and furnaces, the morning was a fine one. Across the street, the breath of a warm house evaporated through a tin chimney into the cold, dry air.

Innes thought the harbor ugly, made so by war and commerce — by fuel tankers, textile mills, railroad yards, and busy wharves — and tried to imagine the land as it might have been a thousand years ago: the natural harbor sparkling, the shores of Dartmouth across the way forested. Two large ships in the harbor, Innes noted, were on the move.

Innes left his room and followed his nose to the dining room. Mrs. Fraser and Louise were seated at the table, each at a different stage in her breakfast. Her plate yet to be collected, Mrs. Fraser was making a list with pen and paper, a cup of tea beside her. Louise had just tucked into a substantial plate of steaming food. Innes reflected that even the dress of the women was vaguely military these days. Mrs. Fraser's blouse had a wide sailor collar. Louise's had epaulets with brass buttons. Innes said good morning and made his way to the mahogany buffet table on which sat several silver chafing dishes. Lifting the lids, Innes found Scotch eggs in one, kippers in another, a kind of porridge in a third. In a silver toast rack were thick slices of brown bread. An array of jams and condiments had been arranged on a platter.

Innes filled his plate with eggs and kippers (the kippers a delicacy) and two slices of toast. Not wishing to presume upon the chairs at either end of the table, Innes sat across from the women. He snapped open his linen napkin.

Louise and Mrs. Fraser had seated themselves so as to allow their guest the view of the harbor. Four arched and paned windows flanked the harborside wall, built especially, Innes imagined, for this view, which might, in peacetime, be more appealing. As a consequence of this arrangement, however, Mrs. Fraser and her daughter were in deep shadow because of the glare. Innes wondered if household etiquette required breakfast conversation.

"Mr. Finch," Louise said finally, "you have a fine day with which to begin your apprenticeship in Halifax."

"I do," Innes said. "The skies are very clear." He paused. "Last night, I asked your sister if she would call me by my first name, and I wonder if I might ask you to do the same."

Mrs. Fraser looked up sharply from her list, and Innes at once regretted the remark. Doubtless, Mrs. Fraser was wondering as to the circumstances in which Innes felt free enough to issue a personal invitation to her eldest daughter.

"If it suits," Innes added.

Louise, who was pleased and who had possibly misread Innes's intent, smiled in his direction. "It would suit me just fine," she said. "Are you at all nervous? Your first day?"

The idea of being nervous had not yet occurred to Innes. Perhaps it should have. "I hope to do well," he said.

"Oh, I know you'll do well," Louise said, unaware that a crumb of toast had lodged on her lower lip. "But if it were me . . . I've never been able to imagine cutting into someone's eyeball." She gave a kind of shiver to emphasize her distaste, and Innes was surprised by the remark. Surely Louise, as Dr. Fraser's daughter, had had ample time to get used to the idea of eye surgery.

The door to the dining room swung open. Innes hoped for Hazel and was rewarded. He stood, but Hazel waved him down. Hazel's dress was decidedly not military. She wore a pale peach silk blouse with ivory lace in the neckline. Her hair was pulled more severely off her face this morning. There was no graceful sweep across the brow. All of Innes's senses were attuned to her presence. For her part, Hazel gave no sign of what Innes took last night to be a kind of intimacy. He forced himself to eat slowly (trying to break his medical-school habit of wolfing down his meal), though he still had to read the papers Dr. Fraser had given him. A clock on the buffet table read 8:36.

Hazel, who selected dry toast and tea only, sat near her mother with the instincts of a chess master. Did she mean only to appear to distance herself from Innes, or was it a genuinely protective gesture? Might it be a generous one, leaving Innes to Louise? (Or might it simply reflect a desire not to be seen so early in the morning?)

"Good morning, Mr. Finch," Hazel said, inadvertently making a mockery of his earlier invitation to Louise.

"Good morning," Innes forced back.

So there were to be no first names at breakfast.

"Mother, I left the clothes for Ellen on the bed," Louise said from her end of what was really quite a long table.

"Perhaps today you will have had a letter, Hazel," Mrs. Fraser said to her eldest daughter, ignoring Louise altogether.

There could be no doubt what was meant by a letter.

"We need soap in the bathroom," Louise added.

"Ellen could fetch that," Mrs. Fraser said. "Hazel, is this your day at the clinic?"

"Yes, I'll be there until one o'clock," she said.

"I can't remember if this is your father's day for surgery," Mrs. Fraser said.

"I can't find my fawn scarf," Louise said.

"Perhaps you lost it on the way home from the shops yesterday," Hazel offered.

"Oh, I hope not," Louise said. "It's a favorite of mine."

Though the homely banter had the unintentional effect of encompassing Innes into the Frasers' household, he didn't think it the right moment to mention either his laundry or his need for a tailor. The door was once more pushed open, and Dr. Fraser, in high collar and bow tie, seemed to swing into the dining room. "Finch," he said, rubbing his hands together vigorously. "Tang in the air. Stings the face. Good for the lungs."

Dr. Fraser's cheeks were pink, and his nose was running. Morning exercise had not occurred to Innes.

"Four miles," Dr. Fraser announced, fingering his mustache and examining the fare on the buffet table. "You have a decent coat, I take it," he added, as if there were no one in the room but he and Innes.

"Passable," Innes answered.

"Good. We walk, of course, to hospital."

Dr. Fraser took his place at the head of the table. "New wounds from France," he added with startling relish and seemingly no memory of having uttered the phrase the evening before. The words had less power, however, in the sunshine; no low gas seeped across the table. Hazel calmly ate a bite of toast. Perhaps she was protected by the thought of a letter.

A massive plume of smoke, topped by a ball of fire, rose above the windowsill.

"There's a fire," Innes said, half standing.

Dr. Fraser turned in his chair. "What on earth . . . ?"

Innes moved to one of the four arched windows. "There seems to have been a collision in the harbor," he announced.

"Good lord," Dr. Fraser said when he had reached Innes.

The smoke was black and thick, with licks of fire appearing and disappearing. Two massive ships were linked in the harbor waters.

"The smoke is oily," Dr. Fraser said. "Phyllis, where are my binoculars?"

"In the library."

"I'll get them," Hazel said. Innes turned in time to see her stand and make her way to the swinging door. She was graceful in her movements — the slide, turn, and rise from the dining room chair — even when on a simple errand. And that, possibly, was the difference between Hazel and her sister. There was no child in Hazel.

Louise and Mrs. Fraser joined the men at the window. In the harbor, objects shot into the sky at angles from one of the ships. "Oooh, it looks like fireworks," Louise said.

Below, on the streets, passersby began to gather in groups to watch the blaze. "Haven't seen anything like this since the war began," Dr. Fraser said. "I'm assuming this isn't some kind of sabotage."

"Germans in Halifax?" Louise asked, her voice rising.

"No, I'm sure not," Innes heard Mrs. Fraser say with slight annoyance.

Innes, his eyesight keen, could see lifeboats being lowered from the burning ship. The smoke was indeed thick and oily. Barrels appeared to ignite from time to time.

Hazel returned with the binoculars and walked directly to the window, where she handed them to her father.

"They're abandoning the ship with some haste," Dr. Fraser said after he had had a moment to adjust the eyepieces.

"The ship is drifting closer to the Halifax shore," Innes said. He thought the calamity, for all its potential horror — were men caught in the fire? — quite beautiful with its tongues of flames and irregular fireworks.

"I see the words 'Belgian Relief' on the other ship," Dr. Fraser said.

Below, on the street, two nursing sisters had stopped to watch the spectacle. A boy, who must already have been late for school, had climbed atop a letter box to get a better view. Hazel was standing so close to Innes that the sleeve of her dress brushed his jacket. Was this by design? For a moment, Innes could think of little else but Hazel's proximity.

"Best to return to our breakfasts," Dr. Fraser said, setting the binoculars on the windowsill. Innes, reluctant to take his seat with Hazel standing so near to him, picked up the binoculars and examined the ship for himself. Hazel stepped away from Innes, as was only proper.

"I'm not sure I've ever seen such black smoke," Innes said to Dr. Fraser.

"They'll get it under control," the doctor said.

But Innes wasn't as confident. He followed with the binoculars a lifeboat in the water. He could see the men paddling frantically toward the Dartmouth shore.

Innes remembered the papers he had to look at before he and Dr. Fraser left for the hospital. He set the binoculars on the sill. "I have some things in my room I must collect," Innes said to Dr. Fraser. "I'll be in the hallway at nine-fifteen?"

"Yes, of course. Earlier if you want to get a good look at the fire."

"I think you probably have as good a view from here as anywhere," Innes said, taking a last sip of coffee and looking at Hazel, who had returned to her seat. She turned, and there it was again: that secretive glance, covert and inviting. Or did Innes simply wish it so? The thrumming, which only Hazel seemed capable of setting in motion, had started up again in Innes's chest.

Innes took the steps two at a time, swung around the newel post at the top of the staircase, and headed for his room. He found the papers Dr. Fraser had given him spread upon the floor near the bed. He'd tried to read them last night before falling asleep, but he couldn't remember a single word. He glanced at the title. *Purulent Ophthalmia in Infants.*

He noticed that the plume of oily smoke had risen higher into the Halifax sky and was drifting with the slight wind. Papers in hand, Innes walked to the window. The glass was smeared in the east light, suggesting it had not been washed in some time. Innes saw a clock tower, a church spire. Dozens, perhaps hundreds, of Haligonians had come out onto the streets to observe the fire. Clearly the garrison city had not seen much wartime action. Without the binoculars, it was more difficult to make out what was happening at the site of the fire. Innes imagined the ship abandoned by now. It would wreck itself on the shore. He glanced down at the abstract. *The inflammation develops in less than three days after birth,* he read.

A blast from a factory whistle caused Innes to glance up. Two streets away, a tram stopped. A woman on a bicycle was passing just under his window.

A brilliant, blinding radiance, a flash of light brighter than anything Innes had ever seen, obliterated everything beyond the glass and had the effect of a blow to the face. In one fluid movement, Innes dropped the papers, raised his arm to shield his eyes, and turned his back to the window.

Innes heard a low rumble, an explosion of great magnitude, and then the sound of glass shattering. He arched his back against the pain — he was being shot — and was blown through the air. He heard the screeching of metal and felt his clothes being torn from his body. In a protective gesture, Innes tried to keep his arms over his head.

He felt a great sucking wind of such ferocity, he thought he might lose his limbs. He was aware of movement, of twisting in the air. He hit what seemed to be a vertical wooden beam and fell. His shoulder took the brunt. He lay stunned and lost consciousness.

When he came to — a minute later? five minutes later? — his nostrils were clogged with dust. For one panicky moment, Innes was certain he was suffocating. For how long had he been unconscious?

He coughed. He blew his nose. He tried to stand, but he couldn't. What had happened? Where was he? He couldn't remember.

When he opened his eyes, he saw that he was both outside and inside a building he didn't recognize. It was as though he had been put through to another world, a hellish place covered with dust. Not ten feet from where he was sitting, the floor had buckled, its wooden boards jagged edged. The air was thick with smoke. The wall next to him was bent inward at an impossible curve that Innes thought could not hold another second. Through a blown-out window, he saw that he had landed on an upper story of a home. Not a house at all, Innes thought, surveying large cones of cotton and wool that had been tossed into a jumble. A textile factory?

Innes looked above him. The entire roof was missing.

For long minutes, Innes heard no sound. It was as though the world had simply stopped.

He could remember a flash of light. Before that, a fire.

He felt a biting pain in his back. He reached to the place where he was hurt and cut his finger on a shard of glass. A splinter had hit him in the back just below the shoulder bone. Removing a sock from his foot — his trousers and shoes were inexplicably gone — he padded his fingers with the sock and tried again to reach the splinter of glass. He pulled it out and flung it, pressing the sock to the wound.

What in God's name had happened?

He remembered the Frasers then. He thought of Hazel. Had he been blown out of the Frasers' home? And, if so, where were they?

Innes reached out with his foot, trying to snag a cone of rag wool. The movement inadvertently pushed the cone away. Innes darted forward with his hand and snatched it, bringing it back onto his lap. He could feel the blood running from the wound on his back and soaking his undershirt. With speed, Innes pressed his other sock up against the wound and tied a length of the rag wool around his body, pulling as tightly as he could without breaking the wool. He must get himself to hospital. He had no idea how deep the wound was.

Oddly, he had little pain, though he was aware now of the cold. He scanned his small corner of the floor that was still intact, looking for a garment of any sort. All this wool and no clothing. He had an image of his mother knitting. A woman from below screamed, a sound that chilled Innes and kept him immobile for a long minute. He tried yelling back, but had no reply. He noted a leather apron with short sleeves on a hook. Trying to stand, he felt the pain of the wound in his muscles.

There was pain in his face as well. He ran his hand along his cheek and discovered that tiny slivers of glass were imbedded from his cheekbone to his jawbone. One by one, he picked them out by feel. He examined the interior of his ear for any glass fragments as well, but he found none. Holding on to a diagonal beam, Innes reached over the blasted flooring and flipped the leather apron off the hook.

Now that Innes was standing, he could see, through the partially destroyed wall across from him, an astonishing sight. Seawater was advancing across a devastated landscape. It was as though the ocean meant to conquer the city. He watched as the water rolled over the city and then subsided.

In the sky, he saw a zeppelin, which turned out to be, upon closer inspection, a thermal cloud, curly in shape and giving off flashes of light. He heard a groan from below. Louise, for all her hysteria, had been right. Halifax had been shelled by the Germans.

Innes surveyed the ruins of the attic he was in, searching for a way down onto the street. It was simply a matter of time before that curved wall collapsed and with it the rest of the building. Fear, which Innes had not felt until now, motivated him to begin climbing down through the wreckage. His entire body began to tremble.

He found a stairway intact, though it had been ripped from the wall and now hung at such an angle that Innes had to descend almost vertically. He held on to the banister with his good arm. He must get directly to hospital, he thought as he felt the blood running down his back — less copiously than before, but still there wasn't enough pressure on the wound.

He searched the bottom floor of the building, a maze of broken objects and chunks of plaster. He tried to find the person who had screamed. He lifted beams and bits of furniture. He called out several times.

When he had no response, he decided to leave the building, reaching the street through what remained of a window, its glass completely missing. He stepped out into a city as still as death.

This couldn't have been the Germans, Innes thought. The damage was too vast, too uniform. The street on which the Fraser house had once stood simply no longer existed. For as far as Innes could see in any direction, houses had been leveled or partially destroyed, their roofs blown off, their walls buckled. From the sky, a shower of ash and debris was falling. Telephone poles tilted at angles. A cloud of smoke rose high over the city.

Forty feet from where he stood, Innes saw a woman pinned under a beam. He made his way with bare feet over scrap metal and glass and wood to the spot where the woman lay. Her face was bloodied, the only color in an ashy landscape. There were splinters of glass protruding from her eyes. He bent to take her pulse, but there was none. The beam had crushed her chest.

A young girl of about ten years walked around the corner from an overturned carriage. She was naked but for a cotton slip. Her face and arms were dirty, her blond hair singed.

"Where's your mum?" Innes asked, standing and walking toward her.

The girl simply stared straight ahead with no expression. Innes wondered if she could see. He waved his fingers in front of her eyes, and she blinked. "Take my hand," he said, reaching for her when she did not respond. "We have to find some clothes for you."

Innes, shivering now, knew that he must find a length of fabric to secure the pressure bandage to his wound. When he and the young girl had gone a few steps, he remembered the dead woman under the beam.

"Stay here," he said to the girl. "Don't move. I'll be right back."

Innes quickly retraced his steps to the body and tore lengths of cloth from the woman's skirt and underslip. He removed her shoes and socks.

Already he was looting the dead.

He returned to the girl and handed her the shoes and socks and told her to put them on. Still she seemed not to be able to hear him. Was she an immigrant with no English? Innes spoke to her in French with no success. Gently, Innes sat the girl down on a bit of upholstered cushion from the overturned carriage and slipped the socks and shoes on her feet. They were, of course, too big for her, but they would have to do.

Innes guessed that the girl would not be able to assist him in tying up his wound. He lowered the leather apron, undid the rag wool yarn, wadded up the material from the dead woman's underslip, and pressed it against his wound. Using his one free arm and his teeth, he wound the cloth from the skirt around the bandage. He tied it across his chest as tightly as his strength would allow and then put the leather apron back on. He brought the child to her feet.

"Come on then," he said, taking her hand again.

Innes and the girl headed up the hill, Innes guessing that the blast would have lost power and momentum as it had moved upward.

The devastation was beyond anything Innes had ever imagined. There were fires everywhere, the city covered with a black oily soot. Power lines were down, automobiles were overturned, and a church steeple lay in the center of what had once been a road.

Innes saw headless corpses, survivors staggering naked. He saw a chair with a dead child still sitting in it, a woman kneeling on a sidewalk praying. He saw a man clawing frantically at the wreckage of a house and stopped to help, but the fire inside was too fierce, and he had to back away. Above him, a white sun began to appear through the soot and ash.

Everywhere Innes looked, faces were blackened, hair was singed, bodies had burned to bone. Innes stepped over a radiator, a piece of crockery, an arm attached to a hand. Signs of the once placid domestic life of the city — a bit of knitting, an intact chair, a Christmas wreath, a fan of papers — were strewn over the streets. Innes hoped the girl beside him would not retain the images now forming on her retina. He stopped once to treat a serious cut on a woman's neck by making a bandage from her skirt. He told her to follow him. In a sight that unnerved Innes, a man sat with his back against a dead horse, cradling an infant in his arms. From the loll of the child's head, it was clear to Innes that the child had perished.

Others moved up the hill in tandem with Innes. The Citadel, a fort on a hill, seemed to be the goal. Innes passed a barrel with a ship's insignia, a man with a missing foot, a house completely flattened. He saw dozens of animals — cats, dogs, cows — some dead, some still alive but bloody. After a time, he spotted an intact building — a house? a shop? — with two men in the doorway. They would help him, Innes thought. At the very least, they would know the direction to the nearest hospital.

As he approached the building, a middle-aged woman came from within and took the child from him. "What's your name, love?" the woman asked. The girl did not respond. Without a word to Innes, the woman carried the child into the build-ing. Above the blown-out windows of the shop, a sign read DRUGGIST.

Innes entered the building. Along one wall, bodies were al-ready lined up as if in a morgue — some disfigured, others with glass protruding from their faces. Many were partially naked. An entire city, Innes thought, had been called to the windows by the spectacle of the fire and then in an instant killed or wounded.

"I'm a doctor," he told the first person he encountered. "I need a better bandage for my wound and some clothes and shoes, and then I can help."

Clothes and shoes were found for Innes. He suspected they had come from the dead, but he didn't ask. The middle-aged woman washed out Innes's wound with alcohol and applied a pressure dressing. "Your daughter is being cared for," she said.

"She's not my daughter," Innes said. "I found her alone in the street."

"She won't speak."

"She's in shock," Innes explained.

A long counter on which the chemist had once mixed his po-tions was now in use as a kind of gurney. Innes learned that the chemist had been making sutures and applying dressings. Innes took over, calling for instruments, antiseptics, and anesthetics. The chemist and the middle-aged woman assisted him with rudimentary medicine. An hour earlier, Innes reflected with a kind of shock, he'd been eating kippers and toast in the Fraser dining room.

Innes worked steadily, the work a buffer against fear and urgent curiosity. He had little time to think beyond the immediate, to speak to the wounded, or even to wonder at their circumstances prior to the blast. With their clothing missing and faces blackened, there were few clues to the occupation or class of the people Innes treated. He removed glass slivers from eyes and faces. He set broken bones. He sutured deep lacerations. His work was not expert; his instruments were rudimentary. Each of the patients would need to be transported to hospital for better care once a vehicle could be found.

The makeshift ward was a cacophony of moans and cries. When the morgue against the far wall could no longer contain all the dead, bodies were laid on the frozen ground outside the door. Men and women searched for relatives, indicating with a cry that a search was over. Innes was told that at St. Joseph's School, fifty children had been killed. Nearly everyone at the Dominion Textile Factory had died. The blast had momentarily emptied the harbor of water. Ships had leaped into the air.

Innes worked until he felt faint. He was made to sit in a chair. He was brought soup, which was on the boil over an open fire at the back of the building. There was no electricity, gas, or water in the city. Innes thought about the Frasers and wished that he could go in search of them. If he had survived the blast, perhaps they had as well.

He could not imagine Hazel's broken body.

In the late afternoon, Innes was relieved by a military officer. Innes asked for and was given directions to the nearest surviving hospital. There, he hoped to find Dr. Fraser, to assist him in his labors.

Innes left the druggist's, happy to be away from the stench. But after a few minutes, he wished himself back inside. He found a school in ruins. A woman with her belongings in a pillowcase appeared to be wandering aimlessly. A block of houses was still burning. Odd bits lay in passageways that had once been roads: the axle of a truck, a sewing machine, a woman's lace corset, a bread tin. Men tugged at timbers. One house, remarkably intact, still had its wash on a line on its porch. A letter, addressed to Craig Driscoll, was wedged between two pieces of wood. Innes noted the presence of soldiers, which he took to be a good sign. It was understood now that the explosion had been caused when the *Mont Blanc,* a munitions ship, had blown up in the harbor. Innes remembered the sailors rowing for their lives to Dartmouth.

Innes reached the hospital to which he had been directed. He announced himself to a nursing sister in a blue blouse, white pinafore, and headdress. He was greeted with relief. He was shown to a room in which doctors were dressing wounds and performing surgeries. They resembled butchers after a long day. Innes asked for Dr. Fraser but received no satisfactory answer. Innes was asked to remove his overcoat and step in for a man who had been wounded but who had been operating for hours. Sixty eyeballs had been removed, Innes was informed. He did not mention his own wound.

The number of blind was indeed staggering, the correlation between curiosity and injury striking. Later, Innes would learn that nine thousand from the city had been injured from the blast. Two thousand had died.

Stretchers came and went. Innes rendered first aid, operated on wounds, administered morphine. The baptism that had begun in the morning turned nightmarish. By evening, all of the anesthetics and antiseptics had run out. For the first time in his life, Innes was forced to operate on a patient without chloroform. If he didn't amputate the girl's mangled left arm, he knew, she would shortly die of her wounds. Giving the most barbaric command of his life, Innes ordered a nurse to lie across the girl's knees. He told another to hold down the girl's free arm. The girl, surprised by the knife, screamed. Mercifully, and as expected, she fainted, allowing Innes to complete the surgery and cauterize the wound.

The injured were triaged, the worst cases sent to a series of stretchers against a wall. Women volunteers walked among the white iron cots, soothing when they could. If Hazel had been alive, Innes thought, she might be doing much the same.

On a break, Innes wandered the wards, stepping over cots and bodies as he went. He had never seen so many injured and dead. Even his worst imaginings of France had been less chaotic, less bloody.

He asked again and again for Dr. Fraser, receiving no answers. Innes thought about leaving the hospital, returning to the place where the Fraser home had once stood, and searching through the wreckage. But he doubted that he could find it in the dark. Through a blown-out window, a high wind had come up, and, with it, snow.

My God, Innes thought. A blizzard.

He was fed with bread and water and dried peas, an odd combination he gratefully consumed. On the second floor of the hospital, Innes was informed, were the patients who had been treated and who were resting. He climbed the stairs and found, in the stairwell, a nursing sister in uniform, curled into a ball, asleep. He did not wake her.

Through swinging doors on the second floor was a vast corridor with wards to either side. Innes searched the first ward, quiet and dark with a single candle and a white pitcher on each bedside table. A nursing sister, ashen but efficient, was the only one on duty for what looked to be at least fifty patients. Innes was struck by the number of children.

From a distant ward, Innes could hear a woman keening.

He made his way through the wards, searching for any of the Frasers, the only people he had known in Halifax. Some of the patients had their surnames written at the foot of the bed. Others' beds were blank, perhaps indicating patients who could no longer speak or who did not remember who they were. Innes examined faces. He thought of the ten-year-old girl who had taken his hand. Would she have begun to speak by now? Would she have been told the fate of her family?

The keening grew stronger as Innes approached the end of the corridor. The sound changed to a frantic squabble, a bird interrupted and screeching. Something in the tone of the voice made Innes pick up his pace, and he was on a run by the time he swung through the door. A woman, her head bandaged, was sitting in a wheelchair, making guttural and frenzied noises and clawing at the air in front of her. Below the bandages that covered both eyes, Innes recognized the fringe of wavy light brown hair, a blouse with epaulets and brass buttons. A nursing sister, in desperation, batted away one of the patient's hands.

"I'll take over," Innes said, reaching the nursing sister's side.

"She's off her rocker, this one."

Innes saw at the nurse's feet a spilled bowl of soup. He crouched and faced the woman in the chair. He caught her hands and brought them together in his own. He could feel the wildness and the panic in her arms as she struggled to break free. "Louise," he said. "It's Innes."

The woman cocked her head so that her right ear was turned toward him. Innes knew, though Louise did not, that this was her good ear, the one with which she would "see" everyone who spoke to her for the rest of her life.

"Mr. Finch?" she asked.

"Yes, Louise. It's Innes."

"Oh God," she wailed, reaching for him. He allowed Louise to feel his face and hair. Her fingers were blunt, unpracticed. Briefly he closed his eyes.

"They are all dead!" she cried. "All dead."

"Who are all dead, Louise?" Innes urged.

"Mother. Father. Hazel. All dead."

"How do you know this?" Innes asked, trying to keep his voice calm. Louise could not actually have seen the bodies, he guessed, not to judge from the blood-soaked gauze at her eyes.

"The man who found me told me. He said they were all dead." Louise began to tremble uncontrollably, and Innes bent forward to hold her. A rank smell rose up from the back of her blouse. She had, in some way, soiled herself.

"Sister," Innes said. "This woman must be bathed."

"Now, sir?"

"Yes, now," Innes said, standing. "In hot water. And then I'll want to remove the bandages."

"Sir, it is two in the morning."

"It is of no consequence to me what time it is," Innes said.

"There is no hot water, sir."

Louise reached out to Innes. "Don't leave me," she cried. Innes took one of Louise's hands as the nursing sister began to wheel her in the direction of the bathing room. The large wooden wheels were nearly silent on the lino floor.

"Why can't she walk?" Innes asked the sister.

"Her anklebone is broken, sir. Crushed."

Innes bent to lift the blanket from Louise's feet. A hastily constructed cast was on her lower right leg.

"I'll be within earshot," he told Louise. "Just outside the door. You'll be able to hear me and talk to me."

Innes watched as Louise was made to lie on a cot. With some expertise, the nursing sister removed Louise's clothing and bathed her. Innes saw that the cast would have to be remade. He hoped the bones would not have to be reset. He did not turn away from the sight of Louise's nakedness. The small white breasts, the taut stomach, the swollen right leg. From time to time, Louise called out to him, and Innes answered her.

"Something will have to be found to calm the woman," he said to the nursing sister.

"There are no medicines," the sister answered.

When Louise had been bathed and put into a hospital gown, Innes moved closer to her and took her hand. "I'm going to remove your dressings and have a look at your eyes," he said.

"They hurt," Louise said, but Innes noted that some of the hysteria had left her voice.

As gently as he could, and with the nursing sister standing to one side of him with a basin, Innes cradled Louise's head and unwound the gauze. The damage was considerable. In the right eye, most of the external muscles of the ball had been severed, and it protruded from the socket. It would have to be removed. In the left eye, a laceration of substantial depth sliced across the cornea and extended into the skin beyond the eye.

"I can't see," Louise said.

Louise, Innes knew, would be blind for life.

Agnes, sitting against the headboard, put the notebook in her lap. It was snowing outside. Had anyone mentioned snow last night? Agnes got out of bed and padded, in stocking feet, to the window. The snow fell thickly. Four to five inches were already on the ground. How amazing! This would be a winter wedding after all.

Agnes crossed her arms over her chest. So Louise was blind.

Well, it had to be that way, didn't it? Agnes knew that she could, in less time than it took to formulate a sentence, make Louise well again, give her sight. But Agnes thought she would not. The reality of the explosion was doubtless worse than Agnes, with all her reading, had been able to imagine. Innes, for example, might easily have found Louise with the glass still protruding from her eyes. Would he then have operated on Louise?

Oddly satisfying, that: Louise blind for life.

Immensely satisfying, too, just to be able to write the story of Innes Finch. Last night, it had been all Agnes could do to stop herself from speaking certain words of another story that had squeezed themselves up inside her throat. She had mentioned Jim's name, and that in itself had been thrilling, but it hadn't been enough. Rewarding, though, to discover how much the others had admired their former teacher. What was it that Jerry had said? Mr. Mitchell was *the man?*

Yes, Agnes thought. He was the man.

Her head throbbed at one temple. If she ate, if she had coffee, her hangover might abate. She didn't just yet want to get dressed, however, and she very much didn't want to see the others at breakfast. Perhaps an Advil was what was needed.

Agnes rummaged through her backpack. She found the bottle of Advil at the bottom, slipped two pills onto her palm, and filled a glass of water at the bathroom sink. Two Advil and forget about it. This was the advice she gave her field hockey girls when they complained of minor aches and pains.

Agnes caught a glimpse of herself in the mirror and was not happy with what she saw. Her face looked haggard, her eyes slightly bloodshot. Her hair was matted on one side from sleep. Her breath was foul. She found her toothpaste in her toilet kit and brushed her teeth. She knew she ought to get into the shower and let the water clear her head, but the idea of a shower — washing the body, shampooing the hair, drying it with the hair dryer — seemed like a tremendous amount of effort just now. Instead, she walked to the desk and sat in the chair. She stared at the snow.

What would she do all day? A baseball game was clearly out of the picture. Visit the outlets? But would the roads be cleared? Sledding? Agnes thought she could get mildly interested in coasting down the long hill that sloped away from the inn. But would that activity completely occupy her thoughts the way downhill skiing used to do? Or would she still feel dogged by the ghost of the man who was with her always? With her and not with her. New activities, new pleasures, must always, by definition, be only half experienced.

She fingered the blotter on the desk. She could write to Jim. Yes, she could. The activity, by its very nature, suggested a kind of satisfactory completion. Agnes would write from Massachusetts. The letter would travel to Wisconsin. Jim would fetch the letter from his mailbox at school. He would tear open the envelope. He would read the letter. Circuit complete.

In the desk drawer, Agnes found the leather folder that held the inn's stationery. There were three large sheets of writing paper, two envelopes, and one postcard. Of course Agnes would not send a postcard.

She reached for the ballpoint pen on the desk. Her handwriting was tiny and very neat.

Dear Jim,

she began.

> *I think I might have written you a few weeks back that Bridget Kennedy (later Rodgers and this evening to be Ricci) is marrying Billy Ricci. Do you remember her? She was always with us*

in our group of friends at Kidd, and I know you and I have talked about her before. Of course, you remember Billy from our Am lit class. Yes, that Am lit class.

I am here now in Nora's new inn. I'm sorry you never saw the old house. I used to sleep in a guest room under a velvet and silk crazy quilt that was quite worn but very beautiful. Nora has done a brilliant job of converting the old house to an inn, and I imagine it's cost her a lot of money. The inn is luxurious, more European than Country Living. *Just now I was in bed enjoying the feel of the silky sheets and the down comforter. I was, of course, missing you.*

And there I've already gone and done what I meant not to do. I wanted to write you a chatty letter telling you of our mini-reunion. I wished to keep this light. But I can't. You are with me all the time. Sometimes I feel as though I have a lover who has died, whose memory I keep alive. Being apart from you is a particular sort of agony: the separations painful, the memories delicious.

The early memories are the most delicious of all. Last night, I was remembering that day before Thanksgiving when I came back from college and drove to Kidd to visit you. I'd been thinking about you ever since graduation, and I believe I went to Kidd with the idea of telling you that. But then, face-to-face with you, I found myself too shy to say much at all. You sat across the desk from me and asked questions, and I answered them, all the time knowing that in a few minutes I would have to get up and leave and that I'd never again have a good enough excuse to visit you. You must have wondered at my bumbling answers, my distracted manner. I was all nerves. Stupidly, I just sat there until finally you said you had a meeting, that you'd walk me to my car.

It was a kind of death walk for me: those slow steps from

your office and along the hallway. I thought of doing something theatrical, turning to you and telling you I loved you. I imagined your shock, the Hollywood kiss, dangerous and thrilling in the corridors of Kidd. But there were people all about, leaving for the weekend. Dean Cropsey came out of his office and said hello and asked me how Mt. Holyoke was, and I thought for one panicked moment that you would excuse yourself and leave me. I was curt with him, but I couldn't help it. And then you and I walked outside, and it was sleeting, the weather delivering that thing we New Englanders like to call a "wintry mix."

You once said that you thought I had slipped on purpose. You used to tease me about it, remember? But I don't believe I slipped on purpose. In fact, I'm positive I didn't. My legs were weak and certainly reluctant, and that may have caused the accident. I still have a hard knot in my butt — scar tissue, I imagine — from the fall.

I don't remember how you got me to your car. I do remember the waiting room of the emergency ward. You held my hand, and I think you meant it to be a kind of paternal and comforting gesture. I was hurting, but the pain seemed somewhere very far away. All of my body was instead concentrated on our clasped hands. I dared not move my fingers even a millimeter lest you let go of me.

I was put into a cubicle and then sent down to X-ray. I was sure then that you had left the building, that you had gone home to your wife and daughter. It was, after all, the afternoon before Thanksgiving, an inconvenient time for any accident. I touched my hand where you had held it, hardly aware of the doctor who came in. He said that nothing was broken, that I'd have a nasty bruise that might take months to heal, that I was lucky. He told me to be careful on the ice.

A Wedding in December

And then, behind him, I saw you with your jacket open, your tie loose. You smiled encouragingly. You stood with your hands on your hips, looking at me. You watched the doctor lift up my skirt, lower the elastic of my underwear, and examine the spot that had taken the worst of the fall. I knew that you could see me. You didn't turn away. You helped me into my coat and held me all the way to your car. The weather was filthy by then, icy and cold. The snow stung my face. You put me into your car and then got in yourself. I was shivering — more from shock, I think, than from the cold. You held me to stop the shivering. "I'd better take you back," you said.

That kiss. Papery and long and admitting everything.

I remember all of it, Jim. Every plane flight, every drive, every hotel room. I used to be able to remember specific dates as well, but I've forgotten them now. I wish I'd kept a diary (all those precious details lost). Our love affair was an entity with a life of its own. It should have been chronicled. And I, Agnes O'Connor, who makes her living off the chronicles of others, did not write about the one thing that has mattered most to me in my life.

Yes, I know there have been difficult times. Your own particular agony, which I've never been able to share with you. But I have had agonies of my own. The long months when you've not called or written. The time you said over drinks in Boston that we couldn't continue the affair. The day you told me Carol was pregnant again. But the very worst for me was the day I drove to Kidd to surprise you with the news of my new job. I would be teaching at my old school, I told you. We would soon be colleagues. I remember your face went hollow, all my lovely news dissipating in an instant. I understand now why you were concerned. Of course I do. I understand your desire to keep our affair separate from your "real" life (as you once called it). But I didn't then. I thought you would be as happy as I was, and when you weren't, I was hurt and angry.

Mostly, I choose not to remember that day, however. Instead, I remember the cottage we rented in Bar Harbor and the meals you grilled on that tiny barbecue on the deck. You even made a pizza, as I recall. I remember that ratty hotel in Portland and making love on a plaid sofa. Later, I wept for the pure joy of it. I remember our walk through the city on a Sunday night, all the shops closed, the buildings shuttered. It felt as if we were the only two people in the world. I have loved you now for twenty-seven years. In all that time, I have not slept with another man. I am your other wife, your second wife, the one who waits for you at her hut. I cherish your visits and feed off them for months. If others knew, they would pity me. So much invested for seemingly so little reward. But I look at other couples and am convinced that what you and I shared — share — was beyond anything they could ever imagine.

I didn't mean to do this, Jim. I know it sometimes angers you when I write of this thing we cannot have. But I can't pretend that I don't long for you. I wish that you were here with me and that we could slip under this duvet cover together. I know that no woman has made love to you as I have. I know that I am still your fantasy.

Agnes put down the pen. She held her head in her hands. The ache was as fresh and as keen as if Jim had just left the room, not to return for months.

Agnes got up from the chair and walked into the bathroom for a tissue. She blew her nose. She would not send the letter. She wouldn't even finish it. She would have to take it with her in her backpack.

She couldn't risk leaving even the torn bits in the wastebasket. But would it be so awful to tell her story to just one person? Nora, for example? Nora certainly would honor her secret. All this time Agnes had lived with her story. Must she live with it for the rest of her life? What if Agnes were to die suddenly? If no one knew about the affair, who would tell Jim?

The memories, jostled and released by the letter, bombarded Agnes now. She remembered bending her head forward and Jim kissing her all the way to the base of her spine. Opening a box two days before Christmas in a motel room in Bangor to find a ring — not an engagement ring, but a small silver band inside. Agnes had worn it every day since. She remembered the feel of Jim's muscles against her palm. And bars, dozens of them. The thrill of the first kiss of the evening. The touching of hands while the drinks were ordered. The relentless talk about themselves, their affair, as if there were nothing else in the universe that mattered. The arrival of the dusky drinks that promised a room with a bed. Agnes remembered a room in Montreal, a cavernous room with many beds. Six or seven of them anyway. Even now, she thought of it as The Room with Many Beds.

Agnes padded back to her own bed and slipped between the sheets. Her head throbbed. She turned on her side, facing the unshaded windows. Yes, perhaps she had had too much to drink last night. It was the cognac that had done it. It was foolish to accept another drink after the meal was finished, but there was Jerry, holding out the bulbous glass, and Agnes was so seldom offered a drink of any kind.

She would like to go back to sleep now. The memories hurt. She understood that they were, in some way, deeply masochistic. Perhaps it would be a good idea to go to a hypnotist to try to erase the memory of Jim entirely. Was such a thing possible? And if she did successfully obliterate Jim from her life, what would be left? A dull sphere with its radiant center missing?

She sat up suddenly and experienced again, at the periphery of her vision, the odd oily blips that seemed to rise up in cylinders at the edges of her eyes. She must absolutely make the appointment to see her ophthalmologist, she thought. Not to be able to see: Agnes could hardly imagine a worse fate. She thought of Louise, blind behind her bandages. How would one manage in the world? Should Agnes change Louise's fate?

No, Agnes thought as she found her notebook in the bedcovers. Louise would remain as she was.

Innes put new dressings on Louise's wounds. It would likely not be he who operated on her in the morning, when a shipment of chloroform was expected.

In a supply room on the first floor, exhausted surgeons found shelter. A half dozen cots had been set up. Men who could barely stand waited for one to become free. Nursing sisters were housed upstairs. Even in calamity, one had to observe certain proprieties. Innes fell into a deep sleep, but was woken four hours later. Other physicians needed the beds.

For three days, Innes worked in the operating theater. Supplies were brought by rail from other parts of Canada. Boston sent a hospital train. Thousands of homeless sought shelter in makeshift camps from the blizzard and the cold, while others searched morgues and hospitals for the dead and injured. When Innes had a few minutes, he studied the lists of casualties in the newspapers. *#221. Female about twenty-five years. Blond hair, blue eyes. French underwear. Rose-colored stockings. #574. Charred remains of adult. #371. Male. Age about five years. Face disfigured. Brown striped sweater, white underwear. Envelope found on body addressed to "Mr. William Finn, 45 Buckingham Street, Toronto."* Innes read these descriptions carefully, looking for mention of a peach-colored silk blouse, a ring of small diamonds. He believed that Dr. and Mrs. Fraser were dead, though only the body of the latter had been recovered and identified. Innes did not believe in Hazel's death. He thought often about where she might have been at the exact moment of the blast. Was she still at the dining table? If so, it was unlikely she would have survived the shattering glass from those four arched windows. But if she'd been in an interior hallway, she might have been able to dig herself out of the wreckage.

At the hospital, Innes acquired a reputation as an excellent surgeon, rising through the ranks more quickly than he would have as an apprentice to Dr. Fraser. There were no apprenticeships now. The days and hours for Innes were a kind of exhausted blur. He lived at the hospital, sleeping and eating there because he, like many of the staff, had nowhere else to go. An entire city was homeless, bereaved.

Innes was appalled by the suffering of the city. He began to conceive the notion of a malevolent God. How else to explain the capricious deaths of children, the suffering of the mothers? Intact families were rare, worthy of comment. Innes could make sense of small moments only — of this moment, he could say, yes, this happened, or no, that did not happen — but he could not comprehend the whole. He no longer thought about music or art or even the war in Europe. Life was reduced to work and food and sleep. He operated by day and read the casualty lists at night. He told himself he was doing it for Louise. Day after day, he checked the lists. *#83. Female. About twenty-five years old. Brown hair. Ivory linen blouse. Insole of boot reads* PARIS. *Wedding ring was found upon the body and may be claimed at Camp Hill Hospital. Previous pitting and scarring on right side of face. Cesarean scar on abdomen.*

During his breaks, Innes visited Louise, who had been moved to the third floor with the most improved of the wounded.

189

Louise cried and reached out for him. Though she had been told that her mother had died, she still called out for her. She repeatedly panicked at the thought of her future. How would she survive if she was blind? She begged Innes for a cure, believing that medicine would save her. The irony was brutal: the daughter of a famous eye surgeon blinded.

Louise had no memory of the blast. Innes quizzed her, asking where she'd been at the moment of the explosion. Louise couldn't answer him. She couldn't say, either, where Hazel had been, whether she was still in the dining room or elsewhere. Innes learned it was the same for many of the wounded. The few moments leading up to the blast had been obliterated from their minds.

On the fifth day, Innes arrived at the ward to find Louise in an agitated state. She had knocked over her water pitcher, and an orderly was cleaning up the mess.

"Louise," Innes said when he had reached her. "What's wrong?"

"She was here!" Louise cried. "And I told her that now she had everything. I told her that I was the more beautiful, but now I have nothing. No home. No husband. No children."

"Who was here, Louise?" Innes asked, sitting on the bed. He rubbed her arm to try to soothe her.

"I told her, she can see, she can walk. It is too unfair. She can see, she can walk, and I can't. I will never get a husband now. Who will love a blind woman? Who will marry a woman who cannot see his children?"

"Louise," Innes said once again. "Who was here? Who were you talking to?"

Louise raised her head from the pillow. "Hazel," she said. "Hazel was here, and now she has gone away."

Though expected, the name, when said aloud, was a blow. "Did she say where she was going?" Innes asked.

"No," Louise said.

"Did she say where she was living now?"

"No," Louise answered curtly, perhaps having heard too inquisitive a tone in Innes's voice.

"Was she hurt?" Innes asked. "Did she suffer any wounds in the blast?"

"She did not say," Louise answered with a distinct note of pique.

"And her father. Your father. Did she have word of him?"

"He is dead," Louise said.

Louise began to wail, and Innes rubbed her arm again. He wanted to comfort her, but it was all he could do to remain at her bedside. If Hazel had left Louise just moments earlier, she might still be in the building. He watched as the orderly finished cleaning up the mess. Innes had Louise sit up and take a drink when a new pitcher of water was brought. He told her, as he had several times before, that many blind women had full, rewarding lives. They had husbands, and they had children. There were schools where domestic skills could be learned and practiced.

Louise would have none of it.

After a time, Innes told Louise that he had to leave. He bartered for his freedom, saying that he would return in the evening and that he would read the newspaper to her. Both the pilot and the master of the SS *Mont Blanc* had been arrested and would go to trial. This fact captured Louise's attention. "If you promise," she said.

Innes searched every room and corridor in the building. He ran out onto the street, believing he had just missed Hazel, that he would see her slender form moving away from the building. He described Hazel to the nursing staff. Each sister shook her head.

During his dinner break, Innes walked the streets near the

hospital. Logic dictated that he would not find Hazel in his wanderings, but now that he knew she was alive, he couldn't help himself. Reluctantly, he returned to the hospital in the evening to read to Louise as he had promised. He wanted to ask her more questions, but he knew they would upset her.

On the following day, when Innes had two hours to himself, he made his way first to the Camp Hill Hospital and then to the surgical train from Boston. He searched through rooms and cars but saw no one who resembled Hazel. He made inquiries and received no answers. Had Hazel already left the city? Had she gone inland? Or was she simply staying with friends in a part of Halifax not damaged?

Innes made a plan. He would search each quadrant of the city until he had satisfied himself that Hazel was not in Halifax. The task seemed as imperative to him as breathing.

Innes returned to the hospital for his afternoon shift. He hung his overcoat in the cloakroom. Just the day before, Innes had found, buried deep in the pocket of the coat, a receipt for a lighting fixture made out to a M. Jean LeBlanc. Innes imagined it was M. LeBlanc's coat that he wore now. He wondered whose shoes he owned? Whose suit coat?

The need for surgeries did not abate. Lately, these had been second surgeries, the first meant merely to save a life. Innes repaired crude work, some of it his own. He visited his patients, most housed on the second floor. The hospital no longer smelled of ash and death as it had when Innes had arrived on the first day. There were no patients lying on the floor between the cots. On the upper floors, the hospital was keeping patients longer than was necessary, simply because the wounded, like him, had no place to go. Hundreds of children had been orphaned.

Occasionally, there were moments of joy as when family members were reunited. Happy cries, rare enough, caused the staff to look up from their work for the source of the jubilation. Just that morning, a father had found his daughter whom he had thought lost, ecstasy turning to sorrow when the father had to tell the daughter that the mother had died.

Innes thought about his brother, Martin, who was still in France. He imagined all the soldiers who would arrive home on transport ships only to find most of Halifax destroyed. Another brutal irony: the soldiers returned safely, but the families waiting at home had been killed.

Innes, reading a chart on his way to the second floor, noted through a double door a woman standing next to a cot. He stopped short and took a closer look. Innes had, in the past two days, mistaken other women for Hazel, once running ahead and accosting a woman who looked very like Hazel from behind but turned out not to resemble her at all. Such scenes, he reflected at the time, must be happening all over the city.

With the folder under his arm, Innes entered the ward. The woman couldn't see Innes, and he fought the urge to call out. He might disturb her. She was in conversation with a female patient. The patient, sitting up in the bed, had an eye patch on her left eye. The woman who looked like Hazel, in a gray wool dress over which she had on the customary white pinafore, lifted a spoon to the patient's mouth. Innes looked for signs of bandages on the patient's hands and found them. Perhaps the woman had been burned in the blast.

Innes waited, pretending to read the chart. He saw nothing but the name Ferguson. A nursing sister asked him if he needed assistance. He shook his head. Finally, he could wait no longer. He moved toward Hazel and cleared his throat. "Miss Fraser?" he asked.

Hazel turned, spoon in hand. "Mr. Finch," she said, and he could see that she was much surprised.

"I am happy to see you," Innes said with great feeling. "I heard only yesterday from Louise that you were alive."

Hazel looked tired about the eyes, and her hair had not recently been washed. She had a bad bruise on her forehead and healed lacerations on her cheek.

"I was sorry to hear about your father and mother," Innes said.

"Thank you."

"I don't wish to keep you from your task. Perhaps when you are finished, we could have a word?"

"Yes," she said. "Of course."

Innes stood just outside the double doors. He checked his watch, aware that he was late to his rounds. None of his patients would die in the next ten minutes. From time to time, he glanced through the window in the door. Nursing sisters were folding blankets. Hazel had settled herself upon the patient's bed. Something she said made the patient laugh. After a time, Innes watched as Hazel got up from the bed and carried the bowl and spoon to a tray near the nursing station.

Innes waited for her, expectant.

"Innes," Hazel said, as she emerged from the double doors, elating him by using his first name. "It's very good to see you. I've wondered what happened to you."

"And I you. I've worried about you rather a great deal in fact."

"Have you?" she asked. She untied the pinafore and slipped it over her head.

"Where were you when the ship exploded?" Innes asked.

She bit her lips together, repressing a smile. "Actually, in the WC."

Innes laughed, the first laugh he had had since the blast. "Saved your life," he said.

"Apparently, it did." Hazel unrolled the cuffs of her blouse.

Innes minded. He had liked the sight of her wrists. "And you?" she asked. "Where were you?"

"In my room, standing in front of the window. It's a miracle, really, that I wasn't killed."

She studied him. "You seem intact," she said.

"A small wound in the back."

Hazel gazed down the corridor. "I imagine you have had quite a time of it."

"Haven't we all?"

"No, I meant with the surgeries."

"It's been hectic."

"Yes."

Innes shifted the folder from his right hand to his left. "Your sister is healing well."

"Was it you who operated?"

"No. No, I didn't."

A frown appeared on Hazel's brow. "It was awful. She became so upset when I visited, I haven't dared to go back. She was screaming at me."

"A certain amount of hysteria is to be expected," Innes said.

"Yes, of course," Hazel said.

"You didn't know that she was here?" he asked.

"I was told she had perished in the fire with my parents."

And now it was Innes's turn to be surprised. "There was a fire?"

Hazel was silent.

"I'm so sorry," Innes said, imagining the horror of burning to death. "One hopes your parents perished at once from the blast. It's very likely they did."

Hazel's chin began to quiver, and she turned away from him. He could see that she was overcome. He waited.

She took a handkerchief from her sleeve and blew her nose.

When she had tucked the handkerchief away, she turned back to him. "Yesterday morning, my aunt received a message from a friend who had seen Louise here. My sister is very fragile."

"She was fragile before this," Innes said, and Hazel looked at him curiously.

"I shall have to find a place for her," Hazel said.

"I'll help you with that," Innes said, though he did not, at the moment, know of any schools for the blind that had survived in Halifax. Schools would be built, however. That much was inevitable. "It may be that she will be able to leave the hospital in a few days," he added. "Is there a temporary place for her?"

"I am staying with an aunt. Their house was not bothered." Hazel tucked a tendril of hair behind her ear. "Of course, there's room for Louise."

"It will be at first a great burden to care for such a patient."

"Yes, I imagine," Hazel said. "It's a kind of hell out there, isn't it? At least Louise has been spared that."

"She will be spared the sight of it forever."

"I never thought such a blast possible," Hazel said.

"None of us could have imagined this."

"And the irony of all those people at the windows."

"A cruel irony," Innes said, reluctantly checking his watch again. "I must go. I have patients waiting for me. When will you be leaving hospital?"

"I have been asked to stay until six o'clock," she said.

"Will you walk with me then?" he asked. "I cannot go far, since I am to be on duty this evening. But I should have at least a half hour."

She hesitated. "Yes," she said finally. "I will walk with you."

Innes was at the front door of the hospital just before six o'clock. He had arranged a thirty-minute dinner break. He waited impatiently, aware that each moment that passed was one he would not have with Hazel.

She came through the double doors wearing an oddly festive blue velvet and fur-trimmed coat with large silver buttons on a diagonal. She had on a black hat with a brim and a short veil. Innes imagined that the coat and hat were borrowed. He hoped they were from the living. Hazel drew on her gloves as she approached him.

Without a word, Innes opened the door for her, and they stepped out into the evening. An effort to remove the debris from the streets immediately surrounding the hospital had largely been successful. Horses and buggies passed by. There was still very little fuel for automobiles. Innes was impressed, as he had been every night he had taken his walks, by how quiet the city was. There were few motors, very little traffic in the harbor. Voices carried for long distances.

"Do you mind where we walk?" he asked.

"Not at all," she said. "I am glad for the fresh air."

"How far is it to your aunt's house?" he asked.

"About . . . maybe five miles from here?"

"How will you get home?" Innes asked, his words making blunt puffs in the icy air.

"My uncle will fetch me. He has a carriage. How about you?"

Innes laughed and pointed back toward the hospital. "My humble abode."

"You live at hospital?" she asked, surprised.

"Many of us do. There are quarters. We are well fed." He left unsaid the fact that he had nowhere else to go.

"I convinced myself that you had not died," Hazel said. "I thought perhaps you had gone back to your family."

Innes felt again a sense of elation. Hazel had thought about him. She had hoped he had not died. "There is so much work to do here," he said. "My place is here. I have cabled my family. They do not expect me."

"Will you make Halifax your home then?" she asked, skirting a pile of slush.

"If Halifax should ever again become a home for anyone."

"I've heard they will erect housing. My uncle is with the council."

"There are thousands homeless."

"One would do well to be a carpenter just now," she said.

Innes laughed, and they turned a corner.

"Did you think it was the Germans?" she asked.

"I did for a moment. Until I got outside and saw the devastation. No bomb could have produced that."

"You were not in the wreckage of the house?" she asked.

"I think I landed in a textile factory."

Hazel thought a moment. "The Looms. You'd have landed there. It was behind our street and one building over. Not a textile factory. More of a crafts organization."

"Would you like to stop for something to eat?" Innes asked.

Hazel shook her head. "I will have a meal waiting for me at my aunt's house. Really, I am just enjoying the fresh air."

The air smelled clean for the first time in days. The scent of death seemed to have vanished.

Hazel stopped short and faced Innes. "My sister," Hazel said. "I don't see how I can visit her again in the near future."

"It would seem unwise at the moment," Innes said, surprised by the abruptness of Hazel's pronouncement. "I do believe that she will calm down. I have seen many other patients accidentally blinded. Few can maintain the fever pitch of terror that seems to grip her now."

Hazel was standing so close to Innes that he could feel her breath.

"I wish to go away," she said. "I wish to leave all this."

Innes wasn't sure of her meaning. "Leave Halifax?" he asked.

"Yes," she said. "I don't want to be here. It's heartless, I know, when so many have suffered. When my sister is suffering."

"But where would you go?" Innes asked, aware of a pressure building in his chest.

Hazel tore off her hat. She shook her head, and her hair fell loose. "Perhaps to America," she said. "I don't know. When the war is over, I could go to Europe. I know only that I can't tolerate this city. I felt this way before the blast."

"Yes, I sensed it," Innes said.

"And now there's nothing for me here."

Innes was stung by the remark. "You don't feel the need to be near your sister?" he asked.

"Of course, I shall take care of her," Hazel said. "There is money. And I will visit her — when she will have me. But, no, I don't feel the need to be near her every minute. I think both of us would do better to be apart for a while."

Innes was not surprised by Hazel's admission. Nor even the heartlessness of it.

"But what about your fiancé?" he asked. "Will he not shortly return from France?"

Hazel played with the hat in her hands. "I have written to him," she said.

"You have written to him," Innes repeated, not at all sure what was meant by the statement.

"I won't marry him." She glanced up at Innes. "A calamity, a catastrophe — it changes everything, doesn't it? It makes you aware that you cannot be indifferent toward your life. You cannot simply give away your life. I didn't want to marry before the blast. This only makes it easier."

"Not for him, I should think," Innes said.

"He must remain in Halifax when he returns. All of his companies are here."

"Some destroyed, I imagine."

"Yes. But all the more reason. They will have to be rebuilt."

"Hazel," Innes said, and her eyes flickered away from him. "It would make me sad to see you go."

"You don't know me," she said.

"I don't think you believe that," Innes said, aware that he had to choose his words carefully. An unwelcome urgency had made it necessary.

"I flirted with you that night," she said. "And I'm sorry. I had no right to do that."

"But you must have felt something," Innes said.

"I imagined," Hazel said simply.

"Would you not then give your imagination free rein?" he asked. "Hazel. Look at me."

Hazel turned her face to him. "I have to leave this city," she said evenly.

If she would leave her sister, surely she would leave a man she hardly knew.

"We only had an evening," Hazel said. "Not really even that. What can be learned in an evening?"

"I think time is of little consequence in and of itself," Innes said and heard the vaguely pedantic note in his voice. "In an instant, an entire city was leveled. Who'd have thought that possible? Might not love be possible in an instant as well?"

Innes was glad for the darkness. His face was hot, his words unpracticed. Surely, he had not intended to use the word "love" so soon. There had been no rehearsal in his life for this moment of reckoning. He had meant only to walk with Hazel, to secure another date. Had he known that his future hung in the balance, he might have practiced his words before they'd met at the door.

"You cannot believe that you love me," Hazel said. "It's simply not possible."

"You can't speak for me," he said.

"No, of course not," Hazel said. "I'm sorry. You've been only kind."

"'Kind' is a cruel word at this moment."

"Yes," she said. "I imagine it is."

Innes knew that he had lost. Unprepared, the battle thrust upon him without warning, he was defeated before the contest had begun. That Hazel had imagined them together in some way, had even debated it within herself, might have given Innes some joy had hope not been snatched away so quickly.

"I shall miss you," he said simply. "I shall miss the possibility of you."

"One has many possibilities," Hazel said. She rose up on her toes and kissed him on the mouth. The kiss, brief and papery, suggested an entire universe he would never know. "I must go," she said, putting on her hat as if the kiss were but one more fact of her long and busy day. "I must be in my regular spot when my uncle picks me up. It would be inconvenient for him to have to leave the carriage and go inside to find me."

"Hazel," Innes said. "Please."

Hazel shook her head. She put her gloved fingers to her eyes, as if to blot out the sight of him. "This is hard," she said.

Innes reached for her shoulder, but already she had turned away. She ran back the way they had come. Innes watched until Hazel was swallowed into the dark. He made a sound that was part anguish, part frustration. His voice, he knew, would carry for quite a distance.

Innes returned to the hospital for the evening shift. He had, of course, missed the opportunity of a meal. An exhaustion he had kept at bay overwhelmed him now, and he performed his duties as if bludgeoned. Another physician asked him if he was feeling poorly. Innes answered that he was tired, but so was everyone else. The colleague agreed, nodding his head.

Innes worked until he was dismissed. Despite his fatigue, he didn't head for his sleeping quarters, however, but rather to the third floor. It was, he knew, an attempt to detain Hazel a moment longer. In seeing Louise, he might see the sister. His hands in his pockets, he shouldered his way through the double doors. He stopped on the other side.

In a corner, by a lantern, Louise was sitting in her wheelchair. Innes wondered why she was not in bed. He meant not to announce himself, merely to watch her sleep. More surprising was the utter repose of her posture. She was sitting erect in the chair, face forward, as if she could see. The features that were visible were preternaturally calm. He wondered if Louise had been given opiates and, if so, why. He took a few steps forward, moving stealthily so that she wouldn't hear him. When he was twenty feet away from her, he saw, with some astonishment, that she was crying. She was very calm, but she was crying.

Innes remembered the small white breasts, the taut stomach. He thought about his mother, who had been blind and who had often needed him.

He took another step forward and bumped into a metal tray on wheels. The sound rattled through the ward, and Louise turned in his direction.

Harrison was first down to the dining room, having been unable to sleep despite the late hour he'd gone to bed. He picked up a *New York Times* on a low table and was led to a seat by the window. The view beyond the glass revealed a vastly different geography from the day before: the blue of the mountains in the distance had been replaced by the whiteout of a thick snowstorm, considerably heavier than when Harrison had left Nora just a few hours ago. The roads would not be good, he thought, and he wondered if Bridget's relatives, who were scheduled to arrive today, would be able to make it to the ceremony. Harrison hadn't seen a weather forecast. Perhaps the snow was slated to end soon.

Harrison needed coffee and a large breakfast. What had been an incipient headache had now settled into his frontal lobes. He glanced at the headline: TALIBAN ABANDON LAST STRONGHOLD: OMAR IS NOT FOUND. He turned to the page where the *Times* was still running its "Portraits of Grief" section, the short bios of those lost in the World Trade Center. He read about a man who had graduated from the Wharton School of the University of Pennsylvania and had developed a proprietary mathematical model for yield curve analysis. He read about another man who had worked evenings at Spazzio's restaurant on Columbus Avenue and had recently bought a house in Union City, New Jersey. Harrison tried, as he did from time to time, to imagine the reality of being trapped in the building, perhaps knowing one was going to die. The flying glass and blocked passageways. The advancing flames and the smothering smoke. The bodies piled in window frames and the cell phone calls to relatives — first to ask for help and then to say good-bye. The fear would have been unendurable. And these images led Harrison to thoughts of Jerry last night at dinner with his odd insistence that if one hadn't been in the vicinity of the disaster one had little right to speak of it. In some small way, Harrison agreed with him. It would have been nightmarish to watch people falling from the towers, and then later to have to breathe in the ashes of the catastrophe. One literally had been made to take it in, absorb it, a unique sort of ownership. If it hadn't been Jerry who'd been arguing the point, Harrison might have jumped in with his support, but Jerry's very tone of voice — his presence even — made Harrison grit his teeth. He didn't like the man, though he had liked the boy well enough. Jerry had been something of a braggart at Kidd as well, but then it had seemed funny rather than annoying. And, of course, the guy could pitch.

A waitress, not Judy, informed Harrison that on Saturday mornings, there was a buffet. She pointed in its direction. Harrison could order à la carte if he chose, but she confided that the spread was really pretty good. She poured him a cup of coffee that tasted watery compared to the rich espresso in the library. After breakfast, Harrison decided, he would wander in there and have a second cup and read the paper. He'd never really had much success trying to deal with a newspaper at a breakfast table not his own — no room to spread out.

Harrison headed for the buffet. He chose baked eggs, well-done bacon, a dish of strawberries (he couldn't help but look for a fly), and a carrot muffin. If this didn't cure his headache, nothing would. As he was returning to his table, he spotted Bill at the entrance.

"Bill," Harrison called out in that louder-than-normal voice men reserve for addressing each other.

"Harrison," Bill said. He advanced toward Harrison and examined his plate. "Looks good, looks good."

Harrison gestured with his bowl to the table by the window. "I'm over there," he said.

"Join you in a minute. Gotta get my daily mg's of cholesterol."

Harrison set his plate and bowl on the table. He folded up the newspaper and slid it into the space between his chair and the wall. In a few minutes, Bill, in plaid shirt and gray sweater-vest, took the seat across from Harrison. Harrison noted a slight paunch under the vest, the thinning steely colored hair (iron filings on a balding pate), more evident in the morning light than at the cocktail party. Bill had chosen berries only.

"So where's the cholesterol?" Harrison asked.

"Trying to lose fifteen."

"On your wedding day?"

"Have to fit into the tux."

"Little late for that."

"I'm saving myself for the dinner," Bill said. "You should see the menu. And the wines." Bill put his hand to his forehead in disbelief. "I'm glad I didn't overdo it last night. All I'd need today would be a hangover."

"That's all right," Harrison said as he spooned the last bit of baked eggs from the white ramekin, "I've got one big enough for the both of us. How's Bridget?"

"Great." Bill paused. "Great," he repeated. "She's sleeping now. The boys won't be up until noon, unless I wake them." Bill glanced out the window. "Doesn't look as though we'll be having a game today."

"Not likely."

"The boys were looking forward to it. They've been listening to me rave about our old team for weeks. I'm afraid you and Jerry and Rob have taken on the status of icons."

Harrison laughed.

"I'm serious. You'll have to sign a couple of the balls I brought for Matt and Brian."

"Sure," Harrison said. "I'll sign 'Nomar.'"

"Bridget's doing amazingly well," Bill said, spearing a strawberry. "They say the worse the chemo, the better the result. It was brutal watching her go through it, though. I kept wishing it was me instead."

Harrison sat back in his chair. "Billy Ricci. I honestly think that might be the definition of true love."

"Years from now, people will look back upon chemotherapy as barbaric, inhumane, a legalized form of torture. At best, as misguided medicine."

"Leeches," Harrison said.

"Worse. But each day, I see more and more of her strength returning."

"That's great."

"Yeah, she's fine." Bill paused. "Really fine."

And Harrison heard in the second repetition a chink in the bravado, a man reminding himself to be optimistic. Bill poured half a pitcher of heavy cream over the berries and sprinkled them with sugar.

"Some diet," Harrison said as he watched Bill tuck into the berries.

"I was worried you'd be upset about Jill and Melissa."

"One always thinks about the kids first. I can't say I was all that fond of Jill."

Bill hitched himself forward in his chair. "You're not the first person to tell me that. It's a little disconcerting to find out after the fact that no one liked the woman you were married to."

"It's not that so much," Harrison said. "I just didn't think the two of you were a good fit." Harrison watched another couple take a table not far from theirs. Both the man and the woman appeared to be slightly fogged, and Harrison guessed that they, too, might have had too much to drink the night before. Perhaps they belonged to the other wedding party.

Bill took a long sip of coffee. "How's Evelyn?"

Harrison had the sense that Bill's question was more polite than curious. "Evelyn's very well," Harrison said. "She has a huge case coming up. Otherwise, she'd be here."

"What about?"

"The case? Greed and human frailty."

Bill smiled. "Thanks for making the trip down for the wedding."

"Actually, I think the direction is *over*, but I'm glad to be here."

"I always think of Canada as up. This whole thing is a little weird, isn't it? Jerry? Agnes? Rob?"

"Very weird," Harrison said. "There's some trick of time and memory at work here that I haven't quite figured out yet."

"And Nora."

"And Nora," Harrison said.

"She's been great with Bridget. God, B's been through some tough times, and not just the cancer. With her ex-husband leaving her and now trying to raise a fifteen-year-old. Matt's a good kid, but, you know, he's fifteen."

Harrison nodded.

"I feel so lucky," Bill said.

Harrison looked up from his muffin. He pondered the bad luck of marrying a woman with advanced cancer.

"Finding Bridget again," Bill explained. "I very nearly didn't go to that reunion. I can't imagine life now if I hadn't gone."

"The things that don't happen to us that we'll never know didn't happen to us," Harrison said.

"The nonstories."

"The extra minute to find the briefcase that makes you late to the spot where a tractor trailer mauled another car instead of yours." Harrison took a bite of buttery muffin and thought about his next cholesterol test.

"The woman you didn't meet because she couldn't get a taxi to the party you had to leave early from," Bill added. "All of life is a series of nonstories if you look at it that way."

"We just don't know what they are," Harrison said.

Bill scraped the sweet cream from the sides of his bowl. "Melissa won't be at the wedding."

"So I heard," Harrison said.

"Why does everything have to be so complicated?" Bill asked. "When I'm with Bridget, I have no doubt I did the right thing. I found Bridget again, and we're together. Period. It feels as right as" — Bill looked around the room as if an object there might prompt an appropriate simile — "as, I don't know . . . rain." He wiped his mouth with his napkin. "But then I look at Melissa, and I feel sick. How does a grown man do this to his kids?"

"Last I looked, Melissa was nearly a grown woman."

"You know what I mean."

"You just have to go with your gut," Harrison said, not at all sure he actually believed this.

"Been doing that for quite a while," Bill said, gazing down at his paunch.

"How's the software business?" Harrison asked.

"We're doing some subcontracting for a company in Boston to provide facial recognition software for places like Logan."

"Hope the ACLU doesn't stop you in your tracks," Harrison said.

"I think the climate has changed. How's your business?"

"Not great. Someone said — I forget who — that it was as if God or Alan Greenspan had pushed the pause button."

"What happens in New York affects what happens in Toronto."

"Absolutely," Harrison said. He had a question for Bill but wasn't sure it should be asked. "You and Jerry Leyden must have stayed friends," he said tentatively. "I was a little surprised to see him here."

"He gives a lot of money to a charity I head up in Boston," Bill said.

At the beach house, Harrison suddenly remembered, Jerry had offered to spring for pizzas for everyone.

"What's with you two, anyway?" Bill asked.

"Not sure," Harrison said. "Nothing, really."

Bill stood. "Going to get some more strawberries."

Harrison watched Bill walk to the buffet. He thought about the notion of nonstories. What if he hadn't signed up for eighteenth-century French poetry and hadn't arrived late to class that morning in October and hadn't sat in the last chair in the last row next to a pretty blonde in a white turtleneck? He would not have met Evelyn. Might he, the next night, or a week later, have met someone else? And what would that person have looked like? Might Harrison have daughters now instead of sons? Or would he, in a kind of wild enterprise, have gone looking for Nora, despite the fact that she was already married? Harrison was still in college when he heard that she and Carl Laski were together. He remembered his tremendous surprise and then his sharp dismay. It was as though a moat had suddenly been built around Nora. One didn't compete with the likes of Carl Laski. Though Harrison had not spoken to Nora since that night at the beach house, she was always there, in his thoughts, and he sometimes imagined himself getting in his car and driving to New York to see her. In the early years, after Harrison had heard that Nora had married Laski, he'd wondered what Nora's life was like. The associated glamour. The cachet of being married to someone famous. Then Harrison found himself in the publishing business and heard the gossip: Laski's misanthropic exile, the stories about the drinking. It seemed to him that Nora had entered a foreign country to which Harrison did not have a passport, that she spoke a foreign language.

Bill returned to the table without the strawberries. "Changed my mind," he said. "Think I better go see how Bridget's doing. Order her room service. Pamper the bride-to-be."

"That's your job," Harrison said.

Harrison, paper tucked under his arm, found the library empty, the espresso machine ready to go. He pressed what he thought was the right button and received a half cup of espresso, the operation immensely satisfying. He settled himself on the sofa on which he'd sat yesterday when he'd had coffee with Nora. When he looked up through the bank of windows, he saw that the snow had almost stopped. A weak sun glowed through a layer of nearly translucent cloud.

For a moment, coffee cup in hand, Harrison merely sat, not willing yet to open the newspaper. He watched the light come up slowly through the thinning cloud, causing the snow-laden bushes and trees to begin to sparkle. In less time than it took to finish his coffee, the view was almost too bright to look at. Harrison briefly closed his eyes.

Like a dark silhouette against a bright background — photographic negatives — Harrison saw Nora as she'd been that spring at Kidd, and, after the summer, during their senior year: a girl in slim jeans and dangling earrings at the sidelines of a game; a young woman with her hair spread all along her back as she hunched over a book in the library, unaware that Harrison was standing behind her; Stephen's girlfriend, lolling on Stephen's bed in the dorm while the three of them — Harrison, Nora, and Stephen — listened to

Lynyrd Skynyrd and Eddie Kendricks. After Harrison's realization that Nora and Stephen were a couple, Nora seemed to be everywhere Stephen was, and as a result, the three of them had become a kind of item. Stephen seemed not to mind Harrison's presence. In fact, his roommate appeared to encourage it. Harrison was an audience, and Stephen, Harrison knew, loved an audience.

By senior year, Stephen had become an icon on campus, albeit a partly tongue-in-cheek one. At the games, an impromptu cheering section would coalesce, yelling, *Steev-en! Steev-en!* each time the shortstop came up to the plate. The cheering was an end unto itself, as were many of the student endeavors that year, Harrison remembered, entirely ironic, a kind of double irony having the effect of actually celebrating Kidd's golden boy. From Harrison's position at second base, he had an opportunity to cast quick glances in Nora's direction whenever the pitcher was warming up. She didn't usually join in the cheering, but sometimes Harrison caught a glimpse of her funny half smile. Once, when Harrison turned a double play, the crowd cheered *Harri-son! Harri-son!* — a triple irony if ever there was one.

Occasionally, when Stephen was at class, or, more likely, sleeping, Harrison found himself alone with Nora. Harrison remembered a day in early May when the two of them came across each other on a footpath.

"Oh, hi," Harrison said. "You off to practice?"

It was a warm day. Nora had on shorts and a T-shirt in anticipation of tennis practice. Harrison was wearing long pants and a long-sleeved shirt as required by Coach D. They would be practicing sliding that day.

"I am," Nora said. "But. Um . . ." She looked out to sea.

"But what?" Harrison asked.

"Can . . . can I talk to you about something?"

Harrison didn't have to be asked twice. "Of course," he said.

Nora dropped her backpack and sports bag to the ground. Harrison did the same. He followed her to a large flat rock that overlooked a cove. They sat.

"Um. Stephen's drinking," Nora said at once.

"I know," Harrison answered, though he was surprised by the abruptness of Nora's pronouncement.

"A lot."

"Yeah, I guess it's pretty bad," Harrison said, having seen what he thought was the absolute worst of it a few nights before: Stephen hugging the toilet bowl. His roommate had wanted an audience for that, too, but Harrison, after one glance, had drawn the line.

"Where does he get it?" Nora asked.

"The booze? Frankie Forbes," Harrison said, referring to a local guy in his early twenties who worked construction in the area. Forbes bought the booze and sold it Thursday afternoons off the back of his truck to students. Cash only. No IDs required.

"You drink," Nora said. "I drink once in a while. It's not the same."

"No."

"Why? Why is that?" Nora hugged her knees. Her legs, from her shorts to her tennis socks, were bare. Harrison remembered his desire to run his hand along her calf.

"I don't know," Harrison said. "Stephen's engine runs at a different speed than mine." Harrison, who was mildly obsessed with the notion of buying a '69 Camaro he'd seen advertised in the local paper, was thinking in automotive metaphors that spring. If he could get his mother to send him the money that his plane ticket home would have cost, and he added that to the cash he'd saved working Sundays at the supermarket in town, he could almost swing the deal and drive home to Illinois for the summer.

Nora swept her hair off her neck and tied it in a knot at the back of her head. "I . . . I don't know, Harrison. Do you think we should get him some help?"

"We all need help," Harrison said.

"I'm serious. I'm worried about him. Last night. Last night, he was so drunk I honestly don't think he even knew I was there."

"Where were you?"

"On the beach."

Harrison didn't want to think about Stephen and Nora on the beach. He forced himself not to glance at the inside of Nora's thigh, perfectly visible to him. "I don't know," Harrison said. "I don't think he'd listen. I'm just amazed he hasn't gotten caught more often than he has. Truthfully, I can't believe he's still in school."

"He's doing better with his grades."

"You're helping him with that."

"Yes."

"Well, I guess it's good you're doing that, because otherwise he's going to blow his scholarship to Stanford," Harrison said. Stephen, whose grades were only average, had been recruited by the school's baseball coach. No one else at Kidd had gotten into Stanford. Harrison would go to Northeastern, Nora to New York University.

"He'll drown at Stanford," Harrison said.

(Harrison, with a heart-stopping pause in the library, checked himself. Had he really used the word "drown"?)

Nora rolled her neck in a lazy, sensuous way.

"Hey, listen," Harrison said, putting his hand on Nora's shoulder, fulfilling a monthslong ache simply to touch her. "If you want to help Stephen, I'm with you."

Nora shrieked, and Harrison let go of her shoulder as if his fingers had been singed. Nora grabbed the sides of her waist where Stephen had goosed her. It had not been a gentle goosing. The pokes, Harrison thought, had been more like jabs. Stephen lifted Nora to her feet and wrapped his arms around her. He kissed Nora on her neck, a long and demonstrably possessive kiss, something Stephen seldom did in front of Harrison. Harrison had, in fact, appreciated the couple's previous restraint in his presence. Their threesome would have been impossible without it.

"So, Branch, what are you going to help Nora out with?" Stephen asked.

Nora pulled slightly away from Stephen.

"We'll be late for practice," Harrison said, checking his watch. He saw Stephen's sports bag twenty feet behind the rock on which Harrison and Nora had been sitting. Had Stephen intended to sneak up on them?

"So, hey," Stephen said with a winning smile that revealed perfectly white teeth, "party Friday!" He smacked his fist into the palm of his other hand. "Binder's beach house."

"Stephen," Nora said quietly.

"We have a game early Saturday," Harrison pointed out.

"Actually," Nora said to Stephen, "if you want to know the truth." She paused. "We were talking about your drinking."

"What?"

Stephen put his hands in the pockets of his pants and stood immobile for a long moment.

"My drinking?" he asked finally. "Really? What about it?"

"We're worried about you," Nora said.

Stephen nodded, as if slowly taking in the new information. "You and Harrison are worried about me." Harrison watched as Stephen's bewilderment turned to something harder. "Well, nice to know my friends are looking out for me," he said. "Um, Harrison? Did you mention to Nora that you were plastered Saturday night?"

"That's different, Stephen," Nora said.

"Oh, really? Cause Harrison couldn't find the toilet and took a piss against Hodgkins, which, as all present know, is the freshman girls' dorm."

This was a fact, one Harrison had hoped to forget.

"Maybe the both of you," Nora said. "Maybe both of you should get some help."

"It's not like we're doing drugs," Stephen said, and Harrison heard, for the first time since Stephen had snuck up on them, a thickness in Stephen's voice. Had he been drinking already?

Harrison walked to the place where he'd dropped his backpack and sports bag and hoisted them over his shoulder.

"So, Harrison, you in for Friday?" Stephen called after him. "Forbes needs five bucks from each of us by Thursday."

And Harrison had felt then an inexplicable kind of helplessness, a desire not to be left out of a party at which Stephen and Nora would be present.

"Sure," Harrison had said, starting off in the direction of the baseball diamond. "Count me in."

"I hear one can get a wicked cup of coffee in here," Rob said from the doorway of the library.

Harrison, startled from his reverie, glanced up. "The best," he said.

"You were a hundred miles away," Rob said.

"Four hundred. You have breakfast?"

"Don't do breakfast. Never did."

"That's how you stay so trim," Harrison said, admiring the long line of Rob's cashmere sweater and jeans.

"Nerves," Rob said, walking further into the room. He appeared fresh from the shower, his hair still wet.

"You get nervous before a concert?" Harrison asked.

"Every time." Rob paused in front of the espresso machine and studied it. "How do you work this thing?"

"It's incredibly difficult," Harrison said, standing. "I'll have to do it for you."

Harrison pressed a button and shrugged. Rob smiled. "Don't know if I can master that," he said.

"Give it a few days."

Rob took a seat across from Harrison and glanced around the room. "Beautiful, isn't it?"

"Very."

"I didn't know Nora had it in her."

"I think we're all learning a great deal about one another this weekend," Harrison offered.

Rob nodded. "You, for example. I didn't know until two weeks ago that you were in publishing."

Should Harrison reply with a comment about his not knowing that Rob was gay? Did Rob want that conversation? Harrison couldn't tell. "I like your friend Josh," Harrison said instead.

"He's practicing."

"He brought his cello with him?"

"Virtual practicing. He sits in a chair and closes his eyes and puts his fingers on imaginary strings and visualizes the playing."

"Really," Harrison said. He thought of Beethoven composing symphonies he couldn't hear.

Rob crossed his legs, and Harrison noted the long trouser socks, the custom-made shoes. That Rob had understated elegance was a given. What interested Harrison was that Rob seemed a man perfectly of his era. The snowy white shirt under the V-neck sweater. The Movado watch. The trim cut of the hair, not drawing attention to itself, yet somehow suggesting with a few spikes in the front an edgier look than most. Harrison made a mental note to catch a concert if Rob should come to Toronto.

"I admire both of you," Harrison said. "I've never had an ear for music."

"I remember that about you."

Harrison laughed.

"Stephen could sing, though," Rob said. "Remember the night he got up and did that Neil Young thing?"

"Wow, I haven't thought about that in years," Harrison said.

"Actually I was jealous of you," Rob said. "I had a wicked crush on Stephen."

Harrison checked his surprise. "Didn't everyone?" he asked casually.

"One day, I saw him running along the beach," Rob said. "I was standing on the cliff near Rowan House, and I could see Stephen approaching from a distance. He had a beautiful stride, stepping in and out of the water with such ease. I always thought of him as a superbly aligned animal. Like a cheetah, maybe. He seemed oblivious to everything but the moment. I envied that."

Harrison said nothing.

"I'm sorry," Rob said. "This must be hard for you. Being here with all of us must constantly remind you of him."

"A little."

"If we'd only known then what we know now," Rob said. "That he was the one guy among us who should never have taken a drink. He used to say that one beer was too many, but twelve wasn't enough."

"Did he?" Harrison asked. "He once told me that having one beer and quitting made him feel lousy."

"You can't outrun that fate."

"No, I guess not."

"But, my God, he was the funniest guy. Remember the time Mitchell got called out of class, and Stephen — I swear he didn't miss a beat — stood up front and pretended to be Mitchell and finished the class? He nailed the guy, just nailed him. That little hitch in Mitchell's walk? The Boston accent? He even did his laugh. It was brilliant."

"I'd forgotten that," Harrison said, smiling at the memory.

"He was something," Rob said.

"He was something," Harrison said.

There was a long silence in the room.

"This is none of my business," Harrison said, "but did you know at Kidd?"

"That I was gay?"

Harrison nodded and hoped he hadn't overstepped his bounds. Did every gay man anticipate and loathe this question?

"Of course," Rob answered.

"You dated . . ."

"Amy Shulkind. Only because Bridget set us up. She was always doing that. Matchmaking." Rob took a sip of coffee. "In the beginning you hope it isn't so," he added. "I don't know anyone who's glad of it as a boy." He set his cup on the coffee table and glanced at a copy of *The New Yorker*. "So what about you, Branch? When did it all happen for you?"

"Sorry?"

"Find yourself. When did you know who you were?" Rob opened the magazine, looked at a cartoon.

"That's a tough one," Harrison said. "Not sure I'm there yet."

"Still an existentialist at heart?" Rob asked, looking up. "That's the one good thing about being gay. It tends to clarify everything in a hurry. Well, not the only good thing."

"Hope not," Harrison said.

"You've got a family," Rob said, closing the magazine.

"I do. And I suppose it's not really fair of me to pretend I don't know where I'm at. I have tremendous clarity about my boys."

"The one bad thing about being gay," Rob said, leaning back and crossing his arms over his chest.

"Not the only bad thing," Harrison echoed lightly.

"No."

"I imagine it's the music that defines you now," Harrison added, wishing very much that he had listened to one of Rob's CDs before coming here.

"That . . . and Josh . . . and, I don't know . . ." He smiled. "The Red Sox."

"You always were a masochistic son of a bitch."

"You wait."

"Wait what? Another seventy, eighty years?"

"The Cubs aren't exactly red-hot."

"They ran out of gas," Harrison said. "Sammy's monster year and Leiber's gutsy performance just weren't enough."

"Hey," a voice called from the doorway. Bill stood in a bright blue parka and hiking boots.

"Billy," Rob said. "What's up?"

"We're on for a game after all."

Rob glanced out the window. "In this?"

"Snow-ball," Bill said, holding up a Wiffle ball and yellow plastic bat. "Jerry's idea. He said he once played snow-golf in Aspen, took him forty-five minutes to finish the first hole."

"Aspen," Harrison said.

"Look," Bill pleaded, "if I have to sit around all day waiting for this wedding, I'll go nuts."

"Okay, I'm in," Rob said.

"You're umping," Bill said, pointing. "We've got the bases covered, as they say. Nora had some Frisbees we can use. Problem is," he added, holding up the plastic ball, "this is white."

Harrison thought a minute. "I might have an idea," he said.

"We're out front when you're ready."

Harrison searched for the boy he'd seen the day before and found him in the dining room wearing a North Face fleece. He

219

apologized to the parents for interrupting their breakfast and asked the boy if he still had the Magic Markers he'd been using the day before at the table. Harrison explained the game of snow-ball and invited the boy and the father to join them. As an afterthought, he invited the wife as well. She sighed and said a few minutes alone in the library would be heaven.

When Harrison returned to the hallway in his jacket and sneakers, the boy was already waiting for him with the box of markers. His father, he said, would follow in a minute. Harrison selected neon green. The boy seemed struck dumb with the gravity of being asked to play ball with grown men, and Harrison tried to draw him out — *Are you having a good time here? Have you ever played Little League? Cool jacket . . . did you get that yesterday?* — to little avail.

The two headed out the door and found Bill on a level bit of snow-covered lawn near the parking lot. Harrison brandished the marker, and Bill gave him the thumbs-up. Harrison colored the ball as best he could, getting nearly as much ink on his fingers as he did on the ball. He wondered idly if it would come off in time for the wedding.

"Okay, let's see," Bill said when everyone was assembled. "Harrison, you and Jerry and . . . what's your name?" he asked the boy.

"Michael," the boy said.

"Hi, Michael, I'm Bill." Bill walked toward the boy's father and held out his hand.

"Peter," the father said, shaking it.

"Okay, great," Bill said, turning to the group. "Peter, Michael, Harrison, and Jerry on one team. Me, Agnes, Matt, and Brian will be the other. Nora, you playing?"

Nora, her coat over her shoulders, looked down at them from the porch. "I'll watch for a minute," she said.

"Julie?"

Julie, in furs, leaned against the porch railing. She shook her head.

The brilliant sun caused a glare from the snow that was tough on the eyes. Everyone but the boy had on sunglasses.

Agnes was up first for her team. Jerry, in his sleek black jacket, went into his windup as if he were pitching to Ichiro Suzuki. The green neon ball whipped through the air and left its traces every- where — on Jerry's fingers, on the bat, in little trails in the snow, like rabbit tracks. After several misses, Agnes hit a pop-up.

"High fly ball to center," Rob intoned, commentating as well as umping. "Branch making his way back to the warning track. Looks as if he's lost it in the sun. No, he's got it. Nice over-the-shoulder catch for Harrison Branch. One out. Matt Rodgers at the plate. Billy Ricci in the on-deck circle. Here's Leyden with the windup. Oooh, nice little sinker just cutting the corner. Rodgers whiffs, swinging for the outlets. Strike one."

Standing in what passed for the outfield and catching the green neon Wiffle ball produced in Harrison a sharp memory of street play as a kid. Players gathering at random, temporarily leaving and entering the game as their mothers called them in for supper and then sent them out again. He could see the vacant lot beside the candy store, the bases scored into the dirt with sticks, the wild swings, the sprints to the bases, the squabbles over close plays. The memory passed through Harrison like a whiff of pure air tinged with the scent of mown grass and rich soil.

"Ricci, who had a nice season last year with the Sox, makes his way to the plate," Rob said with the clipped patter of a sports an- nouncer. "Jerry Leyden's looking for the sign. Good stop by Michael in the snow. Ball one."

Nora appeared and disappeared. Julie simply disappeared. Har- rison, feeling absurdly proud of himself, hit a long fly ball none of the fielders could reach, resulting in a home run. The score grew ridiculously high. Bill thought it was 18–11. Harrison argued that it was 17–13. Rob admitted he wasn't keeping track, and both teams booed the ump. When Harrison turned around, he saw that the boy, Michael, had taken off with first base, using it as a sled to coast down the hill. The kid, legs in the air, got a good ride.

"Not a bad idea," Harrison said.

Sleds and saucers were produced from a storage shed under the porch, and Harrison thought of Nora's comment about men who hadn't been on sleds in years showing off to their wives and kids. He folded his legs into a saucer and took a spin down the hill. The snow was slippery, giving him a slick ride. Why was the pure play of childhood such a highly prized memory? Harrison wondered.

He tumbled from the saucer, narrowly missing a tree. He caught his breath, took hold of the rope, and lifted the lightweight aluminum disk up the hill. He jumped to one side as Bill careened past him, clearly out of control. Agnes, following close behind him, yelled at Harrison to get out of the way.

"You got a good run," Rob said when Harrison had reached the top of the slope.

"Here, take off your coat, give it a whirl. You can use my jacket."

"Can't," Rob said.

Harrison remembered the fingers. "You mind?"

"Sometimes."

Harrison glanced down the hill. Matt and Brian had improvised a two-foot jump. Bill, on a saucer, tried it, getting air and coming down hard on the other side.

"We'll have a groom on crutches," Rob said and turned toward the inn. "I better go get Josh before he strains his virtual fingers," he called over his shoulder.

Harrison heard Bill laughing from down below. He watched as

Agnes climbed up the hill, short of breath at the top. "And I thought I was in shape," she said to Harrison.

Harrison contemplated the jump.

"Go for it," Agnes said.

"You think?"

"You're only young once."

"But I need to be middle-aged for quite a while."

He hopped on the saucer, dug his hands into the snow to get some speed, and saw the jump coming. It looked considerably taller from ground level than it had from the top of the hill.

Harrison sailed up and over, getting air, tumbling as he came down. For a minute, he lay on the snow, the wind knocked out of him. He stared at the sky and felt again the bliss of childish activities, a feeling akin to the joy he experienced when he fielded grounders from his boys or dared to get on the ice with them. Bill, heading up the hill with his sled, said, "Beautiful, Branch. Just beautiful."

Harrison rolled over, snow down the front of his jacket and packed inside his sneakers. He got up onto his knees and looked around. His saucer was halfway down the hill. His feet nearly numb, he fetched the saucer and made his way to the top.

"Quite a spill," Nora said when Harrison had reached the summit. She had her coat wrapped over her shoulders, holding it closed with her gloved hands. Her sunglasses hid her eyes. "The game looked like fun," she added.

"You sound wistful," Harrison said.

"Every once in a while, I wish I was just a guest."

"Seriously?"

"Seriously."

Harrison looked down the hill. "Someone's going to hit that tree there," he said.

"I know. I've . . . I've thought about removing it, but it's such a beautiful tree. Especially in the fall."

"What kind is it?" Harrison asked.

"Sugar maple."

The lone tree at the bottom of the hill triggered a recollection. *"Ethan Frome,"* Harrison said aloud, referring to the novel in which a man and his would-be lover try to commit suicide by sledding into a tree. "That was supposed to take place somewhere around here, no?"

"Starkfield."

"Not a real town."

"No."

Harrison had a further recollection. "In the early stage of your husband's career," he said, "he repeatedly praised *Ethan Frome.*"

"Carl didn't like Wharton's other works."

"That's unusual, isn't it?" Harrison asked. "Most people who care for Wharton prefer the other books. *The Age of Innocence* and so on."

"In any event," Nora said, "he later changed his mind."

"Why?"

Nora moved slightly to one side. "Tepid, Carl said. Artificial. Clunky. A novel shouldn't have its architecture showing."

"And what do you think?" Harrison asked.

Nora shrugged. "It is what it is. A sparsely written novella that high school students can read. Carl . . . Carl admired it at the beginning of his career because he thought he might be a novelist. If you're a poet thinking of becoming a novelist, a sparsely written novella is just the ticket."

Harrison turned his head and studied her. "I was unaware of that."

"You're surprised by this," she said, looking up at him.

"Yes. Tremendously. Did he actually write a novel?"

Nora tucked her gloved hands under her arms. "He began one. He had me burn the pages when he knew he was dying."

"You're kidding."

"I suppose that's upsetting for an editor," she said.

"A *bit*," Harrison said with feeling. "I imagine his publisher would be upset as well. What was the novel about?"

"I don't know," Nora said, drawing her coat more tightly around her. "The first time I ever saw it was the day Carl told me where it was. I never took it out of the box. He made me burn it in the living room fireplace. He supervised from a chair. He was very secretive about his writing. When he was writing it, that is."

Harrison stuffed his hands into the pockets of his jacket. He kicked at the snow with his sneaker.

"I've really surprised you, haven't I?" she asked. "You're struck speechless."

"I was just thinking about the explorer Richard Burton. His wife burned all of his pornographic writings when he died." Harrison paused. "I suppose that's the widow's prerogative, isn't it? To protect the image of her husband?"

"Possibly," Nora said, glancing at her watch. "But in this case, the writer was protecting himself. I have to go."

"Don't," Harrison pleaded in mock distress, holding out his arms. "You're always leaving me."

Harrison meant this as a joke, but the words, once spoken, rang uncomfortably true.

"See you later?" she asked, and Harrison felt a small kick inside his chest. She drew away from him, walking backward in her boots, waving.

"Definitely," he said.

Harrison watched as Nora did a little run up the front steps and disappeared inside the front door. When he turned, Jerry Leyden's face was inches from his own.

"You can always tell when a guy's still carrying the torch," Jerry said.

"What?" Harrison asked. Jerry's nose was running. His teeth were the translucent blue of overwhitening.

"I once Googled my old girlfriend at Kidd. You remember Dawn Freeman? She's a sheep farmer now in Idaho. Whew, glad I didn't go there."

Harrison wished Jerry would back up a step. His breath stank of stale coffee.

"Hey, listen," Jerry said. "I didn't mean to jerk you around last night. About Stephen? I know you loved the guy."

Harrison said nothing.

"Just seems like we all got away with murder, you know what I mean?"

Harrison's hands were fists in his pockets. It was all he could do to keep them there. "You're an asshole, Leyden," Harrison said under his breath as he turned to walk away.

"Branch, wait a minute," Jerry said and caught the sleeve of Harrison's jacket. Harrison looked down at Jerry's fingers. Jerry let go of Harrison, and Harrison faced him.

"Look," Jerry said, "I don't know what happened that night at the beach. I've been needling you, and I really don't know why. To be perfectly honest, I think it's myself I'm angry at. That night, when I got back to the dorm and found out Stephen was missing, I felt so . . . I don't know . . ." Jerry looked down the hill and then back again at Harrison. "Helpless," he said. "Stephen was dead before we knew it, and there we all were — *alive*. Really *alive*." Jerry yanked off his gloves. "It was the same with 9/11. All those bodies falling, and there I was. Alive. I can't describe it. It makes you feel sick inside. Guilty, sure. Angry, you bet. But the really terrible feeling is *helpless*. I fucking hate feeling helpless."

Harrison took a long breath, and Jerry stuffed his gloves into his pockets.

"Stephen was a beautiful guy," Jerry said.

Harrison got behind the wheel of the Taurus and spun out of the parking lot. He had no destination, merely an urge to push the car forward, to have it make some noise.

The long drive to the inn had been plowed, but almost immediately Harrison realized he would have to slow down. He didn't want to end up in the trees at the side of the drive because of Jerry Leyden or Stephen Otis or anyone else from his past.

He shut Jerry's face and voice out of his mind. He hit the road that led to Nora's inn, skidded a bit in the turn, and followed it back to town. When he had driven to the inn the day before, he'd been searching for signposts and had paid little attention to the village. This time, he made note of a post office, a bookstore that looked promising, an elementary school that resembled a factory, and two other inns, both of which he viewed competitively, taking Nora's side. He didn't think she had much to worry about. The first was a pink-and-purple Victorian house that promised "all-you-can-eat" breakfasts. The second was a modest B and B unhappily situated next to a Mobil station.

Harrison parked the Ford on the main street and walked, hands in pockets, snow still melting inside his sneakers. He needed a pair of dry socks. He passed an odd structure and glanced at the sign on the porch. It was the town library, the Holy Grail of his profession. Actually not, Harrison reflected, remembering the bookstore, the true Holy Grail of his profession, with its sales and promise of profits. The library was a curiosity, though, a large yellow Victorian with rounded turrets and stone columns. He imagined the building, during an earlier age, as the home of one of the town's more prosperous citizens — the local doctor, a venerable judge. As Harrison climbed the steps, he tried to picture Carl Laski doing the same. Or stopping at the bookstore. Or nipping out for an early morning doughnut on the way to the college. Would Nora have been with him?

Once inside the library, Harrison headed for the poetry section. He hoped to find a copy of Laski's last volume, *Burning Trees*. The library was quiet on a late Saturday morning. Only a few patrons were sitting at computers or reading newspapers in the reading room. Harrison had always liked the hush of libraries, the antiquated notion that only in silence could one absorb words.

He surveyed the two shelves of poetry volumes (two out of five hundred shelves? a thousand?), and he wondered, not for the first time, why it was he had attached his own star — his work, his editing — to such a marginal enterprise as publishing literary works. Worse, to the most marginal practitioners of it. To date, Harrison had edited a half dozen biographies of poets and two slender volumes of verse: one from the American poet Audr Heinrich, a venture that had brought the man, as well as Harrison's publishing house, some considerable renown, and the other from the Persian-Canadian poet Vashti Baker, a volume that had slipped so far below the radar screen, it had essentially vaporized itself. Of these books, however, Harrison was proud. Certainly prouder than he was of the various self-help books and thrillers he'd had to edit to help keep his company in the black.

Harrison pulled out the Laski volume and took a seat at a polished cherry reading table. He opened the book. He knew the man's work to be arresting and deceptively simple. Harrison skimmed the volume, looking for poems about women. Although he hadn't consciously realized it at the time, Harrison knew now that he was hoping to find, in the verse, references to Nora. The phrase "wet with water" caught his eye. He read the rest of the poem. It seemed to be about a woman washing her hair while a man watches, thinking about his son watching his own wife wash her hair.

Harrison fanned the pages of the book slowly, scanning the type, looking for key words and lines. It was a trick he'd learned as an editor. If he suspected a repetition of a word in a text, he could find the first reference in seconds by using this technique. He fanned once again, starting from the back of the book. He saw the word "tongue." He flattened the book on the table.

The poem was entitled "Under the Canted Roof" and was graphic in its sexual details, somewhat more so than Laski's other works. The verse had the feel of reportage. Although Harrison had not read Laski's final collection, the poem seemed like something of a new direction for the man. The woman in the poem was blond, but Harrison had no doubt that Laski was referring to Nora. *The narrow thigh; the asymmetrical smile.* He thought of Nora's funny half smile.

Harrison closed his eyes, and a kind of prurient jealousy squeezed at him. He had no one to blame but himself. This was what he had unconsciously sought when he'd come into the library, something intimate about the marriage of Nora and Carl Laski. Harrison opened his eyes and read the poem again, as if, hidden among the words, Harrison would discover a detail even more revealing.

Though the poem was about sexuality, there was little joy. Within ecstasy lay the seeds of loss. Was this the glimpse of Nora's marriage Harrison had hoped for?

As Harrison examined the lines again, he remembered an accusation Evelyn had tossed his way during a fight they'd had some six years into their own marriage. He was insulated, she said. He did not know how to love someone else. She meant herself, of course, and Harrison recalled being stung by the criticism hurled in the heat of the argument, immediately taken back that evening. For he knew that something he'd thought resilient — his marriage — might now be subject to all sorts of criticism, as if open season had been declared. After Evelyn had left the bedroom, Harrison had lain on the bed, wondering if Evelyn was correct. Had he, somewhere along the line, lost the ability to love another person fully? But then he'd had the thought that his boys were someone elses, and he certainly loved them, and that realization had been immensely reassuring to him. He had even, he remembered, sat up, feeling a kind of pleasure at this vindication.

Harrison closed the book. He wouldn't be able to take it out. He had no library card, no way of obtaining one. He guessed, however, that the bookstore might have a copy of the volume. The town was, after all, a kind of mecca for devotees of Laski.

Harrison left the library and crossed the street to the bookstore. When he opened the door, a pale young man with a light brown mustache looked up at him. Harrison smiled, and the man nodded. Harrison did not engage in his usual bookstore activity — searching the shelves for his own company's volumes, turning them jacket-side out when he found them — because none of the books in this American store would be his. It was a tiny shop, barely wide enough for two freestanding sets of shelves. Harrison found the poetry section easily (half a shelf) and purchased a copy of Laski's latest. On the way back to his car, he stopped to have a cup of coffee, and as he did, he read several more of the poems in the book. He gassed up the Taurus and headed back to the inn.

In the lobby, Harrison hovered, hoping for a glimpse of Nora, but there was no sign of her. As he climbed the stairs, he imagined she had retreated to her rooms. He pictured her having a long soak in that generous bath with its marble surround, the water tinted a faint chartreuse from the oils in the antique glass cruets.

*   *   *

Harrison woke with a start and, for a moment, felt disoriented. Where was he? What time was it? He glanced at the bedside clock and saw that he had overslept. He sat up quickly. He had a wedding to go to. He took a fast shower and dressed.

In his new suit, bought for the occasion, Harrison checked his tie in the mirror. How long had it been since he'd been to a wedding? His sister's second, he thought. Five, six years ago. Must have been. He couldn't remember anything more recent. He recalled the picture of Nora and Carl Laski on their wedding day, how young and vulnerable Nora had looked, how he'd wanted to put his hand between the bride and groom.

The narrow thigh; the asymmetrical smile.

With his fingers, Harrison brushed back his hair, wishing there was more of it. For Bill's sake, he hoped the ceremony would be meaningful, the celebration festive. Christ, they had a hard road ahead of them.

Harrison took his wallet and his room key from the pants he'd had on earlier and put them in the pocket of his trousers. When he looked down, he saw that his shoes needed a shine. He found the boxed shoe-shine kit in the bathroom, put each foot in turn on the rung of the desk chair, and gave the toes a polish. He washed his hands and dried them with the hand towel. Opening the door, Harrison took one last look around the room, shut off the lights, and headed out.

Before Harrison had reached the library, he could hear the music, an astonishingly lovely piano piece. Chopin? Mozart? Nora's sound system must be remarkable, he thought. But when he turned the corner and entered the room through the double doors, he saw

Rob at a baby grand that had been rolled in for the occasion. Rob's fingers moved over the keys with unearthly precision and delicacy, and for a moment, Harrison stood transfixed. He thought about Rob's comment that he had once had a crush on Stephen.

Didn't we all?

In a kind of hypnotic trance, Harrison took a seat. That one of their own should have such immense talent caused in him a surge of pleasure and pride. Harrison had once known the man at the piano, however long ago, however briefly, however different the incarnation. And how sly of Nora and Rob to have kept this delicious secret from the others. Harrison felt like a guest summoned to an eighteenth-century manor house for a concert, a man invited to attend a performance for the privileged, the elect.

Paradoxically both calm and elated, Harrison gazed around the room. Discreet bouquets of white flowers had been placed at irregular intervals, the hand haphazard. Clearly Nora's doing. Despite the six pairs of folding bridge chairs — three pairs on either side of a narrow aisle — the library had retained its elegance. The overhead lamps had been dimmed, and candles near the windows cast flickering light on the faces. Harrison spotted Agnes in a blue dress, sitting next to Josh in suit and tie (new acquisitions from the outlets?). Two women Harrison did not recognize — one younger and one more elderly — were ensconced in the front row across the aisle from Agnes. Bridget's mother and sister? Julie, her hair done up in a French twist and fastened with a pearl clip, had her eyes closed, as if at church. Jerry, his hair gelled and bristling, was seated just behind her.

Harrison closed his own eyes and wished Rob would play for hours. He vowed to take Evelyn and the boys to the Toronto Symphony as soon as he got home. He couldn't remember the last time he and Evelyn had gone to a concert. He would seek out Rob's CDs as well; there was a good music store a block from his office. He couldn't think how he had let such beauty slip from his life. It was his own fault: too much work, too much getting and spending. He should have introduced his boys to classical music long before this, he thought, and he wondered if it was too late. He would tell the boys about his friend, a baseball player, who had become a famous concert pianist. The CDs, magical totems for the boys, would do the trick.

From a door to one side of the library, Harrison heard murmurs and rustling. He opened his eyes to see Bill and Bridget make their way across the front of the room, followed by the boys, Matt and Brian. Apparently there would be no procession down the makeshift aisle. This was a second marriage for both, and the bridal party was tiny. More to the point, Harrison guessed, neither Bill nor Bridget wanted any fuss.

Bridget, in a pink suit, had her lips pressed tightly together. A deep flush had suffused her skin, giving her a glow of robust health. Bill and the boys were in tuxes, a nice touch, Harrison thought. A woman Harrison did not recognize followed the four to the front of the room. She must be the justice of the peace, he decided. From the piano, the music quietly subsided. Rob sat back on the bench, his hands folded in his lap — the organist at church.

Bill and Bridget turned their backs to the guests and faced the justice of the peace.

We are gathered here today to celebrate one of life's greatest moments . . .

Nora slipped into the empty seat beside Harrison. She gave him a quick smile, a greeting as well as a confession of some excitement. All Nora's work — her choreography, her planning, her secret surprises — was about to be revealed.

"What was Rob playing?" Harrison whispered.

"Handel," Nora whispered back.

Bill reached over and clasped Bridget's hand. Standing beside the couple, Matt and his friend seemed slightly baffled but impressively solemn for the occasion. Bridget's sister got up from her chair and put a hand on Bridget's back. And Agnes — *Agnes!* — was sobbing. Noisy sobbing, with gulps and small head shudders. Josh offered her his handkerchief, and Agnes blew her nose. Harrison wondered at the source of Agnes's dissolution. Joy for Bridget and Bill? Anguish for Bridget? A wedding was an act of faith, Harrison reflected, perhaps never more so than today.

. . . recognition of the worth and beauty of love . . .

The swish and whisper of a door slowly opening caused Harrison to turn his head toward the back of the room. A young woman in a white sweater and a short black skirt, a black leather purse slung over her arm, stood at the double doors. She seemed embarrassed, a concertgoer who had entered the hall during a particularly quiet moment in the symphony. As she scanned the room for an empty seat, Harrison recognized her. Melissa. Bill's daughter.

Bill, turning (perhaps he had secretly been hoping?), spotted the young woman, and on his face Harrison saw a moving picture of emotions. Disbelief. Joy. Pride. Bill signaled to Bridget, who glanced at the small audience. She saw the young woman. On Bridget's face, a look of pure relief.

. . . unite Bridget Kennedy Rodgers and William Joseph Ricci in marriage . . .

During the short ceremony, the groom cried. The bride did not. From time to time, Agnes emitted noisy gulps. Josh kept his arm around the distraught woman and spoke to her in a low voice. Who'd have thought Agnes, who had always seemed to be so very much in control of herself, could so easily be undone by a wedding?

After a few minutes, Josh removed his arm from Agnes's shoulders and stood just to the right of the wedding party. Harrison winced inwardly, thinking that the man was about to recite a poem or give a homily. Josh couldn't possibly know Bill and Bridget well enough to do that. Whose idea had this been? But then Harrison heard the first notes of a baritone voice so arresting it caused chills along the back of his neck. Harrison didn't know the music. The words were in Italian. It must, he thought, be a love song. Harrison saw suddenly that there might have been, before any physical love, an attraction between Rob and Josh that transcended gender or sexuality.

Josh's voice had power and range. It was a voice almost too large for the room, and yet there was a subtlety to the song that was all quiet yearning. Bill seemed more composed now, and even Agnes had taken a deep breath. Harrison gazed at Nora, who had pulled off a choreographic triumph. A service as beautiful and as meaningful as any Harrison had ever been to, shorter by half, and with the music of angels.

"Well done," he whispered in her ear.

Nora, in a moment of pride or affection, took Harrison's hand in both of her own and set it on her lap. And Harrison knew then that Evelyn, years ago, during that long-forgotten and inconsequential fight, had been entirely wrong: Harrison was not in the slightest — not even in the tiniest part — an insulated man.

The trembling started just outside the library when the justice of the peace, a woman Bridget had never met before, began to explain the service. In the background, Bridget could hear Rob's quiet prelude. Josh, whom Bridget had met only briefly last night, would sing toward the end of the ceremony. Rob had said the man's voice was beautiful, but then again, Rob might be expected to be biased. Bridget had been to weddings ruined by wobbly sopranos who couldn't reach the upper registers.

Matt, standing off to one side, looked stricken.

"Matt?" Bridget asked, leaving Bill to absorb the instructions.

"You cool with this, Mom?" Matt gave his hair a quick, nervous swipe.

"The ceremony, you mean?"

"The whole thing," he said, meeting her eyes, one of Matt's finer qualities. Matt had friends whose eyes Bridget had never seen.

"This will be easy," Bridget said. "It's kind of a cross between a church service and a little play. Someone will cry. I'll be nervous. You'll be fine. You don't have any lines. All you and Brian have to do is stand up straight looking very handsome. Like one of the guards in *Macbeth*. Remember *Macbeth?*"

"Mom."

"You'll be fine."

"But I have the rings."

"Yes, we hope you do," Bridget said.

"So when do I give them?"

"The justice of the peace will tell you. If you miss that cue, I'll give you a poke and point to my finger."

Matt sighed heavily.

"You'll love it," Bridget said, patting him on the sleeve of his tuxedo jacket, though she was not at all sure that Matt would be charmed by the ceremony about to take place. She, for example, would not love the service. It wasn't that she didn't want to marry Bill. She did. It was that she wished they could get it over with here and now in the hallway. If the justice of the peace could say the words in anticipation of the ceremony, why not just do it here? Why must an audience be involved? But then Bridget thought of all of Nora's planning, of Rob's lovely music, of the way the library had been transformed into a space in which a wedding *should* take place — so, of course, they would have this ceremony. At least it was not the Catholic service Bridget had had the first time she'd been married, an athletic test of endurance if ever there had been one. Ninety minutes of standing, sitting, kneeling for the prayers, up again for the hymns, down for the homily.

There would be no upping and downing at her short service. A quick ten minutes, then out the door for champagne. And, yes, Bridget would have a glass of champagne tonight. She wished she had a glass right now.

Bridget glanced over at Matt's friend Brian and smiled. The boy whose face looked better today — it appeared as though he had sanded his skin — smiled back. She wondered if Brian had ever been in a wedding before, if he'd even been to one. She would keep an eye on him, make sure he was included in all the festivities.

"Matt," she said, remembering that she needed to speak to her son. She put a hand on his arm. "There's something I have to tell you."

Matt went white-faced.

"No, no," Bridget said quickly. "It's not about me. Well, it is. A small fact. When Bill and I met each other again, he was still married."

Matt's relief was immense. "I *knew* that, Mom."

"What I mean to say is, Bill and I . . ."

Matt put a hand up. "It's okay," Matt said. "Really."

"Really?"

"Yeah, really."

Bridget wasn't sure Matt knew precisely what Bridget had been about to confess, but it was clear Matt didn't want to hear any more. That was fine with Bridget. She'd made her attempt. She was in the clear.

The justice of the peace put her hand on Bridget's elbow, a signal to leave the hallway and enter the library. Bridget would be first in, followed by Bill, then Matt and Brian, and then the justice herself. Bridget's heart did a little tick, and her hands began to shake.

She had to press her lips together to stop the trembling, and — wouldn't you know it — a hot flash was starting. It hit her face first, and then her shoulders and neck. She could feel it in her armpits. She would ruin her suit, but that was all right. She hated her suit, she just hated it. She worried that the panty line of her one-piece would show through the skirt girdle. And why did she and Bill have to stand facing forward? The guests might be distracted by the back of her wig, its least convincing part.

When she entered the room, Bridget saw her mother and sister seated in the front row. Both smiled, and her sister gave her a little wave. They had arrived in time for lunch, which they'd eaten in the dining room, both of them exclaiming over the treacherous drive out from Boston and the hideous condition of the roads, the exaggerated claims an effort to avoid having to mention, on Bridget's wedding day, the word "cancer." It was, Bridget had reflected then, a word almost medieval in its power to evoke fear. She could think of few others that could compete. *Terrorist?* No, too impersonal. *Nuclear war?* No, that was two words. *Death?* Too commonplace, too abstract. It didn't carry with it the sense of a slow and torturous decline. *Terminal?* Yes, possibly. A definite possibility.

At lunch, her sister had admitted that she was impatient to visit the outlets before she had to return to the inn to do her hair. Bridget's mother, suffering from arthritis, went to her room to lie down. Bridget, never one for winter sports, sought the solitude of the bridal suite. Wasn't it natural to want to be alone on one's wedding day? Bridget would have been happy with a single room. She didn't want to see Bill or have to talk to him before the ceremony. But how could she reasonably have requested two rooms? Only young women, virgins, did that these days. Well, these days, no one was a virgin.

Bill stood beside her and took hold of her hand. Behind her someone was sobbing. Her mother? No, wrong side. Agnes? It couldn't possibly be Agnes, Bridget thought. Who else was sitting there? Bill's hand on her own — he was squeezing her — had the desired effect of slowing her breath. She thought the hot flash was subsiding as well. Rob caught her eye and mouthed something Bridget couldn't quite catch. *Love you?*

Do you promise to love, honor, cherish, and protect . . .

Bridget took a quick peek to her side. Yes, it was Agnes who was sobbing. But why? Agnes hardly knew Bridget. They hadn't been exceptionally close at Kidd, and they hadn't seen each other in twenty-seven years. Bill gave her hand an extra squeeze, and Bridget glanced up at him. He signaled with his head to look to the audience. Bridget turned and surveyed the small group. Harrison and Nora seated near the back. Agnes and Josh. Her mother and . . . oh my.

Bridget saw the long dark hair, the white sweater and skirt. Melissa had driven herself across the state to attend her father's wedding.

Bridget glanced up at Bill's face, his eyes wide with the wonder of his daughter's presence, the barely suppressed grin. She could think of no better gift to Bill than this: a sense of all the pieces of the puzzle in place; an absolution greater than any she or a priest could have granted. Melissa would cling to Bill at the reception and might even ignore Bridget altogether, but none of that would matter. The simple fact of Melissa's arrival would be everything to this man who would, in about a minute and a half, be Bridget's husband.

. . . life given to each of us as individuals . . .

When she had been a young woman, Bridget had imagined herself becoming Mrs. Ricci even before she had formally met the boy at Kidd. He'd been a senior and she a junior, and Bridget remembered watching him from afar, admiring the way he'd walk across the campus with his sports bag slung over his shoulder, back straight, face forward, a ready grin for everyone who crossed his path. Bridget had maneuvered her way into his life, often placing herself in his vicinity, and when that hadn't worked, she'd cajoled a friend into making sure he would attend a school dance on a Friday night in late October of her junior year. Bridget didn't exactly stalk Bill, but she knew that he was shy with girls and that the first move would have to be hers. She remembered clenching her fists, walking up to him, and asking him to dance to a song from the Jackson Five during which they wouldn't have to talk. Indeed, they didn't say much that night, the music and student chatter being so loud one had to shout to be heard.

After the dance was over, they left the student center and headed out into the raw coastal night. Both were sweating, and Bridget felt a chill immediately. Because she had worn only a sweater to the dance, Bill gave her his jacket. She remembered that they did not head directly back to her dorm, as would have been expected, but rather walked down the narrow path to the beach, using only moonlight to guide them. There they sat in the damp sand, Bridget ruining her new jeans, watching the tide advance slowly toward them. They'd talked then, but of what? Bridget couldn't remember now. Mostly what she remembered was how it felt to sit beside this boy she had been dreaming about for weeks.

It was, she thought now, a story without drama, a story that doubtless had been repeated hundreds of times that fall on campuses everywhere. Two kids who sensed they ought to be together managed to find each other. Bill did not kiss her that night, but before the week was out, they had snuck once more down onto the beach and had become lovers. The speed with which she had allowed Bill to make love to her might have frightened another girl, made her proceed with caution, but Bridget felt no guilt, no remorse, no need to slow down. That she and Bill had come together in the most primitive sense of the word had felt absolutely right.

There was a small silence now from the justice of the peace and a nod in Matt's direction. With a quick fumble in his pocket, the boy produced the rings and presented them on his sweaty palm. The justice took them from him and gave one to Bridget, one to Bill.

. . . The outward and visible sign of the unbroken circle of love . . .

Just before she'd come down from the room, Bridget had slathered her hands with Vaseline Intensive Care Lotion so that Bill would have no trouble slipping her ring on. She'd been worried that her weight gain since they'd bought the rings might make the gold band stick at her knuckle. But Bill, with a light touch, accomplished his one and only task with ease.

. . . forsaking all others and holding only unto her? . . .

In a few seconds, she and Bill would be well and truly married. She wished their story had been a simple one, a clear shot from the day they'd first met until this day. But it was not. The hiccup that Jerry had referred to in the toast had lasted more than two decades.

It had never occurred to Bridget that Bill might be unfaithful. He was as honest a boy as she had ever met. So when his letter had come during the spring of her sophomore year at college, Bridget had been stunned. Bill had, he wrote, fallen in love with someone else. The girl's name was Jill. Bridget read and reread the letter a dozen times, disbelief turning into a kind of leaden certainty, for Bill, a good man, would never put Bridget through such pain were the news equivocal. If Bill said he had fallen in love with another woman, then that was that.

Bridget didn't like the language of excess or of melodrama, but it was impossible for her to remember that time without thinking of the words "shattered" and "catastrophic" and "disaster" and "wanting to die."

Bridget did not write back to Bill. Her mother and her roommate urged her to drive to Vermont where Bill was at school and confront him, but Bridget would not beg. She could not imagine a scene in which she knocked on Bill's door and found inside the woman named Jill, with whom Bill was now in love. Bridget was quite sure she would not survive that encounter. That even if she lived (well, of course, she would live), something inside of her would be lost. Memory? Faith? The ability ever again to believe in love?

And so she had suffered in silence. The news was dire. Her hormones were rampant. Bridget remembered days spent in the bed with the covers drawn up over her head. Long risky walks late at night, begging someone to mug her. The missed meals, the nearly unbearable weekend nights, the having to explain why she was not with Bill to friends and family. Most of all, Bridget minded the future she would now not have. She had for so long imagined their life together — the wedding, the house, the baby — that it was as though this had been taken from her as well. And, of course, Bridget cried. So much so that she'd had a headache for weeks.

In the library, Bridget slipped Bill's ring on his finger, and she, too, said *I do.*

She was aware then that Josh was standing beside Bill. She prayed that Josh's singing wouldn't be too painful or awkward, ending the wedding on a wincing note.

But Josh's voice, when he began, was glorious. Simply glorious. She glanced at Bill. What was this astonishing song?

She didn't mind now that her back was to the guests. Josh's voice, far more than the words of the simple ceremony, moved her. And how odd, since the song appeared to be in Italian. Not knowing the lyrics, Bridget invented her own: *We had so many years apart, but now we have found each other. I wish that we had had children together. I had a beautiful strong body in my twenties and early thirties, and I'm sorry that you never saw it.*

Josh let the last note linger, and then it faded away. Bill took Bridget's hand. Her son, Matt, was just inches from them both.

This is what I have now, Bridget thought. This is it. A man and a son and a short future, during which I must live every hour as if it were my last.

Agnes knew that she would cry as soon as Rob started to play. She had this reaction at church when a familiar hymn was sung, at the symphony when the violins were exquisite, even at baseball games when the tenor began the national anthem. The music was a kind of trigger that summoned emotions normally kept in check. Reverence. Gratitude. A sense of something greater than herself. Sorrow. Heartache. Loneliness.

Sometimes she cried for the anonymous. For the thousands dead in tribal genocide in central Africa. For the victims of earthquakes in southeast Asia. For the hundreds swept away in floods in India. Occasionally, she cried for all those lost during World War I or on the *Titanic* or at Masada. More recently for those who had died on September 11. What would it take to make yourself jump from the 103rd floor of a building, knowing — *knowing* — that you would die in a suicide more efficient than any other? Only gravity would be necessary. Would one be conscious during the fall, or would the body seize up, causing a blessed blackout? How long would it take to hit the ground? Agnes imagined the woman she had read about in the *New York Times,* the one reaching for the coffee pot, standing in the ledge of a window, looking down, the flames behind her. No, Agnes thought. She would not have jumped.

And, oh God, just the crying itself was a kind of personal horror, wasn't it? Should she excuse herself? Josh handed her a handkerchief, and she tried to smile in his direction, but it was no good. Her body, rhythmically convulsive, would not calm down. Her face would be a ruin, and her eyes would not recover for hours — she would have to dunk her face in ice water to clear them.

But Agnes couldn't stop crying, because now she was thinking about Halifax and all the people who had died there. She pictured the woman pinned under the beam, her chest crushed. That woman would have been a mother. Of course she would have. Or the ten-year-old girl who had lost her family. Imagine — to experience that bright light and then to wake to a hellish universe in which you were utterly alone. And then there was that poor man propped against a dead horse, his child lifeless in his arms. Would the shock of the event obliterate pain? Could a parent's pain ever be obliterated?

Agnes would never know. Agnes would never be a mother. She was forty-four years old, and already her periods were irregular, sometimes two and three months apart. Jim's wife, Carol (such a cold, cold name), was a mother twice over — her children grown now, one in college, one just out. Jim had once said that he might leave Carol when both children were through college (earlier, it had been when both children were out of high school, but, as Jim had pointed out, that clearly wouldn't work: where would the children go when they came home from school on vacations?), but Agnes doubted that Jim would ever leave his wife. Even if he did, it was too late for children, wasn't it?

So a child was out of the question.

Agnes glanced around her. Nora was sitting with Harrison. Nora had never had a child. Carl had already had his children, he'd said. He would not entertain thoughts of another. Rob and Josh would not have their own children unless they adopted. But they all had, or had experienced, something Agnes did not have. Steady companionship. A wife. A husband. A lover with whom one lived. Agnes and Jim had shared motel rooms and cottages, but never for more than three days at a stretch. What would it be like to come home with groceries in a bag to find Jim sprawled on a couch, reading the paper? To wake up morning after morning and see his long back as he bent to put on his shoes? To fold herself into him whenever she wanted to?

. . . union of a man and woman in marriage . . .

And that was another thing Agnes would never have. A wedding. Never a public celebration of herself and Jim. A thing so commonplace and yet so utterly impossible for her. She shook her head. The self-pity was endless. Pathetic, really. And utterly useless. What good did it do to cry over something she could not have? None whatsoever. All she could hope to accomplish would be to draw attention to herself and thus have to invent a plausible explanation for her tears. She hardly knew Bill and Bridget as adults, though she liked them well enough.

(Agnes had a sudden and horrifying thought. Would Bridget misinterpret the tears, thinking Agnes was crying because Bridget might die soon?)

Agnes blew her nose again and sat back against the pew. Josh removed his arm and gave her leg a little squeeze. He stood, and Agnes was confused. Was the ceremony over? She watched as he turned to the assembled. He seemed to collect himself, and Agnes thought that he would speak the way people spontaneously did at funerals. A little weird. A little nervous making. Josh was not one of them, really, for all his kindness.

Instead of speaking, however, Josh began to sing. It was an aria, Agnes thought. It had to be. From an Italian opera. Or an opera in Italian. Agnes might know the work. She often listened to opera on her public radio station. She closed her eyes, and the rhythmic convulsions began to subside. She folded her hands in her lap. Had Nora arranged for this? Well, of course, it would have been Rob's idea. Perhaps Josh sang professionally in addition to playing the cello. No man could be this good and keep it to himself.

(Had Agnes been wrong, she wondered now, to make Louise blind? Had she been too heartless?)

The song was too brief, and Agnes minded when suddenly it was over. She wanted to clap, but one didn't clap at weddings. She felt she needed more of the music. She had a sense of having almost reached something inside herself that needed to be got at.

Agnes blinked. The justice of the peace was pronouncing Bill and Bridget husband and wife. So soon? Was the service over? Agnes had hardly heard a word.

She knew she must compose herself now. There would be a dinner, toasts, a sense of celebration. The entire weekend had been leading to this moment. Agnes would have to say that she always cried at weddings. She ought to have warned them. How pathetic, she would add, trying to make a small joke of it. She would sidestep all questions, exclaiming over Bridget, Josh's singing, Rob's playing. How lucky they were to know such talented people!

Agnes stood, her knee stiff from having held herself so tightly. There was a small crowd already around Bill and Bridget. Jerry, tieless, in a charcoal suit. Julie smoothing the bun at the back of her head. Harrison shaking Bill's hand. Bridget hugging Josh. Rob, standing to one side, barely containing his pride in his partner. No, Agnes thought, she must go back to her room and wash her face. Did she have any Visine in her toilet kit?

"Agnes," Harrison said.

Agnes turned, and with one tug, Harrison pulled her into him. Her face was pressed against his shirt and tie. She could smell his soap or his aftershave. He asked her no questions, for which Agnes was grateful.

Harrison held her for a long time. Agnes was aware of people moving, of voices subsiding.

Agnes drew away from Harrison. "I'm just . . . I don't know," she said.

"You're a mess," he said, examining her. "Where's your room?"

"Twenty-two."

246

"I'll walk you up there and wait for you."

"You don't have to —"

Harrison cut her off. He put his fingers under her chin and tilted her face up toward his — her unlovely, ruined face. It had been years since a man had touched her just this way.

"Agnes," Harrison said. "What's wrong? Why are you so sad?"

She wanted to tell him — oh God, she wanted to tell him — but what exactly would she say? I love a man, have always loved him, but he only loves me back sporadically with long, inexplicable gaps in between? No, that simply could not be said, not to this kind man in front of her.

So," Jerry was saying, "here's the deal. You board a plane and take your seat in first class. After a few minutes, six Arab men get on the plane and take seats, also in first class. Let's say one of them is carrying a copy of the Koran. The question is: do you get off the plane?"

For a moment, the table, which had been noisy with two and sometimes three conversations running simultaneously, was quiet. Agnes pondered Jerry's question.

After the ceremony and the drinks that had followed, the wedding party had settled around the long table in the same private dining room as the night before. No need for place cards this evening, however. No need for Nora's careful planning. Or perhaps the very randomness of the seating had been part of Nora's planning. Though the dining room suggested a wedding, with its anemones and ivory damask linens, the mood was more relaxed than it had been earlier. A half dozen bottles of champagne had been opened. The toasts had been made. A first course of pumpkin-cranberry soup had been consumed. Agnes was drinking a delicate white wine, though she didn't know the name of it. She was hardly a connoisseur.

"I'd only notice if they were good-looking," Josh said from his end of the table, which produced a hoot from Bill, who'd been nearly levitating since the end of the service. He sat with his new wife on one side and his daughter on the other, and though the daughter had barely spoken to anyone else (and noticeably not to

Bridget), Bill was the picture of a happy man. "Basking" was a word that had crossed Agnes's mind.

"I'd get off," Bridget said. "For Matt's sake. When you have a child, you can't make decisions for yourself anymore." Agnes glanced over at Matt, whose face instantly reddened with embarrassment. "But I probably wouldn't be on the plane in the first place," Bridget added, "because I'm terrified of flying. I'd look at it as a wonderful excuse to bolt."

Bridget's sister, Janice, was seated next to Matt. Bridget's mother had stayed for the drinks and toasts but would have her meal in her room, Bridget had explained. The woman's arthritis was apparently so severe she couldn't sit for long periods without pain.

"If Bridget got off, I'd go with her," Bill offered.

"Cop-out," Josh said genially.

"Anyone else?" Jerry asked. He'd shed his jacket and had his shirtsleeves rolled. Agnes wondered if he'd been preparing this question for the group all day.

"I think I'd engage one of the men in conversation," Rob said thoughtfully. "I'd ask him what he did for a living. Where he lived. And then I might base my decision on his answers and his general demeanor and how the others reacted to my talking to the man."

"Sounds sensible," Harrison said.

"I'd tell the flight attendant," Agnes said abruptly, without having given her answer much thought.

"What good would that do?" Jerry asked.

"Oh, I don't know. I guess I'd ask her if she'd noticed that six Arab men had just gotten on the plane."

"That's discrimination, right?" Jerry asked.

"Well, of course," Agnes said. "But the configuration so mirrors what happened on 9/11 that I'm not sure the notion of discrimination applies any longer."

"You wouldn't mind that you were engaging in racial profiling?" Jerry probed.

"I might mind, but being politically correct would certainly never take precedence over trying to save my life. Not to mention the lives of two hundred others. Not to mention the lives of thousands who might be at another ground zero."

"And what if the flight attendant did nothing?" Jerry asked.

Agnes thought a minute. She would already have publically raised the question. The men on the plane might have heard Agnes and the flight attendant in discussion. "Wait a minute," she said. "You said first class, right?"

"Yes."

"Well, then, I'd stay on," Agnes announced. "If I were lucky enough to get a seat on first class — which I've never flown by the way — I certainly wouldn't give it up."

Harrison laughed, and Nora, seated next to him, smiled.

"What about you, Nora?" Jerry asked.

Their hostess had on a black lace shawl over a sleeveless dress. The skin of her neck and collarbones was smooth and white and unblemished. Two black pearl pendants hung from her ears. Agnes had always admired the way Nora, with little obvious fuss, could make herself look so well dressed. "I figure if my number is up, it's up," she said.

"That's it?" Jerry asked. "You wouldn't get off the plane?"

"No," she said. "No. I don't think so."

"I doubt I'd get off the plane either," Harrison offered. He lifted a bulbous glass of red wine to his face and pondered it, as if looking for the answer there. He, too, had taken off his jacket and loosened his tie.

"You're kidding," Jerry said.

"No. Good manners would initially keep me in my seat. I'd feel extremely rude getting off. I'd be thinking, too, about the hassle of missing my flight and having to get another one. Then I'd be figuring the odds. The likelihood that these six men were terrorists would be, I don't know, one in a thousand? One in ten thousand? And the odds that one of them got through security with a box cutter? One in a million? I'd be sweating bullets, but I don't think I'd get up."

"Julie?" Jerry asked, turning his head to his wife sitting beside him.

"I'd take a Xanax," she said coolly. "Two maybe."

The remark was received by the table as a joke, though Agnes was quite sure that Julie hadn't meant it as one.

"You're all crazy," Jerry said. "Me? I'm off that plane faster than a speeding bullet."

"Why?" Harrison asked.

"Even if they're all high-level executives at Schwab, six Arab men in first class three months after 9/11 puts me on red alert."

"And the racial profiling?" Harrison asked.

"I could care less about racial profiling in that situation," Jerry said. "Let's see: if I stay on the plane, I might die. If I get off the plane, I don't die. Sounds pretty simple to me."

"That might be the case even without the six Arab men," Harrison offered. "If you stay on the plane, you might die. If you get off, you won't."

"My point exactly," said Bridget. "Which is why I'm not on the plane in the first place."

"Actually," said Rob, "you're more likely to die in a car accident on the way home from the airport than you are to die on the plane."

"What about you, Melissa?" Jerry asked. Agnes liked the way he had thought to include the girl. She looked to her father, a reflexive gesture, before answering.

"Well," she said slowly. "Assuming I had some time, I'd observe the men before I made my decision. Do they act like people do on a plane? Getting settled, looking for something to read, slightly bored, remembering to turn off their cell phones, looking for a drink? Or do they seem too alert, too observant? Do they notice I'm observing them?" She paused. "But truthfully? If six Arab men got on the plane, I'm not sure I'd even notice."

Bill laughed and Harrison chuckled.

"Do you like school?" Agnes asked the girl.

"I do," she said.

"What are you studying?"

"I think I might major in psychology."

"Do you live alone or do you have roommates?"

"I have two roommates," Melissa said. "We have a three-bedroom apartment."

"Whereabouts?"

"On Commonwealth Ave?"

"Oh, I just love Boston," Agnes said, smiling at the girl.

"Where are you going for your honeymoon?" Julie asked Bill and Bridget, a question that not only silenced the table but seemed odd coming so hard on the heels of bringing Melissa out of her shell. Had Jerry not told Julie about Bridget?

Bill reached over and took Bridget's hand. "Delayed honeymoon," he explained. "We're going to Europe in March. Paris, London, Florence."

"You'll have to get on a plane *then*," Jerry said.

Bridget, with aplomb, asked Julie if she could borrow some of that Xanax she was talking about.

"I'm envious," Nora said, smiling at Bridget.

"You could take some time off," Jerry said, turning in Nora's direction. "Your place here is doing a good business. I read that article in *New York Magazine.*"

"But I can't really," Nora said. "That's one of the pitfalls of running an inn or a restaurant. You have to be there all the time. There are really no days off."

"None?" Julie asked, and Agnes wondered if Julie of the furs and the pearls had ever worked a day in her life.

"Well, I'm exaggerating," Nora said. "But not too many."

"What do you do?" Agnes asked Julie, regretting the question as soon as it was out of her mouth.

"I'm with Credit Suisse," Julie said.

"Not just *with* Credit Suisse," Jerry corrected. "Julie is senior vice president for corporate finance."

For a moment, no one at the table spoke, each guilty, Agnes guessed, of having formed the same set of assumptions she'd made.

"You must travel a lot," Nora said.

"Hence the need for Xanax," Josh said.

"Julie doesn't toot her own horn," Jerry said.

And you certainly don't do it for her, Agnes thought.

"Evidently," Rob said. "It's quite refreshing, actually."

Julie lost herself in a glass of wine. Three waiters arrived bearing large silver trays laden with the entrées. Agnes had ordered the Dover sole. She'd only dabbled at her soup and was now hungry. She attributed her hunger to the sheer work of all those tears, combined with a kind of emotional exhaustion. She noted that she was more than a little tipsy as well.

After the service, Harrison had walked her up to her room. He'd waited while she'd gone into the bathroom and washed her face. She'd run the water as cold as she could, trying to shock her face into some semblance of normalcy. She hadn't wanted to delay Harrison too long, but she had to comb her hair and blot her dress because she'd splashed water all over its front. When she appeared, Harrison, who'd been sitting on the bed watching CNN, said, "That's better," and Agnes had allowed herself to relax a bit.

When they'd arrived at the room in which the dinner would be held, and Harrison had asked her if she would like a drink, Agnes had accepted with alacrity. Drink in hand, she'd finally made her way to Bridget, whom she'd embraced and congratulated.

"Do you have children?" Agnes asked Julie now.

"One," Julie said. "A daughter. She's thirteen."

"Oh," Agnes said with enthusiasm. "Then you'll soon be thinking about schools. Have you considered Kidd?"

Agnes noted a stop and pause between Jerry and Julie, a momentary beat after which Jerry spoke as if for the both of them. "Emily is autistic," Jerry said bluntly, a fact he clearly hadn't volunteered earlier. And one Agnes wished she hadn't inadvertently forced out of him. "She's at a special school in Manhattan. The best in the country."

The information left Agnes momentarily at a loss for words. Should one be sorry to hear that Jerry's daughter was autistic? Or glad that she was being so well cared for? "I didn't know that," Agnes said, marveling at the sheer mass of all that had cumulatively happened to her six friends in twenty-seven years. "I'm glad she's receiving such good care," she added.

Jerry played with his napkin. He set it on the table and then put it back on his lap. He seemed about to say something but didn't. Agnes found this small glimpse into Jerry's vulnerability appealing. For the first time since he had arrived at the inn, she felt sorry for him.

Agnes gazed around the table. Bill and Bridget. Two failed marriages between them. On the cusp of another. A diagnosis of breast cancer. Stage two? Stage three? Children who would have to adapt to being in a blended family. Agnes had watched Matt as he'd surreptitiously (and sometimes blatantly) observed Melissa. The pair were, as of today, stepbrother and -sister, though they seemed hardly to have spoken.

Nora. Married practically as a child to a man who easily could have been her father. A difficult man by all accounts, whose brilliance and fame might have been both thrilling and exasperating. Now a widow with tremendous responsibilities and apparently no partner with whom to share them.

Harrison. Whom Agnes had very much admired as a boy. The only one of them on full scholarship at Kidd. Raised by his mother who'd been widowed years before. On the surface at least, Harrison appeared to have the most normal life of them all: a wife, two sons, a good job, a home. And yet there was about the man some quiet anxiety not accounted for. Perhaps it was only that in this group, he couldn't help but think of Stephen. As, indeed, they *all* couldn't help but think of Stephen, a boy who, outwardly at least, had appeared to have all of life's advantages — good looks, athleticism, charm, money — and yet, at heart, had seemed to lack an essential authenticity that had caused him to drive himself, in a kind of frenzy, to the front of the pack. Unlike Harrison, who'd hung back a bit, been something of a loner, an observer.

Jerry. Clearly enmeshed in a cold, if not a fraught, marriage. One child, autistic.

Rob. Happy now with a calling and a lover, and apparently tremendously successful at both. Rob's early years after Kidd would have been difficult, however. Working for his place at Juilliard. Emerging into gay life. A gay man's existence could not be easy, however outwardly happy and successful it seemed, Agnes thought. Or was she simply profiling once again?

"Rob," Harrison said. "I've been meaning to ask about your folks. Are they still living in Manchester?"

"No, they moved to North Carolina to be near my sister. She and her husband have three kids. How about your mom? Still in Chicago?"

"Still there," Harrison said. "Just retired from teaching a couple of years ago. We see a lot of her actually. She's great with the boys."

"I wonder who among us will be the first grandparent," Nora mused.

"Oh jeez," Bill said, "what a way to spoil a good meal."

Agnes calculated. It would not be Nora or Rob or herself. Unlikely to be Jerry. That left only Bill and Bridget and Harrison. Melissa was staring at her lap, and Matt looked as though he wished himself a hundred miles away.

"Does anyone know what happened to Artie Cohen?" Agnes asked, trying to change the subject. Artie, one of their fellow students in Jim Mitchell's class, had been a particular friend of Stephen's.

"I heard he ended up in Indonesia," Rob said, "but I'm not sure."

"Doing what?" Jerry asked.

"Medicine maybe?" Rob said. "Peace corps kind of thing? I think I might have read that about ten years ago."

"Good for him," Agnes said.

"Does anyone else get the alumni bulletin?" Rob asked.

"I do," Agnes said. She studied the bulletin each time it came out, looking to see who worked where, who had married whom, who had died. "You all knew that Joe Masse died, right?" Agnes asked.

"A car accident?" Rob asked.

"He was in a small plane that crashed at a ski area in northern Italy."

"I heard that," Jerry said.

"Sad," Nora said.

"Does anyone ever talk to Stephen's dad?" Jerry asked.

Nora glanced at Harrison and back at Jerry. "I do," she said. "I visit from time to time, usually on my way to Boston."

"He still in Wellesley?" Jerry asked.

"Yes. In that enormous house. All by himself," Nora added.

Harrison, who had been drinking red, signaled the waiter for another glass of wine.

"What happened to his wife?" Jerry asked.

Agnes could feel the collective tension of the thirteen souls at the table. Harrison, chin resting on his hand, was staring out a dark window. Jerry, perched forward, elbows on the table, was listening intently. Rob cast a look at Josh as if to say, *I'll tell you later.* Even Nora, who always seemed calm, nibbled at her nail. "Gone," Nora said. "Left after Stephen died. I think that's what happened."

Agnes cut into the fish. The sauce was particularly good. Some sort of grain (rice?) appeared to be green, though the light was so low, it was hard to tell.

"Does anyone know what happened to old Fitz?" Rob asked, referring to their art teacher at Kidd. "Remember he just picked up in the middle of our senior year and quit?"

"Jim Mitchell once told me he quit because he'd had this panicky sense he had to start painting," Agnes said.

"You mean like oil painting?" Jerry asked.

"Some kind of painting," Agnes said.

"So what happened?" Jerry asked.

"Couldn't make a living at it. He couldn't get a gallery. Last I heard, he was teaching history in Nyack, New York."

"Wow," said Rob, a kind of hollow and empty *wow.*

"Guys," Jerry said in an animated voice. "Remember the time Mr. Mitchell caught us smoking weed behind the field house after practice?"

"I certainly do," Harrison said.

"Who was there?" Jerry said. "You, me, Rob, Bill . . ." Jerry suddenly remembered Melissa and Matt at the table and quickly amended his statement. "No. Bill. You weren't there."

Bill chuckled.

"But Stephen," Jerry said. "He was there, right?"

"Stephen was there," Harrison said quietly.

"And we're like . . . swallowing the smoke, standing on the roaches. Mitchell knew, right?"

"Of course he knew," Harrison said.

"Yeah," Jerry said admiringly. "Mitchell was the man. Never said a word. We could have been expelled."

"We certainly could have," Harrison said, taking another sip of wine. "Closest I ever came."

Tell them now, Agnes thought, feeling a pressure build inside her chest.

"It was so stupid," Harrison said. He turned and looked pointedly in Matt's direction. "Never smoke marijuana," he added. It occurred to Agnes then that Harrison might be just a little bit drunk.

"On school grounds," Rob added.

"Immediately after a game," Jerry said.

"When a teacher might be around," Harrison cautioned.

"Yeah, Mitchell," Jerry said, sighing. "He was great."

"I love him," Agnes said.

She waited, wrists poised on the table, for the cataclysm she knew was coming.

"We all did," Harrison said casually. "You had him for your senior project, right? It must have been great to have him for a colleague."

"No, I mean I love him," Agnes said, aware that she was sealing her fate, that there was no going back, that she was exposing Jim, and as a result she might never see him again (and was there not just the slightest relief in this?).

"What?" asked Jerry.

Agnes lifted her chin. "I love him," she said. "I always have."

Agnes noted the moment of recognition. Jerry ducking in his chin in surprise. Harrison tilting his head, not quite believing what he'd just heard. Rob nodding slowly.

"That's great," Nora said after a long silence.

"Well. No," Agnes said. "It isn't."

The room was so quiet, Agnes could hear a conversation in the next room. A man was talking about a Lexus. A woman said the word "Anichini."

"Matt?" Nora called from across the table. "You and Brian don't have to hang out with us old folks if you want to go back downstairs and play pool."

"Sure," Matt said, clearly eager for any excuse to leave the room.

"I think I'll go check on Mom," Bridget's sister said.

"Great," Bridget said. "I'll be up soon, too."

Matt looked in Melissa's direction. "You want to?" he asked his new stepsister.

Melissa shrugged. "I'm not very good," she said.

"We aren't either," Matt said.

"Really, really not good," Brian added, grinning.

"Well, all right," Melissa said.

There was quiet chatter around the table to cover the awkwardness of Matt and Brian and Melissa's leaving. Janice told Bridget to stay and enjoy herself. Rob asked Harrison if he wanted another glass of wine. Harrison nodded, drained the dregs in his glass, and handed it over in Rob's direction. An audience settling itself, Agnes thought.

"So what's up?" Jerry asked finally when the others had left.

"I've loved Jim Mitchell since I was a senior at Kidd," Agnes announced simply.

"And does he love you back?" Bridget asked gently.

"Yes. He does."

She could hear the strain in her voice. Her heart kicked hard in her chest.

"Then why isn't it great?" Harrison asked.

"He's married," Agnes said. "He's been married the whole time."

Jerry whistled. "How long are we talking about?" he asked.

"Twenty-six years," Agnes answered, aware that she was sweating under her arms and down her back. She would ruin her dress.

"Oh, Agnes," Nora said, and Agnes didn't know if Nora's distress was because Agnes had never confided in her or because of the sheer weight of all those years.

"I went back to Kidd to visit him over Thanksgiving the year after we graduated," Agnes explained, "and, it's a long story, but I ended up in the emergency room. He took me there. And that night we . . ." She stopped.

"Jim Mitchell," Rob said with a kind of awe.

"The very same," Agnes said.

"I remember his wife," Jerry said. "Not her name, but she used to come to the games. She was kind of cute. Petite? Brunette?"

Agnes nodded. "Her name is Carol."

"This is amazing," Bridget said, shaking her head slowly from side to side. "Just amazing."

"It *is* amazing," Agnes declared.

"And his wife doesn't know?" Jerry asked.

"I don't think so," Agnes said.

"How is that possible?" Jerry asked.

"Jim and I don't see each other all that often. We meet in neutral cities in anonymous hotels for a night or a weekend."

"And that's okay with you?" Nora asked, unable to hide her concern.

"Yes," Agnes said with emphasis. "I don't want what you have. Or have had. I don't want a man in my life every day. I cherish my condo and my solitude. And when Jim and I meet and come together, it's all the better for having been apart."

"Agnes, I'm happy for you," Rob interjected. "If he has made you happy all these years, then I'm all for it. I'd be a hypocrite if I wasn't."

"If he loves you so much," Jerry asked, "why hasn't he left his wife? It's not fair to her either, right?"

Julie snapped her napkin on the table, surprising all of them. "Since when have you ever cared about fair?" Julie asked her husband.

"What?" Jerry asked, either genuinely surprised or very good at feigning it.

"You shit," Julie said, as she pushed back her chair and stood. "You little shit." She gathered up her purse and her wrap. Agnes watched as she left the room without another word.

Jerry sat back in his chair. "Jesus Christ," he said.

"It doesn't matter," Agnes said quietly. "It's over."

"Why?" Nora asked.

"Because I've told all of you about it. I promised him I would never tell. And now I have."

"You're worried about breaking a promise to him?" Jerry asked, quickly recovering from his wife's departure. He certainly didn't seem about to go after her. "The guy's been using you."

"No," Agnes said. "He hasn't. You don't know the first thing about it, Jerry, so just shut up."

"Whoa," Jerry said, holding his palms up. "Easy now."

"We just hate to see you get hurt," Rob said.

"A little late for that, don't you think?" Agnes snapped. She hadn't meant to snap at Rob.

"How do you mean?" Harrison asked quietly.

"I know what you all think of me," Agnes said. "Steady, sturdy Agnes. Too bad she never had a date. Never got married. Never had kids. Is she gay?"

From a hallway, Agnes could hear a woman calling for *Ian*. A waiter moved around the table, filling wineglasses. Nora gave him a subtle signal to leave.

"Agnes," Nora said finally.

"I'm sorry, Bridget," Agnes said. "I told myself I wouldn't do this. It's your wedding supper, and I've spoiled it."

"You haven't spoiled anything," Bridget said.

But of course Agnes had. She could see it in their faces. Jerry's determination to get at the gritty truth. Nora's sadness. Harrison's bewilderment. Rob's desire to put the best face on this for Agnes.

"I just couldn't stand having you all leave after this weekend," Agnes said, "and not know this about me. That I have had a life. It's a different life than most. A life dispensed in moments. But they were transcendent moments, never dull, intensely felt, full of joy. How many of you can say that? I have had riches. I have had my share. Tomorrow, we'll all say that we'll get together again, but we won't, not really. I might die, and none of you would ever have known. Poor Agnes, you'd be saying. A spinster."

"We wouldn't have said that," Nora said.

Having loosed her secret — and her anger — Agnes found that she couldn't stop herself. Later tonight, or tomorrow morning while driving home to Maine, she might cringe at the memory of this moment. But right now all she felt was relief. Tremendous relief at not having to hide the central fact of her life.

"You'd have thought it," Agnes said. "You've *been* thinking it. Just like I pitied you your whole marriage, Nora. Just like I'm wondering what's eating at Harrison. Just like I'm wondering what it feels like to have cancer and still want to get married."

"Agnes, stop it," Rob said.

Agnes ignored the scolding. "Why are we all pretending? We've spent every minute of this reunion hiding the things that are closest to our hearts. We were once all best friends. Now we're as good as strangers to one another. I don't expect you to tell me your secrets — I don't want you to. It's just that I've lived that duality all my life, and I can spot it a mile away."

Agnes knew that she'd gone too far, that she'd offended people she genuinely admired, even loved. She would not, however, take back what she had said. It was too late for that. There was only one more thing to be said before she left them.

"We're all so full of it," Agnes said, standing, "that we haven't even talked about the thing we're all not talking about. That night at the beach. It's a kind of cancer all its own, isn't it? We were all there. We all saw Stephen. We all watched him drink himself into oblivion."

Nora very quietly pushed her chair back and stood. Agnes watched as she walked behind the others to a door that perhaps led to the kitchen.

"We were all complicit in Stephen's death," Agnes added. "We knew he was a drunk, and yet we didn't keep a close enough eye on him. We didn't even notice he was gone until it was too late."

Agnes laid her napkin on the table. It might have been a gauntlet. "It was a lovely wedding, Bridget. I mean that truly. I think you're a brave, beautiful woman, and I wish you a happy life. Many, many years of a happy life with Bill."

Agnes glanced at Harrison and then over at Rob. She would not see them again. She could say good-bye, but the evening had already had more than its share of drama. She pushed her chair into the table.

Tomorrow morning she would wake and pack her orange duffel bag and get into her car and return to Maine. The drive would be long, and already Agnes dreaded it. The trip would be entirely different from the one she'd made just yesterday. Yesterday, she had had a life. She had had hope. She had neither now.

When Bill and Bridget left the table, Harrison stood. He said good night to Rob and Josh and Jerry, the only ones who remained, Agnes's pronouncement and exit having effectively ended the evening. Possibly, the men would move into the library for a nightcap, though Harrison had no intention of joining them.

Harrison pushed through the door at the far end of the private dining room, the door through which Nora had disappeared. He found himself, not unexpectedly, in the kitchen. Judy, who looked up from a small plantation of mismatched cream pitchers, seemed surprised.

"Where's Nora?" Harrison asked without preamble.

"I don't know," Judy said, perhaps taken aback by Harrison's abrupt manner.

"She came through here," Harrison said.

"Came and went," Judy said.

With his jacket hooked over his shoulder, Harrison searched the public rooms of the inn — the library, the sitting room, another room in which a wedding reception seemed to be in progress — but he couldn't find Nora. It was conceivable she had already doubled back and was in one of the rooms he'd just passed through, but he took a chance and headed for the long corridor that led to Nora's suite. When he turned the corner, he noted that Nora's door was half open, as if she'd dashed back to her desk to fetch a list or a bill.

Harrison pushed the door further open. Nora was seated in an armchair facing the double doors that led to the private veranda.

Harrison tossed his jacket onto the foot of the bed.

"You wanted a story?" he asked.

His question was brusque, rhetorical.

Nora said nothing.

"All right," Harrison said, ignoring her silence. "I'll tell you a story."

He stood with his hands on his hips confronting the woman in the chair, aware that his posture and his voice were full of anger. After a few seconds, however, he couldn't look at Nora as she sat with her legs crossed, holding her shawl closed at her collarbone, staring at the various rectangles of glass. He walked toward the double doors, putting his back to her. In the crenellated reflection, he could just make out the features of her face.

"So I'll skip the part," Harrison began, "where I spend most of my junior year and all of my senior year watching this girl — this girl I've had a crush on since that fateful day in October — from a distance. And then up close and personal when I discover, much to my surprise, that she's the girlfriend of my putative best friend, Stephen Otis."

Harrison paused.

"'Crush,' I think, is not an entirely accurate word in this case," he continued. "I could use the phrase 'in love,' couldn't I? But you'd doubt me because you'd think that to love someone, one must have at least the barest beginnings of a relationship. But since this is my story, we'll dispense with semantics and just take it on faith that I was, indeed, in love with this girl, from a distance as I've said, and then rather up close, though not, sadly, close enough to touch, because she was, again as I have mentioned, the girlfriend — true love? — of my roommate."

Harrison crossed his arms over his chest.

"So we'll skip that whole part," he said, "and go directly to that night on the beach, which, if memory serves, was the third Saturday in May. A night when the water temperature would have been forty degrees, which — and you may not know this — will cause a man to die in less than thirty minutes. The air temperature, factoring in the windchill, never rose above forty-five degrees Fahrenheit that night. You with me so far?"

"Harrison."

"So I'm at this party, which is taking place at a beach house that belongs nominally to a couple named Binder from Boston who use it only in the summers, but in essence belongs to the privileged of Kidd Academy, who think nothing of breaking and entering a temporarily abandoned house. Said house being one point three miles from the boarding school, a fact that will take on some significance later on."

Harrison had not remembered that fact in years.

"And let's see," he continued, "who is there with me at this party? At which, I should point out, there seems to be an inordinate amount of booze, courtesy of Frankie Forbes, who had, two days earlier, dropped off at the beach house — for our convenience — ten cases of Budweiser, numerous bottles of wine, and for the hard drinkers among us, several fifths of Jack Daniel's." Harrison paused. "Good old Forbes. Precious friend to the class of nineteen seventy-four. Where would we have been without him?"

And where exactly would Forbes be now? Harrison wondered. Had he become a drunk? No, too canny for that. Forbes probably had a house somewhere on the coast of Maine, all purchased, of course, with profits from the willing students of Kidd.

"So, who's at the party?" Harrison asked again. "Jerry Leyden, who is at all the parties, not because he particularly likes to drink but because he's a student of human behavior. He likes to observe and then draw conclusions about the observed, these tidbits to be stored and parceled out upon occasion for sport or for further advancement. Jerry would have made a marvelous spy, I always thought, but instead elected to parlay his exceptional talents into sharp business skills, wheeling and dealing his way to the top of the food chain in New York City, no mean feat. So there's Jerry and his girlfriend, Dawn, who, I understand, is now a sheep farmer in Idaho. And who else? Rob Zoar, doubtless fully aware of his sexuality though not yet prepared to announce it, nineteen seventy-four being a good two decades before the era of Gay Alliance clubs on high school campuses. Rob, the quintessential good egg, is mildly drunk on beer — buzzed, shall we say — and is also something of an observer of human behavior, though, unlike Jerry Leyden, not for political ends. There is no Josh in his life as yet, though who knows, there might have been — a sophomore boy? a headmaster? — human nature being as various as it is.

"There are perhaps fifteen others — no, twenty, at least — at the party, well into its midpoint by now, curfew dictating the arc of any social engagement at Kidd. The beach house must be vacated by ten forty-five in order to sprint back to the dorm and be in our rooms by eleven. You remember curfew, Nora?"

"Harrison, why are you doing this?"

"I'm telling you a story, remember?" he asked her reflection in the glass. "And, yes, my story has a plot, though a sordid one. But I'm getting to that. I was speaking of the others present at the party. Bill and Bridget making out in a corner. We begrudge them nothing. Agnes O'Connor is sitting on the couch talking to Artie Cohen about . . . what . . . let's see, the Vietnam War? And there are many others, but some of this is a blur, because yours truly was well into his cups by then. Not as drunk as some, mind you. Not as stoned as others. No, I was somewhat more than buzzed but less than wasted. Certainly less wasted than Stephen, who may have been combining Jack with THC. Hence the bloodshot eyes, the faltering steps, the wet kisses. Yes, I did see those, Nora. And let us not forget his fabulously charming laugh, which tended toward the hilarious and infectious, rising above the crescendoing symphony like a piccolo gone nuts."

"You're drunk now," Nora said.

"Do you think so?" Harrison asked, briefly swiveling in her direction. "Not happily, I can assure you. Not in the tiniest bit happily."

He turned back to the windows and uncrossed his arms, a little of the starch leaving him. He put his hands in his trouser pockets and examined himself in the door frame. A mullioned man.

"Also at this party is the aforementioned girl," Harrison continued. "And I, being a seventeen-year-old boy in love — yes, what the hell, we'll use the phrase — with a beautiful but untouchable girl who seems, if I may say so, more than a little annoyed with Stephen — for his drunkenness, possibly, but more, I think, for his crude possessive gestures: the dramatically wet kisses, the public overtures to enter one of the mildewing bedrooms — follow this girl into the kitchen, where she has gone, ostensibly for water, but I think to be by herself. A chance our hero — that would be me — cannot afford to miss. I find her not at the tap but rather sitting on the really-not-very-clean floor, arms covering her head. A girl in distress. Definitely."

Harrison remembered Nora wedged into the corner, a small animal gone to ground.

"I squat down in front of her," Harrison said, "and ask her what is bothering her, though I, who have been watching her every move and being as astute an observer of human nature as are our Jerry and our Rob, already know. I lift the distressed girl to her feet. And as will sometimes happen with seventeen-year-olds, a comforting embrace morphs into something rather more, producing in the boy at least a feeling akin to rapture, if not actually rapture itself. And in the girl? Who knows? One likes to think some rapture recipro-cated. Certainly the kisses, passionate and protracted, suggest strong feelings on the part of the girl — and perhaps even relief? Was there relief? I think so. And then there was a kind of fumbling embrace and the girl's hand is under my shirt, slightly above my waistline, a detail I have remembered my whole life. Imagine that. Twenty-seven years spent remembering one tiny detail."

"I don't want to hear this," Nora said.

"Somehow the girl and I got turned around," Harrison contin-ued, ignoring her, "and my back was digging into the metal band of the molding of the Formica counter, and I was, to put it simply, thrilled to be holding this girl I'd wanted to touch for months. This girl who admittedly did not belong to me — if one human being can be said to belong to another — but who appeared to be giving herself to me with some abandon. So I might be forgiven for think-ing that this girl shared some of the same feelings I was having: namely that we had, albeit by a circuitous and not entirely blame-less route, found each other."

Harrison paused, not wanting to leave this moment in his narrative — a moment he could feel in all its immediacy, a mo-ment he hadn't ever been able to duplicate, despite years of trying.

Nora put a hand to her eyes.

"But such sublime pleasures," Harrison continued, "if stolen, must be paid for, no? And thus the sudden lurching into the kitchen of Stephen Otis, who could not fail, despite his altered state, to note that his roommate and his girlfriend were locked in passionate embrace."

Harrison remembered Stephen's sudden face, his expression of disbelief, the jackhammer of guilt pounding inside his own chest.

"We might have blown apart then," Harrison continued, "but to the girl's credit, she did not move away from me, a nongesture for

which I will always be grateful. Though, in retrospect, that nongesture might have given us both pause, since it was that lingering embrace, that disinclination to untangle limb from limb, that put a
period instead of a question mark at the end of Stephen's exclama-
tion, which, as I recall, went something like, *What the fuck.*"

It went precisely like *What the fuck,* Harrison recalled.

"The girl said nothing, and I said nothing," Harrison added, "a
demonstration of extraordinary poise, I think now, in light of potential calamity. Who knows what a drunk will do when crossed,
when betrayed? Newspapers and TV shows are full of such scenar-
ios. The girl left us both then, I remember, trailing her hand along
my arm, a distinct commitment to a future. A gesture that filled
my yearning heart with joy and perhaps even bravado. I leaned
against the counter, arms braced on the Formica, waiting for the
punch or at the very least some spittle. Stephen, never the most ar-
ticulate of men when drunk, said only, *You fuck,* swinging old Jack
not in my direction but in his, and swigging impressively — I recall being impressed — from the square-cut bottle. And then he
lurched away.

"I was . . . what was I? Elated? Sober? Relieved? Sexually deliri-
ous? I needed to find the girl, to touch her again. To tell her that I
loved her, which seemed as urgent a message as I'd ever had to deliver. Said message still undelivered, I might add. So I went in
search. Quickly darting out to the porch. No Nora there. Then
back through the squalid rooms of the chicken coop that passed
for a beach house. No Nora there. Had she gone back to the dorm?
A decision that would have been sensible, yes, but a dull ending to
my tale."

Harrison studied the floor, reluctant to enter the portal of this
particular part of his story, the only bit that really mattered.

"So I went out again to the porch. And there, to my horror,

was Stephen, whom I was decidedly *not* looking for. Stephen was stumbling and, I could scarcely believe this, *crying*."

"Please, Harrison," Nora said.

"He said — and I quote — *Oh man, oh fuck.* Repeatedly. Not knowing I was standing there. I thought he was distraught at having found the girl and me in the kitchen, and I was moved. I spoke. I said something. Maybe only his name. *Stephen.* He turned and saw me. I was keeping my eye on the empty and potentially lethal bottle in his hand. He said, *Oh, shit, I can't go back in there.*"

Harrison paused.

"I took a step toward Stephen, and he yelled, *Don't come near me!* He started to back away."

Harrison stopped now on the brink of revealing a detail he had never told anyone. But he had come to Nora's room to do this, to tell this story, which had to include this terrible fact.

"And that was when I smelled him," Harrison said quickly.

Nora covered her eyes with her hands.

"*I've shit myself, man,* Stephen said."

Nora rose in one motion from the chair and walked to the bed. She sat at its edge.

"This was a phenomenon I'd heard about but never witnessed," Harrison said, "this extreme manifestation of inebriation. I was struck dumb, astonished, made ashamed by the pure physicality of being drunk. I was, if I'm not mistaken, actually frozen in place.

I'm goin' in the water, Stephen cried. *Wash out the pants. You get me somethin', man. Steal it from the closets. Anything.*"

Harrison glanced at Nora.

"Stephen turned," Harrison said, "and started toward the porch steps that led down to the beach and the water. *Stephen, don't,* I said.

"*What?* he asked. *What?*"

Harrison bit the inside of his cheek and stared up at the ceiling, remembering.

"The water wasn't rough, but it wasn't entirely calm either. You could see the white edges of the waves. What was I to do? Realistically? Stephen had to wash himself off. He couldn't let anyone see. Better to let the others think he'd gone for a quick swim to sober up than that he'd shat himself, no?"

Harrison took a long breath.

"I started down the steps with him, but he turned and shouted at me to stay where I was. He was still crying."

Harrison could hear the tightness in his voice.

"There wasn't much light that night, and I could just barely make him out as he walked out onto the beach. He kind of stumbled to the water's edge and waded up to his knees."

Harrison swallowed hard. "But, you see, *realistically*, I could have helped him, couldn't I? I could have given him my own pants, walked back to school along the beach in my boxers, and snuck into the dorm before anyone saw me."

And Harrison wondered for the thousandth time why he had not done that.

"Stephen kind of lost his balance and sat down in the sand. He let the tide wash over his legs. I could see him struggling to undo his belt."

"Harrison," Nora said, and he steeled himself to finish his story.

"And then I heard this noise behind me," Harrison said. "A door opening. I turned, and it was Jerry Leyden. Come out to find me. Or Stephen. Because the story of what had happened in the kitchen had spread through the beach house like proverbial wildfire, and our Jerry, ever on the scent of the new and interesting in human behavior, wanted to speak to one of the protagonists."

Harrison could remember Jerry's face, the way he'd tried to see around Harrison to the water. The way Harrison had backed him through the doorway and into the house again.

"I turned and stood in front of Jerry, confronting him," Harrison said. "I was conscious only of trying to shield Stephen from Jerry's prying eyes. I don't know what I said. *Have you seen Stephen?* I might have asked to throw him off the trail.

"*What happened, man?* Jerry asked.

"I tossed him a fact or two to mollify him and to get him to go inside the house. *It's fucking freezing,* I said. *Let's go in.* I don't remember exactly what I said, but it worked. I'd given Jerry enough to go in search of someone else to tell."

Harrison moved to the chair Nora had left minutes before and sat down. "When I went outside again, Stephen was gone."

On the bed, Nora was crying.

"I ran down to the beach," Harrison said. "I yelled Stephen's name over and over again. But no one could have heard me over that surf. You remember what it was like when you were on that beach — even on a calm day you practically had to shout to be heard. I looked for footprints, but I couldn't see anything. The tide was coming in, washing whatever might have been there away. I thought Stephen had ditched the pants or washed them out as best he could and then walked back to the dorm. Maybe I'd taken too long with Jerry, and Stephen had gotten fed up."

Harrison rubbed his eyes.

"I know now that I should have gone screaming into the road, found a house with a light on, and called the police from there. They would have alerted the Coast Guard. Would the Coast Guard have saved him? I don't know. A man in the water, as you know, is dead in less than thirty minutes."

He paused.

"I returned to the dorm. He wasn't in our room. I went up and down the halls, shouting his name. When I couldn't find him, I went downstairs and told the proctor. I said the last time I'd seen him, he was on the beach."

There was a long silence in the room.

"The school called the police, who took a spectacularly long twenty-seven minutes to get to Kidd. Irrelevant detail, for by then, of course, it was too late."

Harrison let out a long sigh.

"I tell myself Stephen couldn't have suffered more than a few seconds of helpless panic. But who am I to say? And how terrible those few seconds would have been. I imagine that his feet got tangled in his pants and that he couldn't stand up. Maybe he made it to his knees. A wave came in and knocked him over, and he tumbled in the water and then got carried out with the undertow."

"Oh God," Nora said.

"It's why I've never talked about this," Harrison continued. "That one pathetic detail. I've kept that private. I've even tried to erase it from my own memory. It's my last image of my friend, trying to clean himself in the water. I've tried to persuade myself I've never spoken of it for Stephen's sake. Not to sully his memory. But you and I both know that's bullshit."

Harrison put his head in his hands. Telling the story was a cruel thing to have done to Nora, and for what purpose? To tell the truth? What exactly did that do for a person?

"Did Agnes know?" Nora asked.

"No one knew," Harrison said.

"We're all guilty," Nora said. "That's what Agnes meant. You. Jerry. Me, more than anyone. I owed it to Stephen to watch out for him."

"Me, most of all," Harrison said. "He was my friend. I think about his life — gone. A whole life gone. Twenty-seven years of a life not lived."

"This is unbearable," Nora said.

"As you know, his body washed up on Pepperell Island," Harrison said, "the gruesome detail of a length of rope having risen and wrapped itself around his neck, giving rise to irrelevant rumors of suicide. I never knew anyone less likely to commit suicide than Stephen Otis. Unless you count slow death by alcohol poisoning."

"Oh, Harrison, he'd have been a drunk forever," Nora said.

"I came here to tell this story," Harrison said. "I didn't know it when I drove here, but I know it now. Agnes would be proud of me, don't you think?"

"Harrison."

"And the best part," Harrison said. "I haven't even told you the best part yet. After the funeral, Stephen's father drove to Kidd for the graduation. Don't you remember? There was a tribute to Stephen at the ceremony? After graduation, Mr. Otis came to my room and said he wanted to see where Stephen had died. That he knew that I was the last one to see him alive, and that I would know the place."

Harrison leaned forward, elbows on knees, hands clasped in front of him. "We drove in Mr. Otis's car. I didn't know what to say. I had everything to say and yet nothing. I led him to the house. We parked the car in the driveway. We walked through the sand dunes at the side of the house and then out to the seawall. I just stood. I was shaking.

"*Here?* his father asked.

"I nodded.

"*There was nothing you could have done, son,* he said to me. He called me *son* and put his hand on my shoulder. Trying to comfort me. I was screaming inside. It wasn't true, I wanted to tell him. There was everything I could have done."

Harrison hoped Nora would not echo Stephen's father or say — as so many women might have done — *You did the right thing.*

275

Empty absolution akin to a sin in Harrison's book, a book that strangely had more blank pages the more there was to add to the ledger.

It was crap that confessing a thing relieved one of guilt, Harrison thought. How convenient to think so, how utterly deluding. Confessing a thing, he knew now, made the thing more real.

And how sordid and sad this tale he had confessed. Harrison could not remember Stephen now, not precisely who he'd been. He had images and photographs, some few stills at home, more in the yearbook, where Stephen Otis was ghoulishly omnipresent. Captain of the baseball team. President of the senior class. Class clown. Some images of Stephen Harrison had actively tried to bury. Lying on a bunk with Nora. Wading into the water. Others, Harrison savored. Catching a grounder on a hop close to his chest and leaping with a throw home that saved a run and won the game. But Stephen — the essence of Stephen — was gone, just like the essence of Harrison's father was gone, recalled now only through anecdote or photographs. The man himself had vanished.

Harrison heard a faint rustle on the bed behind him. It was time for him to go. The classy move would be to stand and leave without a backward glance, without the few exchanges that could only be banal, that would cheapen all that had gone before. But Harrison knew he'd told the story badly, perhaps making more of it than there was at the time, using threads of pure emotion for his tale, so that leaving without a word might be stagy or false. Friend to friend, Harrison ought to comfort Nora. Ought to say, at the very least, *I'm sorry.*

Nora put her hands on Harrison's shoulders, and he flinched. Two warm delicate entities with the energy of bombs. Signaling what? Forgiveness? Or was this meant simply to be a calming gesture, to soothe, to still conversation, her ear as attuned to the banal as his was.

The hands moved inside his collar, electrifying Harrison, and then around and along the skin of his chest until her head rested on his shoulder, her cheek next to his ear. The decision — to clasp her hands in a firm *no* and allow her to remove them; or to turn and kiss her mouth, an emphatic *yes* — was made in a split second. Harrison stood and held the girl, now a woman, after twenty-seven years of intermittent imaginings, the reality so vivid it made his breath tight. He kissed her, the kiss more mature as well, speaking of years of experience he would have to imagine now for the rest of his life.

Nora disengaged herself and walked to the door. Harrison thought, for one heartbreaking moment, that she meant to leave him, as she often did, but instead, she locked it. When she turned to him, no funny half smile on her face, his heart took off in a sprint. She stepped out of her shoes. How beautiful she was. Harrison saw Evelyn slipping a nightgown from her shoulders, and he pushed the image — that parallel story — from his mind, a deliberate act of betrayal. And once banished, Evelyn was gone for the duration, the duration as yet unclear. An hour, possibly. Perhaps a night. Conceivably a lifetime. Though the word itself, "duration," suggested not only this glorious beginning but, on the horizon, a necessary and finite end.

Before the wedding, Bridget had set aside the tissue-wrapped lingerie to have ready when she and Bill returned to the suite. She shut the bathroom door, leaving Bill to light the candle beside the bed. They were both exhausted from the long day of waiting and then the service itself (Bill nearly collapsing with Melissa's unexpected arrival), and then the dramatic finale of Agnes's astonishing announcement (which certainly explained the woman's tears during the ceremony), but Bridget knew that Bill would not fall asleep until she was in the bed with him. It was, after all, their wedding night.

She wondered how Matt and Brian and Melissa had got on playing pool. She and Bill had said good night shortly after Agnes's exit, assuring everyone that they would see one another in the morning for a farewell breakfast. By the time Bill and Bridget had left the room, only Jerry, Rob, Josh, and Harrison remained, and whether the men repaired to the library for more drinks, Bridget didn't know. She thought not, that like Bill and her, they had gone back to their respective rooms to ponder the essential opaqueness of their fellow man.

Bridget glanced quickly in the mirror. She unclipped the wig, shook it a bit, and set it back on her head to unsettle the hair, give it more of a tousled look. Her face was pale in the overbright light — good for putting on makeup, frightening when catching a glimpse of oneself late at night. She divested herself of the hideous pink suit and hated underwear, enjoying for a moment her physical freedom. She would lose the weight after the chemo. Her doctor had said not to worry, that he had patients who had returned to size two with little trouble. Bridget would never be a size two, but an eight would be lovely.

She unwrapped the pink tissue paper and held up the antique silk nightgown, cut on the bias, nipped in slightly at the waist. This was a treasure for a bride, a young bride, but when Bridget had seen the elegant black gown in the window of the vintage clothing store, she had thought, *Why not?* Why should she deprive Bill of something that would please him? Why should she not treat this wedding night as she'd have done had they married in their twenties?

She tried on the gown and examined herself in the mirror. The lace-trimmed slip-dress gently shaped her breasts and hid the fact that her nipples, as a result of the surgery on her right breast, were pointing in different directions. She brushed her teeth and put on gloss that would undoubtedly get all over Nora's lovely linens. She blotted her mouth. She still had her makeup on, and that might smear itself all over the pillows, too, but what was a girl to do? Some mess ought to be expected in the bridal suite, no?

She opened the door from the bathroom and was surprised to find all the lights still on. When she turned the corner, she saw that Bill was perched at the edge of the bed, dressed in his shirt and socks and boxers. Had she come out from the bathroom too soon? Had he been busy, calling Matt's or Melissa's room to see if they had had a good time? She took a step further into the room, and he looked up at her. He was crying.

Bill was crying.

"I didn't have you for so long, and now I might lose you," he said simply.

With a chill, Bridget realized that Bill thought she would die. Possibly, he had had this thought all along.

It was one thing to imagine one's own death, quite another for someone else to imagine it. Worse, for someone to say it out loud.

Bridget wished she had a robe. But she couldn't leave her new husband crying at the edge of the bed to go in search of one. Bridget took a few steps toward Bill and then stopped.

"Bill?" she asked.

"All my life I've wanted this," he said, "and now we'll have what . . . ?"

The question went unanswered. Bridget's chill was quite real now. She wrapped her arms around herself to stop the shivering but felt only the thin silk of the nightgown.

"It seems so unfair," Bill cried. "So brutally unfair. And *I* caused this."

My God, Bridget thought.

Bill crossed his arms over his chest and began to rock back and forth at the edge of the bed. In his black socks and boxers, he looked unmanned. For too long, he had put at bay the ugly facts of her illness. Why they had chosen this moment to push themselves forward, Bridget didn't know. Perhaps it had been the arrival of his daughter, his happiness complete, that had unraveled him. The fraudulence of that happiness apparent only when he was alone in the suite for the few unguarded minutes Bridget had been in the bathroom.

She and Bill could not spiral apart, Bridget thought. There was simply too much at stake. There was Matt for one. There was her health for another. And then there were all those years they had not had. This one chance to make up for them. Reaching past Bill, Bridget lit the candle at the bedside and turned out the light.

There was one last thing.

She unclipped the wig from her scalp, slid it off, and tossed it to the floor.

"Why don't you get under the covers," Bridget suggested.

She walked to the other side of the bed and slipped between the sheets. She could hear Bill undressing. A man crying was a frightening sight. She hadn't minded at the wedding, because she'd known those were tears of joy, of relief. These, however, were tears of despair. Terrifying and frightening. Bridget must, whatever happened, stop them. If Bill disintegrated, Bridget would disintegrate. If Bridget disintegrated, Matt would disintegrate. That chain reaction could not be allowed to happen.

When he'd undressed, Bill slipped between the sheets. He reached for her at once, a small involuntary sob escaping him. "It wasn't supposed to be like this," he said, holding her close.

"I know," she said.

"You look beautiful," he said, a small laugh catching itself inside a hiccup. "I'm going to have to kill myself tomorrow when I remember this."

"Don't do that," she said. "I can't be a widow."

He ran his hand over her hip. "I didn't mean . . ." he said.

"No," Bridget said. "I know you didn't."

Though of course he had. He had meant that he believed that she would die soon, and that he would be left alone. And it *was* sad. Why should Bill not be allowed to feel the pain of it? He and she might have had twenty-seven years together. At best, now, they would have two, maybe three, and most of that time would not be good time. For all she knew, this night might be the best they got.

"Can you ever forgive me?" Bill asked.

"For what?"

"For leaving you. For marrying Jill."

"I forgave you a long time ago."

"You did?" he asked. "When?"

"Oh, I don't know," Bridget said, "last week maybe?"

Bill kissed her in the way that he did, a way she liked very much. They were old lovers even though they'd been together for less than two years. They had their routines. They were not adventurous. Perhaps tonight Bill might have tried a little something different. But sorrow — that most effective antidote to sex — had got the better of him.

Bridget took her husband's hand and brought his fingers to the side of her head. "Touch me here," she whispered.

She had never made love to Bill without her wig. She knew what her scalp felt like — the frighteningly thin hair, the patches where she was bald — but she believed that this must happen now. For them to be truly married, he must touch her head. For a moment, his hand rested where she had left it. Perhaps he wasn't exactly sure what she intended. She waited for him, knowing that in a moment he would understand.

He smoothed the side of her head, above her ear, near the temple, and then around to the back of the neck. As he did, Bridget thought about the girl at the *sheitel macher* and wondered what her wedding night had been like. Had she ceremoniously removed her wig to reveal her own shorn head? Had she wept? Did her husband, a nameless, faceless man, caress her head as lovingly as Bill was doing now, recognizing his wife's sacrifice?

Bill was gentle, for which Bridget was grateful. Her scalp was sensitive, a fact she hadn't known before she'd lost her hair. He removed his other hand from under her body and held her head in both. He pulled her to him and kissed her, a long and protracted kiss.

This was better, Bridget thought. Why pretend that she was not sick? Why not love her exactly as she was? Wasn't this what every woman longed for?

Sunday

She said his name, as if in a dream. Harrison drifted back to sleep. He was unconscious only seconds, minutes at best.

The room was dark, the shades drawn. He was curled toward Nora, who was lying on her back. Harrison remembered now, the memories jolting his heart and causing instant heat throughout his body. What had been urgent last night was, in retrospect, astonishing.

He reached for her and found her arm. Her skin was warm and dry.

He saw Nora above him, her knees cradling his body. On her back, her arms flung toward the headboard. He was more than astonished that he and she had made love: he was thunderstruck.

Harrison could just make out Nora's profile. He must have dreamed that she'd spoken his name, because she was still asleep. His side of the duvet was crumpled near his waist. He brought the covers to his chest. The inn was quiet. Harrison could not hear music or voices. For how long had he and Nora been asleep? Behind closed doors, in other rooms, people lay in beds, restless or dreaming.

Harrison could smell Nora in the bed beside him. Sex, when taken out of context — even when in context, he thought — was both a bizarre and a wondrous activity.

Last night, Harrison had given in to temptation. This morning he sensed another temptation — to view what had happened between him and Nora as a fulfillment. In 1974, they'd kissed each other. Harrison remembered the promise of the hand beneath his shirt. Had Stephen, in his involuntary but macabre scene-stealing way, not ended what had begun that night between Harrison and Nora, would their romance have played itself out by the end of their freshman year in college — Harrison in Boston, Nora in New York City? Might Harrison have one day found himself Carl Laski's rival?

Impossible thought.

Beyond Nora's shoulder, at the edges of the shades, Harrison could see the light coming up. It was Sunday morning now. He remembered the wedding, the dinner, Agnes's confession. It had been, he reflected, a dreadful send-off for Bill and Bridget, who certainly had deserved better. Though, in the end, Harrison knew, the send-off would not matter. Bill and Bridget's battle would be intensely personal now.

The light grew brighter in the room, and Harrison could make out the armchair in which he had sat. Through the bathroom door, he could see the tub. The sun was making rectangular patterns on the shades. He thought about how he had seen his own reflection in the dark glass. It would be a sunny day, one he did not want to enter.

Harrison had felt some relief in finally telling Nora what had happened that May night nearly three decades ago. To have shared that burden with her and then to have felt her hands on his shoulders, the forgiveness that implied. Harrison had thought, prior to the weekend, that he would never again feel that intense mingling of desire and love he'd known as a young man. He had never been unfaithful to Evelyn, a fact that occasionally had seemed a kind of failure on Harrison's part, a failure of the imagination. Last night, Harrison had rejoiced in temptation, glad simply to feel alive.

Alive at Evelyn's expense. He remembered the way in which he had pushed Evelyn from his mind. She would never know, but

Harrison would, and that would change everything. He would have new, fresh memories now.

A loud, intrusive sound made Harrison flinch. Nora rolled away from him.

"You set the alarm?" he asked.

"I had to," she said, lying back, trying to wake herself. "I have to be up to see to the breakfasts."

Nora turned her head on the pillow to look at Harrison. She touched his face, as if she did not believe he was in her bed. "This is extraordinary," she said.

Harrison hitched himself closer to her, but she put a hand on his chest. "I really do have to get up," she said.

"Do we need to talk?"

"We will," she said. "Later."

Nora stood and put on her robe. She had to shower and dress. Harrison watched as she raised the shades. He covered his eyes with his arm. The sun's reflection from the snow was harsh.

In his room, Harrison paced. He still had on the clothes he'd worn to the wedding. His suit jacket and tie were tossed upon his bed, still made, not slept in. His face felt grainy, and he knew he should shower.

He thought that for the good of his family he ought to leave the inn as soon as possible. He would arrive in Hartford early for his flight, but better to be at the airport than to remain here. He was too agitated, however, to perform the simple task of packing. He walked from the bathroom to the far wall and back again.

He had not even held Nora this morning. He had not kissed her good-bye. Would they leave each other this way?

He sat on the bed and stared out the window. He could hear water dripping from the roof. He needed a cup of coffee to clarify his thoughts, and he remembered the machine in the library.

Would it be primed and ready to go at such an early hour? What time was it, anyway? He checked his watch. Nearly seven. Early for a Sunday morning. Might coffee be set out in the dining room?

Harrison, unwashed, left his room and walked downstairs in search of the library. As he did, he could hear the sounds of an inn waking itself up. Voices from a distant room. Footsteps on a wooden floor. The swish and thunk of a large door closing. A man in the lobby had a newspaper spread out on a low table, cup of coffee in hand. Harrison thought of asking him where he'd gotten it. Judy, Nora's assistant, walked into the hallway carrying a stacked set of linens.

"Good morning," she said.

"Good morning," Harrison said.

She had her blond hair pulled tight against her scalp, and once again she had lipstick on her prominent eyetooth. Harrison wondered why no one had ever pointed it out to her.

"You're up early," she said.

. . . the asymmetrical smile . . .

"Yes," he said.

"You found Nora?"

"Excuse me?" he asked.

"Last night," she said, "you were looking for Nora."

"No," he lied, his mind racing. "I didn't find her. I wanted to thank her, but she'd gone to bed."

"Well, she'll be up soon enough," Judy said. "Shall I tell her you're looking for her?"

"No, that's all right," Harrison said. "No. I'll be around for a bit. I'm bound to run into her. I'm looking for a cup of coffee actually."

"In the library," Judy said. "I just fixed it up."

"Thanks," Harrison said.

He headed in the direction of the library, but then he stopped. He took a turn at the stairway.

It couldn't be, he thought.

He had his key out — that hefty gold key — before he'd even reached his room. Once inside, he tossed the key on the bed and searched for the book he'd bought yesterday. He lifted a sweater from the desk and found the slim volume. He sat on the bed and turned immediately to the poem he'd been reading in the town library, the one that had so intrigued him, tortured him, for its sexual images. "Under the Canted Roof."

The woman in the poem was blond and had bad teeth. Yesterday, the word "tongue" had caught his eye. He found the line again: . . . *caressing your tooth with my tongue . . .*

A small confirming jolt straightened Harrison's spine.

He read the lines again, certain as he did so that Carl Laski was writing about the woman who had served Harrison the salad with the fly, the woman who had just passed him in the lobby.

. . . the asymmetrical smile . . .

Harrison could hardly imagine the cruelty on Laski's part to have written this poem, then to have made Nora type it. Finally to have published it.

Quickly flipping to the front of the book, Harrison checked the copyright date. 1999. The volume had been published posthumously.

Harrison sat on the bed, thinking. Five minutes passed. Ten.

He stood with the book in his hand. He walked to the window and then back again. He scratched his head. How was it possible that Nora had allowed this?

Harrison pocketed his key and left the room. He retraced his steps back to Nora's suite. He remembered Nora saying that Carl had been unfaithful to her only on the page.

When Harrison reached the end of the corridor, he saw that Nora's door was shut. He might simply have opened it — didn't last night give him the right? — but he knocked instead.

Nora was in her robe, still wet from the shower. On the bed — neatly made, its taut lines breaking Harrison's heart — was a bra and a pair of underpants, a pair of black slacks, a white blouse, two black socks.

Nora's face was pink, her hair flat against her scalp. Her eyebrows were pale, her lips naked.

"Harrison," she said, surprised.

"May I come in?"

"I'm . . . I'm a bit late," she said, but then she stepped aside. "Of course," she added.

Harrison embraced Nora and kissed her. Her breath smelled of toothpaste. He let her go and sat on a cedar chest at the end of the bed. He held the book in his hand, and he could see that she was looking at it. "There's a poem here, toward the end," he said.

Nora said nothing.

"The one called 'Under the Canted Roof.'"

She put her hands into the deep pockets of the plush robe. Harrison studied her pale legs below the hem of the robe, her bare feet. Her hands, he knew, were the only roughened part of her, callused from hard work.

"I think maybe you need to tell me a story," he said quietly.

Nora walked past him and sat on the bed.

"I love you," Harrison said.

And instantly, he minded the hollow words — trite and saccharine — the stuff of greeting cards. How strange to discover, after all these years of waiting to deliver his message, that it simply was not enough. Not enough at all.

"Last night," he said, "might have been the most intense sexual experience of my life."

"You don't really believe that," she said, laying her hands in her lap.

"It feels that way right now," he said.

There was a long silence in the room.

"I was the one for whom Carl had left his wife," Nora said. "He'd never done that before, never even thought of it. He had so many students, so many beautiful young women throwing themselves at him. Right up until his late fifties, he could make a twenty-year-old turn her head."

Nora paused, and Harrison could hear the heat come up through the registers.

"We moved from the city," Nora said. "Carl did it to get away from the horrible mess with his wife. I think he believed he could purify himself by coming to the country. With yoga. By giving up meat. By taking long walks. I could have told him it wouldn't work, that mere geography couldn't alter who he was."

Harrison set the book down beside him on the chest.

"Some men need women to complete themselves," Nora continued. "I've said that."

"You were the helpmeet," Harrison said.

"Carl was voracious in that way. He demanded my presence, my attention, every minute he was home and not actually writing. You had to know him to understand this. I believe there are many men like this. Perhaps Jerry is this way. Bill is not. You are not."

"No," Harrison said.

"Yes, I was the helpmeet." She paused. "Is that so bad? To subsume one's life to another's? If giving myself to Carl meant that his art was all the better, wasn't that sacrifice worth it?"

"Worth it to him, perhaps," Harrison said quietly. "I can't see how it can have been worth it to you."

"You don't?" she asked, genuinely puzzled. "Can you say that pursuing what I might have wanted to do was a greater good? I don't think one can. There's much to be said for sacrifice. Whole religions are based on this premise."

"It's just not the way women live now," Harrison said, knowing,

291

of course, that this wasn't entirely true. Many women sacrificed themselves for others.

"I thought he was a brilliant poet," Nora said. "If I could be part of that in any way, it seemed worth it at the time."

Harrison tried not to think of Nora with Carl Laski, a man who had been in his late sixties when he'd died. Harrison knew what a man of that age looked like. He'd seen plenty of them at the gym.

Harrison noticed suddenly — the way one might look up and register the absence of a particular sound — the lack of a stutter in Nora's speech. She was calm, resolute.

"I was even more isolated than Carl," Nora said. "We lived here, in this house, so far from town. It seemed I existed only for him. I worked for him. He was everything to me."

It was hard for Harrison to picture the particular Nora she was describing, the one for whom Carl Laski was everything. But when Harrison thought about the girl Nora had been, the one who had lived in Stephen Otis's shadow, he could perhaps believe that she might have allowed herself to be subsumed by another.

"There were many rumors about other women," Nora said. "But it was all based on the poetry. In his imagination, Carl was unfaithful to me every day. I could read it in the work. There would be a paean to a woman, and I'd have a suspicion, but there would be enough similarities to me or to those who had gone before me that I could never be absolutely sure."

Harrison winced for this image of Nora studying Laski's poetry for clues to his imaginary infidelities.

"But I knew," she said, "in all the banal, commonplace ways that women know. Carl was voracious sexually as well — I know you don't want to hear this — and there would be a slight falling off following a heightened interest in sex. It became a pattern. I could sense it, feel it. In his imagination, he had many affairs. I suppose all men do. But in this case, he was writing them down, and I was typing them."

She took a long breath.

"Curiously, I never thought of leaving," she said. "I'd married him, and we were isolated. Leaving never seemed an option. Where would I have gone? And with whom?"

You could have come looking for me, Harrison thought.

"One day Carl came home with a young woman," Nora said. "She was blond and nineteen and not at all what you'd expect as a student. Carl called her a 'townie,' even to her face. He found her fascinating. Her accent. Her bad teeth. She was different from any-one he'd ever known before. A girl on a scholarship. Brilliant, Carl said. But raw and unpolished. She had terrible table manners, I re-member. I used to think she played to his image of her — the working-class girl made good — and that the wretched table man-ners were part of her act."

Harrison was struck by the seeming ease with which Nora was telling her story. No tears. No hesitations.

"When I say he brought her home," Nora explained, "I mean he brought her home to stay. He said it was temporary, that she had nowhere to go. That the scholarship covered only tuition. That she'd been living part-time in her car, part-time with friends. She was dirty enough that I believed him. We had so many bedrooms, he said, we could certainly spare a room for her until she got on her feet. He presented it in such a humane way, I could not say no."

Nora turned to face Harrison.

"You see, that's how it works," she said. "In increments. In the beginning, one has such high expectations. And then life, in small increments, begins to dissolve those expectations, to make them look naive or silly. You realize that marriage will not be what you thought it would. That the romance is intermittent at best. That perhaps the man you have married at such a young age is a difficult man. That hopes of constant intimacy are, to use a word Carl was fond of, bourgeois."

Nora began to nibble on a nail.

"I could sometimes hear them making love," she said. "The walls were thin, and even from the end of the hall, I could hear them."

The image shocked Harrison. Nora lying alone in her bed. The first wife listening to the husband visit the second.

"It's one of the things I took great care with when I did the renovation after Carl died," she continued. "I made the bedroom walls sturdy and thick, so that from room to room one cannot hear a thing."

It was true. From his room, Harrison had been unable to hear a sound.

"What Carl hadn't told me was that Judy was pregnant. Within a few weeks, it became obvious to me. Perhaps it was obvious even before I realized he was visiting her bed. I heard her retching in the bathroom in the mornings. I could see her waist begin to thicken. One day I asked her. She said, yes, she was pregnant. I stopped short of asking her if it was Carl's. I knew, but I didn't want to hear it said aloud."

"Nora," Harrison said, "I'm so sorry."

"That day, I realized that Carl Laski was a monster. For years, he had forbidden me to have a child. He had had his children, he said, and doing so had brought him nothing but heartache. He wouldn't do that to himself again. Besides, he would always add, he was too old for children. But, you see, I wasn't too old, was I? I had longed to have a child. And here was evidence that Carl had allowed himself to have a child with this . . . this schoolgirl."

Harrison struggled to take in the reality of what Nora was telling him. A girl living in her house, a girl pregnant by her husband. He remembered the way in which Nora had spoken of Carl Laski just two days earlier: *He was a wonderful man. A wonderful poet and a wonderful man.*

Harrison had read the Roscoff book, and though he had not liked the work, he'd been persuaded that Laski had been, at the very least, a difficult and troubled man. But then Harrison had listened to Nora's somewhat defensive and laudatory comments about her husband, and he'd begun to see the man anew: the wonderful husband, the good teacher. And now, like someone whose first hunch has turned out to be the correct one, Harrison saw the man finally for what he'd really been. A self-absorbed tyrant.

"I was furious," Nora said. "I confronted him. He denied the child was his. He pretended surprise. Carl was capable of betrayal, but not of lying. He was absurdly bad at it. I threatened to leave. I think I actually packed a suitcase. I've never told anyone this."

"I'm glad you feel you can tell me," Harrison said, but he wasn't sure if this was true. Last night, his feelings had been simple, pure, imperative.

"I said I would stay only if he got rid of her," Nora continued. "That I would not live under the same roof, that I was tired of hearing them make love at night. That got Carl's attention. I think he'd imagined that I hadn't heard, hadn't known. He said he would find her a place." She took a breath. "And then he discovered he was sick."

"The cancer," Harrison said.

"He'd had a terrible sore throat for weeks. I thought he had strep. I urged him to see a doctor, but he wouldn't go. He had an arsenal of herbal remedies. There used to be a place in town he went to buy them. He swore by them. But eventually, the pain got so bad, he finally went to the clinic at the college. They advised tests. The word terrified Carl. 'Tests.' He became a child then. A kind of willful and destructive child."

Harrison imagined an old man raging, a kind of Lear.

"In the end," Nora said, "it was I who had to find the girl a place. I visited the college and talked to the dean and told him she'd been living out of her car and now was living with us. The dean knew that Carl was sick. Carl was revered at the school. The dean said he would arrange to have the girl's scholarship increased to include room and board. I didn't tell him she was pregnant."

Would the dean have known, Harrison wondered, that the girl and Laski had been lovers?

"And then Carl became very sick," Nora said. "Howlingly, terrifyingly sick. He raged. He cried. He named every woman who'd been the inspiration for every poem. He confessed every sordid imaginary affair he'd ever had. He enjoyed it. He wasn't looking for forgiveness. He was looking to hurt me because I was young and because I was going to outlive him. Some of the girls, he said, were only seventeen. He said he liked it especially when they were freshmen. I was merely one in a string — a long string, he said. That I'd been the one he married, the one he'd stuck with, really said more about me than it did about him. I had no character of my own. I was nobody. An empty cipher. He trampled over every good memory I'd ever had of the two of us together."

Harrison wanted both to comfort Nora and to shake her. How could she have been so willing?

"Once I learned that Carl was sick, I couldn't leave him, could I?" Nora asked. "Well, clearly not. Possibly I was relieved that our whole false marriage would have a finite end. And perhaps Carl sensed that in me, because as the days passed, as he realized he would not get better, even with all the chemo and the radiation, he grew furious. Unspeakably furious." Nora paused. "It's remarkable how fast love can turn to hate," she added.

"Nora," Harrison said.

"You cannot imagine how relieved I was when he died. How grateful I was that he'd taken care of it himself."

A silence in the room stretched to minutes.

"After the funeral, I went looking for Judy," Nora said. "I think I had an idea of taking the baby and trying to raise it. But she had given him — it was a boy — away to a Catholic charity."

Harrison could hear, finally, the effort to ward off tears.

Nora took a long breath and looked up at the ceiling. The loss of the baby, then, had been for Nora the true tragedy.

"And that was when I conceived of the idea of an inn," she said.

"You hired Judy," Harrison said.

"I brought her here to live. And then I trained her."

"The two of you run the inn."

"Yes," Nora said. "I pay her well."

Harrison wished he had one more day. One more week. "I don't want to go back to Toronto," he said. "It's awful to feel that way — it's terrible to feel that way — but it's true. I want to stay here with you."

Nora got up from the bed and stood in front of him. "This is my fortress," she said. "It is as I want it to be. As I need it to be."

He stood, and she kissed him.

"I have to dress," she said.

Harrison knew now that he and Nora would not see each other again. Not at their thirtieth reunion, in three years, nor at the fortieth, nor at the fiftieth, should Harrison still be alive for that one. One day, a man — like Harrison but unattached, a man with no shared history — would come to the inn and see Nora and talk to her, and that would be that.

"Your husband was right," Harrison said. "There are no words to describe a certain kind of pain."

He walked to the double doors and opened them. He stepped

out onto the veranda. His children would never know of their father's treachery. Harrison would go home and play baseball and skate with his boys, and they would never know that for a period of time — for the duration — he had been willing to leave them.

The sun was unexpectedly warm on his face. He moved through the slush toward the front of the inn. As he did, he thought about melting glaciers and all those birds flying north.

Through her window, Agnes saw Innes coming around the corner, walking through the snow in his shirtsleeves. Of course, it wasn't Innes, but rather Harrison Branch in the same shirt and pants he'd had on last night. But it might have been Innes, as Innes would have been at forty-four. The same upright but diffident posture. The slightly thinning hair. Why was Harrison walking in the snow?

Behind Agnes, on the bed, was her neatly packed duffel bag, her coat lying in folds, her backpack topped up with the free soaps and shampoos the inn (Nora?) had generously provided. She glanced at the letter to Jim Mitchell sitting unfinished on the desk, the one she'd written yesterday before her confession at dinner. Agnes would tear it up and discard it (no need to smuggle home the pieces now). It was possible, Agnes supposed, that Jim would never know of her treachery, that he would imagine that Agnes had simply faded away. And that, she decided, was precisely what would happen. She would fade away. She would return to Kidd, a place from which, physically and in her thoughts, she had rarely left. She would later this afternoon correct a set of papers for her U.S. history class, after which she would attend a meeting with the girls' varsity basketball coach. Agnes was the assistant coach. In the spring, Agnes would be the assistant track coach, and next fall she would coach field hockey, making her girls chase balls and complete drills in preparation for what she hoped would be a winning season. They had a chance this year. Molly Clapper would be returning. Molly had good cutting and even better drives and had the instinct always to be in the right place at the right time. And so it would go — on and on and on — until what? Agnes died? Retired? Her life — her *life* — which had seemed so full of potential just two days ago, felt frighteningly empty now.

A white limo made its way up the curved driveway. Jerry and Julie stood at attention at the foot of the front stairs. The car stopped, and a driver emerged. Immediately he opened the rear driver's-side door, and Jerry, with a spring in his step — as if he were delighted to be leaving — rounded the back of the car and slid smartly inside. Julie waited patiently for the driver to open the rear passenger's-side door. Her fur rolled over her arm, she slipped gracefully in. Before the driver closed her door, Agnes could see Julie pushing the fur onto the seat, a small animal separating husband and wife.

Harrison had stopped in the middle of what might be a lawn. What on earth was he doing? Perhaps he didn't want to have to say good-bye to Jerry and Julie as they drove away from the inn. Agnes would say good-bye to Nora. She wanted to thank her for the weekend, for the dinners and the lovely room. But might it be possible to leave without having to see anyone else? Bill and Bridget would know Agnes wished them well. She would write to them when she returned to Kidd. Yes, a good idea. So much more could be said in a letter than in a brief farewell.

Harrison still had not moved. He seemed poleaxed, just staring out at the Berkshires. Agnes could hear the dripping from the eaves, the occasional slide and thump of snow from the roof. The glare was almost blinding, and Agnes knew it must be warm out. The snow seemed to disappear even as she watched. Was that possible? Could one actually observe snow disappearing — melting and evaporating?

Harrison — Innes — took a step forward. The doctor wouldn't

be at an inn in the Berkshires, however, but he might be in a city. Not Toronto, Agnes decided. New York City. She could see Innes walking along Madison Avenue, pushing Louise in a wheelchair. The year would be — Agnes calculated — 1934. Had the Empire State Building been built then? Agnes changed the venue to Fifth Avenue and Thirty-fourth Street, where the tallest building in the world had recently been erected. Perhaps Innes and his wife had come to New York precisely to see this astonishing sight (well, not Louise, of course, who could not see). Louise and Innes were on a small vacation from Toronto, from his practice, from their children. Or might their children — Angus, fourteen, and Margaret, eight — be with them? Well, not with them, but back at the hotel room with Louise's maid?

It was a warm day in early December, a day close to the seventeenth anniversary of the Halifax blast, about which neither Innes nor Louise ever spoke, as if Louise had sprung, fully blind, from the streets of Toronto, to which the couple had emigrated after having been hastily married — much to Louise's delight — in Halifax. Louise needed the wheelchair, not because she was blind, but because she was both blind and lame, her ankle never having healed as it should have. With her husband's attention and a considerable amount of help (yes, definitely, a maid back at the hotel), Louise had borne and raised two children, established herself as the wife of a well-known eye surgeon (Innes's reputation preceding him to Toronto), and even, upon occasion, appeared in society, such as it was in the early 1930s in Toronto. (Had the Depression affected that Canadian city as it had American cities? Well, yes, it must have, Agnes decided.)

Despite these achievements, however, Louise had, upon closer inspection, the look of a woman who couldn't see, who couldn't entirely take care of herself. There were, of course, the sunglasses: two dark circles connected by a thin gold bridge. Her hair was somewhat drier and flatter than it might be on another woman. Her hair clips were affixed slightly askew, and her lipstick had been applied by feel rather than by sight. Could Louise imagine what her green cloth coat looked like on her, the color not entirely flattering? Did Louise go to department stores in her wheelchair, a friend pushing her through racks of dresses? Did the doctor's wife, who was nearing forty, rely upon her husband to choose her shoes and hats?

Agnes could see clearly this pair who had been together for seventeen years. Dr. Finch in a long brown coat and hat walking behind the wooden wheelchair with the rubber wheels, pushing his wife, who had grown heavier with the years, up the slight incline. Innes didn't show the strain. He looked, in fact, almost happy. Not necessarily because he was with his wife, Agnes decided. More because of the adventure of the trip, because of the simple delight of being away from Toronto — from Canada, if Innes were to be entirely truthful. There was a vitality in New York City, even in the midst of the Depression, that could not be, and was not, reproduced in Toronto, however civilized that northern city might be.

Louise was saying (Agnes listening intently) that they ought to visit Macy's. Joan had told her the department store was marvelous. Did she and Innes have time? When did the concert at Carnegie begin? For Louise, who could not see, a concert was just the ticket.

Agnes moved toward the desk.

Innes answered her questions, always unfailingly polite to his disabled wife, even when she spoke in querulous tones, which seemed to Innes to be happening more often lately. He could see and she could not, which she was inclined to remind him of from time to time. Her voice had a touch of the querulous in it today, in fact, despite this lovely trip. Louise was tired. She was often tired. It was such a strain being blind. One had to listen so intently. One had to imagine. As always, Innes felt sorry for his wife, who could not view the breathtakingly beautiful spire of the Empire State Building. Who could only hear the crowds that surrounded them. Who could not admire the holiday window displays, marvelously ornate and detailed.

Innes stepped carefully through the slush, not only minding where he put his own feet but steering Louise out of the path of the spray from the oncoming buses and taxis. Innes and Louise seldom took taxis. The sheer struggle to get Louise into an automobile made the enterprise a fraught and time-consuming one. They walked when possible. Innes had developed strong arms, a firm upper torso. He was aware, as most were not on this crowded street, of the five-degree incline, which one experienced when pushing a 150-pound woman in a wheelchair. Innes did not complain. He minded only when a passerby stared at Louise, at first with distaste and then with pity, the boldness of the stare not only rude but uncomfortably reminding Innes of barely buried feelings of his own.

Innes idly wondered if Louise and he might have been better off living in New York City, the society less closed, less insular. In Toronto, Louise had her friends and her family, but she was often unoccupied, the unemployment creating a constellation of unpleasant symptoms: boredom, irritability, occasional whining, a tendency to drama. She could not while away the hours the way other middle-class women could, with needlework or with reading. Louise had at first resisted Braille but now understood it about as well as a normal seven-year-old knew how to read.

But these were thoughts for later, for the return trip by train to Toronto. For now, Innes wanted to enjoy his short vacation. The hotel, with its fascinating model of itself in a glass case in the lobby. The dinners out with Margaret and Angus, Margaret in a grown-up dress with a black beaded belt. A lunch with a colleague from medical school followed by a tour of the city in that physician's Buick. Innes especially liked the solitary wandering through the city when Louise was resting. The aimless yet dedicated walking with no agenda produced in Innes a sensation close to freedom.

"I needed the scarf after all," Louise said.

"You're cold? It seems such a warm day. Unseasonably warm, in fact."

"Yes, but I am sitting and you are walking. I might be expected to be somewhat colder than you."

Innes did not answer, having learned years ago that Louise would seldom let a thing go.

"Talk to me," she insisted.

"The streets are crowded," he began.

"Yes, yes, I can hear that. The buildings. The windows."

"Well, here, let me back up a bit."

Innes parked in front of a Dickensian diorama and described the "burning" fireplace, a lighted Christmas tree, and the nineteenth-century costumes on the family members gathered around it. He glanced at another window. "There are some pretty robes for sale," he said. "Margaret might like one of them."

"Describe it."

"It can't be wool," Innes said, "because it looks too soft. Very plush. I'm not good with fabrics."

"Can we go inside? Is it manageable? I could feel the fabric for myself."

"Yes, of course," Innes said, though he did not want to leave the open air, the melting snow, the masses of vehicles on the streets, the words that floated out to him from the crowds. *Forbearance. Much at stake. Scandalous.*

Innes shouldered the door, putting his back to it. A young

woman with a fur scarf smiled at Innes, a moment that added to the day's sum of unexpected pleasures.

Innes asked a salesgirl in a green silk suit behind a glove counter where he might find the blue robe in the window.

"Lingerie on seven," she replied with an indifferent nasal twang.

Innes negotiated the wide elevator without difficulty and emerged onto seven, a universe of slips and girdles and peignoirs and negligees. He searched for a rack of robes and steered Louise in that direction. He placed the skirt of the robe in her hand.

"Chenille," she said at once. "What colors?"

"Pink and white and pale blue and . . . let me see . . . yellow."

"Which would look the best on Margaret?"

Louise had never seen her daughter.

"The pale blue, I think," Innes said. "Her eyes."

"Joan said they'll do a bang-up job with the wrapping. Be sure to get the smallest size."

Innes waited patiently in line at gift wrapping, his wife parked against a wall, ear cocked to the women around her. The package, when delivered, presented a challenge to Innes, who had to ask Louise to hold it on her lap. He could not maneuver the chair and manage the large box at the same time.

Negotiating the elevator once again, Innes pushed his wife past the perfume counter and the glove counter and out into the bright sunshine, which Louise could feel on her face. He turned the corner to head up the sidewalk.

The throng was thicker than it had been just a half hour before. Everyone, it seemed, wanted to experience the warmth of the day. Across from Innes, a crowd of people stood at the curb, waiting for the traffic to pass. Innes stopped short.

She had stepped off the curb and was crossing the street in his direction. She had on a felt hat with a short brim, a wool coat with a fur collar. She was oblivious to his presence, instead making her way carefully through the slush. The several seconds Innes watched Hazel come toward him seemed the most intensely felt of his life.

It was the wheelchair that caught her attention, as it did for almost everyone who passed by. The quick glance at the occupant. Then another up at the companion. Hazel did the same, her eyes sliding over the woman with dark glasses, once, twice, and then stopping. Innes watched Hazel's expression change from one of mild daydreaming to shock. She glanced up at Innes.

He hadn't seen Hazel since the day she'd walked away from him in Halifax. Louise, jealous since childhood, had found reason to be furious with her sister, who wasn't blind or disabled. Louise would not tolerate even a mention of Hazel's name in the house. In the beginning, there had been letters from Hazel to her sister. After Innes had read the first two aloud to Louise and had endured the resulting tantrums, he'd stopped sharing them with his wife. Eventually, the letters themselves had ceased, and even Innes had stopped writing with word of Louise. Hazel's envelopes had been postmarked from Boston, which had, for seventeen years, remained a magical city for Innes.

"Why are we stopped?" Louise asked.

"Traffic," Innes said, barely able to summon sufficient breath to answer her. "We have to wait for the traffic to clear."

"Is it really so busy?"

"Yes, I'm afraid it is."

He would have known Hazel anywhere. For years, he'd imagined her as she'd been at twenty-two. She was thirty-nine now. Was she married? Did she have children? All the questions that had crowded his thoughts for nearly two decades pushed themselves forward in a rush, and yet he couldn't ask a single one. Indeed, within seconds, he would have to leave her. Louise was nothing if not canny.

Innes reached out and clasped Hazel's forearm, getting the cloth of her coat. She didn't flinch. He remembered her lustrous eyes.

"Innes?" Louise was asking with a slight whine. "This box is getting heavy."

Innes wanted to mouth a word to Hazel. But what word? What word?

He released Hazel's arm.

Wait, he said silently.

With great reluctance, Innes turned and pushed Louise forward in the chair.

He walked, but he didn't know where. His thoughts were chaotic, urgent. The glister of the city blinded him.

"Innes," Louise said sharply.

"Yes?"

"*Where* are we going?"

"I have some errands to run," he said. "I'll take you back to your room and let you rest."

"What sort of errands?" Louise asked.

"Tobacco," Innes said. "A book I need."

"Yes. All right," Louise answered, happy to be returning to her temporary nest. She would order tea and pastries, Innes knew. When he returned to the hotel room, there would be flakes dotting the bodice of her dress.

Hazel was standing precisely where Innes had left her: poised, handbag over her wrist, the brim of her hat hiding her eyes.

"How long would you have waited?" he asked when he had reached her. His breath was short from running.

"Perhaps another hour."

"I could hardly mask my impatience."

"She looks very different."

"How so?"

"Angry, I think. I was sad to see that."

Innes nodded. Yes, Louise was angry. She always had been. It did a man little good to sacrifice himself for a woman if he couldn't love her enough.

A man jostled Innes's elbow. "We are here on a trip," he said.

"You live in Toronto still," she said.

"At the same address. Yes."

"I stopped writing."

"She wouldn't allow me to read the letters to her," Innes said.

Innes moved Hazel out of the path of a cyclist. He let his hand linger on her arm. "Is it always this crowded?" he asked.

"This time of year, it is."

She looked up at him from underneath the brim of her hat. He saw that she was self-sufficient. Time or experience had done that.

"I have a room," Hazel said.

Innes was astonished at the bold invitation. And then he was not. They couldn't stand on the street corner.

"You live here?" he asked. "In the city?"

"It's rather far uptown."

"Should we take a taxi?"

"If you like."

"I have very little time."

In the taxi, Innes took Hazel's gloved hand in his own. It was not enough. He removed his glove and then Hazel's. She didn't protest. He clasped her hand and held it tightly.

They drove up the avenue, past the mansions and the park. Innes could see the city only in the periphery of Hazel's face.

They parked in front of a modest brownstone building. Emerging from the taxi, Hazel climbed a set of steps and waited for him in front of a door set with panes of rippled blue glass.

"This is yours?" he asked, looking up at the four-story building. She smiled. "I have an apartment," she said.

They took a small elevator to the fourth floor. In the elevator, Innes reached out to hold her arm, unwilling to let her go, even for a moment. They stepped out into a dark corridor. Hazel led him to her door and unlocked it.

He held her coat while she slid her arms from its sleeves. Innes shed his own. He didn't know where to put them.

"There," she said, pointing to a cracked leather chair and betraying an impatience that sent Innes's heart soaring.

Hazel, standing before him, had on a belted dress of thin brown fabric. Her hair was cut short and had been waved. The brown dress fell just below her knees. She was slender. Many women were slender these days, Innes thought. He hadn't remembered the sturdy legs, muscled.

"I've thought of you often," he said.

She nodded. "Has it been very difficult?"

"Louise? My life?"

"Louise."

"No," he said. "Not very. Sometimes."

"You did it for me," Hazel said. "To let me go."

"My reasons seemed complicated at the time," Innes said.

"Are you bitter?" she asked.

"No, I'm not bitter."

He followed her into the penumbra of a small dark room. On the bed was a fabric he now knew was chenille. Innes, even in his exalted state, took note of a skirted dressing table, a pearl necklace hooked around a post attached to the mirror. Later he would notice the small economies: the lovingly washed silk stockings hanging from a towel bar in the bathroom, a single orange in the icebox, the paper sacks saved in a drawer.

That she had been here all these years scarcely seemed possible.

"I teach at a girls' school in the city," Hazel said.

"Did you marry?" he asked.

"No."

"I thought you might have," Innes said. "I was sure you had."

"No."

"There must have been . . ." Innes stopped himself. He could not ask about other men. Not in this room, not under these circumstances. "I have a son," he said instead. "A lovely boy. He will study engineering, I think. Architecture perhaps. We've been to the Empire State Building twice together. I also have a daughter. Her name is Margaret. She's quite tall for her age. She's very good at the piano."

"What's the boy's name?" Hazel asked.

"Angus," Innes said and paused. "My father's name. You are their aunt."

"Do they know about me?" Hazel asked.

"A little. That you exist. We have said that you were injured at Halifax," he explained with some shame. "That you live abroad."

Hazel nodded.

"I have perhaps twenty minutes at best," Innes said.

Through the thin cloth of her dress, he could feel the bones of her spine. He drew his shirt up over his head. She carefully unfastened her garters. He felt the ridges of the chenille along his back. Her breath was sweet. He gave no thought to Louise, for whom he had sacrificed a joy he might have had for years. For Innes had always believed that, given time, he could have

310

persuaded Hazel to go away with him. Had he not seen Louise sitting in the chair that afternoon.

They lay naked on the bed facing each other. Hazel's thighs were wet. He could see the fine lines of thirty-nine now that the sun had come around the corner of her building. He had been gone nearly an hour. Hazel was not a virgin. How could he even have imagined that she might be? He smoothed her face, her hair.

"What do you teach?"

"History."

"Have you been here all this time?"

"I was in Boston for a while. I returned to Halifax. And then I came here."

"You went back to Halifax?" he asked, surprised.

"Briefly."

"I haven't gone back," he said.

"I found it depressing."

"You have had . . ." Innes hesitated. "Lovers," he said finally.

"Yes."

Innes discovered that he was glad, that he would not have denied her this pleasure. He was equally glad he could not put faces to the men.

"One who mattered?" he asked.

"Yes," she said.

How strange that Innes had known Hazel for only a night, a morning, and an afternoon, and yet he had missed her all this time. The resemblance between the sisters might have kept Hazel alive for him.

"I haven't the strength to leave you," he said.

She pulled him to her breast. Innes had a sense of needing to remember every second so that later he would be able to re-create this hour in all its wonder. The ease with which she had undressed. The lack of shame. The sense of inevitability.

"Did you ever think about me?" he asked.

"Of course," she said.

"That night, in Halifax, before the blast," he asked, "did you know?"

"I didn't know enough to know," she said, "but in retrospect . . . yes, I did." She paused. "You have been happy in your marriage?"

"'Happy' is the wrong word. 'Content' maybe. 'Accepting.'"

"Would we have been happy?"

"Yes," Innes said. "I'm sure of it."

"She has borne children," Hazel said.

"Yes. Well, in one case. With difficulty in the other."

Innes reflected how strange it was that it had been Louise who had cried out that day in Halifax that she would never have a husband and children, and that Hazel would have everything — when actually the opposite was true. Louise had the husband and the children.

"You have been all right without children?" Innes asked Hazel.

"Yes. Most of the time. I'm sometimes afraid of the future."

"Louise would not have been all right," Innes said. "She is barely all right even with all of us around her."

"That day," Hazel said. "It doesn't seem possible."

"The blast, you mean."

"Yes."

"You were engaged."

"He came home," Hazel said. "He had to stay in Halifax, but I didn't."

"It was that simple?"

"No."

"All those years . . ." Innes said, and in that moment, he came as close to despair as he ever had.

"We can't think about it," Hazel said.

"I have to go back to Toronto," he said. "The day after to-morrow."

"It will be all right," she said, soothing him, drawing her fingers along his back. He wanted to sleep. God, how he wanted to sleep in this bed. With this woman.

He would have to tell Louise that he ran into a friend, lost track of time. If he waited any longer, she would miss her concert. Louise knew that Innes, short of a catastrophe, would not cause her to miss her concert.

This was a catastrophe, he thought.

With a wrenching movement, Innes stood. He found his clothes, the various pieces, putting them on as he discovered them. When he looked again at Hazel, she was sitting at the edge of the bed in a cotton robe. He pulled on his jacket, slipped his feet into his shoes. He sat beside her while he tied them. His coat and hat were on the chair in the front room. He took her hand.

The feeling was visceral, a physical pain. Hadn't he sacrificed enough? But then, it hadn't been all sacrifice, had it? If he were to be truthful? He had had his very satisfying practice, his family. He had had a life.

He couldn't leave Louise. It would be wrong.

He kissed Hazel and stood. He walked to the door and put his hand on the knob.

Agnes rested her head in her hands. She couldn't decide. Did Innes turn the knob and leave the room? Never to return? Would that be right? Would Innes then be a good man?

Agnes could see Innes hesitating, his hand on the cut glass. Perhaps he noticed the panels in the door, could hear a siren from outside. He didn't know exactly where he was. He would have to find a taxi and make the torturous ride back to the hotel, which just an hour ago had held for him a luminous candescence.

Hazel waited patiently behind him. This couldn't be her decision. She couldn't influence the man at the door or try to persuade him. Agnes could only imagine what she was thinking.

Agnes knew what she was hoping.

So, *no,* Agnes decided, setting down the pen with a snap. Innes wouldn't leave Hazel. He might have to leave her for now, Agnes determined with a kind of wild joy in her heart, but he would return. Perhaps even tomorrow he would return for an hour. Yes, that was it. Innes would see to Louise, and he would raise his children, but he would never be without Hazel again. He and she would meet in New York City and in Toronto. At Niagara Falls and in Chicago. They would be lovers until one of them (surely it would have to be Innes; Agnes couldn't allow the man any more heartbreak) died.

Her heart full, her imagination satisfied, Agnes picked up her notebook and put it in her backpack. She dropped the pen onto the floor and bent to retrieve it. She stood up quickly and saw again the oily cylindrical blips at the periphery of her vision. Maybe they had more to do with blood pressure, she thought now, than with vision.

She would finish the story when she got home. Perhaps she might even send it out to be published. Why not? For what was the point of fiction, Agnes wanted to know as she hoisted her duffel bag to her shoulder, if not to edit reality? If not to rewrite history? If not to soothe one's fevered dreams?

Bridget was ravenous, having had little to eat the day before — the wedding, her nerves, the ironclad underwear — but she hadn't wanted to wake Bill. She opened the dining room, taking a seat by the window, the sun beginning to scorch its way up the hill. After a time, Bridget caught the eye of a woman she'd seen around the inn performing various chores: waitressing, registering guests, and, once, carrying a suitcase.

"Can I get you something?" the woman asked.

"I know you're not ready," Bridget said, "but if you could just bring me whatever is easiest. Coffee, juice? Cereal if you've got it?"

"You're the bride," the woman said.

"Yes, I am," Bridget said.

There ought to be a word, Bridget reflected, for "bride-who-is-forty-three." It was the sort of word the Inuit might have.

Bridget watched with fascination as the woman placed the order on a dumbwaiter and sent it down to the first floor to the kitchen. Had Matt and Brian seen the contraption? It wasn't so long ago that one of them would have dared the other to get in and take a ride.

Bridget would wake the boys at 10:00 so that they could dress and pack. She hoped they still possessed all the various parts of their tuxedos. She imagined cummerbunds and studs and bow ties sprinkled over the floor of the basement room in which the pool table apparently was located. Bridget would pack up her own things and let Matt and Brian take all the bags out to the car. And then she would go in search of Nora to thank her. For her kindness, for the extraordinary meals, for all the arrangements. Nora had been more than generous. Bill was paying something (he had not told Bridget the precise sum), but she knew that Nora had heavily subsidized the cost of the weekend. Not just for Bridget and Bill, but for all of them.

Bridget thought of Jerry and Julie. Would their marriage survive the ride home? She thought, too, of Agnes's surprising confession (truly surprising, there had been nothing to suggest it) and wondered what the woman's future would hold. Having revealed the affair, would it now be over, or might it spur Jim Mitchell to action? It was hard not to dislike the man for having kept Agnes on a string all these years. Or was one meant to admire Jim for his loyalty to the family he had made? Bridget worried that her wedding might inadvertently have caused the dissolution of two other couples. How potent these reunions were. Was that why so many refused to go?

And then there was the mystery of Nora and Harrison. Clearly a charge there — anyone could see it. Nora had sat next to Harrison at the ceremony. Did that mean anything? Bridget couldn't ask. She didn't know Nora well enough. She thought about the way Nora had left the room after Agnes's extraordinary challenge to the table.

Bridget could remember some things about that night so long ago. She recalled making out in a corner with Bill (it had been too cold, they had agreed, to go down to the beach), keeping it discreet, occasionally getting up to get another Coke. She remembered that the party was loud, that the boys seemed to be getting drunk faster than usual. There was a sense of everything coming to an end. In a week they would have exams, and in two weeks they would all be gone. Bill to his family in Albany, Bridget to her family in Foxboro. Weeks might go by without her seeing Bill, and if he did manage to come visit Bridget, her parents would keep a close eye on them. In September, Bill would be off to college.

Bridget remembered hearing the news that Nora and Harrison had been seen kissing in the kitchen. Bridget had thought at the time, *as it should be,* not having previously recognized the fact, but knowing that Harrison and Nora were a good fit, a more comprehensible fit than Nora had ever been with Stephen. That relationship had baffled Bridget right from the outset. And she had realized something else that night: that Harrison had all along been waiting for Nora.

Bridget's wants were simple now. She wanted to stay alive until Matt entered his senior year in college. After that, she would have to trust that Matt could make it on his own. It was a lot to ask for, Bridget knew. The odds were slim that she'd even make it to her son's high school graduation.

It wasn't enough time. Her death would send Matt into a tailspin. She hoped Bill would have the sense to hang on to him for a year after high school and delay his admission to college. Get the boy working, have him come home at night, talk to him incessantly. She would speak to Bill about this when she thought Bill was ready to hear it. In a year, perhaps, if all went well.

Bridget heard the pulley of the dumbwaiter. The blond woman brought Bridget her breakfast. There was cereal on the tray if she wanted it, but there was so much more: eggs with crisp bacon, a delicate brioche with sweet butter, a dish of berries with a pitcher of cream. A silver pot of coffee.

A feast for a bride.

Bridget laughed and asked the woman her name. She did not say to Judy, as she might have, "I'll never finish this," because she knew that she would. Bridget would eat every morsel.

A movement at the entrance to the dining room caught Bridget's eye. The young woman there mirrored her glance and instinctively crossed her arms over her chest. Bridget thought it a testament to Melissa's character that she did not turn and walk away. She'd come, Bridget guessed, for a meal and a quick getaway, thinking that the bride and groom would be sleeping in.

How lovely she was, even in her embarrassment. She had on a white boatneck T-shirt that hugged her narrow rib cage and waist, her slim jeans breaking just so over the toes of her black boots. There was a thin silver chain at her neck.

Bridget half stood and called the girl's name.

Reluctantly, Melissa turned in Bridget's direction.

"Join me?" Bridget asked.

Well mannered, the girl crossed the dining room, but she refused eye contact. Slowly, with some poise, she unfolded her arms and took the chair across from Bridget. "Where's my dad?" she asked at once.

"He's sleeping," Bridget said.

"Oh," Melissa said. "I'm not really hungry."

"You have a long drive back," Bridget pointed out.

Melissa shrugged.

(Old people, of course, always thought drives were too long.)

"There will be a buffet later," Bridget explained, "but you can order à la carte from the menu. As you can see, they've brought me quite a spread." Bridget glanced at the food in front of her. Melissa would think her gluttonous. "I ordered cereal, and they brought this."

Melissa nodded.

"Did you sleep okay?" Bridget asked.

The girl fingered the silverware. "I slept okay," she said.

"How was the pool?"

Melissa seemed not to understand.

"Billiards?" Bridget asked.

"Oh, pool," Melissa said. "Good. Brian beat us all."

No more questions, Bridget told herself, until Melissa volunteered a statement or a question of her own.

Judy came to the table to take Melissa's order. She handed Melissa a menu and positioned herself for a wait, but Bridget doubted the girl read beyond the first item. "Oatmeal," she said nervously. "And some tea, please."

"We have Earl Grey and . . ."

"Earl Grey," Melissa said quickly.

When Judy left them, Melissa sat with her hands in her lap, staring out the window, doubtless grateful for the view.

"I'm glad you came to the wedding," Bridget said. "It meant a lot to your father."

Melissa nodded.

"I know it can't have been easy."

"Matt was nice," Melissa said, and Bridget's heart lifted. The remark was more than just a polite lob back to Bridget. A chink, maybe. Something to work with.

"You have a remarkably high tolerance for fifteen-year-old boys, then," Bridget said. "They can be . . . well . . . you know. Pretty awful sometimes."

"No," Melissa said. "He was nice. We talked a bit."

Bridget forced herself not to ask, *What about?* Though she'd have given a lot just then to know. "You should come to the house one day," Bridget said, knowing the suggestion was risky.

Melissa looked away. There would always be, Bridget knew, a fierce loyalty to the mother that Bridget would not interfere with. A quality one could only admire.

"Maybe," Melissa said, leaving the door open but not committing herself.

It was enough, Bridget thought. It was quite a lot, actually.

Bridget asked questions then and Melissa politely answered

319

them, once offering a question of her own, which astonished Bridget. "How are you feeling?" the girl asked.

Bridget thought a minute. She took a sip of coffee. She decided to tell Melissa the truth, unedited.

She worried about the tentacles of the star shape, she told the girl. She had a 50 percent chance of a recurrence, the correct term for the cancer's return. If it did return, it would show up in the bones or the brain or the liver. She hoped to make it until Matt was Melissa's age. This was the bargain she had more or less made with God: Let Matt get to twenty, and then you can do whatever you want with me. One could never really use the word "cure." One had to think of oneself as "a work in progress."

All this she told Melissa, who seemed startled at times by some of the revelations, but who appeared to take it in with concern. She was, Bridget thought, the perfect person in whom to confide. A woman who might want the information but who would remain essentially detached. The stranger on the plane to whom one confessed everything.

"That answer you gave last night at dinner," Bridget said, "about the Arab men on the plane. I thought it was the best at the table."

Melissa tilted her head. She would know, Bridget thought, that Bridget meant what she said, that she was not pandering, that a woman who had confessed being afraid of a recurrence in the bones might be expected to tell the truth.

The sun was hot on Bridget's back as she packed the car, Matt and Brian ferrying suitcases and suit bags and presents to the back of the van. (Presents! Bridget hadn't anticipated those.) Bridget had said to Bill when he'd found Bridget and Melissa in the dining room (quickly forestalling what she feared might be another collapse on Bill's part, her new husband decidedly unhinged this weekend) that he should drive back with Melissa so that the girl wouldn't have to make the journey alone. Bridget would take Matt and Brian. She had then gone in search of Nora to thank her but had no luck. She'd been reluctant to disturb the woman in her suite. Nora had to sleep sometime.

Bridget would write her a long letter when she got home.

"And then they lived happily ever after."

Bridget turned to find Rob and Josh, identical suit bags hooked over their shoulders.

"Where's the groom?" Rob asked.

"We're separated," Bridget said.

"So soon," Rob lamented, smiling at the joke.

Bridget embraced him. "Thank you for coming," she said.

"Wouldn't have missed it for the world."

"A long and happy life," Josh said, giving Bridget the quick hug of an acquaintance who might soon become a good friend.

"I'm calling you next week," Rob said. "After a suitable period of marital bliss."

"You're in Boston for a while?"

"For twenty days. Count 'em."

"And you're going to London," Bridget said, addressing Josh.

"In four days."

"Good luck with that."

"Thank you."

"So, we're off," Rob said. He turned to Matt. "You take care of your mom," he said and shook the boy's hand. "I'll send you that CD we talked about," he added, "and you keep working on your chords."

Matt nodded, and Bridget knew her son would be immensely pleased to have had his own music acknowledged by such a gifted musician.

Rob turned, a wave beginning. But then he stopped. He walked to where Bridget stood by the van and embraced her again, this one lasting seconds. This one saying what he had not said all weekend, what he would not say in front of Bridget's son.

I know you'll beat it.

Rob stood back and hitched the strap of his suit bag a little higher on his shoulder.

"Me, too," Josh said.

Bridget slammed the rear door of the van. "All right, that's it," she said to Matt and Brian. "Climb in."

Though either of the boys could have had the front seat, they'd chosen to sit together in the back. Bridget put the car in reverse. She had not said good-bye to Agnes or Harrison. Had they left already? Bridget made the turn, and as she did she caught sight of a branch of a tree glistening. It might be a trick of light, she thought, for it was just the one branch. Bridget stopped the car. It was a sight too beautiful to pass by. The branch pointed toward the mountains and glittered as if encased in jewels.

The limb must have been in shade, but now that the sun had hit it, the gemlike casing would last only seconds in the warmth.

Bridget had a thought. An extraordinary thought.

There was every possibility that she might live.

She might see more of Matt's baseball games. Melissa might come for Christmas. Bridget might one day be sweltering in the bleachers watching her son graduate from college.

Bridget and Bill might grow old together. Really, really old together.

The thought was so astonishing that Bridget glanced back at Matt to see if he, too, had seen the glittering branch, if he, too, had had a similar realization. But her son already had on his earphones and was fiddling with his Walkman. He smiled at her and gave a little wave.

The wonder of it, Bridget thought as she put the van in gear and pulled out of the parking lot.

Harrison returned to his room and began packing. On the desk was his letter to Evelyn, written two days earlier. He read it and tore it up, dropping the bits into the wastebasket. With her lawyer's eye, she would note the repetition of Nora's name, and she might wonder.

His suitcase packed, Harrison glanced around the room to make sure he hadn't left anything behind. He stepped into the corridor. He let the heavy door close and click behind him.

He started for the lobby and the registration desk, but when he had descended the stairway, he took a quick detour into the library. He gazed out at the view (now familiar, now losing some of its charm), at the high-tech coffee machine, at the framed photograph of the house as it had been years ago. He studied again the race-track, the train a blur in the distance. The place had been here long before there was a Nora or a Carl Laski or a Harrison Branch or the ghost of a Stephen Otis. How many other stories might there be, Harrison wondered, in a house so old?

He walked out into the lobby, but there was no one at the desk. He waited a suitable interval and then placed the heavy gold key on the blotter. He'd already given his credit card. They would send him the bill. How odd it would be to receive that piece of paper in Toronto. To have an envelope from Nora's inn sitting on his kitchen table. One world intruding painfully into the other. Would Harrison be able to open it, or would he simply drop it into a file of bills, to be glanced at later — months later, perhaps?

It would sting, that bill, just the way a quick memory of Stephen could reach out and sting at any moment.

Harrison hoisted his bag over his shoulder and stepped into the sunshine.

The pavement was wet. The maze was revealing itself. Even the wrought iron fence shone in the sunlight.

Harrison walked quickly toward his car. It would take him just under two hours to get to Hartford. Another hour until his plane left. Two hours to Toronto. He'd be home in time for Sunday dinner, an old-fashioned ritual Evelyn and Harrison had decided to maintain, thinking that the boys needed one immovable feast in the week. Evelyn would do up a rack of lamb (his favorite) or a pork loin (the boys' favorite), and they would take their time over the meal, allowing nothing to interfere. Today that dinner would be a kind of torture for Harrison, though next week's would be slightly easier, and easier still the week after that. And finally his memories of this wedding weekend would not be with him all the time, but would come only intermittently — at lunch, say, while waiting for a colleague and trying to draw from memory on a paper napkin the jumbled roofline of the inn.

Tell me a story, she had said.

Harrison opened his trunk and tossed in his bag. He heard a commotion behind him and turned to look. A couple, surrounded by friends and family, was on its way from the inn to a waiting car, the car done up in tin cans attached to the rear bumper, colored streamers wet and clinging to the hood. Harrison had only a glimpse of the couple, who must, he thought, be the bride and groom of the Karola-Jungbacker party, the parallel wedding to that of Bill and Bridget. Casually dressed in a T-shirt and jeans, her body small and lithe, the young bride skipped down the steps, flashing a lovely smile and stopping to hug a friend. The groom had his hand on her back, as if guiding her to their new life. Solidly built and wearing a sweat-shirt that read DARTMOUTH across the front, he turned to shake a hand. His back was thumped, and he laughed. A man in the crowd with a movie camera called out, *Over here, Ian. Look over here.* Harrison heard other cries rising aloft from the send-off.

Be good, someone said.

Don't be good, said another.

From the doorway, Nora waved. Harrison didn't know if the wave was for himself or for the couple, and not knowing, Harrison waved back. A small movement of his hand that might have gone unnoticed.

The groom helped the bride into the car and started the engine. Harrison watched as the vehicle, tin cans tumbling noisily, made its way around the circular drive and passed by him. The young woman, still smiling, glanced at Harrison, and he smiled back.

They had it all before them, he thought. Uncommon beauty. Thrilling risk. The love of children. A sense of rupture. A diagnosis. Relief from pain. Great love. Betrayal. Grand catastrophe.

When he turned to open the door to the Taurus, he suddenly felt quite hollowed out. For a minute, he couldn't breathe. He hadn't anticipated how much it hurt physically to be separated from Nora.

Leaving might be all wrong, he thought — all wrong for all the right reasons. He glanced up at the entrance to the inn, but Nora had gone inside.

Would it be possible to start again? he wondered. Could he and Nora rewrite their own history? Bill and Bridget had done so. Might he and Nora make a life together after all these years?

He felt a wild recklessness within him.

Charlie, he thought. *Tom.*

Harrison leaned against the door and waited just a moment longer.

Acknowledgments

I have many people to thank. Katherine Clemans, natural-born editor. Chris Clemans, who introduced me to the joys of baseball. Molly Osborn, who talked to me about field hockey. Celeste Cooper, with whom I love to brainstorm. Elinor Lipman, dear friend, literary and otherwise. Jennifer Rudolph Walsh, to whom I owe so much. Michael Pietsch, beloved captain of the ship. Asya Muchnick, whose sharp eye and gentle nature I much appreciated. Heather Fain, who makes the public side of the writing life so much easier to bear. Karen Landry, who appears to love baseball even more than I do. And John Osborn, who always sees the bigger picture.

Most of all, however, I would like to thank my father, Richard Shreve, to whom this book is dedicated, for persuading me and my sisters, Janet Martland and Betsy Shreve-Gibb, that we could be or do anything if only we tried hard enough. Sometimes life taught us otherwise, but we never wanted to let him down.